ISOBELLE CARMODY

ASHLING

Random House 🏠 New York

Copyright © 1995 by Isobelle Carmody
Cover art copyright © 2007 by Penguin Group (Australia)
Map copyright © 2008 by Penguin Group (Australia)

The text of this work was originally published by Penguin Books Australia Ltd,
Camberwell, in 1995. Published here by arrangement with Penguin Group
(Australia), a division of Pearson Australia Group Pty Ltd.

Visit us on the Web!
www.randomhouse.com/teens

Educators and librarians, for a variety of teaching tools, visit us at
www.randomhouse.com/teachers

Library of Congress Cataloging-in-Publication Data
Carmody, Isobelle.
Ashling / by Isobelle Carmody. — 1st Random House ed.
p. cm. — (Obernewtyn Chronicles ; bk. 3)
Summary: Elspeth travels to the lowlands to seal an alliance between
Obernewtyn and the rebel forces that oppose the totalitarian Council, while still
being pulled by the need to learn more about the weaponmachines that
destroyed the Land during the Beforetimes.
ISBN 978-0-375-85769-0 (pbk.) — ISBN 978-0-375-95769-7 (lib. bdg.)
[1. Voyages and travels—Fiction. 2. Persecution—Fiction. 3. Human-animal
communication—Fiction. 4. Extrasensory perception—Fiction. 5. Science fiction.]
I. Title.
PZ7. C2176Ash 2008 [Fic]—dc22 2008020301

Cover and map design by Cathy Larsen
Cover background artwork by Les Petersen
Cover photographs by Getty Images

Printed in the United States of America
10 9 8 7 6 5 4 3
First Random House Edition

for Helen Stannard-Williams,
for the most enduring love of all:
friendship

and

for Scott
Do you now fly the spirit trails
you sought in life?

✦ CHARACTER LIST ✦

Alad: Beastspeaking guildmaster

Angina: Empath guilden and gifted musician; twin brother of Miky

Ariel: sadistic enemy of Obernewtyn, previously allied with both the Council and the Druid

Atthis: Elder of the Agyllians, or Guanette birds; blind futureteller

Avra: leader of the Beastguild; mountain mare; bondmate to Gahltha

Brydda Llewellyn (aka the Black Dog): rebel leader

Cameo: true-dreaming Misfit, killed by Ariel

Ceirwan: Farseeker guilden

Daffyd: former Druid armsman; farseeker; unguilded ally of Obernewtyn

Dameon: blind Empath guildmaster

Darga: Jik's canine companion, lost in a firestorm; of the Herder breed, but atypically small and docile

Domick: Coercer ward; Obernewtyn's spy at Council-court, where he goes by the name Mika; living in Sutrium safe house with bondmate, Kella

Dragon: powerful Empath guilder with coercive Talent; projects illusions

Druid (Henry Druid): renegade Herder Faction priest

and enemy of the Council; charismatic leader of a secret community that was destroyed in a firestorm

Elspeth Gordie (aka Innle, the Seeker): Farseeker guildmistress; powerful farseeker, beastspeaker, and coercer, with limited futuretelling and psychokinetic Talent

Enoch: a coachman; ally of Obernewtyn

Fian: Teknoguild ward

Gahltha: Beast guilden; bondmate to Avra; a formidable black horse sworn to protect Elspeth

Garth: Teknoguildmaster

Gevan: Coercer guildmaster

Gilaine: mute daughter of the Druid; farseeker bound to Lidgebaby; beloved of Daffyd

Gilbert: former seaman; former leader of the Druid's armsmen

Grufyyd: bondmate to Katlyn, father of Brydda

Hannay: Coercer guilder

Idris: young rebel formerly of Aborium; trusted companion to Brydda

Jaygar: roan stallion of the Beastguild

Jes: Elspeth's older brother; Talented Misfit killed by soldierguards

Jik: former Herder novice and Empath guilder; died in a firestorm

Jow: former follower of the Druid; farseeker bound to Lidgebaby; Daffyd's brother

Katlyn: herb lorist living at Obernewtyn; bondmate to Grufyyd, mother of Brydda

Kella: Healer guilden with slight empath Talent; living in Sutrium safe house with bondmate, Domick

Lidgebaby: powerful coercer-empath; an infant bound to the Druid's Misfit followers

Louis Larkin: unTalented highlander; inhabitant of Obernewtyn; honorary Beastspeaking guilder

Maruman (aka yelloweyes): one-eyed cat prone to fits of futuretelling; Elspeth's oldest friend

Maryon: Futuretell guildmistress

Matthew: Farseeker ward

Miky: Empath guilden and gifted musician; twin sister of Angina

Miryum: Coercer guilden

Nerat: Agyllian eldar and healer

Pavo: former Teknoguild ward; died of the rotting sickness

Reuvan: rebel seaman from Aborium; Brydda's right-hand man

Roland: Healer guildmaster

Rushton: Master of Obernewtyn; latent Talent

Sallah: rebel mare; companion to Brydda

Zade: stallion; member of the Beastguild

Zarak: Farseeker novice with beastspeaking Talent

PART I

✦

THE DAYS OF RAIN

✦ 1 ✦

AT FIRST SIGHT, the gypsy woman appeared to be embracing the stake. Her languid pose and mocking smile made it seem impossible that she was about to be burned. Blood dripped steadily out of slits that ran from elbow to wrist, yet she showed neither pain nor fear.

The gray-gowned Herder before her lifted his palms to the sky as he chanted the purification prayer. He was old, bald, and toothless, but his eyes glowed like live coals as he made the warding-off signs.

"Beware, demon," he hissed. "You have found an easy vessel in this foul gypsy's body. Yet I will drive you out."

Shockingly, the woman laughed aloud.

"You know I am not possessed, Herder. Say the truth and be done with it. Tell them that you burn me because I tried to heal a baby when your own worthless treatments had done more ill than good."

The villagers, standing in a cluster about the stake, rustled like leaves in a windblown tree, but no one spoke in the woman's defense, and none met her eyes.

"You used herb lore," the Herder said. "It was such dabbling in forbidden arts that brought Lud's wrath upon the Beforetimers for their conceit. The Herder

3

Faction heals with humility, trusting to Lud's guidance instead of sinful pride. The plagues were Lud's warning that the Landfolk tread the same dangerous and prideful path when they close their ears to the Faction, for Herders are the voices of Lud." He blinked and seemed to rein in his religious fervor. "The woman who allowed you to defile her child will also be burned for heresy."

A woman screamed and fainted, but no one moved to her aid.

"You are a fool," the gypsy's voice rang out. "You will not be allowed to burn her when the Council can have her sweating her life out in one of their stinking farms."

"I am a Herder. Lud and the Faction rule me, not the Council," the priest snapped. There was a sullen mutter from the crowd, but the Herder glared them to silence. "She invoked the black arts. Council lore grants me the right to burn her and any who treat with her."

"What black arts?" the gypsy demanded contemptuously.

The Herder turned back to her. "You told the woman her child would die, and one day later it did. You cursed it and thereby revealed the demon within."

"I treated the babe but saw quickly by its symptoms that it was too late to save it," the woman said. "It could not tolerate the potions you fed it. I told the parents it would die so that they might say their farewells and not waste the child's final hours."

"Do not waste your *own* final moments with lies," the Herder jeered, pushing a gloating smile into the woman's face.

Her hand snaked out suddenly as if to grab him,

and the priest wrenched back with a strangled cry. She gave a throaty laugh of triumph. "What are you afraid of, old goat? Do you think my gypsy skin might be catching?"

"Beg, demon! Proclaim your guilt, and the cleansing will be swift," he screamed, almost hysterical with fury.

She laughed again, a humorless bark. "Cease your ranting, old man. Kill me so that I don't have to see your ugly face anymore."

Even from the back of the crowd, I could see the Herder mottle with outrage. Then his lips folded into a vindictive smile. "Evil must not be permitted to think itself triumphant," he said silkily, and then turned to speak a word to his acolyte, eyes glittering with malice.

The boy proffered a selection of long-handled metal tools.

"Th' bastard's goin' to brand her before he burns her," Matthew hissed into my ear, his highland accent thickened with anger.

"Am I blind?" I snapped. The amount of blood pooled about the woman's feet told me she would likely not live long enough to feel the flames of purification, let alone to be rescued. Despite her boldness, her face had grown as white as smoke.

"We mun do somethin'," Matthew whispered urgently. He gestured to our gypsy disguise, as if it made some point of its own.

"Be silent and let me think." I sent the thought directly to his mind.

The sensible thing to do would be to accept that it was too late to save her and withdraw before anyone noticed us. I looked at the gypsy again. Her chin lifted in defiance as the Herder approached with the brands.

I cursed under my breath and slid down from Zade's back, mentally asking the horse to stand quietly until I called. I told Matthew to turn the carriage around and go back to the main road, not trusting his instinct for drama.

"What will you do?" he asked eagerly.

"I'll think of something," I said shortly. "Wait for me out of sight."

As soon as he was gone, I pushed my way through the crowd, at the same time extending a delicate mental probe. Fortunately, the Herder was not mind-sensitive, so he was not aware of my intrusion.

"Where is her wagon?" I demanded aloud.

The Herder swung to face me, his eyes narrowing into slits at the sight of my gypsy attire. "By what right do you question a voice of Lud?" he snarled.

"By right of blood," I said.

It was Council lore that blood kin might speak in defense of their own. In the past, this had not stopped Herders doing what they wished and later making excuses to the Council for excessive zeal. But with the growing rift between Faction and Council, the priests' power had waned, and they were less wont to openly flout Council lore. In any case, it was only a stalling tactic, since I had no proof of kinship to the gypsy.

"Her wagon has been burned, as have all her Luddamned utensils and potions," the Herder said grudgingly, but his memory showed him riffling through the wagon and removing various pieces before the thing was flamed. My probe slid sideways into a memory in which he tortured the gypsy's bondmate to death, and I shuddered inwardly.

"You have proof that you are related?" he demanded.

"All gypsies are brothers and sisters," I answered, not wanting to be caught openly in a lie.

"Do not taint my ears with the practices of your foul breed," he hissed. "I asked for proof of kinship—you have shown me none, therefore be silent."

I saw his mind form a plan to report me to the soldierguards for sedition, thereby ridding himself of me in case I *was* related by blood. He turned back to the gypsy and snorted in annoyance to find her hanging limply from her bindings.

Alarmed, I reached out a probe, but her body still pulsed with life. She had only fainted.

The Herder cast down the brand and reached for a torch to fire the woodpile at the foot of the stake. A great rage seared me. Throwing off caution, I reached into the bottom of my mind for the darkest of my Misfit Talents.

But before I could stun him, an arrow hurtled through the air to bed itself in the center of the Herder's chest. He sucked in an agonized breath and clawed at the wooden stave, trying vainly to withdraw it. Then his eyes clouded and he collapsed, blood bubbling obscenely from his lips.

I disengaged my probe with a scream, almost dragged to my own doom by his swift spiral into death. Panting, I stared down at him in astonishment, and for a moment, silence reigned in the village clearing.

"The Herders will kill us all for this," a woman wailed, shattering the stillness, her eyes searching the trees for the archer.

"Not if we kill these gypsies and throw the bodies in the White Valley. We can say we saw nothing of what happened," a man began, but before he could continue, another arrow whistled through the air, piercing his neck.

He crumpled to the ground with a rattling gurgle.

That was enough for the rest. It was one thing to watch someone else die, and quite another to risk your own life.

People scattered in all directions, crying out in terror.

I did not know who had loosed the arrows, and there was no time to find out. Situated on the border of the highlands and lowlands, Guanette was visited regularly by off-duty soldierguards seeking amusement. At any minute, several might be drawn by the screams to investigate.

I rushed forward to the stake. Fortunately, the cuts on the gypsy's arms were shallow, since the aim of bloodpurging was to exact a full confession, not to kill. Still, the cuts were enough to drain her blood slowly. I ripped at the hem of my skirts and bound the torn strips around her arms, automatically setting up a barrier to repel the chaotic wave of unconscious thought that flowed from the gypsy as our flesh met. Then I cut through her bonds with shaking fingers, staggering as she fell heavily into my arms. A thick pot-metal band around her upper arm grazed my cheek.

All at once, my hair was wrenched savagely from behind, and I was pulled over backward, dragging the unconscious gypsy on top of me. For a second, I lay still, winded; then the acolyte launched himself at me, renewing his attack, raining blows on my head, his eyes alight with fanatical rage.

"Demon gypsy! Holocaust scum! Halfbreed!" he screamed in a reedy voice. "They've killed my master! Soldierguards!"

Fighting free of the gypsy's dead weight, I shoved the boy hard, toppling him to the ground. He glared up at me, a handprint of the gypsy's blood on his chest.

"You will die for this," he hissed. "Lud has granted my masters great power to kill their enemies. One day we will destroy all of your kind, even the stinking Twentyfamilies."

I turned from him in disgust and hauled the woman to her feet. This was no easy task, for she was tall and full-bodied, and her arms and upper body were slicked with blood. By the time I had her upright, Zade had responded to my mental summons. From the corner of my eye, I saw the acolyte's eyes bulge in astonishment as the horse knelt to receive the woman's body.

I groaned aloud as two soldierguards burst through the trees, wielding short-swords.

One dropped like a stone, pierced by another deadly arrow from my mysterious helper. The other soldierguard gave the dead man a sick look and flung himself behind a cart, scanning the treetops fearfully.

"Quickly, climb/get on my back," Zade sent, rising to stand upright. "Gahltha will be angered if you are harmed in my care."

Obediently, I vaulted onto him and wound my fingers in his mane, clamping my knees around the unconscious gypsy.

"Go!" I shouted, and he leapt forward.

Using coercion inwardly, I locked my muscles in place to ensure stability. Then I turned my head, sending an outward coercive bolt at the acolyte to erase all that he had seen. The block slammed into the boy's stunned mind, but not swiftly enough to prevent him from throwing the bloodpurge knife.

It pinwheeled toward me with uncanny accuracy: blade, hilt, blade . . .

There was no time to summon the mental energy to deflect it, but instinctively, I threw my head backward.

A split second later, the knife hammered into my temple.

I'm dead, I thought, and the world exploded into painful pieces, sending me into the abyss.

◆ 2 ◆

I WAS STANDING on a high plateau at the beginning of a path that led down into the terrible seared deadness of the Blacklands. It was night and darkly quiet. The distant noise of liquid dripping slowly into liquid was the sound of seconds dissolving and falling away into the sea of time.

Far across the Blacklands, I saw a flash of dull, yellowish light. I blinked, and suddenly I was down in the valley; the bleary gleam I had seen from afar shone from the gaping maw of a tunnel cut into a rocky outcrop.

Entering, I walked until I reached the source of the light: two great carved doors set deep in a granite arch in the tunnel wall. Incredibly, though made of stone, the doors were ablaze. Opposite them, illuminated by the glow, was a small grotto. I felt a surge of terror, for within it, dead and stuffed, was the Agyllian Elder, Atthis.

Then a voice spoke inside my mind—Atthis's voice from the past.

"Long ago . . . I dreamed one would be born among the funaga, a Seeker to cross the black wastes in search of the deathmachines, one who possessed the power to destroy them. . . . You are that Seeker. . . ."

The voice had grown steadily softer until it faded altogether.

11

"Atthis?" I whispered, but the bird in the grotto was as cold and silent as the rock, her clouded eyes gleaming with reflected flame.

I turned to face the doors again, for there was something about them that tugged at me. Before I could understand why, they swung open. Standing in their fiery embrace was a radiantly beautiful boy with gleaming yellow hair.

"Ariel . . . ," I whispered disbelievingly.

He gave a prim, cruel little smile. "Of course it is I. Did you really think we were done with each other?" His voice was as I remembered: high-pitched and taunting. "You cannot hide from me. But my revenge will wait, because there is a thing you must do for me."

"I won't do anything for you," I hissed.

"Do as you wish and you shall still do my bidding," he said with an angelic smile. "And when you have served my purpose, I will kill you. Until then, let me give you a gift of pain to remember me by."

I backed away from him, but before he could do anything, Maruman leapt from the darkness into the tunnel. The old cat was huge—the size of a wild wolf—and he positioned himself between Ariel and me, tail twitching back and forth. Tattered ears flat to the skull, he gave a yowling cry. The sound lifted the hair on my neck.

Ariel's eyes widened with terror. He made a warding-off shape with his fingers, and all at once, as if by moonfair conjury, it was not Ariel on the threshold of the burning doors but another blond boy—Jik.

The sight of the empath filled me with sorrow, and I barely noticed that Maruman had vanished.

"Promise," Jik murmured, the word barely audible against the crack of flame.

"Jik—" I began.

"Promise!" His voice drove into my mind, his eyes bright with dread.

Before I could summon the wit to answer, he lifted a hand to me. Instantly, fire licked at his sleeve and leapt into his hair.

At last I found my voice.

I screamed, but the noise that came from my mouth was a slow, rumbling growl that shook the world.

I opened my eyes and squinted in the dim light, my heart pounding sluggishly. The stone walls and tapestry hangings told me I was in the Healer hall at Obernewtyn.

I frowned. I had dreamed a long, oddly chaotic dream. And before that? The effort of trying to remember made my head throb.

Thunder rumbled ominously, and I looked out the window. Storm clouds darkened the horizon, and distant flashes of lightning threw the edges of the high mountains into sharp relief. Closer, in the gardens, the treetops whirled in a dervish dance in the rising wind.

As if my waking had been a cue, it began to rain heavily. I started as someone moved to the window, blocking my view.

"So the Days of Rain begin," Rushton murmured.

The sadness in his voice startled me, for the Master of Obernewtyn rarely displayed emotion. I felt immediately uncomfortable at his presence.

"It is just as well this season is brief, for, in truth, it casts a shadow on my spirits." Dameon's voice rose out of the darkness. The blind empath spoke with the slightly stilted formality of the highborn, for so he had been before being charged Misfit. Why were the leaders of Obernewtyn at my bedside?

"They feared for you, ElspethInnle," Maruman's voice whispered into my mind.

The old cat was curled by my head in his usual position. "You were in my dream!" I beastspoke to him. "But you were much bigger."

"Things are not always what they seem on the dreamtrails," he sent composedly.

"I wish it were summerdays all th' time." Matthew's voice came from a chair alongside the window. "I wish it were summerdays all th' time."

"Softly," Rushton murmured. "You will waken her."

"I'm awake," I rasped. My mouth felt dry and furry.

Rushton turned on his heel to face the bed, and I could not see his face at all. After a momentary stillness, he crossed to a table, poured water into a mug, and brought it to me. I was careful not to let our hands touch as I took it from him. Lifting my head slightly, I drank a mouthful, then froze at a sudden vision of a knife spinning through the air toward me.

"What happened in Guanette?" he asked.

I reached up to touch my temple. There was a slight lump on my head but no broken skin. Odd. I explained the sequence of events in Guanette after Matthew's departure, assuming he had told the rest. "The Herder's acolyte threw a knife at me just as I mounted Zade," I said at last. "The hilt must have hit me."

I had thought the blade struck me. I even seemed to recall the feel of it cutting into me. Or had that been part of the dream?

"Who would've thought that weedy acolyte had such a throw in him," Matthew marveled with what seemed to me tasteless relish. "It's just lucky ye'd locked yer muscles in place. Zade brought ye to th' wagon absolutely frantic. I near died meself when I saw ye covered in blood. I thought ye were mortal wounded and raced back to Obernewtyn. It were only when I got ye here that I realized it were th' gypsy's blood on ye, fer ye'd nowt a scrape."

Something in his description bothered me, but I could not pinpoint it. I sat up, wincing as a bolt of pain struck my temples. Instinctively, I set a suppressing barrier, a kind of mental net, to capture any hurt. It was a useful measure that enabled me to put off enduring pain. It was dangerous, however, to let too much pain build up.

The Healer guildmaster entered the chamber. "Is the gypsy all right?" I asked him.

"It is difficult to tell," Roland answered gravely. "Because she lost so much blood, she is weak, but the problem is more that her body appears resistant to healing."

I frowned. "How long have I been asleep?"

"Only a night. But you slept like the dead, if you will forgive the expression," the Healer guildmaster added dryly. "Obviously, the blow concussed you, for there is only a slight abrasion at your temple. But you always did heal fast." He let a little pointed silence form, reminding me that he still believed there was more to the healing of my scarred legs the previous year than I had told.

"Fortunately, it was not a serious wound," he went on, "since your mind will not allow healing access. But I suppose you know that well enough."

I hadn't known. Since a healer's talents required access to the unconscious levels of the mind, it must be some sort of instinctive reflex.

Roland shrugged. "Speaking of healing, you should be resting now." He looked around at the others.

"I'm goin'," Matthew said, rising. He looked down at me. "I'll tell Alad yer awake. Gahltha is madder 'n hell that he was nowt with ye. He's convinced ye'd nowt have been hurt if he were."

"I hope he hasn't blamed Zade for what happened," I worried as the Farseeker ward departed.

Dameon came to the bedside, and as he bent to touch my hand, I kept a tight hold on my emotional shield, wary of the Empath guildmaster's phenomenal Talent.

"I am glad you are safe, Elspeth," he said in his soft tones.

I nodded, forgetting he could not see, but he did not wait for an answer, gliding from the room with the slow grace that was a sign of caution but that sometimes appeared to be an uncanny instinct guiding him in compensation for his blindness.

Roland glared at Rushton.

"A moment," the Master of Obernewtyn said.

The Healer guildmaster shook his head in exasperation and moved away.

"You seem to go out of your way to try to get yourself killed," Rushton admonished gently, pulling a chair to sit by the bed.

From this angle, a lantern on the far wall cast enough light to show me the craggy plains of his face, but it was not possible to make out his expression. Nevertheless, there was an intimacy in the moment that filled me with discomfort.

Maruman snorted derisively and curled back to sleep, for human emotions irritated his senses.

"I had no choice," I told Rushton awkwardly, wishing Roland had not left us alone.

Rushton's feelings for me had been distorted during a partial mindbond we had undergone during the battle for Obernewtyn. Once, injured and delirious, he had called me his love. To my relief, he had not spoken of it since. Rushton had Misfit Talent, but it was latent, and I reasoned that his feelings for me were the same. Nearly suffocated already by his solicitude, I had no desire to face the restrictions that would surely arise from waking his overt affections. Besides, there was no room in my life for such things so long as I secretly awaited a summons from Atthis.

"You know, you talked in your sleep," Rushton said.

My heart beat faster at the thought of what I might have said. "I dreamed. It made no sense."

"You called out Ariel's name."

I heard again the dream—Ariel's promise to kill me—and felt chilled.

"He can't hurt us while he is locked up in the Herder cloisters as an acolyte," Rushton said.

If *he is in a cloister*, I thought. That was what we had heard, but I could not believe that Ariel would have tied himself to an organization weakened by its estrangement from the Council. Ariel had always sought power, and a Herder acolyte would be little more than a lowly servitor for his masters.

"You said Jik's name, too," Rushton went on.

I felt abruptly depressed. "I dream of Jik often. I wonder what it means."

"Too much death is all it means," Rushton said sharply. "That is the way of the world, and you have to accept it. What happened to Jik was not your fault,

Elspeth. No one could stop a firestorm. You should not judge yourself so harshly."

"I don't," I snapped. "My dreams judge me."

"Well, what are dreams but tricks of the mind?"

"Are they?" I asked coolly. I was less convinced of that. Sometimes dreams were gateways through which messages might come. Beasts called them *ashlings:* dreams that called.

Thunder rumbled again, and Rushton glanced back over his shoulder at the slanting gush of rain, just as a distant flash of lightning illuminated the clouds.

I took advantage of his inattention to turn the conversation to less personal matters. "Did Matthew make sure he wasn't followed when he brought me back here from Guanette?"

Rushton turned back from the window. "The only person he saw leave was an older gypsy who rode hell for leather toward the lowlands. He is almost certainly the one who shot the arrows. I don't know whether he had any interest in you, but fortunately, he did not try to track the wagon. Just the same, I will ask Gevan to have his coercers keep their eyes open so they can turn him aside if he does appear."

"I'm surprised the other soldierguard didn't come after me."

"I expect the gypsy put an end to him and to the acolyte. The villagers are probably still arguing about who should report the whole thing. It wouldn't surprise me if they had not even removed the corpses."

"The queerest thing was how frightened the villagers were of the Herder. I thought the Faction had lost influence, but you would not have thought so to see them cowering."

"I must send word to the safe house in Sutrium and ask Domick to investigate the relationship between the Herders and the Council. At his last report, they were still at odds, and I will be happier if that is still so," Rushton murmured.

To my relief, he rose, his thoughts absorbed by these larger concerns. "I was thinking of sending someone down to make contact with the safe house anyway. Domick's reports have been scant of late, and he has sent no word yet about how our offer of alliance was received by the rebels. I will speak of it at the next guildmerge if I have no word from them by then."

Briefly, his eyes returned to me. "We will have to decide, too, what to do with your gypsy when she wakes."

"*If* she wakes," Roland said, coming over determinedly. Rushton nodded and allowed himself to be ushered out.

I lay back, weary and curiously depressed. Rushton had been right about one thing—there had been too much death. Grieving had drained the heart and soul out of me, and sometimes I felt as if all that was left of me was a pale, shadowy wraith. And now the gypsy might die, too. Well, I had known that even as I strove to save her.

I looked out to the mountains, which were almost lost in the blackness of the stormy evening, and wished for the thousandth time that Atthis would call and that I might begin to live and act, instead of waiting.

❖ 3 ❖

LANTERN LIGHT GLIMMERED on patches of wet, black stone, dulling the pallid glow that emanated from a thick phosphorescent crust on the rock wall.

Fian reached out and prodded gently at one of the scabbed mounds, and a cloud of glowing insects rose, exposing uneven patches of bare rock as they flitted away into the echoing darkness.

"Do ye know these little beggars eat th' holocaust poisons but are nowt poisonous themselves?" he murmured.

I was startled at that but did not comment. There was no reason to be silent, yet the thought of the mountain of stone pressing down on top of the subterranean cave network seemed to compact the darkness and thicken it, leaving no room for words.

I looked back, searching in vain for a glimpse of daylight, but even the rock shelf we were walking along vanished into the shadows a few steps behind. The teknoguilders had laboriously cut the ledge out of the cave walls, it was designed to run from the White Valley entrance, shaped by the flow of the upper Suggredoon River, around the cavern walls just above the level of the subterranean lake. In spite of the constant flow of water from the Suggredoon, the lake remained at the same level, because a steep channel offered an outlet through the other side of the mountain to the lowlands.

The only other way to move about the caverns was by raft, poling between buildings and along the straight, narrow waterways that, leagues below, had been streets. Clusters of the strange, glowing insects that were the cave's sole inhabitants lit segments of the stone walls and crumbling buildings, reflecting them in pale disconnected shimmers on the dark water, but the majority of the dead city and the caves that contained it were sunk in eternal night.

As ever, I could not help wondering how the city had survived the shifts in the earth that had buried it under a mountain. How had the enormous dwellings, hundreds of floors high, not been crushed in the geological upheavals of the Great White? Was it yet another impossible feat of technology of the Beforetimers that kept the city intact?

Or had fate saved the ancient city for some purpose of its own?

I shivered.

"This way," Garth panted, an undercurrent of excitement in his tone. He moved along the path and around the perimeter of the ancient city with an energy and agility that belied the Teknoguildmaster's bulk.

Behind him came the Teknoguild ward, Fian, with Rushton and myself at the rear. We were moving in single file, because the ledge path was too narrow to walk two abreast. I stared at Rushton's back, wondering what had possessed him to permit an expedition of guildleaders into the least accessible water caves. Ordinarily, he was violently opposed to our taking part in anything dangerous, considering us too valuable to be risked. Garth must have presented a compelling case.

It would have been nice if either of them had thought to tell me what we were going to see, I thought with a flicker of irritation. I glared up at the broad space between Rushton's shoulders. As if he felt my gaze, he glanced back, but I let my eyes fall quickly.

"Damn!" he muttered as he stumbled in the darkness. "How much farther is this?"

"Nowt far," Fian assured us, holding his lantern higher. His eyes, gleaming with amusement, met mine fleetingly over Rushton's bowed head. In spite of my mood, I found myself smiling in response. There was something irrepressible about the highlander. His eyes sparked with intelligence and a wry humor that stopped him from being as painfully earnest as so many of his guild in the pursuit of knowledge. And he was one of the few at Obernewtyn who had not treated me with stultified awe since my return from the high mountains last wintertime, which had been deemed miraculous by some, since I'd been assumed dead.

We came to a place where only a brief, murky stretch of water separated the ledge from a sloping island of rubble formed by the collapse of one of the towering Beforetime monoliths. Dark water lapped sluggishly on the makeshift landfall. Garth leapt across the intervening space with a grunt, and on the other side made his way to the foot of an intact building. The light from the lanterns reached no farther than the row of square windows on the second level; black shadows obscured the floors above. At this end of the caverns, the ground sloped up so that most of the towering building was above the water line.

"This is it," Garth wheezed, flapping his hand in a flourish at the construction. "All five hundred floors. Oh, you needn't worry," he added, seeing my look of horror. "It's quite stable, because a good deal of it is buried in the rock above and behind, including what would have been the front door. The astonishing thing is that we discovered this at all, especially with so much of the city underwater or tainted. Of course, the very fact that so many buildings are still standing is incredible in the first place. We are becoming convinced that this city was one of the last built before the holocaust. The degree of technology here is far superior to that of other ruin sites and may well explain how this city survived when so many others did not. But there are certain strange facets to the architecture. . . ."

"Garth, get on with it," Rushton said brusquely.

Garth gave Rushton an offended look and turned to enter the building through a hole that had been cut in one of the immense walls. I glanced up, and the row of empty windows seemed to look down like eyes.

"It took an age to knock th' hole in the wall," Fian said, coming through after us with the second lantern. "Them Beforetimers built solid."

"And we had to be careful. Our main fear was that we might destroy something irreplaceable," Garth explained.

The building was cast along the lines of all Beforetime constructions, walls and floors bare, squared and uniform with no ornamentation. The Beforetimers were admittedly inspired at construction, but they lacked imagination.

Garth led us along the hall and up three featureless gray flights of stairs. Stepping out of the stairwell onto a small landing, the Teknoguildmaster lifted his lantern to reveal that the wall facing us had words carved into it: "Reichler Clinic Reception."

I stopped dead.

My mind rushed back to the moment when I had found the book called *Powers of the Mind* in a Beforetime library . Standing in the darkness of another ruined city, I had read enough to understand that there had been Talented Misfits before the holocaust. The book had spoken of tests performed at the Beforetimers' Reichler Clinic that proved conclusively that human beings of their era possessed Talents not unlike our own, though these had been largely latent. The clinic had claimed that, in time, more and more people would be born with such powers, though it would take a great catalyst to awaken the conscious mind to latent abilities on a grand scale. We had taken this as proof that we were not mutated freaks, as the Herder Faction and Council claimed, but a natural progression in human evolution. And what greater catalyst could have occurred than the Great White?

However, the teknoguilders had regarded the book with skepticism after their initial euphoria, fearing it might merely be one of the fictions the Beforetimers had produced in such number. But the discovery of the actual Reichler Clinic must resolve all doubt.

"Worth a bit of a walk through the dark, eh?" Garth sounded pleased by our reactions. He poked at my arm. "I thought since you discovered the book and argued so strongly that it was true, you should see this, my dear," he added.

"Strange to think of Beforetimers comin' here to be tested to see if they was Misfits," Fian said dreamily.

I felt a strange chill at the thought that, a thousand years before, a girl like me might have come to the clinic, wondering if she was a freak because she could use her mind to speak to animals or to other people.

Garth led the way through a door, and we found ourselves in a large room with metal benches. Windows along one wall opened to the darkness of the caves, while along another wall was a line of boxlike metal structures that were unmistakably Beforetime machines. These were smaller than the ones in the Teknoguild cave network in the mountains to the north.

"We know the Reichler Clinic was a paranormal research center," Garth said in a lecturing tone of voice. "*Paranormal* was a Beforetime word for 'Talented' or 'Misfit.' As Fian said, people would come here to be tested. We had no expectation of finding the clinic, and once it was found, it never occurred to me that we would find much in the way of information, because damp has destroyed all but the most impervious materials in the city. And even they will not resist decay forever."

"Garth . . . ," Rushton began.

"Patience," Garth said, as if Rushton were an importunate novice. "As I was about to say, I did not expect to find anything here, but I was wrong. It appears that the people who ran the Reichler Clinic were forward-thinking, and they sealed much of their information in a slippery, waterproof, transparent material they called *plast*." He bent down with a grunt and opened a cupboard, lifting out a sheaf of what first appeared to be pieces of paper. On closer examination, they proved to be made of some sort of pliable material. There were words on the sheets, but I could make nothing of them.

"The plast-covered paper is absolutely impervious to water, although it is not resistant to heat. As you see, a good deal of the matter contained on the sheets is in one of the peculiar linguistic codes the Beforetimers were so fond of using. Hiding their information in this way always seemed to me a paranoid and pointless business, but as it transpired, they had cause to be careful and secretive. My guild is beginning to fathom many of the codes, and these sheets are in one that the Beforetimers called *Jerman*. Fian has specialized in this code, and he was able to translate enough to come up with some very odd intelligence—not about the Reichler Clinic but about another Beforetime organization." He nodded regally at Fian, who took up the narrative.

"I believe th' code was used to store information that th' folk who ran th' Reichler Clinic wanted to keep secret," the highlander said. "I've only just begun decodin' th' plasts, but it's clear from what I've read so far that they wanted to conceal th' fact that some of th' Misfits they tested were not latent."

"Conceal it from whom?" I wondered, and Fian nodded.

"That's what got to me, too. Why would they want to hide what was basically proof of th' things they wrote in that book ye found? Th' answer was in th' plast sheets. Th' Reichler Clinic were bein' investigated by a powerful organization called *Govamen*, which was connected to huge weapon-tradin' houses that made a profit out of sellin' weaponmachines. Govamen was supposed to be stoppin' wars an' findin' other ways to resolve conflict between Beforetime factions, but in reality it reaped coin from th' very people who wanted th' wars to go on—namely th' weaponmakers. Of course, th' connection between Govamen an' th' weapon-tradin' houses was illicit. Th' Reichler Clinic folk learned of it by chance when they was tryin' to find out why they were bein' investigated."

"You mean this organization conspired to promote war for profit?" Rushton demanded.

"I would not go that far," Garth said. "However, it does seem to offer an explanation as to why the Beforetimers had so many wars. It is a thing that has always troubled me about them."

"I still don't understand what this had to do with the Reichler Clinic hiding things," I said. "It wasn't forbidden to be a Misfit then, was it?"

"No. But th' Reichler Clinic people learned that th' part of Govamen investigatin' them was devoted to research an' development of paranormal abilities as weapons," Fian said. "This was th' symbol of th' research cell from Govamen."

He stopped to point to a tiny picture atop one of the plasts. It showed three minuscule birds flying in an endless spiral around a word I could not interpret.

"Look closely," Garth invited.

I did, and my eyes widened at the realization that the birds pictured were Agyllians—Guanette birds, as Landfolk called them.

"Fascinating, eh?" he demanded.

"Yes," I agreed faintly, thinking he had no idea *how* fascinating.

The Land resonated with myths about the huge red birds, which were believed to be virtually extinct. But I knew that they dwelt in nests on high citadels of stone in the tallest mountains to the north, because they had once brought me there to save my life in the hope that I would one day destroy the Beforetimers' remaining weaponmachines. I wondered if it could possibly be a coincidence that their image adorned material produced by the mysterious organization called Govamen, with its sinister connections to the weaponmakers.

"Th' section in Govamen that used this as their mark"—Fian tapped the design—"had apparently gone a lot further in its paranormal research than simply testin' th' minds of volunteers. It had actually tried to alter th' brains of animals to produce artificial Talents. Seems they had some spectacular initial results that came to nowt. From what I have translated, th' Reichler Clinic people feared Govamen's interest in th' clinic meant they had th' idea of usin' th' people that they had tested as latent Talents. An' by usin' I mean kidnappin' an' experimentin' on, against their will."

I felt sick. That meant Misfits had been no safer in the Beforetime than we were now. Perhaps it would always be so.

"This is all very interesting," Rushton interrupted. "But you could have told it to us safely and simply back at Obernewtyn. I presume there is some reason you have dragged us into this miserable place?"

Garth sighed. "All right. I could have told you what I am about to show you, too, but it is so momentous I felt you would wish to see it. Perhaps I was wrong."

The stocky teknoguilder moved to the other end of the room, and as the light from the lantern he carried reached the far wall, I could see a mural had been carved there, depicting a mountain scene in perfect relief and intricate detail. It was a magnificent work, and it seemed vaguely familiar.

"It's Obernewtyn," Rushton said in a stunned voice. "Or at least, it is where Obernewtyn is sited. The same spot. The trees are different, but you can tell by the positioning of the mountains. But why on earth would its image be carved here?"

"I think ye'll find th' answer to that when ye read th' inscription on th' wee plaque," Fian said, pointing to a small metal square with raised lettering on the wall beside the mural.

Rushton leaned closer, and I heard him suck in a startled breath of air.

"What is it?" I demanded.

He gave me an unseeing look, and I slipped past him to see for myself. The words read "Presented to the Founder of the Reichler Clinic, Hannah Seraphim, by her devoted admirer, Jacob Obernewtyn."

"Seraphim," I whispered, staring at Rushton. "That's your family name. And Obernewtyn . . . What can it mean?"

He opened his mouth to speak, but abruptly the dazed look of amazement faded into a frown. "Listen," he said, tilting his head.

Then we all heard it. Someone was calling out.

"It's Matthew." I recognized the farseeker's voice. "He can't farseek underground."

I crossed to a window and peered out. From above, the watery caverns looked even more eerie. I spotted the ward by his lantern light bobbing along the ledge path and shouted to him that I would come down. My voice echoed weirdly, reverberating between water and rock.

"I told him to do a routine scan of the villages for new Misfits," I explained to the others. "Maybe he's found someone."

"Be careful," Rushton cautioned.

I nodded impatiently and hurried back downstairs, wondering why after so many Misfit rescues he felt the need to warn me to take care.

Matthew looked so relieved when I joined him on the ledge that I realized he had something more than a wild Misfit Talent to report.

"What is it?" I demanded, panting slightly.

"Ceirwan farsought me," the farseeker said. "He says ye mun all come back at once. Maryon's had a futuretellin' vision about th' gypsy woman we rescued—an' it sounds like trouble."

We rushed back to Obernewtyn, only to discover that Maryon had fallen into a second futuretelling trance from which she had yet to emerge. The Futuretell guilden had been unable to tell us anything more about her guildmistress's futuretelling, other than that it concerned the gypsy I had rescued and the future of Obernewtyn.

We could do nothing but go on with other matters until Maryon awoke. The whole affair completely overtook the excitement of finding the Reichler Clinic, and as we made our way to the kitchens for a late nightmeal, Rushton asked me not to speak of the finding until the Teknoguild had prepared a presentation.

"It seems strange to think of your being related to the very people who were interested in Misfit powers in the Beforetime," I murmured. "Do you suppose Jacob Obernewtyn built this place?"

Rushton shook his head. "My grandfather, Lukas Seraphim, built Obernewtyn as it is now, but Louis Larkin once told me that it had been built on the ruins of an older building. It's my guess this Jacob built the original house that stood here."

"I wonder why Hannah Seraphim started the Reichler Clinic in the first place." The discovery meant Rushton could trace the line of his descent back to the Beforetime—he must surely be the only person alive who could do that.

But Rushton only gave me a look. "It is a long time past, and her world is dead. The Teknoguilders' discovery of the Reichler Clinic is useful only in that it confirms absolutely that there were Misfits like us in the Beforetime. We have the present to deal with, and that is quite enough without wasting time on historical puzzles. I am far more concerned to find out what a nameless gypsy could possibly have to do with Obernewtyn."

I did not sleep that night for wondering what had been so important it had necessitated our immediate return.

The following morning, Matthew came to my chamber before firstmeal to inform me that Maryon had awakened. Rushton had called the guildleaders to his chamber.

I was careful not to wake Maruman as I dressed, and on leaving had to resist an urge to gather the bedraggled cat into my lap and stroke the rough fur and misshapen head of my first and dearest friend. Every time Maruman disappeared, I worried, knowing he wandered far from Obernewtyn in the throes of his occasional strange fey fits. On his previous disappearance, he had been gone for almost a full cycle of the moon. When he had returned, his already damaged right eye had been so severely infected that Roland had no alternative but to remove it.

If he suffered for the lack of it, he made no complaints.

I hurried then to Rushton's chamber. His face was stony as he opened the door and stepped back to let me enter.

The other guildleaders were seated about the small room, their faces grave. My eyes flew to the Futuretell guildmistress standing in a shadowed corner. Her dark eyes glinted enigmatically across the room at me, and my heart began to beat unevenly.

"What has happened?"

"All in good time," Rushton said tightly, gesturing to an empty seat. I flushed, for he did not normally speak so sharply to me.

He opened his mouth, then shook his head as if thinking better of whatever he would have said. Instead, he turned to the Healer guildmaster. "You'd better begin, Roland," he growled, flinging himself in a chair.

"Elspeth, as you know, the gypsy you rescued is resisting healing," Roland said. "We cannot work against her body to force her to heal, and it is impossible to enter her mind, because she has a natural mental barrier."

"Are you saying she is dying?" I asked.

"Right now, we are keeping her stable. However, if this goes on for much longer, she will die."

"Maryon?" I said, turning to the tall woman in the shadows. "What did you see in your futuretelling? What has the gypsy to do with Obernewtyn?"

Rushton rose and began to pace about the room.

The futureteller made a graceful gesture with her long fingers. "I saw many things. A journey over th' great water; a gray stone fortress wi' a Guanette bird flying o'er it." Maryon spoke these words in a high oratory tone, but now she dropped into a more normal voice, and its very flatness gave her words greater power. "I saw yon gypsy woman mun be returned safe to her people within a sevenday fer th' sake of Obernewtyn."

"Seven days!" I cried. Futuretellers often came up with obscure deeds they said must be performed for this reason or that, or for no reason at all that they would divulge. But this was the most dramatic I could remember in some time.

"Futuretellin' is nowt an exact study," Maryon said. "There is much to see that defies understandin'. But I did see that th' gypsy's people may be found in Sutrium."

"Sutrium!" That was almost worse than not knowing. Sutrium was the largest town in the Land—and the most dangerous, being the base of the main Council-court.

Belatedly, I realized no one else had reacted to the mention of it—they already knew this. I wondered why Rushton had not waited for me before telling what was to be told. It was not as if I had delayed coming or had been difficult to find.

"Given that they are gypsies, I dinna know how long her people will bide there," Maryon was saying. She shrugged. "All I can tell ye is that they are there now." She broke off suddenly and there was an awkward silence.

"Are we voting on whom to send with the gypsy?" I asked at last.

"There will be no voting on this matter. *You* will take her," Rushton said tersely.

I was genuinely astonished. Rushton had managed to convince the guildmerge to ban guildleaders from trips to the lowlands, because there was too much risk. Now he commanded me as if I was a novice to make a journey to the most oppressive city in the Land, with an unconscious gypsy fugitive!

"I will impose a sleepseal on her," the Healer guildmaster said in such a way that let me understand this had been discussed, too. "It will slow down her heartbeat and her dying. Kella can remove the seal in Sutrium, just before you hand her over."

"Why am *I* to take her?" I asked slowly.

Rushton's green eyes stared into mine for a moment; then he turned to Maryon. "Tell her."

The futureteller drew herself up to her considerable height. "Fer Obernewtyn's sake, Elspeth, th' gypsy mun be returned to her people. This was the futuretellin' fer which I sent to recall ye from the city under Tor. But yesterday, when I fell into a second an' deeper trance, I learned another thing: *You* mun be th' one to take her back. Nowt fer Obernewtyn's sake but fer yer own."

"Mine?" I echoed.

Maryon went on, her face grave. "On th' journey, you—an' only you—will have th' chance to learn what the word *swallow* means. If ye fail, I have foreseen . . . that ye'll die afore th' next Days of Rain."

❖ 4 ❖

ON THE SIDE of the road were patches of scrub and a
few of the immense white-trunked ur trees that charac-
terized lowland terrain. Matthew had not seen many of
them before, but the trees had grown in great profusion
around my childhood home in Rangorn.

I thought fleetingly of picking berries in their shade
with my mother. Then I sighed and shook myself.

Rushton, Dameon, and Ceirwan had seen us off at
first light, the gravity of the expedition diverted at the
last minute by a hysterical tantrum of the young
empath-coercer Dragon, whom we had rescued on a
previous expedition. She had suddenly realized she
would not be going with us, and it had taken all of
Dameon's empathy to prevent her from flinging herself
after us as the gypsy wagon pulled away in the gray
mountain dawn.

My last sight of Rushton had been of him frowning
after me, arms folded across his chest.

Thunder rumbled now, and I looked up at the lowering sky, wondering if we would reach Sutrium before
the storm broke. We had not long passed Glenelg Mor,
its sodden earth invisible beneath a veil of mist.

I sent a brief command for Matthew to take up the
reins, rather than letting them hang down loosely. "It

will look odd if someone comes along and sees no one is steering the wagon."

"Gypsy horses are trained to stay on the road while their owners sleep. Besides, who in their right minds would be out so late with a storm brewin'?" Matthew grumbled, but he did as I bade.

A few minutes later, a horse galloped around a bend behind us. I gave Matthew a pointed look, though in truth he was right about seldom meeting anyone on the road. He did not notice, because he was all agog at the sight of the exotic-looking gold-skinned rider—wrapped in a purple cloak and bent low over the horse's neck—who thundered past and out of sight around a bend in the road ahead.

"That were one of them Sador tribesfolk," Matthew said excitedly. "I'm goin' to visit Sador someday." His eyes glowed at the thought.

The road to the remote region had only just been opened up in the last year, as the Blacklands taint along the eastern shore of the Land faded, allowing a slender, and some said dangerous, passage along the coast.

The Council had always maintained the Land was all that remained unpoisoned of the world, while the Herders preached it was all Lud had seen fit to spare of the corrupt Beforetime. Seafarers had long known this to be a lie, but they had a rigid code of silence imposed by the Council. Even so, word had leaked out, initially as gossip and rumor. But with Sador suddenly accessible and known to all, it seemed more likely than ever that there was a world beyond the Blacklands.

Looking before us to where the Sadorian rider had disappeared, I remembered Gahltha, who was scouting ahead for danger. I asked Matthew how long the horse had been absent.

"Nowt long. He won't go too far with you here."

I ignored the questions implicit in his tone. There was no way of explaining Gahltha's transformation from a vicious human-hating fury into my devoted guardian without relating the whole fantastic story of my deliverance from death by the Agyllians. It was Atthis who had called the black horse to carry me down from the high mountains, and whatever the ancient bird had said to keep him waiting through the long months of my convalescence had altered Gahltha completely. Gahltha now believed utterly that I was to rescue beasts from their long slavery to humans. No surprise that he and Maruman both had insisted on accompanying me to the lowlands.

I sighed, sick of living my life at the directive of the vague whims of fate and futuretellers.

At the conclusion of our impromptu meeting the day before, Rushton had suggested I say nothing of Maryon's predictions concerning myself to the general population of Obernewtyn. I had been only too glad to agree. Success would simply add to the myth surrounding me, and if I failed, it would not matter what had been predicted. Matthew had been told that the purpose of the journey was to return the gypsy to her people, which was true enough, and that while in Sutrium we would inspect the safe house and inquire as to whether Brydda Llewellyn's rebels would accept us as allies. Rushton still had no answer since his visit to Sutrium, and he feared missing an opportunity to ally ourselves with those who could very well be the next rulers of the Land.

If only they would accept us.

I glanced back over my shoulder to where the gypsy lay on one of the wooden pallet beds, Maruman curled fast asleep at her feet. I judged her to be about forty years of age. Her features were too strong for beauty, but she was handsome and her hair was as black as my own. One sleeve had ridden up to reveal the potmetal bracelet she wore above her elbow.

Her stubborn resistance to healing had begun to take its toll. Despite Roland's sleepseal, there was an unhealthy pallor to her skin.

"She's nowt dead yet," Matthew said defiantly.

I frowned at him. "Let's hope she lives until we get to Sutrium and that we have no trouble getting her through the gates."

"We have papers," Matthew said.

"Yes. False ones. But, Ludwilling, the soldierguards will not have a description of her yet—or of me."

The farseeker paled. As usual, he had given no thought to the realities of the situation in his dreams of heroic deeds.

"I wonder where th' gypsy who shot them arrows in Guanette rode to in such a rush. I dinna see him very well through the trees, but he were tall and well-muscled. He had gray hair in a gypsy plait, an' he were wearin' a blue shirt," Matthew said dreamily. Beyond his sloppy shielding, I caught a glimpse of a vision in which a tall gypsy hero thanked us regally for the return of his companion.

"There's no possibility of us chasing after this gypsy and just handing the woman over as if it were a public play," I said sharply.

Matthew flushed and his shield slammed into place.

"Ye said ye'd give her to her people, an he mun be one of them."

"And so I will, but discreetly." *If she lives*, I thought. *And if I can find them.*

Matthew let out a formless exclamation of surprise, dragging me back from my worries. We had reached the top of a long rise, and Sutrium lay before us in the blighted light of the gathering storm.

It had grown much bigger than I remembered, spreading farther west until it joined up with settlements along the side of the Suggredoon River and stretching east and north into straggling outlying districts and farmlands. Beyond the city lay the great sea.

In some ways, Sutrium was not unlike the coastal town of Aborium. We had journeyed there on the very expedition that had led to the rescue of the empath-coercer Dragon. Whether it was my imagination or the knowledge that Sutrium was the home of the main Councilcourt, it seemed a dark and menacing place.

Unlike Aborium, there were no watchtowers. It was too big for such things to be of any use. But in any case, there was no need, since there were three huge soldier-guard camps on the city outskirts. One lay slightly inland on the banks of the Suggredoon; another closer to the sea, near the ferry port; and the third to the east, among the farmlands.

How would the very first Councilmen, who had sworn not to follow in the steps of the Beforetimers, view the sprawling city? I wondered. Surely all their fears that humans might tread the same doomed path of progress would be realized at the sight of it. In my mind's eye, I saw for a moment the shadowy, half-drowned city beneath Tor.

Thunder sounded again, and as if it were some heavenly signal, Gahltha emerged like a shadow from a thick copse of Ara trees a little way down the slope. He waited, a dark shape against the pale speckled trunks and tremulous clouds of foliage, until Jaygar brought us close.

"The way to the funaga-li barud is not watched by danger," the black equine sent in his stringent mental voice. "Funaga" was the closest rendering of the beast thought symbol for human. The form used by Gahltha was subtly derogatory, for though the old acid bitterness had vanished from his nature, there were still traces of it when he considered humans outside of Obernewtyn.

"It would be wise for ElspethInnle to ride this equine," Gahltha sent. "Only the funaga walk without shackles/burdens in this place."

"Wait a moment," I sent, and climbed into the back of the cart to change my skirt for trousers. Coming out again, I stood up on the wagon's bench seat, and the black horse came alongside, allowing me to transfer smoothly to his bare back. Sensing his approval at the ease of my mounting, I felt smug. Gahltha had taught me to ride as gypsies did. And there had been many times during his painful lessons that I had felt certain they were simply a sadistic way to murder me. Yet I had survived, and there were few now at Obernewtyn who could match my skill. In fairness, that was because few rode as frequently. None among us rode a horse except at its invitation, since all thinking beasts were regarded as equal to humanfolk. I would as soon ask Matthew to carry me as ask one of the equines. Horses took part in expeditions at their own choosing, masquerading as beasts of burden. They never carried humans other-wise, except at great need.

Gahltha was the exception.

After bringing me from the high mountains, he had insisted on going back into them often; whether out of nostalgia or to remind himself of his promises, I never knew. Each time he went, he asked that I ride on his back. At first I had refused, disliking the way it in-creased the mystique my activities had already woven about me, but his determination had worn me down. And like him, I had come to love the headlong gallops over the whispering grasses, flattened to his back and feeling as if the two of us were, in those moments, a sin-gle wild spirit.

This had the unexpected result of causing the proud Obernewtyn equines to question whether carrying hu-mans must always be a sign of slavery. More than one of the beasts had suggested that a time might come when it would be useful to have Misfits who rode well. The matter was still under discussion among their kind.

"We must be nearin' th' outer gate," Matthew sent as we reached the first shingled dwellings at the outer edge of the sprawling city. He got into the back to cover the woman's face, and I concentrated on summoning the mental focus I would need to coerce the soldier-guards at the city gates if there was any difficulty.

I reached out to take Gahltha's reins in my fingers as Matthew returned to his seat. My hands and body, like his, were stained a light gypsy tan. Brydda Llewellyn's mother, Katlyn, who had come to live at Obernewtyn, was a skilled herb lorist, and to aid our most common disguise, she had perfected a dye that simulated gypsy skin tone and that would not wash off easily. Despite prevailing prejudices, it was far safer to move about the Land as homeless gypsies than to pretend to be normal Landfolk, for they rarely traveled.

I concentrated on the disguise, enhancing it slightly with coercion so that people would see a boy in the gypsy clothes—just in case news of the incident at Guanette had spread to Sutrium.

With a mental apology to Gahltha, I pulled the reins tight. They did not drag at his mouth, being a modified bridle that only looked as if it would control and direct a horse. The old bit and bridle were anathema to human and beast alike at Obernewtyn, but even so, I wondered if it would not have been wiser to use it on expeditions that would take us into the heart of Council territory, where spies would be watching for any deviations.

Well, it was too late now.

To my relief, there was a crowd at the gate; traders and farmers and the odd green-clad jack returning after a day's work trading outside the city. The number of people lined up to show papers would mean a longish wait but less individual attention.

Approaching the end of the line, we fell in quietly behind the rest, ignoring cheeky signals from a cluster of children. Such a reception was so common for gypsies that we would have stood out if we had reacted to it.

For the most part, the people about us were grim-faced and sour-looking, and many bore the ugly marks of plague survivors. There was no chatter or end-of-day banter, only a brooding silence. People did not look into one another's eyes, and the few words spoken were punctuated with wary, sliding glances.

It was a timely reminder that Sutrium was a dangerous city, filled with a treachery that must not be underestimated. The main thing was to get past the gate without any sort of fuss that would draw attention to us.

I looked up at the dark clouds, willing the storm to break. The soldierguards would scarcely glance at us if it was pouring rain on their heads.

Jaygar's mental voice speared into my mind without warning. "I will kill/trample funaga-li!"

As if suddenly mad, the horse began to push his way through people in front of us, dragging in his wake the wagon containing the unconscious gypsy, Maruman, and a helpless Matthew.

✦ 5 ✦

I SENT OUT a coercive mental bolt, forcing Jaygar to a halt. Then I looked around frantically, trying to see what had provoked the normally placid equine to such a dangerous outburst.

I did not need to look far.

My own fury swelled at the sight of a small mare ahead of us trembling under the weight of a load of wood. But what made my blood boil and what had surely incensed Jaygar, was the sight of a fat youth sitting on top of the load, unconcernedly eating a bun.

Even as I watched, the mare staggered sideways under the weight of her burden, and the lout cursed her unsteadiness, whacking her with casual cruelty over the head.

"Release me!" Jaygar raged. "You have no right."

I did not loosen my mental hold. "I have the right to restrain any beast/funaga who endangers the rest," I sent, quoting from the expedition charter Rushton had made us draw up over long guildmerge sessions. Jaygar knew as well as I did that Avra had approved it on behalf of the Beastguild. "Now will you obey/calm?"

The horse snorted angrily. "You would risk us/all for an unknown funaga but not for this beast?"

44

"Risk comes from acting in thoughtless haste," I gritted. "I will help the beast my own way. Now, will you obey, or must I waste more time in arguing with you?"

Chastened, Jaygar agreed, and I asked Gahltha to come up beside the mare. To my astonishment, he refused.

"I will not let you endanger yourself," he sent. "This equine is one alone, and your life's purpose will save/help many more than one life."

"She is your kind," I sent. "Surely you don't set my life above hers?"

"Protect Innle before/above all," Gahltha sent.

"Is that what Atthis told you?" I fumed. "Well, I am not Atthis's servant/slave. I won't spend my whole life waiting to perform a single deed, Gahltha. Not for you, nor for Atthis. I will do what I can now, because tomorrow might never come. Now take me up beside the mare, or I will get down and walk!"

After a long moment, Gahltha moved forward, but there was an offended stiffness in his bearing. I wished I had the empathy to show him what I felt. So often words said only half of what you wanted to say, even words sent directly from mind to mind. But empathy was the one power I lacked utterly.

As we drew level with the mare, I made myself calm down. I did not want to show an interest that would be remembered later. From the corner of my eye, I noted the exhausted sag of her head and the scars on her knees and fetlocks from previous falls. Taking a deep breath to quiet my outrage, I reached out a probe to examine the bindings on her load. When I detected a weakness, I began to work at it with my mind, backward and forward.

This was exhausting, because the probe had to be densely focused to produce even the slightest physical force, but anger gave me additional determination, and in a short time, the tie snapped with an audible twang.

The lout on top of the load gave a bellow as he and the wood crashed to the ground.

A second after, a streak of lightning split the sky. People looked up fearfully, ever mindful that this might be a firestorm. But it began to rain, and it was not the burning rain of a firestorm.

The lout got to his feet, red-faced with embarrassment, and flayed the mare viciously. She was so exhausted that she barely flinched under the onslaught.

"Get out of my way," I said insolently, pushing Gahltha forward to distract him. I blinked to clear the rain from my lashes.

"Halfbreed trash!" he yelled. "Don't tell me what to do."

"Then do something of your own will," I rejoined promptly. "Show us you can move your fat bum as fast as you flap your lips."

He stepped forward, lifting his stick to strike me, but Gahltha snorted and reared, pawing the air. The youth cried out in fright and cowered back.

Thunder cracked again and lightning slashed above, shedding an eerie light on the motley crowd as the rain gathered force. The storm created a mental static that interfered with my Talent. I concentrated hard and prayed it would not get any worse.

"What's going on back here?" demanded the gate soldierguard, striding back along the line.

"The stupid horse lost its load," the lout blustered.

"Then that gypsy tried to set his horse on me. Savage brute of a thing."

"T'was the lightning affrighted him," I said, lowering my voice.

"He overloaded the mare and the ropes broke," a woman said, spurred by a coercive prompt. I did not want the soldierguard to focus his attention too specifically on me.

"Look at the poor thing," another woman shouted after a mental prod. Then she blinked and looked startled with herself.

"It's a wonder it didn't keel over in the very path," someone else growled of his own accord.

"And what if it did?" the lout demanded truculently. "It's my property. I'll kill it right now if I feel like it." I felt Jaygar's anger like the sun on my back.

"Do that and you'll be fined," the soldierguard snapped.

"Fined?" he squawked. "I've a right to do what I want to my own horse."

"I don't give a damn what you do to the beast, just so long as its corpse don't clutter up the way. Now get this mess out of the road. Load it to one side and be quick about it."

Muttering and cursing, the lout dragged on the mare's bridle to shift her onto the grass verge and began to move the wood. She stared out unseeingly, her eyes like dusty pebbles.

"Greetings, littlesistermind," I sent.

She blinked and turned her dull gaze to me.

"This funaga is cruel to you," I continued.

"All your kind are so. Your blood is curdled with cruelty." Her mental voice was infused with a dreamy

47

kind of hopelessness. She didn't seem surprised to have a human talking to her. Perhaps she thought she was hallucinating.

"Not all funaga are this way," I sent, but the mare was silent with disbelief or lethargy. I sighed, thinking this was not the moment to convert her. "If you hate this funaga, why not run free?"

"Funaga are everywhere. The wind spawns them. If not this one, another would own me," she sent without bitterness. "When I take the longsleep, I will run free."

Beastspeaking was often difficult to understand, because sometimes animals used words differently than we did. Equines called *sleep* the "shortsleep" and *death* the "longsleep," believing the two states to be related.

I shook the wetness from my face and licked my lips. The rain tasted sweet and cold.

"If there were a barud for freerunning in thiswaking, would you dare to run? Could you escape?"

"There is no such place," the mare sent flatly.

"Littlesistermind, I tell you such a place does exist, and if you go there, you may run free and nevermore wear the coldmetal in your lips."

"A barud with no funaga? That is as likely as skyfire without its roar." The flash of cynicism told me not all of the spirit had been beaten out of her.

"There are funaga," I admitted. "But these have the power to speak with beastminds, as I do. And none of them thinks of owning or breaking or hurting. They think of equines as brother/sisterminds."

She showed her disbelief again. I asked Gahltha and Jaygar to speak to her mind and convince her. Only when the black horse came close and showed her the false bit did she believe, and then she listened carefully as he described a route that would bring her to Obernewtyn.

The lout glared at me. "Get that black demon away from my horse, halfbreed."

I shrugged and drew Gahltha away at once, resigned to the knowledge that he would remember me when the mare disappeared. I sent to her, warning her to be careful she was not followed when she escaped from her human masters. "Run safe, littlesistermind, and perhaps we will meet again in thiswaking."

"I am called Faraf," the mare sent. "And I swear this will be so: nevermore shall I curse the funaga as one, for I know now that some burn with the heartfire."

My eyes pricked with sudden startled tears, for the mare had paid me a great compliment. Beastlegend told of a heart that burns eternally with the souls of all beasts who die or are yet to be born. This shared heart symbolizes the harmony between beasts, no matter what their physical form or how they prey on one another.

Beasts excluded humans from this cycle of harmony, believing they have no true soul. This offered an explanation for humankind's terror of death and their desire to dominate.

In implying that I shared the heartfire of beasts, the little mare was naming me her equal and the bearer of a true soul.

I felt my spirits lift, for the rescue of the gypsy and the exchange with the mare reminded me that no matter what Atthis or Maryon or Gahltha thought, I was the mistress of my own life.

We had drawn almost level with the gate now. In front of us, the soldierguards were checking the soggy papers of a jack.

"Ye'll be lucky to find buyers for that lot," one of the soldierguards told the green-clad trader. "No one's got much coin these days, an' them that has coin wants exotics from Sador or lavish trinkets from the Twenty-families. Even with the Herders sayin' it's all Lud-curst." I was surprised at the accent, for most soldierguards came from lowlander stock. I also wondered what sort of trader a Twentyfamilies was. I did not know what the word meant, but I was sure I had heard it before, and recently.

"We're away next," Matthew sent.

I saw that he was nervous. "Remember, don't be apologetic or humble. It isn't the gypsy way, and it will seem odd."

The Farseeker ward had been on plenty of expeditions, but this was his first visit to the lowlands. It was one thing to fool a highland villager and another entirely to lie barefaced to hardened soldierguards.

"There may nowt be humble gypsies, but there's plenty of silent, surly ones," he said. "I'll be one of them, an' you can do th' talkin', same as ye did when we was caught by Henry Druid that time."

Henry Druid was a rebel Herder who had disappeared after being driven from the Faction for refusing to destroy his collection of Beforetime books. On a previous expedition, we had stumbled onto his secret camp, but it had since been destroyed by a firestorm, the Druid and his people killed or scattered.

"My talking didn't stop them taking us prisoners," I pointed out. Gahltha twitched, as if reproaching my inattention. The soldierguards had finished with the jack and were waving him through the gates. I noticed a man staring at Gahltha and realized the rain had washed away the dirt I had rubbed into his coat. Even at his most unkempt, the black horse had always been magnificent to look at. More than once, there had been trouble on expeditions because someone had coveted him. I had gotten into the habit of daubing his coat with filth as a safeguard.

I sent a swift message to him as the soldierguard gestured for us to come forward. Gahltha's smooth gait became an uneven, lopsided lurch, his head drooped low, and I was amused to hear him wheezing loudly as if his wind were gone.

My amusement faded as the soldierguard reached up for my papers, for the other with the highland accent had turned to the wagon and bade Matthew pull the curtains open. We had decided to pretend there were only two of us, just in case the Guanette incident had been reported and they were looking for an injured gypsy. If either moved to examine the rig, I would have to coerce them.

My heart leapt into my throat as the highland soldierguard climbed onto the running board and peered inside the cabin.

"Nothing to trade?" the other soldierguard asked me.

"Some beads and braiding," I said, trying to pay attention.

The soldierguard sneered. "No market for low-quality halfbreed work."

I shrugged, riveted to the wagon. One step farther and the other soldierguard could not help but see the gypsy. But there was a loud hiss and the man fell back in fright.

"What's that? Some sort of fangcat?" he demanded of Matthew.

"It . . . it's injured," the farseeker stammered.

"Looks like it needs knockin' on th' head," the highlander growled, drawing out a short-sword.

"Perhaps, but it is said Lud curses them who hurt cats," Matthew said in a desperately sinister voice.

He had gauged it well. The soldierguard was a highlander and fortunately was as superstitious as the best of them. He backed away hastily, letting his sword drop.

At that moment, the light rain became a drenching torrent, and with a curse, the soldierguard examining my papers thrust them unceremoniously into my hand and reminded me that gypsies had to report to the Councilcourt for an extension of permit if we stayed more than a sevenday.

"We won't be here more," I said, hoping that was true.

"You did well," I told Matthew when we had been passed through the gate. "Maruman says to thank you for preventing the man from knocking him on the head."

"Thank Lud for Maruman," he said fervently. "Another step an' that soldierguard would've seen th' gypsy."

In a few minutes, we had reached the outer rim of the labyrinth of narrow streets that was the city center of Sutrium. Dwellings here were built right up against one another, often with no more than a single dividing wall to separate them, and had steeply thatched roofs that hung in shaggy fringes over doors and windows. Most were several floors high, which meant the streets weaving through them were shadowy and cold, seldom touched by the sun's rays. But there were gaps, too, where nothing stood. I saw several before their significance struck me: They marked where dwellings had been burned. In some places a whole row of houses had been burned, while in others a single house had been razed and those on either side left untouched.

"'Tis ice-cold out." Matthew shivered. "Feels like wintertime rather than the Days of Rain."

"Better to be cold here," I said, turning my attention back to the road. "Stops us getting comfortable and careless."

"I dinna think there's much danger of that," Matthew said. "Besides, I was nowt thinkin' of myself." He jerked his head toward the wagon's cabin.

"Look there," I interrupted, pointing to a striped awning. "Just as Domick described it."

"Were we supposed to turn left or right now?"

"West toward the Suggredoon. That would make it right." *I hope*, I thought.

Responding to my mental directive, Jaygar veered away from the main road down the next right-turning side street. It proved to be a narrow lane lined with workshops and frowsy, dilapidated apartments. Even in the rain it stank of urine and refuse.

Without warning, a window opened and a bucket of swill was hurled across the stones.

A little farther on, a man opened a door and stared out at us. He bore the scarring of a plague survivor.

The plague had erupted the previous year in Aborium or Morganna, spreading rapidly to Sutrium and all the other populous coastal cities and killing one in three who contracted it.

In the aftermath of the disease, there had been almost no one to work the farms, and this had resulted in terrible shortages that had seen hundreds starve. The shortages continued, as many of the farms still lay abandoned and unproductive.

Uneasily, I realized that meant there was little to sell in cities other than information. The sooner we located the safe house and got off the street the better.

We came around the corner and groaned at the sight of the sea, a seething gray mass in the rain. "We should have turned left back there," I said. I was surprised when my senses detected powerful static from the direction of the water. There had to be something nearby tainted with holocaust poisons, I thought.

Gahltha turned around so that I could direct Jaygar in maneuvering the cumbersome wagon from behind. I opened my mouth to speak to Matthew and almost bit my tongue off when Gahltha suddenly leapt forward and galloped at a breakneck pace back along the lane. I managed to keep my seat thanks to our mountain rides, but I almost flew straight over his head onto the cobbles when he came to an abrupt halt and swung sideways, facing into a short dead-end street.

"What the hell are you doing?" I demanded. Then I faltered, feeling the panicky shift in my mind that could mean only one thing.

Someone was tampering with my thoughts!

The alien probe sensed my awareness and fled from my mind. As an immediate consequence, I could see what I had been prevented from seeing sooner.

Crouched in the middle of the alley was Dragon, dripping wet and staring up at me with defiance and fear.

• 6 •

"WHAT DO YE mean ye followed us?" Matthew shouted.

Dragon backed away from his fury into the corner of the wagon, bumping the bedshelves. The blankets fell from the gypsy's face; I was startled anew by her pallor.

"Have ye any idea how worried they'll be at Obernewtyn when they find ye missin'?" Matthew raged aloud, for Dragon's formidable and instinctive mindshield made farseeking her nearly impossible.

"Keep your voice down," I snapped.

We had climbed inside the wagon. It got us out of the rain, but it was hardly the safest place for a screaming argument.

"Did ye hear—" Matthew began wildly.

"I would have to be deaf not to," I interrupted in a cold, quiet voice. "Whatever Dragon did or didn't do is not going to matter a damn if someone calls the soldier-guards on us for causing a disturbance."

The empath-coercer gave me a mutinous look. "Dragon come, too," she said.

Even dirty and wet, her glorious mop of red curls dangling in rattails, she was still incredibly lovely in the wagon's lantern light. I prayed we were not the only ones she coerced out of seeing her. Once seen, Dragon would not be easily forgotten.

What puzzled me was how she had followed us. We had made good time to make it to Sutrium in a day, so she could not have kept up on foot. She must have been in the wagon the entire time.

"Won't go back," she added mulishly, as if she feared she had not been clear enough.

Since there was no question of simply sending her back, I might have reassured her, but she must not be allowed to think she had won.

"This is a bad thing you have done, Dragon," I said sternly. "I am very angry. Dameon will be terribly worried about you."

Dragon adored the gentle Empath guildmaster who had taken her under his wing. With a stricken look, she burst into noisy tears and choked out that she had left a message with Louis Larkin to say she had gone to visit some of her animal friends. That mollified me slightly, for no one would worry overmuch to begin with. At least she had not gone away completely heedless of the trouble it would cause. Everyone would assume she was sulking over our departure for a little while, and since she had fended for herself alone for most of her life, no one would think of finding her and forcing her back to Obernewtyn too soon. But we would have to send a message back as soon as possible.

Dragon was staring at me with a woebegone expression. I put my arms around her thin shoulders with a sigh, knowing there was no use in trying to treat her as if she were any other disobedient novice. Despite her beauty and incredible illusion-making Talent, only the thinnest veneer of ordinary human behavior lay over the wild, half-starved waif I had coaxed from the Beforetime ruins outside Aborium.

And the truth was, had I not been so preoccupied with my own thoughts, I would have felt her clumsy coercive manipulations and sent her back long before we had reached Sutrium.

"Surely yer nowt goin' to let her gan away wi' this?" Matthew demanded.

"No, I'm going to turn her over to the soldierguards to teach her a lesson," I said sarcastically, wondering at the extent of his reaction. Did he think I would blame him for her presence simply because she'd grown attached to him? "What's done is done. Now let's move."

Dragon promptly turned her head and stuck her tongue out at him.

"Enough," I said firmly. "Lud knows how many tales will be told tomorrow about a gypsy wagon lurking in a side street. I think we have done enough to get ourselves noticed. Now let's find the safe house. Get the wagon turned around, Matthew."

The farseeker obeyed begrudgingly. Dragon's eyes were huge with apprehension when I turned to face her. "Not go back," she begged.

"I won't send you back," I promised. "We're going to the safe house now to see Kella. You remember Kella?" Dragon's eyes warmed and she nodded eagerly. "Good. Now you must be very quiet or else the soldierguards will stop us. Can you do that?"

This time she nodded solemnly. "Quieter than Maruman stalking a squeaker," she vowed.

Hearing his name, the cat stretched luxuriously and peered down at us, his good eye glowing in the darkness.

"Maruman, will you keep her/*mornir* quiet?" I sent. *Mornir* was the name the animals at Obernewtyn had given Dragon. It meant "brightmane."

The old cat assented and began to wash himself industriously. I looked at the gypsy. Her breathing was labored, her eyes sunk into their sockets. If she did not get help soon, she would die in spite of Roland's sleepseal.

Well, I could do no more than I was doing.

Cautioning Dragon again to stay quiet, I climbed out of the wagon, pulling the curtain to the cabin shut behind me. The lane ahead was empty, and it was still raining hard, but it was too much to hope we had not been noticed. I remounted Gahltha, and we retraced our steps as swiftly as we could, but it was full dark before we reached the small trading market that Domick had described as the nearest landmark to the safe house. In the daylight on a good day, it would doubtless be a pleasant spot to linger, but tonight it was a wet and windy pool of darkness and completely deserted.

We crossed the square to a street leading off, abutted by a trader office on one side and a huge wagon-repair shed on the other. A sign glistening wetly in the wagon light told us the entrance to the repair yard was from the side street.

The gates were standing ajar, creaking slightly in the wind, when we came to them. Beyond, the place was sunk in darkness. The shapes of half-dismantled wagons were standing about in the open, and the shed was nothing more than a square of shadow.

"Are ye sure this is it?" Matthew sent. "It dinna look as if anyone is here."

"They wouldn't advertise their presence," I replied, though in fact it did look deserted. Jaygar pulled the wagon into the yard.

"There's a light in there," Matthew sent. I looked where he was pointing, and sure enough there was a dim glow from one of the shed's windows, hidden from the street.

"I'll go," I sent, and slid off Gahltha.

Inside, the shed smelled of damp metal and sawdust, but at least it was dry. The light was coming from a small room set in a far corner of the enormous structure. Through a doorway, I could see a youth sitting at a table, the light from a lantern glancing off his cheeks.

He jumped to his feet when he spotted me. "What do you want, halfbreed?"

"I . . . I have a wheel rim that needs some attention," I stalled, startled by his aggressive tone.

"You'll have to go somewhere else. We don't fix halfbreed wagons," he said.

Before I could think how to respond, a door opened beside him and Kella stepped out. Seeing me, the healer's mouth fell open.

"Elspeth! By all the heavens! How did you get here?" Without waiting for an answer, she rushed across and flung her arms around me.

I stiffened instinctively. Misunderstanding, the healer let her arms fall to her sides and stepped away awkwardly. "I'm sorry," she said.

"No, I'm sorry," I said. "I'd forgotten how it feels to be treated like an ordinary human being."

She looked bewildered. "What do you mean?"

I laughed dismissively. "I don't mean anything, except that I am glad to see you." I looked pointedly at the strange youth.

"This is Balder," Kella said lightly. "He is one of Brydda's people, lent to us as a watchman. Balder, this is a friend of mine and of Brydda's."

The boy nodded politely, but his eyes were cold.

I drew Kella out into the great shed on the pretext of seeing the wagon. "Why is he here?"

"I told you, he is guarding the safe house. It's all right," Kella said. "He doesn't know anything except that we are friends of Brydda's and that I am a healer. Brydda always sends someone when Domick goes out of the city on errands for the Councilcourt."

There were a dozen questions I wanted to ask her, but now was not the time. "We'll talk about this later. Matthew and Dragon are in the wagon—"

"Dragon!"

"There is also a woman who needs healing," I said.

Kella stiffened. "Take me to her," she commanded, imperious in her healer role.

Dragon was sitting wide-eyed in the corner of the wagon with Maruman, who had solved the problem of keeping her put by sitting on her lap. With barely a glance at them, Kella climbed into the cabin and pulled the blankets back from the pallet bed. Her eyes widened at the sight of the unconscious gypsy, but she composed herself swiftly and laid her fingers lightly on the woman's neck. A moment later, she shook her head.

"It's impossible to treat her here. Let me send Balder away, and then you can bring her in."

She left, and a few minutes later, the rebel came out of the shed wrapped up in a dark oiled coat. When I was sure he had gone, I jumped down into the rainy dark and between us, Matthew and I carried the gypsy inside.

"On th' floor?" the farseeker asked as we reached the smaller room within the shed.

"Through here," Kella directed, opening the door she had come through earlier. Beyond was a rickety set of steps going up into the darkness. Seeing the expression on my face, she gave a faint smile. "Things are rarely what they seem. You, of all people, should know that."

At the top of the steps was a dark landing and a door with blistered whitewash. Kella opened it with a flourish, and bright light and warmth flowed out.

"The safe house," she said proudly. "You can't tell from below, but the whole top of the shed is another floor. No light shows outside, because all the windows face the sky or else are blacked out with heavy cloth."

She stepped into a short hall and opened a door. "This is our healing chamber. Bring her in."

The room was long and narrow, with a row of straw mattresses made up as beds. The healer drew back the blankets on the nearest of these, and we lay the gypsy on it.

"I'll unharness Jaygar and take the bridle off Gahltha," Matthew said, turning to the door.

"Bring Maruman and Dragon up, too," I requested, crossing to the door and closing it behind him. When I returned, Kella was kneeling by the mattress, holding the gypsy's hand.

"These are not fresh wounds," she said, a question in her tone.

In as few words as I could manage, I explained my rescue of the gypsy, Roland's diagnosis, and the sleepseal he had imposed.

"I don't understand why you brought her here," Kella said, beginning to unravel the stained bandages. "If Roland couldn't help her, I doubt I can do better. I daren't take the seal off yet, but at least I can bathe her wounds and change the bandages." She moved to a small cooling cupboard, took out a stone jug of whitish fluid, and returned to bathe the gypsy's arms.

"Maryon said her own people will be able to treat her," I said. "That's one of the reasons we're here."

"Gypsies know a great deal about healing," Kella agreed. She rebandaged the woman's arms deftly and pulled the blankets up. "That is all I can do for now," she said, rinsing her hands in a bowl. "At least it will stop any infection from setting in. You will have to move swiftly if you are to return her alive to her people, though. Even with a sleepseal to slow everything down, an injury drains life energies, and she does not have much left to lose."

We went back into the hall, and she indicated another door. "That is one of the sleeping chambers, and there is another closer to the kitchen." She opened the door alongside. "The bathing room. There are three bathing barrels, and we even have water piped in. Fire heats the water while it's still in the pipes, and then it comes out of tubes to the barrels once you remove the stoppers. Unfortunately, it takes ages to heat. I'll light it if you like?"

I shook my head and gestured for her to go on.

Despite its considerable size, the kitchen was cozy and welcoming. It had been whitewashed so that even without windows, it seemed light. The air was warm and redolent with the odor of hundreds of tiny bunches of drying herbs hung in neat rows along all the walls. There were shelves of foodstuffs and in the center of the room, on a woven rug, a thick scrub-wood table and some stools. A fire blazed in a narrow hearth. As I crossed at once to warm myself, Kella filled a kettle and bent to hang it on a hook suspended over the flames.

"It's like a breath straight from Obernewtyn to see you here," she said with sudden fervency. "I miss you all so much. I dream of the fields and mountains, and then I wake and am still here."

The depth of longing in her eyes made me feel ashamed. In spite of Maryon's doom-filled predictions, I had been glad to get away from my cloistered existence at Obernewtyn, while poor Kella lived in constant danger to keep it safe.

"Sutrium is awful," she went on. "I never imagined people could be dragged so low. Even before Rushton took over, there were times for laughter at Obernewtyn. Here no one laughs, and if they do, people stare at them as if they have gone mad. And it is a hundred times worse since the plague. I pity these people their gray lives."

"Don't pity them too much," I said dryly. "Those same pitiable souls would stand by and watch us burn without lifting a finger."

"It's true enough. We're nowt but freaks to them," Matthew said, coming through the door carrying Maruman. The cat leapt to the ground and began prowling about the room, smelling it. Kella knew better than to react to his presence and pretended not to notice him. Instead, she beamed at the ward.

"Lud, but you've grown now that I see you properly, Matthew. Has Brydda's mother been using herb lore on you instead of her garden?"

Matthew laughed. "Seems to me it's yerself who's shrinkin'!"

I thought his jest curiously apt, but Kella only slapped playfully at his arm and urged him to dry himself in front of the fire. Then, catching sight of Dragon hovering in the hall behind him with her shoulders hunched miserably, the healer gave an exclamation and held out her arms. Dragon rushed at her, and it was some minutes before she could pry herself loose from the girl's impassioned embrace.

"What a grub you are, love," Kella laughed. "It's a miracle you manage to stay dirty in so much rain. Will you let me wash your face?"

Dragon froze, her blue eyes livid with fear. "No bath."

"No bath," the healer assured her, knowing as well as anyone Dragon's inexplicable terror of water. "Just a bit of a damp cloth."

Kella ushered her from the kitchen, and Matthew scowled after them.

"What do you want done about her, Matthew?" I snapped. He was as bad as Dragon, I thought, with less excuse for it.

There was an awkward pause. "They've done a good job here," Matthew said at last. "There is even a special yard where th' horses can graze without bein' seen."

I drew off my soaked boots and poured some of the boiling fement into two mugs, handing him one as a peace offering. "They've had quite a bit of help from Brydda Llewellyn by the sound of it."

"Of course," Matthew said easily; then he gave me a sharp look. "And why not? Surely ye dinna worry he'd betray us?"

I shook my head. Brydda's father, Grufyyd, and his mother, the herb lorist Katlyn, had come to live at Obernewtyn after the Council learned their son was the notorious rebel the Black Dog, so betrayal on Brydda's part was completely out of the question. "It's not Brydda. It's the others. That rebel boy who was downstairs, for instance. Did you see the way he looked at us? If he feels that way about gypsies, how is he going to react when he discovers we're Misfits? There's no point in us pretending we're all allies until it has been agreed to officially by the rebels. We don't really know where we stand with them."

"Is that really why we're here? Did Maryon's prediction have something to do with the rebels?" Matthew demanded.

I was glad when Kella's return prevented my answering. "I've put her into bed," Kella said. "The poor little mite was asleep before her head brushed the pillow. But why on earth did you bring her here?"

I explained, and the healer shook her head in wonder. "She must be very attached to follow you all this way, Elspeth."

Matthew rose, pulled on his coat in one ferocious motion, and went out the door, saying he was going to unpack the wagon.

Kella stared after him in astonishment. "Whatever is the matter with him?"

I laughed and, even to my own ears, it sounded bitter. "I am beginning to suspect it wasn't me Dragon followed but Matthew. I think he volunteered for this expedition specifically to get away from her."

"Oh, poor Dragon," Kella said compassionately. "I remember she followed him everywhere when I was last at Obernewtyn, but I thought it was just a fleeting infatuation."

"More's the pity it wasn't," I said, suddenly emptied of ill humor. I stood up. "I am going to wash and put on some dry things."

"There are clothes in a trunk in the bathing room,"

65

Kella said. A lantern was lit in the bathhouse from Dragon's wash, and as I peeled off my soaking clothes, I caught sight of myself in a mirror hanging on the wall: a long, lean girl with irritated moss-green eyes and thick, black hair falling past her waist. I glared at myself and realized abruptly that I felt less pity for Dragon's love than exasperation at the inconvenience of it.

What a terrible business loving was. It was a troublesome and tiresome emotion destined more often to enrage the recipient than to please them. Rushton's love for me, if that was what it could be called, had him determined to shut me up like a bird in a gilded cage, while Dragon's love for Matthew had driven him out of his home. What right had people to love you when you had not wanted it or asked for it?

Of course, in Dragon's case, the only wonder was that no one had foreseen the outcome of throwing together a volatile girl, who had spent most of her life in wretched loneliness, with a boy of Matthew's easy charm. Yet Dragon had ultimately saved Obernewtyn with his help. Her heartache and his irritation must be considered a small price to pay for that.

It seemed there was always a price to pay for loving.

I had a sudden vivid memory of a time when, taken in by Dragon's illusions, I had thought Obernewtyn destroyed. From my hiding place, I had spotted Rushton. He had been haggard, grim-faced with burning eyes, and I had imagined he was despairing over the loss of Obernewtyn. Only later had I understood that his sorrow arose from his belief that I was dead.

I shook my head and turned to rummage for dry

clothing, not liking the tenor of my thoughts nor the way Rushton's face haunted me.

I fled to the kitchen, bringing the lamp with me, and pulled up a stool to join Matthew and Kella in front of the fire. Maruman came over and leapt onto my lap. His mind was closed, and I did not try to force entry to it.

"How long before Domick comes home?" I asked Kella, wincing as the cat's claws penetrated cloth and flesh. "Are you expecting him tonight?"

The healer nodded, the smile fading from her lips.

I guessed she was wondering if our arrival would put Domick in danger, and for the first time, I was aware of the strain in her face. There were lines around her eyes, and her hands fidgeted constantly in swift, nervous gestures. I had been surprised at the strength of the longing in her voice as she talked of Obernewtyn, but now I truly thought of what her life in the safe house must be like. Every day she watched her bondmate leave, knowing he went to work under the very noses of the Councilmen. If discovered, he would be killed.

It seemed far easier to take action than to sit and wait. People like Kella had the worst of it—the waiting and wondering and being helpless. In asking when Domick would return, I had surely voiced a question she never dared permit herself to ask.

Hearing the stair door creak and heavy footsteps in the hall, I felt an echo of the profound relief I saw on Kella's face.

But when the kitchen door opened, I did not recognize the dark-clad man who stepped inside.

◆ 7 ◆

I T WASN'T UNTIL Kella crossed the room to embrace the man that I realized it was Domick.

The last time I had seen the coercer was at Obernewtyn just around the time he and Kella had established the safe house. Then, Domick had been on the edge of manhood, brown as a gypsy, with shoulder-length dark hair and bold, serious eyes. There was no sign of that youth in the man who now stood before me.

His skin was milk pale, and his long hair had been cropped very short. But most of all, it was his expression that made him a stranger—or the lack of expression. His face was a gaunt mask, the eyes two hooded slits. If he felt any surprise at seeing us in the safe house, it was not evident.

As a coercer, Domick had possessed that guild's characteristic aggression, but his love for Kella had seemed to temper his intensity. I could not begin to imagine what had happened to turn him into this hard-faced man.

"Has something gone wrong at Obernewtyn?" he asked in a voice as even and emotionless as his expression.

"That is a harsh greeting for old friends," Kella

scolded him gaily, and I saw that she had not mentioned his transformation because she did not perceive it. It seemed that love was truly blind.

Domick exerted himself to produce a semblance of liveliness. "Kella is right. Forgive my abruptness. It has been a bad night, but it is good to see you both." He smiled, but his eyes remained remote, and again I found myself wishing for empathy—this time to tell me what seethed under the stoniness of his face.

The coercer removed his oiled cloak, and I saw the tension in his movements as he crossed to hang it on a peg beside the fire. Sitting down, he reminded me of a spring coiling tight for a hard recoil. Maruman watched him, then hissed and sprang from my lap to prowl about the room.

"You have chosen a bad time to visit," Domick said, glancing up to indicate the rain thundering down on the roof.

"Needs must," I said.

He gave me a swift look. "Need?"

For the second time that night, I told the story of the rescue of the gypsy, and of our decision to return her to her people when Roland could not heal her.

"It was a risky thing for you to have gone in alone to face the Herder," Domick reproved. "Those villagers might have killed you at once."

"Not with th' gypsy shootin' arrows at them from th' trees," Matthew said gleefully. "Besides, we could hardly leave her to burn, now, could we?"

An odd expression flitted over the coercer's face. "Sometimes you have to endure a lesser evil in dealing with a greater one."

Kella stared fixedly into the fire, as if disengaging herself from the conversation, but Matthew was openly indignant.

"Ye mean we should have left her? I doubt she'd call that a lesser evil!"

Domick shrugged. "If you had been caught, it would not have helped her, and it may well have done great, even irreparable, damage to our cause. Which, then, would be the greater evil? To let an unknown woman die, or to intervene and see your friends perish for it?"

"We got her free, didn't we? An' we weren't caught," Matthew returned stubbornly. "If we thought like you, we'd nowt even have tried. *There's* evil fer ye. Nowt even tryin' to fix somethin' that's wrong."

"You are naive," Domick said dismissively. "If the woman is as sick as you say, there is every likelihood she will die despite your help."

Matthew flushed. "Maybe I am naive, but rather that than bein' someone with ice fer blood an' a clever tongue an' shifty brain instead of a heart!"

They stared at one another for a moment; then Domick relaxed back into his seat. "And is that the reason you have come to Sutrium, Elspeth? To take an irrelevant gypsy back to her people?"

I suppressed a surge of anger at his callousness and the temptation to tell him what Maryon had futuretold about this "irrelevant" gypsy. But with the woman so near death, there was enough urgency without piling the burden of a portentous vision on their heads.

"I would also like to see Brydda Llewellyn," I said mildly. "Maybe he could suggest some safe way to locate her people."

"I am not sure there is any way that is safe," Domick said. "Is she a halfbreed? I suppose she must be," he answered himself.

"I think so. Yes," I added more positively, remembering the Herder had called her that. "Does it make a difference?"

Both Kella and the coercer nodded.

"A Twentyfamilies gypsy would not break the Council lore forbidding healing," Domick explained.

"Twentyfamilies?" I echoed, surprised to hear the odd word again. "What does that mean?"

"It is what pureblood gypsies call themselves," the coercer said. "It was not a name any but traders of expensive trinkets knew until the Herders started bandying it about. They hate gypsies and Twentyfamilies most of all, because it was they who negotiated the safe passage agreement with the Council that exempts gypsies from Herder lore. Herders preach that gypsies ought to be made to settle. They claim the plague was spread by their wanderings."

"The Herder in Guanette said the plagues were a punishment from Lud because of people ignoring the Faction," I said.

Domick shrugged. "Same thing. There is a lot of talk to that effect encouraged by the Herders, but it will not give them power to force the Council to make the Twentyfamilies settle. The halfbreeds are not so lucky, for the safe passage agreement no longer includes them, yet nor are they allowed to settle. They are persecuted by Landfolk and Herders alike, as you know. But it is worse since the plague."

I began to see that returning the gypsy before Maryon's futuretold deadline would be even harder than I had anticipated. Hitherto, I had imagined I understood something of gypsy society, but in truth, what I knew arose solely from memories of a single friendly troupe that had come through Rangorn every few seasons when I was a child. I did not even know if they had been pureblood or halfbreed.

"You talk about Twentyfamilies gypsies and halfbreeds as if they were two separate races," I said.

"That is very nearly what they are," he answered. "The division between them has its origins in the days when gypsies first came to the Land. Some say they walked here; others say they came by sea. Either way, they didn't want to be ruled by Council or Herder lore, so they came to an agreement with the Council to remain as visitors, never settling or farming the Land, never owning any of it."

"I know all of that," I said, faintly impatient.

"I suppose you know, too, how they got the Council to agree to let them remain as visitors?" Domick snapped.

Abashed, I shook my head. "I'm sorry. Tell it your own way."

He went on. "In exchange for safe passage status as visitors, the gypsies offered a yearly tithe: a percentage of the craftwares their people produced. Their works were rare and beautiful, and for a time everyone seemed to benefit from the arrangement.

"In those early days, some gypsies mated with Landfolk, so halfbreeds were born. Initially, there was free trade of knowledge and blood between full and halfblood gypsies. But that ended with the Great Divide," Domick said. "Purebloods do not now teach their skills to halfbreeds; therefore, halfbreed wares are pale echoes of their work, based on half-recollected formulae and recipes. Invariably inferior, they bring scant coin, whereas the purebloods make more than enough to live well from what remains of their work after the tithe."

"Why dinna Twentyfamilies gypsies teach th' halfbreeds th' craftskills?" Matthew demanded indignantly. "A halfbreed mun have at least one pureblood in their line of descent. Dinna this tie mean anything to them?"

"It was a matter of survival for the purebloods," Domick said. "On the whole, halfbreeds weren't as scrupulous about obeying Council lore as the Twentyfamilies. That caused a lot of strife. Finally, the Twentyfamilies leader had no choice but to announce the Great Divide, cutting halfbreeds off absolutely from purebloods. The Council accepted the division, because it allowed them to control the troublemaking halfbreeds without breaking contract with the Twentyfamilies. And the purebloods had to maintain the exclusivity of their work, because it was their only leverage with the Council.

"And that keeps them safe even from the Herders," the coercer added. "The Faction wants gypsy traveling stopped, because they want all in the Land under their power. Of course, the Council has a vested interest in keeping things as they are, because if they make the purebloods settle, the bribe tithe will cease."

"Naturally, greed would decide th' day," said Matthew with a flash of cynicism.

"The halfbreeds should be so lucky as to have something the Council wanted. It is hard on them. It would not be so bad if they were permitted to settle and become ordinary Landfolk, but in spite of the division, people regard gypsies as gypsies. They resent the wealth and inviolability of the Twentyfamilies gypsies, and they take it out on the halfbreeds."

"There have been a number of incidents just recently in which halfbreeds have been beaten or attacked," Kella said, her eyes worried. "Your disguises are now dangerous, because you are obviously not Twentyfamilies and as halfbreeds, you are fair game."

Why had Domick not warned us of this in his reports? Before I could ask, Matthew spoke. "Why can't we say we're Twentyfamilies? Fer that matter, why dinna th' halfbreeds say it? There's enough color variation for that not to matter."

"Twentyfamilies gypsies would know you were an impostor regardless of skin color," Domick said.

"How could they know?" Matthew persisted.

The coercer shrugged. "They just do. You might farseek them and find out how, if it mattered enough. Yet, what point would there be in it? Your gypsy can only be a halfbreed. To reach her people, you must be one of them."

That was true enough.

"And even among the halfbreeds, you will have trouble getting information, because gypsy or not, you will be unknown to them," Domick said. "Given the climate, they are understandably wary of strangers. If, by chance, they discover you are not a gypsy, they will probably kill you, thinking you are a Herder spy."

I frowned into the fire.

"And that is another thing you must consider," Domick went on inexorably. "I have heard no report of the affair in Guanette at the Councilcourt, but just because it has not reached the Council does not mean the Faction is ignorant of it. If they do know, they are certain to have spies watching the gypsy greens with descriptions of you in their pockets."

"I will keep the gypsy woman out of sight and go about as a boy," I said firmly, stamping ruthlessly on a little flutter of fear in my stomach.

"Best to abandon the gypsy disguise altogether, but of course the tan would give you away," the coercer said.

"I can brew something that will fade it faster," Kella offered.

I nodded. "It would not be a bad idea to have such a mixture on hand. However, given what you have said, I doubt any gypsy would speak to me unless I was obviously one of them, so I will have to remain as I am for the present. Maybe I can coerce them into thinking they know me."

Changing the subject, I told Domick how Dragon had come to Sutrium and asked if he could send word back to Obernewtyn that she was safe.

"It will take a sevenday at least," he warned. "My reports go through Enoch, and he daren't let himself be seen going up to the mountains, since they're supposed to be deserted and Obernewtyn a tainted ruin."

I nodded. "Rushton had worried at the lack of news from you. It's good to know you were just being cautious."

Domick glowered. "I am always cautious. And we have had to be even more so lately. At the height of the plague, Enoch would have been stoned if he traveled openly enough to cause people to fear he carried the disease from place to place."

"The plague seems to affect so many things," I mused.

"How was it at Obernewtyn during the plague?" Kella asked, and I realized how little she must hear of home and everyday events in Rushton's businesslike missives. It would not occur to him that his spies might need to hear the small details of life in the mountains.

"It was not so bad in the highlands," I said, "though Rushton insisted we stay in the mountains for some time. How did you manage?"

Kella's expression was suddenly haunted. "It's so dirty here that people went down with the disease in the hundreds. So many died that there were not enough left to bury the dead. The corpses bloated and stank, and the disease spread and spread. And all to the Herder Faction's benefit," she added in sudden anger.

I was surprised. "You don't believe Lud sent it on their behalf?"

"That's not what I meant," she said. "I am sure it was nothing more than a disease born of filth and ignorance. But the Herders were quick to warp it to their purpose. They claimed only those hated by Lud would die." There was a terrible bitterness in her voice. "Are babies and old dodderers evil? Does Lud hate children and sick people? For they were the first to fall."

"The strange thing is that so few of the Herders died," Domick said pensively. "It seemed to prove their claim that Lud was protecting them. They did not care at all when plague killed off the sickly and the weak, but when it began to eat up the strong, they were less delighted. After all, if everyone was killed, who would be left to be preached at?"

Kella laughed. "They really started to worry when

76

the crops were ready and there was no one to harvest them. What would they eat? Would they have to till and labor for food with their own white hands? The Councilmen were panic-stricken, of course, and right from the beginning, the majority of them had barricaded themselves in their homes with supplies. But still many of them died as well."

She fell silent.

"What happened in th' end?" Matthew asked, as if looking for a happy ending to a bedtime tale.

Domick answered him. "It went on and on, until half the city was dead or dying, and finally the Herders told the Council to lock up the houses of the dead and burn them with the corpses inside."

Kella gave a sob. "Yes. That was their solution. They told the Council to employ the purifying flames of Lud. So the soldierguards went out, burning any house where there had been plague and quite a few where there was nothing, whether there were people inside or not. Dozens were burned alive."

I swallowed back horror as Domick moved to take Kella in his arms, his expression more masklike than ever.

"I did what I could," Kella whispered into his shoulder. "But there were so many. . . ."

The coercer met my eyes over her bowed head, and for a moment there was a flare of some emotion in his eyes, but it was gone too quickly for me to interpret it.

"It was difficult," he said in a cool voice. "Brydda was bringing those of his people who had contracted the plague here. Most arrived too late to be helped. Other times there were so many needing healing that Kella had to choose which lives to save and whom to let die. She almost killed herself trying to heal them all. She would not rest or eat."

"How could I rest with people dying every minute I slept? How could I eat in the midst of all that death?" she whispered.

Domick rose and led the weeping girl out, leaving me and Matthew to stare at one another.

"I dinna know it had been so bad," the farseeker said in a subdued tone.

I said nothing, for though horrified by Kella's story, I was concerned that people had been brought so haphazardly to the safe house. Yet the thought gave me hope, for surely the rebels would not use it and Kella's healing skills so freely if they did not mean to ally themselves with us.

Maruman appeared from behind a cupboard and climbed into my lap again, making himself comfortable before the fire. I was fascinated to feel his mind curling around mine in much the same fashion as his body shaped itself to my lap.

"Maruman/yelloweyes guards ElspethInnle," he sent, as if I had posed a question.

Domick returned.

"I have coerced Kella to sleep," he said in a somber voice. His eyes met mine. "She is exhausted in body and spirit. You cannot know what it was like for her. She nearly went mad when she learned of the burnings. You must take her with you when you go. She cannot bear it."

"It doesn't seem to bother you," I said.

"I am not Kella," he responded flatly. "I am a realist. There was plague, and the burnings ended it. Therefore, the method worked."

"It was a brutal solution," I snapped. I did not like the coldness in his voice when he spoke of Kella, nor his apparent acceptance of the Herder Faction's murderous solutions.

"Brutal?" he said. "Perhaps. But this is a brutal world. Yet it did not endear the Faction to the Council, for all its success. Too many Councilmen died and too few Herders."

Diverted, I frowned. "Then there is still conflict between the Faction and the Council?"

Domick nodded. "There is a feeling among Councilmen that the Herders have too much hysterical power over the masses, that they are fanatical and dangerously extreme. Of course, since the plague, they command the power of life and death—or so the ignorant are led to believe—so there is no question of the Council doing anything immediately to limit their power. But, I daresay, they will find a way to curb them in the end."

"Do you think the Council would ever disband them altogether?"

He shook his head decisively. "I doubt they will do more than pull a few teeth. The Faction serves a purpose, and the Councilmen know it. They have just recently sent a pack of Herders to soften up the Sadorian tribespeople. Why bark yourself when you can have a dog do it?"

And if the dog turns on its master? I wondered.

Domick stood up abruptly and reached for his cloak. "Come."

My bones ached and I was still cold, but I stood, lifting Maruman from my knee. The old cat gave me a haughty look and stalked away. I pulled on my sodden boots and took the cloak the coercer handed me.

"We will be back before midnight," he told Matthew.

The farseeker nodded and leaned forward, lifting both hands to the fire. I felt a stab of envy.

"Where are we going?" I asked, clumping down the dark stairs.

Domick's eyes glimmered in the darkness as we stepped out into the windy night, and his words were an echo out of the distant past: "You wanted to talk to Brydda Llewellyn, didn't you?"

✦ 8 ✦

THE STREETS WERE all but deserted as we passed through them like two shadows. Houses were everywhere sunk in darkness, but here and there were more of the blackened gaps I had noticed that afternoon. I shuddered, now understanding them in the light of Kella's story.

A woman peered out of a window at us, and I wondered whether I should have insisted we take the horses. Gahltha would be angry that I had gone without him, but Domick had argued that we would draw more eyes on horseback than on foot. Because of a rising trade in stolen horses, few rode at night.

Even so, Gahltha had ways of defending himself that would discourage any thief.

With a shock, I realized I had grown so accustomed to the black horse's presence that I felt curiously vulnerable without him.

A curtain twitched as we passed another window and a memory surfaced. "Is there still a curfew in Sutrium?"

Domick lifted his head as if to dispel a dream, and I wondered what he had been thinking about. "There is a curfew, but it does not come into effect until midnight," he said. "It is not strictly enforced, because there are worse things than soldierguards to contend with. Only fools asking to be robbed or murdered wander the streets after dark."

"Marvelous," I said sourly.

"Since the plagues and the loss of crops, there is no work and little food," the coercer went on, as if I had not spoken. "There are a legion of poor in the city. Some beg for their needs, and others take what they want. Hard times make for hard folk."

Involuntarily, I smiled, recognizing in the phrase Brydda's love of neat sayings. "One of the Black Dog's homilies?"

Domick gave me a startled look, then said defensively, "He has a way of putting things that makes them memorable. It is a fine and useful quality in a leader."

There was not the slightest flicker of humor in his voice. He had always been serious, seldom speaking more than was necessary or laughing aloud, but now it seemed he had built a deep wall of reserve around himself. I wanted to ask why, but his manner did not invite intimacy.

"Do you see much of Brydda?" I asked instead.

The coercer gave me a wary look as we passed under one of the few lit street lanterns, and it struck me forcibly that something was very wrong.

"I see him," he said noncommittally.

"How is he, then?"

Domick was silent so long, I thought he meant to ignore the question, but at last he spoke.

"Superficially, he is the same as ever: brave as a lion, swift to laughter, loyal, proud, and silver-tongued. But to my mind, his policy of elusiveness is affecting his mind."

"You mean he is going mad?" I asked, startled.

Domick gave me a pale echo of a genuine smile, which fleetingly stripped the years away from his face. "I mean, it is affecting his way of thinking. He is the kind who needs to trust. He is happiest with loyal comrades constantly about him. He remains close to Idris and Reuvan, who you'll remember came with him from Aborium. Yet even those friendships are strained. For the sake of security, the Black Dog has chosen a lonely path."

He fell silent and I considered what he had said. No one knew better than I how loneliness tainted a person's thinking. Solitude could become an addiction, a canker of the soul, ever hungered for as much as it was loathed. All the years I had spent in the orphan home system after my parents were killed, I had kept myself apart—even from my brother Jes. With informants about, friendship was dangerous in the best of cases, and I had extra reason to fear, being a Misfit. This had made it hard for me to trust or to relate to people, even when it was safe to do so. And, in spite of all the years of longing for friends, now that I had them, part of me yearned to be by myself again.

But Brydda had not learned the orphan's lesson. I could well imagine the effect enforced solitude would have on him. It saddened me to think of the laughter dimmed in the merry giant.

"And you?" I asked impulsively. "Do you think of your path as a lonely one?"

Domick gave me a strange look but made no response.

We fell silent as we passed an open veranda where an old woman swept her porch. She watched us go by, as if poised to run inside and bar the door. I felt her eyes following us through the rain until we passed out of sight.

We came into a street running right alongside the shore. A boardwalk was built level with the cobbled street, but beneath it the ground dropped away to a narrow, rocky beach. Rain fell into the water with a hissing susurrus. Again, I was conscious of a strong mental static, which indicated the water was tainted in some manner. I did not recall this from my previous visits to Sutrium. Perhaps there had been a recent firestorm?

The sea was so dark that it seemed as if we traveled along the rim of an abyss. This would be a good place for an attack, but I resisted the urge to look over my shoulder.

Thoughts of one fear begot another, for without thinking, I asked, "Have you heard anything of Ariel lately?"

The name evoked in the coercer the same heavy silence it caused anyone who had been at Obernewtyn before Rushton became its master.

"He went to Herder Isle just before the plague struck," he said at length. "It seems that he remains in the Herders' good graces, though I do not know why. They were as angry with him as the Council when the soldierguards he sent to Obernewtyn found nothing. I would have expected them to cast him off as the Council did."

"You know, it has always bothered me that Ariel was so certain Obernewtyn had not been destroyed by firestorm that he sent the soldierguards to catch us in the lie," I mused.

"His Talent must have given him the knowledge," Domick said.

I gaped at the coercer, astonished. Why had it never occurred to me that Ariel was a Talented Misfit?

Domick went on, unaware of my reaction to his words. "Kella thinks he has empathy because of the way he generated fear, but I think he is a latent coercer—it would explain his skill at manipulating his way into power. I doubt he's a futureteller, for he's been caught off guard too often; a true dream would have been enough to tell him that Obernewtyn still stood."

True dreams were common among Misfits and often contained fleeting flashes of the future.

My mind circled back to my own question: Why had I never thought of Ariel being Talented? I had known he was a Misfit, but above finding him morally corrupt and sadistic, I had never considered what it was that had *made* him a Misfit. Why?

The answer came swiftly.

Because I did not want it to be so.

I wanted to believe that all Talented Misfits strove for right and justice. The thought of someone so wicked having a Talent, being part of our community . . . It left a bitterness in my mouth.

The rain began to fall more heavily. The coercer looked up with a muffled curse and lengthened his stride. I drew up the hood of my cloak to stop water dripping down my neck and hastened to keep up, my thoughts running ahead of me.

Ariel as a coercer—even as a weak and unaware coercer—was a fearsome notion.

In the early days at Obernewtyn, there had been

much concern over the morality of coercion and even talk about trying to convert it to healing or some other use. But in its aggressive form, it had proven too necessary to our survival.

Instead, there had been a move away from separatism. These days, guilds aimed to train novices to use all their powers, though Misfits still generally chose to specialize in one specific Talent as part of the process of becoming guilded. There had been some resistance to crossguilding, until it was realized that development of a lesser Talent often enhanced the primary ability. For instance, as a farseeker with coercion, I could coerce from a distance, instead of needing to be close to a subject, as a typical coercer must. And the combination of beastspeaking, farseeking, and coercing meant I could coerce animals without being close to them physically.

Domick plucked at my arm and pointed across the street to a dingy inn whose signboard proclaimed its incongruous name: The Good Egg. "That is where we will make contact with Brydda."

"The last time I went into an inn looking for Brydda Llewellyn, I was nearly arrested," I said, following him reluctantly across the street.

"We will not ask for him openly," Domick said. "It is just a matter of ordering a certain obscure brew, which will not be in stock, in a particular quantity. Then the Black Dog will be signaled and will send someone for us as soon as he is able."

There was no time for more talk, as the door swung open and a group of drunken revelers stumbled out into the night. Domick grasped my elbow, steering me past them and into the inn.

Though cavernous, it was poorly lit—as all such

places were, for the people who came to drown in their cups seldom wanted to be seen doing it. The inn was surprisingly crowded for a city supposedly full of the poor, but perhaps there was always enough coin for oblivion. The room reeked of cheap, sour fement and old sweat, but I was grateful for the warmth created by the throng.

I took my cloak off with some trepidation, having no alternative but to let myself be seen as a girl because of the clothes I had put on in the safe-house bathing room. The garments were not necessarily that of a gypsy, but my tan skin marked me, so I made the room see me as a full-grown gypsy woman rather than as a girl.

I could have completely coerced one or two people into seeing me any way I chose, but not a whole roomful. Coercing a large number of people was more of a general influencing, or accentuating what existed already in their minds. It was a surprisingly effective trick even when those with natural mindshields were about, because a group of people tended to operate as a single—and not very intelligent—mind. Still, I had to work within reasonable limitations.

Domick apparently had his own feint in mind. To my surprise, he suddenly reached out and drew me into the circle of his arms.

✦ 9 ✦

"Ho, Mika!" someone cried.

Domick turned, digging his fingers into my shoulder.

"Join us," said a lean man with close-set, crafty eyes that moved over me like prying fingers. "Who is your companion, my friend?"

"Her name is Elaria," Domick said in an arrogant voice that startled me almost as much as his putting an arm around me. He slid into a seat, pushing me before him, and I found myself crushed up next to an old man with a grizzled face and faded blue eyes.

"Elaria, I am Kerry," the lean man opposite introduced himself with a leering smile. He stabbed a blunt finger at the old man beside me. "That is Col, and by me here is Oria."

Col merely grunted, but the blond woman, Oria, gave me a friendly nod, which filled me with suspicion. Since when were people remotely civil to a gypsy?

As if accommodating my doubts, a thick-necked youth farther down the trestle scowled at me. "Half-breeds are thieves an' plaguebirds," he said loudly in a highland accent.

"You are a fool, boy, blighted with stupidity—which is a greater affliction than plague, since one cannot even hope for recovery from it." Domick's eyes were contemptuous. "Would I walk about with a carrier of the cursed plague?"

Oria and Kerry roared with more laughter than the witticism deserved. As the blond woman moved her head, I saw that her face was disfigured on one side by the savage spore of the disease.

"Ruga, you've been put in your place fair enough." Kerry leaned across the table toward me, and I fought the urge to slap him away. "She's comely enough," he approved. "But my taste don't run to gypsy flesh. Specially not one with a face as sober and sour as a judge."

"No doubt she finds you a sour eyeful, too," laughed the woman.

"Well, like I was sayin'," said the young highlander somewhat huffily from farther down the trestle, "I'm thinkin' of joining th' soldierguards. I'd just as soon step on a few necks as have mine stood on."

The oldster beside me gave a sneering laugh. "Join up and you'll just as likely find yourself warring with the tribesfolk in distant Sador. And I've heard they roast over their temple fires and eat those they take prisoner."

"There will be no war against Sador," Kerry said swiftly, his eyes flickering to Domick's face and then quickly away.

"The Council has sent Herders on a mission to make peace with the Sadorians," Domick said.

"Peace?" echoed the bleary-eyed Col. "The Council don't want peace, 'cepting maybe a big piece of Sador. And who knows what them Herders are after?"

An awkward silence ensued; then Kerry said with

forced joviality, "Best keep your words for other company, old man. There's some here who might not take kind to your speculation."

"You have no need to worry about me," Domick said. "Fools blow air out of their mouths as often as their bums, and either way it causes a stink and comes to nothing."

I looked around at the people at the table and, seeing their expressions, understood suddenly why Kerry and the woman had behaved so oddly, fawning on Domick and being civil to his gypsy companion.

They were afraid of him.

Abruptly, Domick rose and left the table, saying he wanted to order a drink. I tried not to look disconcerted at being left alone there, but I sensed the others at the table studying me covertly. Unnerved, I shaped a general coercive probe suggesting that I was defective. Given the general prejudice against gypsies, it was not difficult to plant a negative thought, and as the idea took root, they relaxed.

Only the plague-scarred Oria continued her scrutiny. I entered her mind and discovered she believed me to be a spy left by Domick to garner information. It was clear this disturbed her, but I did not trouble to delve deeper to learn why. I merely grafted into her thoughts a memory of having seen me before with different men at different inns and of having observed enough of my behavior to judge me defective.

Her disquiet faded, and she dismissed me from her mind. Turning to the old man, her brow creased with exasperation. "You are a fool with a mouth big enough to lose yourself in, Col. Don't you know who that was?"

He shrugged. "Some official or other. What do I care who he is? I've seen him here before."

"And that makes him safe?" she hissed. "He works for the Councilcourt."

"He sweeps the floor an' runs messages," said the highlander, Ruga, from down the table. "I heard him say so once."

Oria sneered at him openly. "Of course he would say that."

The old man frowned. "Well, what does he do, then? Is he a spy?"

I felt myself start, but no one noticed. The blonde leaned across the table and lowered her voice. "You heard what happened to Jomas?"

Col merely nodded, so I was forced to read the memory evoked by the woman's question directly from his thoughts.

A man called Jomas had spoken out against a Councilman, claiming the official had charged his father with sedition in order to obtain his farm. Jomas had been arrested and charged with sedition the very next night and was tortured so savagely that he had never walked again.

"So what? Everyone knows they torture seditioners," Col said.

Oria looked around before speaking. "Neither Jomas nor his father were seditioners and well you know it. But the point of the story is that Mika was here when Jomas was mouthing off about that Councilman."

Col snorted. "And for that you'd have me fear him? This place is full of folk who'd sell their mother for the price of a mug. Anyone could have reported Jomas's mouthings."

"I went to see Jomas when he recovered," Oria said fiercely. "He told me he was there when they tortured him."

"He?" the oldster echoed, confused.

"He," Oria repeated. "Mika." She lowered her voice. "He is a torturer."

I was so shocked that my probe faltered in its hold on the group.

"We should not talk of such matters," Kerry said, his tone suddenly anxious. "People who talk too much have a way of disappearing into the interrogation rooms beneath the Councilcourt."

"Sometimes elsewhere," Oria added darkly as I regained control.

I could barely follow the turn in conversation as someone else asked if there were truly prospects for war in Sador.

"That's not why they're recruitin'," retorted Ruga. "They want more soldierguards because of them rebels with Henry Druid gettin' too big for their boots."

"Henry Druid is dead," Oria interrupted. "He died in a firestorm in the highlands. The rebels they're after now are those led by Brydda Llewellyn."

"Not Brydda. Bodera," Kerry said.

"What does it matter who leads them?" sneered Col, glaring into his mug. "I hope there *is* a war, whether it is with them demonish-looking Sadorians or the rebels, and they all kill one another."

The table fell silent again as Domick reappeared bearing a small jug.

"I don't know how you drink that mucky syrup," Oria said brightly. "But if you ordered it more often,

92

old Filo would keep some for you instead of your having to wait while he sends out."

The coercer made no comment. He drank with every evidence of enjoyment, then set the mug down and looked around the table.

"You should be careful of loose talk," he said casually. There was something in his voice that brought everyone in the immediate vicinity to silence.

"There are those who are not what they seem," he went on in a sinister tone. My heart began to thump. *Now* what was he doing?

"Take that man." He pointed to a drunkard at the nearest table, staring about owlishly. "He seems no more than a sot. But is he really? Perhaps he is something more than he seems. Perhaps he has drunk less than he makes out and flaps his ears for seditious talk."

Oria laughed uneasily. "You jest."

Domick smiled and sipped at his golden mead.

Suddenly the oldster beside me slammed his fist down. "I'll not pretend! I am no seditioner to sit here cowering. You think we don't know what you are?"

The room fell silent, and all attention was on Domick, waiting to see what he would do.

"And what am I?" he asked in a soft, dangerous voice.

"I've a right to speak," Col blustered, the silence penetrating at last.

Domick sipped the last of his drink; then he dabbed fastidiously at the edges of his mouth with a handkerchief. "You should use your tongue for less dangerous talk, old man," he said at last. "Fortunately for you, I sweep, I write letters, and sometimes I deliver them.

That is all I do. Anyone who would say otherwise . . .
should think twice."

He rose, pulling me up with him. I kept my head
down, trying to look moronish and insignificant.
Domick nodded languidly to Kerry and Oria. "Perhaps,
when next I come, the company will be better."

Kerry smiled stiffly and bade us walk safe.

Outside, I pulled on my cloak with suppressed fury.
"Are you crazy? There is not a person in there who will
forget your face or mine after that little display. And
how is it so many people know you work for the
Council? Is this some brilliant new strategy based on
telling your business to every stranger you meet?"

Domick was looking out into the night, his face
empty of expression. "A Council employee is often investigated in the interests of security. If I had no life to
investigate, I would be instantly suspect. I must have a
background to fit my role, and those people are part
of it."

"You might have warned me," I snapped. "What if I
hadn't been able to improvise?"

"Guildmistress of the farseekers, veteran of hundreds of daring and brilliant rescues unable to improvise?" he demanded dryly. "Yet I would have warned
you, had I expected them to be there."

"Perhaps they deliberately came tonight to avoid
you," I snapped.

He shrugged. "That is likely true. They have no love
for me. Why are you so angry? I would have warned
you if I could, but once inside, it was too late."

I opened my mouth to deny anger, then realized he
was right. My temper had risen from fear.

"That was unnecessarily dangerous," I said, forcing myself to be calm. "You deliberately frightened them. Why?"

Domick's eyes were like the holes of the Blacklands as he stepped out into the night. "The people back there are not bad folk. They are just poor and ignorant. They speak too freely of matters better left unsaid. I am trying to teach them to keep their mouths shut."

"And what if there had been trouble in there? What would Mika have done? Would his job protect him if someone decided to take offense to his bullying?"

"You don't seem to grasp what it means to be employed by the Council," Domick said softly. "There is little it would not protect me against."

I snorted in disbelief. "Only those high up in Council employ warrant that sort of protection. Not a sweeper of floors."

"You think that after so many seasons of faithful service the Council would not reward a loyal worker?" Domick asked quietly.

A chill crept along my veins. "You mean . . ."

He laughed hollowly. "Let us say that it has been some time since I have swept a floor in the Councilcourt, Elspeth."

I licked my lips. "The people back there believe that you are a torturer. Why didn't you coerce them against believing such a rumor? It can't help you to spy. What possible advantage could it give you to let them think it?"

"The protection and power wrought by fear," Domick said. "But even if the rumor had served no purpose, I cannot stop it. I could not coerce everyone to disbelieve a rumor that is so universal."

"This . . . this rumor that you are a torturer . . . how did such a thing begin?"

He did not answer, and my heart began to beat unevenly. "Domick, what is it you do at the Council now?"

"I am not a torturer," he said at last in a grim voice. Then his eyes went over my shoulder. I turned to see a hooded figure standing in the rain.

"Look, there is our man," Domick said. "Brydda has sent him to collect us."

· 10 ·

Idris bowed, his round face lit by the sunny smile that I remembered from my last journey to the coast. "It is good to see you again, Elspeth."

The young rebel had appeared outside The Good Egg wrapped up in a cloak and gestured for us to follow. It was not until we reached a small dark hovel, a few streets away from the inn, that he had drawn back the hood of his coat to greet us.

"What is this place?" I asked as the blond rebel turned to the door of the hovel. It seemed to be nothing more than an abandoned husk and was surely far too small to be useful as a safe house.

"It is just a house," Idris said, forcing the sagging door open and ushering us before him. Inside the front hall, it was dark, and we stood in silence as he found and lit a lantern. The hall was empty, its walls scored black from fire. Idris removed his cloak and carefully hung it on a wall peg. Following suit, I remembered that he had always been meticulous and slightly plodding.

He brought us through empty, musty rooms to the back of the place, saying, "There are any number of houses standing vacant since the plagues." He pointed to an outbuilding's door, under which a slice of light showed. "They have proven very useful to us as temporary residences."

"Don't people wonder at seeing lamps in abandoned houses?"

Idris shrugged. "No doubt, but it does not matter. We rarely spend more than a few days in any one. This is the last night we will spend here." He pushed open the door.

The room behind it was a complete contrast to the great, warm homelike place Brydda had used as a headquarters in Aborium. It was bare but for a number of rough stools and chairs drawn around a little fire, a table piled with scrolls and maps, and a small supply of firewood stacked up on the floor. It was clearly hastily assembled, and no attempt had been made to render it comfortable. The room was dimly lit by a single guttering candle stuck in a mug on the table and by the warmer glow of the fire. Black cloth had been tacked over the only window, but as soon as we entered, Idris extinguished the brighter lantern he carried, the gesture belying his unconcern about being seen.

"Where is Brydda?" I asked.

In answer, the large-backed chair directly before the fire swiveled to reveal the big rebel holding a knife.

"Little sad eyes," he said in his rumbling voice.

Watching him sheath the knife and rise, I thought the old nickname suited him better than it had ever suited me. The rebel leader seemed more hugely bearlike than ever, his hair falling almost to his shoulders in a great shaggy pelt of midnight curls. Yet there was a tinge of silver amidst the darker hair at his temples and in his beard, and fine lines about his eyes that I did not remember. The unsheathed knife told its own story.

This life was taking its toll on him, as Domick had said. Brydda was like a lamp, with the flame burning dangerously low.

He gathered me into the affectionate ursine hug I remembered so well. That at least was unchanged, and my heart swelled with a gladness that startled me and made me feel absurdly like bursting into tears.

I watched as he greeted Domick with warmth and was interested to see that, for a moment, even the coercer lost some of his icy reserve.

"Let me give you both something to eat." Brydda gestured to the fire where a battered pot hung. "It is only a broth, I am afraid. These days we do not have the time or leisure to feast." The note of regret in his voice was palpable.

"I will do it," Idris said, pushing Brydda's hand aside and lifting the pot from the hook. He opened the lid and a delicious odor wafted out. My stomach, ever ready to herald its state, growled loudly.

Brydda burst out laughing.

"I have not eaten for ages," I defended myself. "I do not feel so hungry when I am traveling, and we have just arrived."

"I am the opposite," Brydda said ruefully. He accepted a mug of soup from Idris and handed it to me. "I eat as though for ten men! Ah well, we are what we eat; that is evident. And how was the road?"

His eyes sharpened at this. He had switched effortlessly from friend to seditioner chief seeking information. I drank and thought a moment before answering. "It was emptier than usual. More soldierguards and fewer ordinary travelers. Toll gates were heavily guarded. I would say the Council is tightening up on travel, trying to keep a record of who is going where and why." I glanced at him from under my lashes. "Perhaps trying to prevent rebel groups from liaising with one another. And from what I heard at the inn tonight, your people are, at least in part, the reason for an increase in soldierguard recruitment."

Brydda nodded approvingly. "'Little sad eyes' I called you, but perhaps 'sharp eyes' it should have been. A good summation. And what do you think all these clues suggest?"

"That you have stepped up your activities and have been careless enough to let the Council know it," I said promptly. "Or maybe you meant the Council to know it, for some reason. Or . . ." I hesitated to voice the third and obvious possibility.

"Or we have a traitor in our midst telling the Council they had best get ready for a fight," Brydda finished bluntly.

"And had they?" I asked quickly. "Are your people planning to move openly against the Council?"

Brydda made a vague gesture. "I suspect the increase in recruitment is less for fear of us than the Council's way of dealing with the number of people without work since the plague. So many who would have found work on farms have come to the city. The Council would have been wiser to restore the farms. But they are also making sure there are plenty of soldierguards if it comes to war over Sador—they covet the spice groves there." Here his eyes sought Domick's, and the coercer nodded confirmation.

I frowned at this further evidence of close interaction between the rebels and the safe house.

"The crime rate in the cities has tripled since the

plagues," Domick said. "And the Council reasons that employing more soldierguards will reduce the number of people out of work and will control those who have chosen robbery as a way of filling their bellies."

The rebel chief drank some soup. "Not a bad stratagem, but of course one wonders where the coin is coming from to pay them." He paused, seeming lost in thought for a moment.

"Then the increase in soldierguards has nothing to do with seditioners?" I persisted.

Brydda gave me a swift look. "I did not say that. It is true the Council have begun to regard us more seriously as a threat, and that may be another reason for their increase in recruitment. In part, this is unavoidable. We have heightened our profile among the people, for we will need them behind us when . . ." He stopped.

I turned to stare at the rebel chief squarely.

"Are you planning to attack the Council, Brydda?" I asked flatly.

"Of course. You knew that all along."

I felt my temper rise. "Do not play word games with me."

I heard Idris and Domick gasp aloud but did not take my eyes from Brydda's.

"You mistrust me?" he asked sorrowfully.

"Never," I said. "But I think you mistrust us. Or you think of us as fools to be put off. Don't underestimate us, Brydda. We can read the signs as well as anyone, and rumor says the rebels prepare for rebellion."

There was a charged silence; then Brydda sighed heavily. "Will you believe me if I tell you that no date is named as yet for rebellion?" he asked.

I hesitated, then nodded. "If you say it, I will believe it."

"Good, for I do say it." The rebel leaned forward to throw some wood on the fire; then he looked at me again. "Rushton sent you to ask about the alliance, didn't he? That is why you are here?"

"One of the reasons," I admitted, ignoring Domick's involuntary movement at my side. "He wonders why you delay in responding to our offer of alliance."

Brydda gave me a penetrating look, then sighed. "Perhaps I *have* underestimated you. There is a problem with the alliance, and that is why I have evaded Domick's queries. I had hoped to be able to present Rushton with a united acceptance of your offer, but . . ."

My heart did an unpleasant dance. "You won't accept us, then?" My tone was colder than I had intended, but it was too late to retract it. And in light of his words, perhaps it did not matter.

The big rebel leaned closer. "Elspeth, you talk as if it is *my* decision. It is not."

"You are their leader."

To my surprise, he shook his head.

"When first you knew me, I was the leader of a small rebel group in Aborium devoted to bedeviling the Herders," he said. "But I was compromised. Just after we met, as you know, I left the Aborium group to be run by my second, a stolid, reliable fellow named Yavok. I took no one with me but Reuvan and Idris."

Brydda was silent a moment, his eyes distant as he looked into the past.

"While in Aborium, I had come to know the leader of the Sutrium group, an old fox named Bodera, whom

I learned to admire. I had told him my dream of uniting all the rebel groups, and when he heard I was to leave Aborium, he invited me to work toward that end with him in an organized effort to overthrow the Council. The most difficult thing is that each rebel group operates almost in isolation. Fortunately, Bodera was one of the first rebel leaders, and he knew all the others. They respect him tremendously, so he was exactly the right person to serve as a focus. It was only because Bodera asked it that the other rebels listened to my ideas."

"Then he is the leader of the rebels?" I asked.

Brydda sighed. "No single person is the leader. That is what I am trying to tell you. But Bodera has great influence on the men who lead the various groups, and because of this, he was able to get the rebels to accept me as a sort of roving overseer whose task is to bring everyone together long enough to fight the Council. But it has been an uphill battle. And when Bodera dies, it is very possible the whole thing will fall apart."

"Is he so old, then?" I asked, fascinated by this glimpse into rebel affairs.

"Old, yes, but it is not age that kills him. He has a peculiar slow form of the rotting sickness contracted when he was a boy on Councilfarms. In those days, they sent children with their parents if they were charged with sedition, rather than sending them off to orphan homes."

From my own experiences in the orphan home system, I knew children mined whitestick, a poisonous residue of the Great White. In its raw state, the substance had to touch the skin in order to transmit its poisons, and we had been given gloves to collect it.

Sometimes I still woke at night sweating because I had dreamed of touching it by accident, as so many orphans did.

Once collected, whitestick was sent to the Councilfarms where it was treated to strip away the poisons so that it could be used in medicines and as a power source. The transformation of whitestick was dangerous, because during the process, it emitted the poisons that, over time, caused the dreaded rotting sickness. This was why a long Councilfarm sentence was, in effect, a delayed death sentence.

Brydda blinked, searching for the tail of his narrative. "I have convinced Bodera of the need for an alliance with your people. But the leaders of the two largest rebel groups reject you."

"Do they give reasons?"

Brydda ran a huge hand through tousled curls. "You come to the heart of my reluctance to present you with the matter. Of the two who oppose you utterly, the first is Tardis, who runs the rebel organization in Murmroth. He has taken over recently from his father, who was a stiff-necked bigot. Tardis responded to the proposal of an alliance between rebel and Talented Misfit forces with predictable repugnance. He wrote that, Talent or no, Misfits are not true humans and he will not make an alliance with mutants. The one bright note is that, unlike his father, Tardis does not favor wholesale extermination of your people. His note said that we do not make contracts with cows or horses, and neither do we kill them for being less than human." He smiled wryly. "I am afraid Tardis regards your ability to communicate with animals as further proof of your inhumanity."

"And the other rebel leader?" I asked quietly.

"Malik. He is based in Guanette and runs most of the rebel groups in the upper lowlands and around the Gelfort Range." Brydda's voice held a flatness that told me he disliked this man. "He is more violent than Tardis in his rejection of Misfits. He thinks you are freaks and should be eradicated like poisonweed in a kitchen garden.

"There are others who oppose you, too, but they might be argued around. If not, they are less important. Tardis and Malik are the keys. Without them, there will be no rebellion."

Brydda tugged at his beard, a familiar signal of his inner disturbance.

"Then there is to be no alliance?" I strove to sound undeterred.

Brydda sat forward in his seat in sudden agitation. "Do not think that! It is the very reason I have hesitated to tell Domick what has been happening. There is always hope."

"What hope?" I demanded. "That boy you had guarding the safe house reacted like I was poison because he thought I was a *gypsy*. How is he going to react when he knows I am a Misfit? We can't make your people accept us."

With a wave of bitterness, I wondered what hope there was for Misfits to ever live normal lives if even our own allies thought of us as freaks. If we did trick them into standing beside us in battle, what would it ultimately achieve? Not the acceptance we dreamed of. And how long would it take before loathing tolerance became hatred and, once again, persecution?

"There is hope in gaining Bodera's support of you,"

Brydda insisted. "And there is always the possibility that we can change the minds of the other rebels. One of the main problems is that the rebels still think all Misfits are shambling mental defectives. Second," he said swiftly, forestalling my outrage, "your youth has convinced them that there would be no military gain in an alliance with you."

"And in the face of this, you can say that there is hope?" I asked incredulously.

"I believe so," Brydda reiterated firmly. "The first thing is to make my comrades think of you as human beings."

"A simple matter."

Brydda ignored that. "I think you should meet with them."

"Rushton already did that, and it was obviously no use."

He patted my arm. "I meant you specifically, Elspeth. Rushton was introduced to them as your leader, but the rebels think of him as your keeper, as if you were a troupe of trained bears. I think they need to meet a real Talented Misfit."

"To what end?" I snapped. "Would you parade a freak before them to confirm their prejudices?"

The rebel shook his head. "I would have them meet and speak with a lovely young woman gifted with remarkable abilities. Not a mutated monster. I have not dared explain Misfit abilities in much detail, because they would only increase your monstrosity in the rebels' eyes. But if they could meet you and accept you, then we could show them what you can do. After that, your age will not matter, I warrant."

I sighed. He was right. It was worth a try, only

because the alternative was too bleak to contemplate. "When would such a meeting take place?"

Brydda's eyes sparkled. "There is to be a meeting of the rebel leaders soon. The day is not yet set, but it would be within a sevenday."

I felt a sick thrill of nervousness. "Where?"

"It must be held outside Sutrium," the rebel said promptly. He looked over his shoulder at Idris, who, though silent, had stood close to Brydda throughout our conversation.

The boy nodded, and Brydda reached out to ruffle his hair. In the wordlessness of this exchange, I saw the depth of the friendship between the pair.

"It is my strict policy to keep the locations of rebel meetings secret until the last minute so they cannot be revealed to anyone." The big man shifted forward in his eagerness. "Think of it, Elspeth—all you need to do is convince one or two rebel leaders to regard you as human. At the worst, it will be a positive beginning."

I thought it more likely such a meeting would simply confirm the rebels' prejudices. People had a way of seeing what they wanted to. And in spite of all Brydda's precautions and countermeasures, the big man had said there was a possibility of a traitor being in the rebels' midst. Which meant a definite risk.

On the other hand, if by some slim chance he was right and I did manage to change the rebels' attitude toward us, the risk would be a small price to pay.

"I will send word to Obernewtyn to see if the guild-merge will condone this meeting."

Brydda frowned. "I am not sure there will be enough time to send for approval. It is a great pity you have no birds here."

Idris smiled at my expression of bewilderment. "We have learned that if some birds are raised in a certain place, they will return to that place unerringly, no matter how far away they are released. Each of the rebel groups now raises birds, and we exchange them so that we always have the means to send messages swiftly. These are carried in tiny cylinders fastened to a bird's leg. It was done this way in the Beforetime."

Brydda slapped his leg. "But wait! You would not need a homing bird, Elspeth. You could simply beast-speak your message to a bird and ask it to fly to Obernewtyn."

Before I could respond, the door burst open behind us.

Brydda whirled, drawing his knife in one smooth-flowing movement and landing in a crouch. Idris had just as swiftly taken a sword from his belt.

It was only the seaman, Reuvan, whom I had met before in Aborium. His handsome face was red from exertion, and he was so intent upon delivering his message that he did not notice me or Domick. "There is a drunk in an inn who claims Salamander is in Sutrium," he panted.

Idris was at the edge of my vision, and I was startled to see his pleasant features twist in a spasm of hatred.

Brydda slid his knife home and turned to us. "I am sorry to cut short our supper, but I must go at once. I will come to you soon at the safe house, and we will talk again. But think on what I have said, Elspeth. The only hope of an alliance rests with your being able to alter the way rebels see Misfits. A meeting may be the only means of achieving that."

A moment later, we were outside in the dark, alone.

"Who is Salamander?" I asked Domick.

"It is the name of the man who runs the slave trade," Domick said. His tone was stiff. "Why didn't you tell me you were here to find out about the alliance? Doesn't Rushton trust me now? Has he sent you to check up on me?"

I shook my head helplessly.

◆ 11 ◆

I WOKE NEAR dawn to the muted sound of rain falling. The air felt clammy, and I wondered what had disturbed me.

I let my thoughts drift and had the fleeting impression of an unfamiliar mind touching mine as lightly as the shadow of an intruder might fall on a sleeping form. I then realized Maruman's mind was curled up around mine and gently extricated myself. I wondered if I'd simply mistaken Maruman's presence for something else.

The door opened and Kella peered in, holding a lantern high.

"What's wrong?" I asked, sitting up.

Maruman stirred on my pillow and opened his golden eye. I had the odd impression that he had been awake all along.

"It's the gypsy," the healer said softly so as not to disturb Dragon. "She woke me screaming."

I jumped out of bed and pulled a thick shawl around my shoulders.

We ran along the corridor and into the healing chamber. As I approached the gypsy's bed, I saw that her eyes were open but unfocused, just as Maruman's were when he was in the midst of his mad dreams. One eye was blue and the other a mottled brown. Kneeling by the mattress, I forced myself to be calm as her queer gaze swiveled to me.

"Can she see me?" I asked.

The healer shook her head. "She's broken the sleepseal but isn't really awake. She's having some sort of nightmare, but her system won't be able to take the strain for long."

"She's going to die?"

"If this goes on, yes. I need to get into her mind to relieve some of the pressure, but as a healer, I can't work against her will, and her mind is refusing me access." Kella's eyes narrowed. "*You* could get into her mind through her subconscious."

I looked down at the gypsy and felt a ripple of unease at her steady regard. "And do what?"

"Wake her," Kella said. "I'll do the rest."

I licked my lips. They felt dry and rough.

The subconscious could not be shielded, so if I did as Kella wanted, the deepest thoughts and desires that formed the basis of the gypsy's character would be laid bare to me in all their seething disorder. We had agreed unanimously in guildmerge that we could establish no system of dealing with the unTalented until they regarded us as equals. As long as they saw us as freaks, we could not afford to have any scruples about using our coercive abilities to plunder their minds and use what we found there against them. It was war, Rushton had said, and we must win before making terms.

Yet this gypsy was not my enemy, and the thought of entering her undermind filled me with revulsion. My reaction was emotional and instinctive. When I had first been sent to Obernewtyn, Ariel and his masters

111

had invaded my mind using a coercive machine. My only defense had been to enter into a partial mindbond with Rushton and use his latent abilities to strengthen me and shield my mind from their torture. Such a bond had meant a kind of mental nakedness, the thought of which even now made me tremble. Rushton had not abused the mindbond by blending entirely as bondmates might, but the affair had left us uncomfortable, intimate strangers, and me with an abiding dislike of mindbonds.

"Elspeth," the healer murmured, drawing me out of my thoughts. "I know this is hard for you, but healers enter unconscious minds all the time and do not regard it as a violation. It's simply a matter of not absorbing while you are in there—of separating yourself mentally."

I ground my teeth together. She was making a good point. To enter for healing purposes was hardly a brutal invasion. And in doing so, I would be saving Obernewtyn—and myself, if the gypsy could help with Maryon's second prediction.

Steeling myself, I leaned closer to the gypsy.

"Do you hear me?" I asked aloud, still reluctant to begin. She made no response, either by word or gesture, to indicate she heard what I was saying. I sighed. "All right. I'll deep-probe her and bring her out if I can."

I closed my eyes and extended a probe delicately toward the gypsy. My mind butted gently against her shield, then slid down the outside of it, seeking the point at which it would dissolve in the maelstrom of the subconscious.

I was astonished to find the shielding continued

right down into the subconscious. I quested against it. It was definitely the sort of shield unTalented minds produced naturally, but it had been somehow displaced from the upper levels of the gypsy's mind. It was scarred and buckled, and I began pushing coercively, testing until I found a weak place where I could enter.

Almost immediately, I came upon a wall of forgetting. Again, this was not usually found at a subconscious level.

The wall was eroded and had fused in places with the mindshield. This suggested the original forgetting established by the mind had begun to give way, allowing whatever had been repressed by it to rise to the conscious level. From what I could see, the gypsy's mind had reacted instinctively to protect itself, collapsing its shield on top of the memory in an effort to bury it. Obviously, this had worked for a time, though it had left her unconscious. Now the memory had begun to erode the fused barrier made up of wall and shield, causing the fit that had so alarmed Kella.

Curious, I pressed myself lightly against the fused barrier, wondering at its strength. It was paper-thin, and before I could stop myself, I had slipped through into . . .

. . . a small room. I/we are alone. My/our hands and legs bound tightly. I/we cringe at the sound of Caldeko's screams. What are they doing to you, my love?

The Herder and the boy are bringing me/us to him now. Showing him to me/us. The thing that was once Caldeko is barely recognizable as human. The mindless keening that rises from it fills me/us with horror/fear.

Caldeko opens his eyes. His soul reaches out of them to me/us, begging for release.

The Herder smiles coldly. "Tell me about the Twentyfamilies."

(How does he know?) I/we shake my/our head but I/we are afraid. (Block)

He waves his hand at the boy, who has a brand.

Caldeko's shrieks fill my mind. Split me open.

I/we scream and struggle to reach him.

"Tell me his given name," the Herder says.

I/we dare not speak. Must not. But Caldeko is my/our soul's joy! I must answer.

Caldeko is suddenly silent.

"Fool," the Herder snarls at the boy, "you have killed him. If she will not speak to save her bondmate pain, she will never speak to save herself. Well, we will make her an example. . . .

Caldeko/beloved is gone in terrible agony because I/we would not speak.

The pain of the tearing/the guilt/the grief is unbearable. I/we push it down into the darkness, because I/we cannot exist with it burning at me.

I/we make a wall of forgetting to bind it.

Peace.

Now I am at the stake. My arms are cut and bound. I am to die. I do not fear. I go to join my beloved. But, oh, the thought of Caldeko gives the memory/the monster life, and it rises to savage me. (I betrayed/I failed)

I panic and reach. Again I have it trapped, but the new barrier is flimsy. It will not last long. No matter. Soon the flames will come, and it will be ended.

But they do not come. I live. There is only one escape. Now I must go down and down into the deepest darkness. But something opposes . . . me. . . . Everything . . . slows . . . down. . . . I . . . am . . . weak. . . . But . . . I . . . fight them and now, now it is easier. Soon it will be over.

The spiral begins. I go down. I want to go to escape the memories (I failed to speak/I betrayed/he died/I killed him).

I fall. I dive.

I hear the song. Death sings my name.

I felt myself pulled down, dragged with the gypsy woman in her search for death. I fought against her, struggling frantically to disentangle our minds. We were too deep. I sensed the humming magnetism of the mindstream, which offered the oblivion she sought.

Desperate, I drew on the dark strength of the violent power at the depth of my mind to tear us free from the pull of the mindstream.

I wrenched us away into . . .

. . . a pale shining room. She/we are looking at a man with skin as black and polished as an old tree root. He wears odd clothing. His eyes are frightened. He takes her/us by the shoulders and shakes her/us hard.

"We have no choice, Emma," he whispers. "We have to escape. Their actions have already set it all in motion."

"But if what Cassandra foresaw is to happen, we will give them what they seek," she/we say.

"She said one of our number will give in. One will reveal what we have kept hidden. But it need not be you or me. We can escape."

Emma/we opens her/our mouth. "But where can we go? There will be radiation sickness when it comes—better to die at once."

"There are places that won't be hit so badly, where humanity will go on. We will join them. But Cassandra said we must make sure no one ever knows about us or what we can do."

"Oh God, why? Tell me why this has to happen?" Emma/we cry hysterically.

The man squeezes her/our arm awkwardly, as if he is not used to such gestures. "I don't know. Come with the rest of us. We're going to the Reichler Clinic first. Hannah and Jacob believe the mountains will be safe. . . .

. . . The mindstream tugged, dragging me/us free, pulling me/us down. . . .

A familiar voice called to me, harsh and intrusive.

"ElspethInnle! Remember your promise. You must live to come when the oldOne calls!"

It was Maruman.

"How are you here?" I asked dreamily, drifting downward, mesmerized by the shimmering siren call of the mindstream.

"You must not go down any more. Stop!" he sent

116

urgently. I felt a searing pain on my hand, and I suddenly realized that I was on the verge of sharing the gypsy's suicide.

I fought to free myself, but again Maruman spoke. "Bring the funaga. Bring her, for she is needed."

I reached back and dragged the gypsy up with me. She screamed in fury and fought me. I drew again on the murderous power hidden in my mind for the strength to reject the mindstream. I gripped her tighter still. I could not hold her so close and remain separate. Our minds merged again. . . .

Something is holding/pulling. I am caught/ something makes me live/stay/suffer.
Let me go. Let me die. I cannot bear it.
WHO ARE YOU?

I screamed and opened my eyes.

"Elspeth!" Kella was shaking me, white to the lips.

"What?" I felt dazed, confused, shattered. My mind churned with grief and guilt. Disjointed, impossible memories seethed in me. And my hand! Blood welled from three savage slashes across my palm.

"What happened?" the healer demanded. "One minute you were sitting there calmly, and the next you started to convulse. I thought . . ." She sank down on the edge of the gypsy's bed. "Lud, but you scared me!"

"I scared myself," I said shakily, pushing the heaviness of my unbraided hair from my face. I felt hot and cold at the same time, and my hands were trembling uncontrollably. I dabbed at the blood.

"Maruman scratched you," Kella said. "He climbed onto your lap when you were in the gypsy's mind, and when you started to shudder and groan, he scratched you. He must have been frightened. I . . . I slapped him, and he ran out."

"He saved my life," I murmured. "I had gone too deep, but he brought me out of it."

"Oh no," Kella said, aghast. "And I slapped him!"

There was a small moan from the bed, and I turned to look at the gypsy. Her eyes were open still, but tears now coursed down her cheeks. Her expression was aware, anguished. "What have I done?" she whispered hoarsely.

"It doesn't matter," I said wearily. "Everything will be okay now."

The gypsy buried her face in her hands. "Doesn't matter? You don't know. You can't imagine . . ."

Her eyes glazed over, and her eyelids shut. I looked up to see Kella frowning in concentration. "I've put her back to sleep. It's just a light sleepseal— not like the one Roland put on her whole body. She is out of immediate danger but still terribly weak. I have closed her wounds and hastened the healing, and her body is responding. What on earth happened?"

I took a deep shuddering breath and looked down at the gypsy. There seemed no connection between the tempestuous, desperate will I had encountered inside her mind and this passive form.

"She had locked a memory behind a wall of forgetting, but it was leaking all over the place. She was trying to die so as to escape it. Roland's seal slowed her down, but she broke through. I was testing the wall, but I had neglected to erect a separating shield around myself. Our minds merged."

Kella's eyes widened. "And?"

"I relived the memory she was trying to escape. The Herder we rescued her from had tortured and killed her bondmate in front of her to make her tell him the name of some Twentyfamilies gypsy. She refused to speak. When her bondmate died, she was convinced she had betrayed him."

I felt a surge of sorrow for the loss of a man I had never known, a residue of the accidental joining. "She thinks if she had talked, he would have lived." I shook my head sadly. "But the man was on the verge of death before they brought her in. I don't think he even knew what was happening."

The healer was ashen. "Monsters," she whispered. "They are monsters to be capable of such barbarism." Kella bent to draw the covers up around the gypsy. Abruptly, I remembered the odd sideways shunt that had hurled me into the depths of the gypsy's mind and into one of the racial memories that Maryon said arose occasionally from the mindstream like bubbles. The memory was already blurred at the edges like a dream, and even as I groped for detail, it dissolved.

But I did remember one thing. There had been something in the dream about the Reichler Clinic.

I shook my head. The foray into the gypsy's mind had drained me, and my wits drifted with weariness. The previous day and night seemed to have been going on for years.

Kella washed the scratches Maruman had inflicted, worrying all the while about her treatment of him.

"He will understand," I said. We went into the kitchen, and I took a poker and stirred to life the embers of the previous night's fire.

"Domick told me you met with Brydda last night," Kella said, hanging up a jug of mead to warm.

I nodded. Domick had spoken little on the journey back to the safe house, furious at the lack of faith Rushton had demonstrated in sending me to speak with Brydda directly. And though Brydda had accepted the blame for the lack of news, I still felt uneasy with Domick since seeing how much he had changed.

"Greetings, ElspethInnle." Maruman was sitting under the table, his yellow eye glinting. "I am glad you did not take the longsleep."

"You saved me."

"Of course," he sent complacently. "Maruman guards the dreamtrails."

"Elspeth?" Kella prompted, unaware of my exchange with the cat.

"I'm sorry. What did you say?"

"I said surely there is no hurry to return the gypsy to her people, now that she has wakened. You will be able to wait until she recovers completely."

I sighed. "It is more complicated than that. I did not want to worry you, but Maryon has futuretold that we must return the gypsy to her people in a matter of days. Otherwise, Obernewtyn may be in great peril."

She was aghast. "But that is impossible!"

"I meant to ask Brydda about the best way to do it, but I didn't get the chance. I'll find a way."

"That's not what I meant," said Kella. "You cannot move her. Her system has undergone a terrible shock, and she was already weak. She needs to be allowed to rest. . . ."

"There is no time," I snapped.

"Then she has even less time, for you will kill her if

you move her in the next couple of days." There was a deep crease between the healer's eyebrows. "Does she have no rights of her own, Elspeth? Is Obernewtyn more important than her life?"

I bit my lip in sudden shame. I had not thought of the gypsy at all, only of myself and Obernewtyn. I felt sick. "You are right," I said. "I will not move her until you say it is safe. But, Lud, pray it is soon."

Kella's face softened. "I did not mean to criticize you. After all, it is not for yourself but for Obernewtyn that you fear." I flushed but held my tongue. "In any case, you cannot return her until you find her people. That is your task, and mine is to heal her. I'll do my very best to have her well enough to be shifted before the days are up," she vowed, squeezing my hand.

Just then, Dragon came in, and I was glad of the distraction. Her face and hands were unusually clean and her hair roughly braided. Her beauty struck me anew, and from Kella's expression, she felt the same.

"Hungry," Dragon said.

My stomach chimed in agreement. Kella laughed and rose to carve some slices of bread and cheese. My mouth watered as she toasted them; then for a time there was silence as we ate. Kella did not join us but fed crumbs of cheese to Maruman as an apology. He sent to me that he felt no ill will for the slap she had administered, but he accepted her offerings with feline fastidiousness, seeing she needed the reassurance.

"Good," Dragon announced at last, patting her distended stomach. Then she gave me an anxious look. "Dragon stay?"

"I suppose you must, but you're an awful nuisance," I sighed.

"Nuisance," she echoed with an identical sigh.

I stifled a grin and put my arm around her. "Dragon, I'm going to let you stay, but only if you promise to do exactly as you are told."

"Promise," she agreed after some thought. "Promise and stay."

"Is Domick still asleep?" I asked Kella.

At once the strained look returned to her eyes. "He went early to the Councilcourt."

I nodded and looked into the fire, reflecting on his behavior at The Good Egg. Kella would be a great deal more worried if she understood more about what Domick did when he was not with her.

I wondered how the healer, with her horror of torture, would respond to the knowledge that people thought her bondmate a Council torturer. My own wild fear, that the rumors had been true, now seemed absurd in light of what I'd seen in the gypsy's memory. No Misfit could stoop to that, not even a coercer.

Then Ariel's lovely, vicious face floated into my mind, giving lie to that certainty. But I thrust it away. Domick was no Ariel.

Only then did it occur to me that Domick had still not told me what he did now at the Councilcourt.

◆ 12 ◆

"Do you understand me/ElspethInnle, who stands before you?" I sent, framing the thought carefully.

The bird tilted its head and eyed me, but I could sense no thought from it other than an instinct to eat and a subliminal memory of flight that filled me with restlessness.

"Well? Are you buying the creature or communing with it?" the stallholder demanded.

Resignedly, I handed him a coin, and he passed over the cage. "You must be starting up a breeding pen with all them birds you keep buying. Store them in your wagon, do you, boy?"

I took the cage and turned away, ignoring him.

"You found one?" Kella whispered eagerly, coming over from another stall.

I shook my head. "I can't get any sense out of it."

The healer stared at me. "Oh, Elspeth! Are we going to free this one like all the others?"

"What else?" I asked in a disgruntled voice.

Brydda's suggestion of using a bird as a messenger had seemed a marvelous one. It was always easier to communicate with tamed or partly tame animals, so I had decided to search the numerous markets for a captive bird that would agree to carry a message to

Obernewtyn. This search would also give me the opportunity to randomly probe a large number of people for information about gypsies.

I found an astonishing amount of Herder-induced superstition and wild surmise but very little real information. Landfolk despised all gypsies but hated and envied the Twentyfamilies with a passion that surprised me.

Kella had accompanied me to the market to replenish her supply of herbs, leaving a disgruntled Matthew to watch Dragon and the gypsy, but she had lingered, drawn into my search for a messenger bird. In many ways, she was of more use here than I, for I had quickly discovered that the birds available in the market were not sentient in the way that Maruman or Gahltha were; they used a mode of communication closer to empathy than farseeking. I was able to receive only the vaguest images from their minds. Kella was able to use her slight secondary empathic ability to muster some response from them, but it hadn't been enough to convey what we needed.

Those few who were able to comprehend farsought speech seemed to have no grasp of time and had very short attention spans.

However, having felt, even dimly, a bird's longing for freedom, I had not been able to leave it caged. So far, I had purchased fifteen of the wretched creatures and set them free, running our store of coin dangerously low.

Kella made a strangled noise, and I thought it a sign of frustration.

Then I realized she was trying not to laugh.

I sighed, wondering why I was still trying, when it had been perfectly obvious for some time that the idea was doomed. After trying so many, I was beginning to believe that the Agyllians had the only avian minds capable of full communication with humans.

"I'm sorry for laughing," she said contritely.

"It's good to hear laughter," I said. "It helps me to forget Maryon's deadline and that I must make some reply to Brydda, when he comes, as to whether I will meet with the other rebel leaders. Since these birds will not lend themselves as messengers to carry word to Obernewtyn, I will have to make the decision myself."

"Domick will have sent a message off this morning," Kella said.

"Nevertheless, it will take too long to arrive to give me any direction. I will be back at Obernewtyn by the time it gets there."

And perhaps I will return only to die before the next Days of Rain. The thought crept insidiously into my mind.

I wished I'd had the chance to tell Brydda about the gypsy and ask his advice. Lud only knew how long it would take him to call on the safe house. I racked my brain for some sensible way to find the gypsy's people, but nothing came to me other than finding out where they set their wagons up in the city and going among them. The other obvious alternative was to have Kella waken the gypsy again so I could ask her. But I was reluctant to do that. I still felt a twinge of shame at the selfishness of my attitude toward the gypsy. Let her waken when she would.

Maneuvering the cage through the market throng, I noticed a ragged gypsy lad trying to sell something to a stallholder; a halfbreed, as evidenced by his poverty, the lad was clearly receiving short shrift from the trader and departed finally with a doleful expression.

If I could coerce some general information out of this gypsy about his people, I would be able to face any number of them without quaking in my boots for fear that I was about to give myself away as an impostor. It was odd how blithely I had gone about pretending to be a gypsy, when I thought I knew all that needed knowing about them. Now, awareness of my ignorance terrified me. Swiftly, I shaped a light probe and sent it after the lad.

The probe slid away from his mind, blocked by a natural shield.

"Damn," I muttered, withdrawing.

The Teknoguildmaster, Garth, had a theory that normal people were developing unconscious shields that keep us from reading them. Even back in my days in the orphan homes, I had known there were unTalented people with natural mindshields that kept me out or mind sensitivity that warned them if they were being read.

I did not like the idea that such natural defenses were developing in response to and alongside our own abilities. Not just because it would make our work more difficult, but because it would put paid to the theory that Talented Misfits were simply the next step in human evolution. It would mean instead that we were simply *one* strand in human evolution and the unTalents another. That practically brought us back to the Herder theory that Misfits were mutant deviations from "true" humanity.

"The poor thing," Kella murmured, her eyes following the gypsy lad. "They are not allowed to farm or settle, and no one wants to buy from them. No wonder they take to thievery. What else are they supposed to do?"

I thought again of our gypsy and of the whole question of half and pureblood. She was a halfbreed, but she had let her bondmate suffer torture rather than speak the name of a Twentyfamilies gypsy. Yet Domick had told me with absolute conviction that Twentyfamilies were estranged from halfbreeds.

I scowled. For a moment, I forgot my guilt and indulged anger instead. I had saved the gypsy from the Herder flame only to see her attempt suicide—and draw me with her! Even if I had broken free and let her go, her death would have meant my own if the futuretelling was true. It angered me that my life should hinge on a woman who valued her life not at all.

"Does it have to be a bird?" Kella asked.

I blinked at her, having lost the thread of the conversation.

"Does it have to be a bird you use as a messenger?" she reiterated.

"Any other animal would move too slowly and would be as vulnerable on the ground as a human messenger," I said. "I might just as well send Matthew."

"Gypsy pig!" a man hissed as I brushed past him.

I ignored him, but Kella paled. Belatedly, it occurred to me that I was endangering the healer by being with her. There was a definite antagonism in the eyes of anyone who looked at me. The Herders' slur campaign against gypsies had been more than effective.

The sooner we got back to the safe house, the better.

Gahltha whinnied softly as we approached the public holding yard, and in spite of my tensions, I smiled at the sight of him. I had asked Dragon to dirty him, and the empath had surpassed herself. His coat was so matted and filthy that it was impossible to tell his color, and he smelled truly disgusting. For once, there had been no need to worry about leaving him alone since he looked and smelled far too disreputable to be worth stealing.

"Is the bird/sahric useful/capable?" Gahltha inquired politely. *Sahric* meant "those who sing." I noted the coolness in his mental voice and realized he had not forgiven me for going to The Good Egg without him the previous night. I had promised not to do it again, knowing he felt his guardianship to be a sacred trust from Atthis, but clearly he still felt slighted.

"I'm afraid this bird/sahric is no more capable of hearing me than any of the others," I sent, looking glumly at the cage.

I mounted him and then offered my spare hand to Kella. She wrinkled her nose in distaste and volunteered to walk.

Suddenly, her eyes shifted to something beyond me, her smile vanishing.

"What is it?" I resisted the urge to swing around and look for myself.

"That gypsy who was watching us before. He's on the other side of the holding yard on a horse. I'm sure he is following us."

I forced myself to be calm and think. Mistakes were made when people panicked.

"Are you sure it is the same gypsy?" I asked at last. Kella was easily agitated and much given to morose reflections. When she had first claimed a gypsy was watching us, I had dismissed it as overactive imagination. Gypsies were too much on both our minds.

"I was sure before and am surer now. He is looking directly at us," the healer said forcefully. She looked near to fainting.

"Perhaps I should beastspeak his horse and ask it to tip him on his head," I said. As I had hoped, her fear evaporated into concern at my flippancy.

"Be serious, Elspeth. He has obviously followed us through the market, and he might now follow us to the safe house."

"He probably follows us because he finds you attractive," I said robustly.

She colored. "But I . . . I . . ."

"Oh, never mind. I won't tell Domick you have been flirting with gypsies. Or perhaps I will, since he neglects you disgracefully."

Her color deepened and then fled. "Oh, Elspeth, he's coming around this way! I'm sure he's trying to see your face."

My heart bumped against my breast, but I kept my voice calm for the healer's sake. She sounded on the verge of hysteria. "This is what we are going to do," I said. "You are going to go back into the market and pretend to shop. If the gypsy follows you, I will ask his horse to drop him on his head. If he follows me, Gahltha and I will lead him out of the city and give him a run for his troubles. Either way, stay at the market a little while and then make your way carefully back to the safe house."

Kella nodded, eyes wide and frightened.

I handed the birdcage down to her. "Take this."

She took it and moved off as I had bid. I waved, turning my head slightly and scanning the area with peripheral vision.

Sure enough, he was there—the same tall, rangy gypsy in costly blue silk that Kella had pointed out earlier. I was puzzled. What reason could he have for his interest in us, other than the slight curiosity value of a halfbreed gypsy boy walking with a Landgirl? He did not fit the description of the gypsy Matthew had seen leaving Guanette. And that would have been odd in any case, since in Guanette he would have seen a girl when now I was disguised as a boy.

From the corner of my eye, I studied him. His dark hair was bound back in a plait, and the band of fabric about his brow was stained to match his shirt. Kella had said the elaborate and expensive garments marked him as Twentyfamilies, but this did not seem conclusive evidence to me. After all, a halfbreed gypsy might be vain enough to spend his coin on such things.

I pretended to adjust my trousers, watching to see if he followed the healer. Sitting astride his gray horse, he stared intently after her. But as she walked off, his eyes moved toward me.

I pretended to spur Gahltha. "Head out of the city."

The black horse wheeled, and after a moment, I looked back as if I had remembered something to say to Kella. Seeing her gone, I shrugged and turned forward casually, but my heart was beating wildly. "He's right behind us," I sent.

"The gray equine ridden by this funaga who follows is named Sendari," Gahltha sent suddenly. "He/Sendari tells that he has not been owned/ridden long by this funaga. He says this one's hands and feet are skilled and gentle."

I frowned. His ownership of many horses seemed to confirm Kella's surmise that our pursuer was Twentyfamilies, but it still did not tell me why he was following me.

"Does Sendari know why this funaga follows?" I asked, just in case he did.

Gahltha paused, then reported the answer to my question. "He/Sendari tells that this funaga has ridden about much in these days soonest past, but he has arrived nowhere. He has spent much time standing/idle."

Watching, I thought uneasily. *Looking for us?*

I decided to probe the gypsy and sent my mind questing, but to my frustration, I encountered yet another mental shield. Cursing, I withdrew, thinking it an odd coincidence that all three gypsy minds I had tried to enter possessed natural mindshields. Garth's theory that more unTalents were developing mindshields was beginning to look as if it might be true.

I was indecisive. There was no subtle way to find out the gypsy's motives. His natural shield would prevent my coercing him except at a subconscious level, and there would be no gain in that. I could ask him outright what he was doing, but I would have no way of coercing the memory of our meeting from him.

"Let's lose him," I sent to Gahltha. Obedient, he broke into a fast canter along a road leading toward the farmlands east of the city.

I could hear the clatter of hooves behind me, but Gahltha did not increase his pace, saying it would confuse Sendari's rider if we behaved as if we were being followed. He was right, for the gypsy made no attempt to overtake us but rode at a distance.

Only when we reached the edge of the outlying farmlands surrounding Sutrium did Gahltha break into a full gallop, and I flattened myself to reduce wind resistance, thrilling to the race.

"He/Sendari follows," he sent.

"Can you outrun him?"

"There is no need," the black horse sent, with a faint echo of his old haughtiness. "Only the funaga race one another for no reason. Equines race for mate or lifesaving. Sendari knows that you are Innle. He will do what is needed."

I was discomforted by the thought that the gray horse would let us get away because he believed I was a figure from beastlegend. I had tried endless times to convince Gahltha I was not their heroic savior. It was enough that the Agyllians had incorporated me into their dreams and futuretellings without finding the animals were trying to do the same thing.

We rode swiftly along the dirt road; then, without warning, Gahltha turned sharply, cutting across a long, sloping grass plain. I clung tightly in case he stumbled on the rough tussocky ground, leaving it to him to decide how to proceed.

Looking ahead, I saw that he was making for a thick copse farther up the slope. He slowed only fractionally as we entered the trees, and in moments, we thundered out the other side of the stand onto open ground.

A rush of exaltation filled me as the ground blurred beneath us, and I gave a wild cry as we crested the hill.

Glancing back over my shoulder, I saw that the gray

had fallen into a limping walk, just short of the copse. Even as I watched, his rider dismounted.

"He/Sendari has pretended lameness," Gahltha reported, coming to a halt, too.

I saw the rider kneel to examine the leg and was impressed. Most men would have lashed their mount half to death rather than lose a quarry.

As if he sensed my thoughts, the gypsy stood and looked up to where I sat on Gahltha. I could not see his expression, but as we turned to ride away, I had a mad urge and held up my hand to wave in a cheeky salute.

The city center lay visible on the other side of the hill, and we went straight overland, jumping farm fences and hedges at a full gallop and making for a main road snaking through the hills and trees. We came out wider than I realized, for when we reached the road, we were in full view of a gate—from outside the city. There was no possibility of withdrawing without looking suspicious, for the soldierguards manning the gate were gazing at us.

My heartbeat quickened as we approached for the second time in a few days. Fortunately, it was not the same gate I had entered before.

"Papers, boy," a burly soldierguard demanded. It was an expedition rule that each of us carry papers on us at all times when we traveled away from Obernewtyn, so that was no trouble. I dug in my pocket and proffered them without a word, concentrating on reinforcing the coercive suggestion that I was a boy.

The other soldierguard stared at me narrowly, but it was not until his eyes dropped to Gahltha that I became concerned. He sauntered over and rubbed at the dried filth on the horse's coat.

"Got some white, does he, under all that muck?" he asked.

It was such a strange query that I probed his thoughts.

He was comparing Gahltha to a description that he had been given of Zade. Fortunately, Zade was smaller and had white markings on his forehead and back legs.

"All black," I said. Digging further in the soldier-guard's mind, I found a description of a gypsy girl that was clearly me, and, to my horror, there was also one of Matthew and the wagon.

Word of our rescue of the gypsy in Guanette had finally reached the Council.

"Been in the highlands recentlike?" the soldier-guard asked, moving around and casually taking a hold of Gahltha's rein. I told myself firmly that there was no reason to fear—Gahltha did not fit the description he had been given, and I was nothing like Matthew. Even so, my heart pounded.

"I came from Murmroth way just yesterday, and just now from Kinraide by Rangorn," I said in a bored voice, coercing the soldierguard who eyed my papers into seeing yesterday's date on the entry stamp and a watermark from the Suggredoon ferry. I wrinkled my nose and gestured at Gahltha. "Mud keeps away the flying biters, but it smells none too good."

The two men exchanged a glance, and the one with the papers nodded. The larger soldierguard's thoughts told me he had decided that neither Gahltha nor I fitted the descriptions they had been given.

He shrugged, releasing the reins. "All right, then, boy. Get on."

I rode off, trembling with reaction, and not just because news of the incident in Guanette had reached Sutrium at last.

While in the soldierguard's mind, I had learned that the Council intended to institute a gate search for the missing gypsy and her two rescuers the very next day. Each gate would have a copy of the original Normalcy Register—which recorded each child at birth after Herder inspection—against which to check the authenticity of travelers' papers.

This told me that either they thought we were heading for Sutrium with the gypsy woman and hoped to trap us as we entered the city . . . or, worse, they knew we were here already and meant to stop us getting out.

• 13 •

IT WAS JUST on dusk as we rode into the market square alongside the safe house. I had taken a circuitous route from the city gate.

I asked Gahltha to stop and took a long careful look around the market. He moved restlessly under me, sending that his flesh itched and stank abominably and asking why we had to go so slowly.

"I have to make sure we weren't followed," I sent firmly.

He trotted into the lane leading to the wagon-repair yard without comment. I slid off his back and removed the false bit and bridle, lighting a lantern. "I'll wash/ brush you down," I sent.

We walked together to the high gate leading to the grassy courtyard. At the far end of the yard was a shed where hay and oats were kept. Jaygar was a shadow grazing in the deeper darkness alongside it, and he lifted his head to greet us.

I hung the lantern from a nail and stepped into the shed to find a brush.

"Clean Gal-ta?"

I started at the voice rising from the shadowy interior of the feed shed.

"Dragon?" I called softly.

The empath-coercer emerged carrying the curry brush. She looked even dirtier than usual, her face woebegone and tearstained.

"What are you doing here?" I asked her.

She held up the brush. "Dragon dirty Gal-ta. Dragon clean Gal-ta. Dragon waiting and waiting."

"Does Kella know where you are?"

"Kella sad," Dragon said earnestly. "Cryingcryingcrying here." She pointed to her slight breasts. "Water here." She touched one of her eyes. "Not see. Not hear Dragon."

I frowned. The empath's ability to perceive emotions was improving dramatically if she could sense inner tears. "And Matthew? Where is he?"

Dragon scowled. "Matthew say, 'Dragon go away.' Dragon go. Not need Matthew. Dragon wait here with Jaygar. Dragon loves Jaygar!"

I sent an inquiry to the roan.

"Mornir has been here since sundeath," he confirmed. "Water came from her eyes."

Dragon's tears did not surprise me. Matthew had been unremittingly cold to her since our arrival at the safe house. He was being childish, but it was a personal matter between them, and I did not wish to intervene. Better if he and Dragon resolved their own difficulties.

Poor Kella's tears were somewhat more worrisome, for her emotions were already stretched taut.

"See if you can do as good a job at cleaning Gahltha as you did in dirtying him," I told Dragon absently. "Come inside when you have finished."

She nodded and set to work with the brush, seeming glad of something to do. I was sorry for her boredom and loneliness, but perhaps she would learn from it that disobedience did not always produce what was desired.

Domick, Kella, and Matthew were in the kitchen. The Farseeker ward spotted me first.

"Thank Lud," he cried fervently, jumping to his feet. "We've been worried sick. I tried to farseek ye, but there is so much static about. Maybe it's just from all these minds crammed together, but it feels like trying to see over Blacklands or tainted ground."

"Kella said a gypsy followed you at the market," Domick interrupted. There was no sign of the previous night's anger over what he perceived as Rushton's mistrust.

I told them what had happened.

"Perhaps this gypsy simply mistook Elspeth for someone he knew," Domick said dismissively. "In any case, you lost him, and I have more important news. The Council is about to institute stringent new measures for checking papers in an attempt to catch two renegade halfbreed gypsies who set another gypsy free in Guanette, killing a Herder and two soldierguards in the process."

There was a tinge of righteousness in his tone.

"You realize this will make it more difficult for you to leave Sutrium. And as soon as you begin asking questions of gypsies, the Council or Herder Faction will hear of it, because information is as good as coin. Someone will talk, and then the gates will be nets, waiting to catch you. And the soldierguards within the city will look for you as well. There will be random street searches, and if you are wandering about . . ."

"I have no intention of wandering about," I said crisply. "Nor will I be asking indiscreet questions. If

I had to, I could simply have Kella wake the gypsy woman, and she could tell me whom to contact."

To my surprise, Kella nodded easily. "If you want, I can break it now. It's only a light seal, and it will not harm her to talk."

"I do not like the idea," Domick protested. "Why not simply put her in the street before waking her? She can make her own way to her people."

Kella gave Domick a fierce look. "What if she is recognized before she has time to find them? And how will she make her way anywhere in her condition?"

"Her welfare is not our concern," he answered coldly. His eyes shifted to me again. "I don't understand why you are so determined to deliver her personally. Or why you have risked so much for her. She could report us."

"And what will she have to report?" Kella asked. "A wild story about being saved by gypsies who live inside a building in the city? In any case, she is hardly likely to march off to the Council to tell her story, is she? And since we will not be dumping her in a street, she is unlikely to be caught by them and forced to speak." She stopped abruptly, staring at her bondmate. The tension between them was fraught with unspoken angers.

"As for letting her creep away herself," I said gently, "it would be a waste. I want to find out more about the gypsies, and this will give me the perfect opportunity. Or so Maryon advised," I added.

"Maryon did?" Domick echoed, his belligerence lessening. "You did not say that the Futuretell guild-mistress had spoken of this."

"Didn't I?" I asked offhandedly. I stood up and

looked pointedly at Kella. "Shall we go and wake her, then, and see what she has to say?"

The healer laid a gentle hand on the gypsy's forehead.

The woman stirred almost at once and opened her eyes. I was startled anew at their queer coloring. She gave me a deeply suspicious look, her heavy brows drawing together over the bridge of her nose.

"Who are you?" she rasped hoarsely. "Where am I?"

"You are in a safe house," Kella said soothingly, giving her water to moisten her throat. "You have been very ill."

The woman's head turned sideways, and she frowned up at Kella for a long moment before her odd eyes shifted back to me.

"I do not know you."

"I am a friend," I said, relieved that she had no memory of her previous brief wakening.

Her chin lifted. "I would not forget the face of a friend. Yet your voice sounds . . . familiar." She sounded as if this were more cause for suspicion than comfort. "What is this place?"

"As she said, it is a safe house."

"Whose safe house? This Landgirl's? Or yours? A gypsy girl dressed up as a boy."

"I am no more gypsy than I am a boy," I said bluntly. "I dye my skin and dress like this so as to travel unnoticed about the Land. I was traveling through Guanette when I came upon you. I stole you from a Herder who was about to roast you, and he was killed. Now the soldierguards are hunting me and you both. Your friend in the trees shot that Herder, not I, but the Council believes I did it."

Her eyes were suddenly wary. "My friend?"

"The gray-haired man who helped me get you out of Guanette," I said, bending the truth slightly.

Her eyes widened with alarm. "He helped you?"

I nodded, still narrowly skirting a direct lie. "If you tell us how to contact him, we will send him word that you are here."

Her eyes narrowed. "Where is here?"

"We are in Sutrium."

Her eyes darkened with mistrust. "You brought me all the way to Sutrium? Past the city gate and the soldierguards?"

"I hid you in our wagon."

She nodded as if such trickery were commonplace, and perhaps it was among her kind. "Why did you bring me here?"

"Why not?" I could not tell her Maryon had commanded me to bring her to Sutrium.

"Why did you help me in Guanette?"

"Perhaps because we may be of some use to each other and might even become friends."

She closed her eyes. "I have no friends."

"Then a stranger did you an unbelievable service if that gray-haired man was not a friend," I snapped.

Her eyes opened, glinting. "As you have done? If he was a friend, why would he ride off and leave me with strangers?"

I felt my cheeks redden and realized I had underestimated her intelligence. "We became separated. He rode toward Sutrium," I said less aggressively. "Look, all I want to know is how to bring you to him."

Her eyes were abruptly cool. "I do not recall asking for aid. Then or now."

"You were in no condition to ask for help then. Nevertheless, I gave it and thought you would be pleased," I added, unable to prevent irritation from seeping into my tone.

"You interfered of your own free will," she snarled. "I was not afraid to die."

"No," I agreed shortly. "You were afraid to live."

There was a flare of pain in her eyes then. "I am not afraid of anything," she said, but there was a frayed edge to her tone. I guessed she was remembering snatches of her attempt to die and wondering at her dreams, for so would she judge my communications with her subconscious mind.

Her eyes went from me to Kella and back again. "What do you want of me?"

"No more than to return you to your people." That was almost true. I tried to get into her mind again, now that she was conscious, but the block remained firm. Any further pressure and she would feel me.

"Why?" she demanded flatly. "I am no Twenty-families with a fat purse to reward you."

I decided to take refuge in indignation.

"You are a fugitive wanted by the soldierguards and the Herder Faction, and they are no friends of mine. I helped you and I expected no more than a little gratitude. Well, that is too high a price for your life, it seems. Instead you insult me and accuse me of sinister motives. Well, if you want to die, that is your business, but I have vowed to return you to your people, and that is what I will do. With or without your help."

There was a prickly silence.

"Help me to dress and show me a door and you will not need to trouble yourself," she said stonily.

Again she had outmaneuvered me. "No."

She nodded, as if she had anticipated the answer. "If you will not let me go, then I am your prisoner."

I thought quickly. "In your weakened state, you are bound to be picked up by the soldierguards and questioned. You would speak of us and this place. I cannot risk it."

"Who are you?" she said again, her expression openly baffled. Then she seemed to think of something and glared at me anew. "You needn't think I will tell you anything. . . ." She stopped.

"Anything about your Twentyfamilies friend?" I asked without thought. Instantly, her face changed, and my heart sank.

Angry at my own mishandling of the matter, I said bitterly, "I don't suppose you know what *swallow* means either?"

Her eyes widened in shock, the pupils swelling to devour the color. "Where . . . where did you hear that?"

My mind raced. "You said it in your sleep," I lied.

"It must have been gibberish," the gypsy said, closing her eyes again, her voice indifferent. "I do not know what it means, and I am afraid I can tell you nothing about my blood kin since I remember nothing more about myself than that I am a gypsy. If that gray-haired man you saw was a friend, I do not remember him either. Or even my name."

She was lying, but there was nothing I could do to make her speak.

"Well, perhaps in time you will remember," I said icily. "Just as I might recall why I bothered to save your life!"

I made a sign to Kella to put her back to sleep.

"Wretched, ungrateful woman," I snapped as we left the chamber.

Kella shrugged. "You can't really blame her, the way things are for halfbreeds. For all she knows, this whole thing could be an elaborate trap. You must admit it would look odd."

Which is the closest she would come to telling me I had been clumsy. I sighed and my temper faded.

"Will you try talking to her again?" Kella asked, stopping outside the kitchen door.

"I think not. If she will not be forced to speak by the torture of her bondmate, there is no way she will tell her story to a pair of strangers with no good reason for helping her," I said. "Damn the woman for being so difficult. I will have to find her people the hard way."

"The hard way?"

I nodded. "I will have to go among the gypsies and probe at random people in the hope of finding some clue as to where she might safely be taken. It *must* be time for luck to work for me rather than against me. Where do gypsies camp when they stay in the city?"

Kella gave me a quick, comprehending look. "They are permitted to camp on any green, but most go to the largest green over near the Suggredoon."

"Both half and pureblood gypsies?"

She nodded, clearly troubled. "Gypsies don't think in terms of physical boundaries, so in spite of the Great Divide, Twentyfamilies camp alongside halfbreed wagons. But that does not happen often. Twentyfamilies gypsies come to Sutrium only in the Days of Rain, when they are to tender the yearly tithe. Otherwise they avoid cities." She hesitated. "If you go there, you might encounter the Twentyfamilies man who followed us.

Perhaps you could wait a few days until they have gone."

"I dare not wait," I interrupted. "I will have to risk it."

Domick and Dragon were seated at the kitchen trestle when we entered, but Matthew had gone. No doubt he had departed when Dragon came in. I shook my head.

"What happened?" Domick asked.

"She will tell me nothing. I will have to go among the gypsies after all and see what I can winkle out."

"You must be careful," Domick said worriedly, and for a moment, he seemed like his old self. "I spoke to you of Faction and Council spies, but remember, the gypsies themselves are dangerous to cross. They may value the woman, but your knowing about her makes you a risk. The best way to protect her and themselves would be to kill you. Thinking you are a gypsy might stay their hand, but if they guess for a moment you are not what you pretend to be . . ."

"I will be careful," I promised.

"Have you decided whether to meet with the rebels?" Domick asked as I ladled a mug of fement from a freshly boiled and fragrant pot.

"I have," I said. "I am going to do it. Rushton wants to know where we stand with the rebels, and this meeting will give us an answer one way or the other. As soon as it is over, we will go at once to Obernewtyn."

Domick nodded soberly. "That is best. But be careful tomorrow, for all our sakes." He rose and reached for his cloak.

"You are going out again?" I asked, surprised.

"I have to go back to the Councilcourt. There is some sort of delegation from Sador arriving tonight."

"Sador," I murmured. There had been a lot of talk

about the distant province of late. A year ago, only the few seamen who plied that part of the coast had even known of it.

He nodded. "They are coming by ship. I expect they will request the removal of the Faction mission from their domain. They have been sending delegations to that effect from the first sevenday the Herders dwelt among them." He pulled on his cloak. "The Herders were sent not long after the road was opened. They are interfering in the Sadorian religion, and the Sadorians don't like it. The Earthtemple in Sador regulates how much spice is harvested, and it will allow only a small yield. It is my guess the Herders have been sent by the Council to erode the power of the Earthtemple and take it for themselves. Then they will increase the spice yield."

The coercer then departed with a perfunctory farewell that obviously distressed Kella. I felt for her, and spoke to give her time to compose herself.

"I should alter my appearance again. I dare not go out as a girl since the soldierguards have my description. I would need to have a coercive cloak the whole time, and that's a risk. Since that Twentyfamilies gypsy saw me as a boy, I will have to think of something else. Perhaps I could remain a boy but cut off my hair. . . ."

"No!" Kella looked horrified. "It is so long and beautiful. Like black silk."

Glad to have distracted her, I was nonetheless embarrassed by her words. "I don't care about hair."

"But gypsies do," she said insistently. "They do not cut their hair—men or women."

That was true enough. I had forgotten for the moment.

"Cut?" Dragon said. She was holding a knife in her

hand and looking so hopeful that both Kella and I burst into laughter.

Dragon hooted along happily.

"What's so funny?" Matthew asked lightly, coming in with his hair wet from a bath.

Dragon's laughter died, and her eyes followed the ward as he moved across the kitchen and peered into the pot.

"I hope that is not for us," he quipped, sniffing at the herbal preparation.

He could not have helped being aware of the empath-coercer's obsessive regard, but he made out that he had not noticed her.

"What about something to drink?" Kella asked Matthew. He sat down and nodded.

"And will you sit and be waited on?" I snapped, disliking the lazy way he expected the healer to bring him his mug. He flushed and rose to help her, and I found myself thinking of him as he had been when first I came to Obernewtyn, with his thinness and his limp and his quick dark gaze. A child then, and not yet a man now, for all he looked like one.

"Dragon will drink," Dragon said, looking up at him with pathetic eagerness.

The farseeker scowled, but he filled a mug with the steaming liquid and handed it to her ungraciously. Dragon took it and drank with the solemn air of a Herder acolyte performing a sacred rite.

Matthew turned pointedly away, and I felt my temper stir. He might not relish Dragon's adoration, but there was no need for him to be so unkind. He had used all of his charm to make her obedient when he was developing her powers so that she could defend

Obernewtyn, but now he was refusing to deal with what he had set in motion.

I forced my anger back, knowing Dragon would detect it if I was not more careful.

Matthew went to refill the empty pot from a stone jug on a bench, and Dragon trailed across the kitchen in his wake, drawn as if by some force she could not control. The farseeker did not notice her standing at his elbow, and when he turned back, he cannoned hard into her, sending both the full pot of fement and Dragon's mug smashing to the floorboards.

"Fer Lud's sake, ye idiot!" he exploded. "If ye'd drunk th' stuff instead of gollerin' at me like a fool, this wouldn't have happened!"

Dragon's face was white as paper. She turned and ran from the room without a word.

Matthew was left standing amidst the debris of broken mugs and steaming fement, looking from one to the other of us. "Ye dinna understand!"

"I understand that was unnecessary," I said coldly.

He paled and ran his fingers distractedly through his hair. "Ah, Luddamn it. Yer right. I'll go an' apologize."

"Why?" Kella demanded fiercely. "She should not be surprised. More fool her for expecting anything more of you."

"Kella, I'm sorry . . . ," Matthew began, but the healer tossed her head, her blue eyes flashing.

"Don't tell me!" she said stonily. "I'm not the one you should be talking to. You don't deserve her love, Matthew. She's worth ten of you, but you're too stupid to see it."

"She's a savage," Matthew flared, stung by the disgust in her voice.

Kella laughed contemptuously. "You don't have the slightest idea who or what Dragon is, even after all these months you've spent with her. She's a lot of things, but she's no savage. Eating with fingers and having dirty clothes doesn't make a person a savage. Cruelty and thoughtlessness do. That makes *you* the only savage here."

I was amazed to hear the gentle healer speak with such passion. Matthew glared at her, then turned on his heel and stalked out. A moment later, the stair door slammed.

I felt as though a firestorm had roared its destructive way through the room.

Kella let out a great sobbing breath and sank into a chair. I crossed to sit by her and lay a tentative hand on her arm. "Dragon will be all right. It wasn't as bad as all that. . . ."

The healer shook her head. "It's not Dragon, Elspeth. Matthew was wrong, but I should not have spoken to him like that. It . . . it is Domick. You saw how he was tonight. I've tried and tried not to see, but I can't lie to myself anymore. He no longer cares for me. Sometimes I think he hates me." She looked at me with tormented eyes. "He's changed. That is why you did not tell him what Maryon said, isn't it? I know it. Of course, I know. Oh, Elspeth, I just want to go home to Obernewtyn."

She began to weep in earnest.

I stared at her helplessly. After a long minute, I crossed to the sky window and stared up. Rain fell lightly but steadily on the glass.

"Perhaps it is time for all of us to go home," I said softly to the night.

· 14 ·

I SANK INTO the hot, soapy water with a sigh.

My backside and legs ached from hours of riding about Sutrium, and I was chilled to the bone by the constant icy drizzle that had fallen.

It had been altogether a miserable and fruitless morning. I had gone to the biggest green and then to as many other greens as I could find. At each, I had tried to far-seek gypsies at random—but every single one I had tried had been mentally shielded! The Twentyfamilies gypsies were even more tightly blocked than the halfbreeds. I had been forced to assume that all gypsies possessed natural mindshields, though of varying strengths.

As I had done with the gypsy woman, I could have entered any of the gypsies at a subconscious level, but there was simply no point. I would not find what I needed in their underminds.

In desperation, for by now there was no other course, I had tried talking to some gypsies clustered around a well, thinking to draw them gradually to talk of the woman who had escaped the Herder fires; but Domick had been right—they were impossibly suspicious of strangers, including gypsies who were unknown to them. I had not needed empathic Talent to be immediately aware of their hostility.

I might have kept on but for the patches of static arising from the buildings. This had puzzled me until it came to me that the Council might be using stone from Oldtime ruins to build within the city. The amount of residual poison was not high enough to cause the rotting sickness, but having to circumvent it stole my energy. The other problem was the mysterious, stronger static given off by the sea and the Suggredoon. There were several smaller greens close enough to these to make farseeking difficult, if not impossible.

I had returned to the safe house exhausted, disheartened, and convinced the only hope of success now lay in letting the gypsy go and following her. I was not sure that would qualify as returning her to her people, or even if it would enable me to learn the meaning of the word *swallow*, but what else could I do?

Kella had interrupted my depressive account to suggest a bath. "You can't think properly when you are all tied up in knots, cold and tense and miserable."

I had been too tired to argue, though when peeling off my garments, I had wondered how I could possibly relax.

But I sank deeper in the hot water and felt some of the stiffness melt from my bones. I closed my eyes with a sigh.

My mind drifted a little, and I found myself wondering if snow had fallen in the highest valleys yet. Gahltha and I had loved to ride through the light snowfalls, scattering the powdery whiteness high.

My thoughts moved down to the valley where Obernewtyn lay, as if I rode there on Gahltha's back. I visualized the farms and orchards visible from the foothills of the higher mountains. The last crops would be readying themselves for harvest, and Alad's beast-speakers would soon be working hard.

Unbidden, the image of Rushton came to me with a queer ache.

I blinked and the image faded, leaving me to ponder what it was about Rushton that made me feel suffocated and tense whenever I was with him, and yet think of him so often when we were apart. A queer contrariness, yet it had always been that way between us. When we had met, he had been pretending to be a farm overseer at Obernewtyn, hiding his true identity from Ariel and his masters. My first sight was of him carrying a squealing, struggling piglet.

The memory made me smile, though at the time, I had feared he could somehow sense my powers and would report me. I had been no more content at his attentions than the pig! But he had not reported me, and in time we had become allies. Yet, in truth, we had never been friends.

I thought of Dragon trailing helplessly after Matthew and shuddered. Starkly, I heard the words Rushton had rasped to me once in delirium: "Elspeth, love." I had tried to rob those words of their meaning and to tell myself his emotions were latent or distorted—that he did not truly feel love but some lesser thing because of our mindbond.

But it was not true. None of it.

He loved me and I knew it. Had always known it. And I?

I became aware that my hands were trembling violently where they rested on the rim of the bathing barrel. I thrust them under the water and wrenched my mind forcibly away from Rushton.

I thought of guildmerge, and my emotions calmed.

There was something infinitely reassuring about the thought of the huge circular room lined with books where guildmerge was held. It was the heart of Obernewtyn. The memory of it was so real that I could almost smell the smoke from the fire and hear the crack of mountain pine above the hum of conversation. I seemed to feel Avra's breath tickling the hair at my neck, for the mountain mare always stood at my side during guildmerge. Sometimes she would reach down and touch her nose to Maruman, who invariably slept on my lap when not away on his travels. Other times she would nudge Alad, signaling her desire to communicate or to reproach him for failing to interpret her clearly enough.

Life at Obernewtyn revolved around the guildmerge and what it stood for: community and purpose. In contrast, Sutrium was dark and chaotic, devoid of hope or purpose. All at once, I felt a longing to be home at Obernewtyn that was as savage and powerful as a hot knife in my belly. The strength of it took my breath away.

Then the irony of it struck me just as forcibly, for I had been only too ready to leave for Sutrium. Ever had it been my way to long for Obernewtyn when I was severed from it and yet to hate it when I was there.

I blinked in surprise, seeing this was exactly how I felt about Rushton.

How strange.

But perhaps not. I loved Obernewtyn and the feeling it gave me of being part of something larger than myself, but often I felt absorbed and devoured by it as well. In many ways, I had used my secret quest to raise a barrier between Obernewtyn and my lone self. My fear of Rushton—if that was the right word for it—was the fear that giving myself to him would cause me to lose myself, that in some queer way I would be absorbed and no longer myself.

Shivering—and only partly from the chilled water—I climbed from the barrel and toweled myself vigorously. Better to worry about what to do with the gypsy than to think of Rushton. That was a far more immediate problem.

Dressing hurriedly, I went to the kitchen. A fire had been lit, and Matthew was repairing a tear in his breeches.

Before I could speak, Kella rushed in behind me. "Dragon," she cried breathlessly. "She's gone."

Matthew jumped to his feet. "Gone? What do ye mean, gone?"

"Just what I said," Kella answered. "She refused to answer the door to her chamber this morning. I thought she needed time, so I left her. But just now I noticed that the door was open, and she wasn't in there!"

"Well, for Lud's sake," Matthew said impatiently. "She'll be downstairs with—"

Kella gave him a look of such searing fury that he flinched. "Stop telling me and let me tell you! I've checked everywhere. The horse yard, the healing hall, the bathing room, the repair shed. She's gone, I tell you."

Her eyes accused Matthew, and he paled. "It's my fault. I meant to apologize for shoutin' at her when she came out," he whispered.

"You should have gone in to her," Kella blazed. "That's the usual way to go about an apology. Or did you expect her to beg for that as well?"

"Kella . . ."

The healer swung to face me. "We have to find her!"

"Do you have any idea where she might have gone?" I asked them.

"To Obernewtyn!" Kella said at once, voicing her own longings.

"She . . . she might have gone to th' market," Matthew said hesitantly. "I . . . she's been pesterin' me since we got here to take her."

He flushed crimson under the healer's scathing look. "What are ye lookin' at me like I murdered her for?" he shouted, his highland accent thickened with anger. "I'm nowt responsible fer her. She shouldn'a be here in th' first place."

"Well, maybe you'll be lucky and she'll be killed. That would teach her obedience, wouldn't it?" hissed Kella.

Matthew whitened to the lips.

"That's enough," I said, shocked at the cruelty of her words. "The thing is to find her, not to decide whose fault it is that she's gone. Matthew, you go out and look for her on foot. I'll farseek her, and if I can't find her, I'll go out on Gahltha. Leave a channel open for me. I'll reach out to you," I said, knowing he might not be able to farseek me in the fog of static that was Sutrium.

He ducked his head and hurried out as I turned to the healer. "Have another good look around the safe house. See if she has taken anything from the chamber with her."

She nodded and ran out.

I sat down on a chair and composed my thoughts, blocking out all apprehension and shaping a probe to

Dragon's mind-set. If she was near, and not on badly tainted ground, the probe would locate her.

It took less than a minute.

She was wandering through the stalls in the central trade market of the adjoining district. I fixed her position in my mind and then farsought Matthew.

"I will go there straightaway," he sent, his mind leaking emotional surges of relief and anger.

Kella came in. "She has taken nothing with her."

"She is in a market in the next district. Matthew has gone there on foot. I'll go over with Gahltha and bring her back."

"Thank Lud," Kella murmured.

I hurried along the hall and down the stairs, far-seeking to Gahltha as I went. Fortunately, I was clad in boyish clothes, so there was no need for me to waste time in changing. Only the gypsy who had followed me would know me in that guise, and if I had outwit-ted him once, I could do it again.

Gahltha was waiting, snorting with impatience at my slowness.

"You have forgotten the coldmetal painmaker," he chided as I vaulted onto his back.

With a curse I dismounted, found a bridle in the wagon, and buckled it on him with an apology.

"Do not sorrow for forgetting the fetter, ElspethInnle. Would that all the funaga would forget. Where is the lit-tle mornir?"

I sent Gahltha an explanation as I remounted, and as soon as we were clear of the little square, he broke into a brisk trot. It had stopped raining, but the drains ran swiftly, filled to overflowing after a day and night of rain. In seconds, the chilly breeze had leached all the bath's warmth from my bones.

I resisted the urge to ask Gahltha to go faster, knowing it would attract too much attention. I could have used a coercive cloak to stop anyone noticing us, but the more obtrusive the behavior, the more energy required to hide it. The effort of cloaking a wild gallop over any distance would virtually drain my immediate energy, and I had the sudden, uneasy premonition that I was going to need my powers very soon.

I chafed at the delay, my mind filled with visions of Dragon wandering through the market with her unforgettable face and hair. If anything alarmed her, she would resort instinctively to her phenomenal power, calling up the dragonish illusions for which she had been named.

I breathed a sigh of relief as the market came into view at the street's end, but drawing nearer, I felt a stab of dismay. This was a far larger market than the one beside the safe house. If anything happened here, hundreds would witness it. The feeling of danger increased as Gahltha brought me to the perimeter of the crowds.

The empath-coercer could not have chosen a more perilous time to come to the market; late afternoons were traditionally the busiest part of the day. Hoping for a bargain, men and women shopped as late as possible, for it was well known that traders believed that a day without a sale offended Lud and that they would be punished by another poor day to follow.

I never ceased to be amazed by their paltry image of a Lud who would care for the sale of a bit of fish or a stretch of cloth.

The horse-holding yard was filled to capacity, which meant I would have to tie Gahltha to the less secure bars along the outer edge of the corral. Gritting my teeth at the delay, I led him into a side lane and scooped some mud from the bottom of a drain. I had almost finished smearing it over him when I heard footsteps.

I knelt and pretended to examine his fetlock. Peering covertly behind, I nearly fainted at the sight of a troop of soldierguards marching along the lane.

There was nothing to be done but to concentrate fiercely and produce a general coercive cloak that would stop them noticing me.

"Seems as if we ought to have more to do than play nursemaid to some Herders," grumbled one of the soldierguards at the front of the column.

"Council wants to keep them happy because of them financin' th' Sador business," another muttered.

The Herders were financing the invasion of Sador? Could it be so? Where would they come by such coin?

"More like they don't dare move against them, for fear they'll get Lud to send another plague."

"It was nothing more than coincidence that they predicted pestilence and the plague came," snapped another soldierguard. "Council'll put them in their place before long, and that'll be an end to our nurse-maiding them."

"Will it? Herders have coin aplenty, so I've heard, and they ain't averse to greasin' soldierguard palms. I ain't fussy as to where coin comes from, long as I get some."

"Shut up and get a move on," called a lean, surly-looking captain at the back of the column.

Their voices faded as they passed out of the lane,

and I leaned against Gahltha's noisome flank, weak-kneed with relief.

Gathering my wits, I farsought Matthew to warn him that soldierguards were in the market and possibly Herders as well. As my probe touched him, a panicky burst of images and words surged painfully into my unprepared mind.

I blocked the chaos and requested the use of his eyes. Instantly, Matthew made himself passive so that I could literally see through his eyes. It was a difficult maneuver but one we had perfected.

He was standing in the midst of a crowd of people facing one of the market speaking stones, onto which people climbed to advertise wares or make announcements. Standing atop it was a Herder, his red armband marking him as one of the more important priests in the Faction hierarchy. Two brownband Herders stood on either side of the speaking stone like guards.

But none of this explained Matthew's panic.

"Look!" His voice rose in my mind. His head turned, and I saw Dragon. Standing out in the open between the crowd and the speaking stone, her blue eyes ablaze with fury, the flame-haired empath-coercer was standing protectively in front of two small children. She resembled some avenging goddess out of a Beforetime story, the sun burnishing her red-gold curls and her face glowing with unearthly loveliness.

Her mouth moved, and only then did I realize that she was shouting at the Herder priests!

· 15 ·

Sick at the magnitude of the disaster unfolding, I flung myself onto Gahltha's back, bidding him to carry me to the other side of the square. Passing through the center of a trade market on horseback was forbidden, but I used my coercive power recklessly, forcing people not to notice us and clearing a path.

I saw that the group of soldierguards had taken the easier and longer route around the perimeter of the market, and I prayed for something to delay them.

"What in Lud's name has happened?" I demanded of Matthew.

Rather than explaining, he sent a vision of a woman and the two children being manhandled by the Herders. The woman had shouted something at the redband priest and had been struck to the ground. One of the brownband Herders had grabbed at the little boy, who had screamed in terror and clung to his sister.

Dragon had flown from the crowd of watchers like a spitting fangcat defending its young, and the beleaguered Herder had retreated with alarm.

"I arrived just as it began," Matthew sent. "The priests were collecting boys to be taken and trained as acolytes on Herder Isle, and the mother refused to let them take her son." There was a pause before he

160

continued. "The senior Herder has just told the brown-bands to take both children. I'm afraid Dragon will . . . uh-oh!" Matthew sent frantically.

By now, I was close enough to hear the empath-coercer's childish voice, and I craned my neck in order to see her over the heads of the crowd. She had her arms around the two cringing children and was glaring at the approaching Herders purposefully.

"Don't," she cried in a warning voice that froze my blood. "Don't dare!"

Then she dropped into a fighting crouch she must have learned from watching the coercers train and bared her teeth at the priests.

They fell back again in astonishment, and there was a murmur of amazement from the crowd.

I could not repress a groan. Dragon would vision. I was amazed she had not done so already. I had to stop her from unleashing her incredible powers in front of so many witnesses.

"Lud preserve us," Matthew sent despairingly along the probelink between us. "Th' soldierguards are here!"

I turned. Sure enough, the troops had reached the speaking stone. Their captain was looking around, taking in the fracas at a glance.

"What is going on?" he demanded, marching up to the senior Herder. But before the Herder could answer, the captain's eyes fell on Dragon. He gaped, thunderstruck.

For a moment, I thought I saw recognition in that look, but then I realized that was impossible. Dragon had led a solitary, feral existence before coming to Obernewtyn, and she'd not left our sight since. Still, something in that look filled me with fear, and I directed a savage coercive bolt at Dragon, augmenting it with the destructive power at the depth of my mind—a power I had once used to kill but had since been able to keep in check, swearing never again to take a life. Still, I had no time to fashion a subtle arrow of it, and my probe clubbed through her shield, obliterating it and knocking her instantly unconscious.

She slumped to the ground, and the two children screamed in fright.

Their mother leapt to her feet and pulled them away from Dragon, just as the soldierguard captain stepped toward her.

Without hesitation, I stamped coercively on his will. The rough nerve control I imposed would fade swiftly, so I had little time. I sent a swift instruction to Matthew and another to Gahltha.

Immediately, the black horse reared up with an ear-shattering scream. People on all sides scattered wildly to escape the flailing hooves.

"Someone has fed my horse prickleberries!" I cried, pretending to have no control.

Gahltha rolled his eyes and bucked, lashing out with razor-sharp hooves, and the three priests dived away from the speaking stone with cries of terror, apparently convinced he was on the verge of the hysterical rage caused by ingesting the poisonous weed.

"Captain?" One of the rank-and-file soldierguards tapped his superior, and the captain stirred, for this was enough to break the trance I had imposed. He looked around; then his eyes widened in fury, and he cracked his fist into the other man's face. "Fool!" he raged. "The red-haired girl. Where is she?"

Time had run out.

"Go!" I sent, and Gahltha bolted out of the square and down a feeder lane.

"A gypsy youth took her!" someone cried out.

I cursed, for I had hoped no one would notice Matthew scoop up the unconscious Dragon in all the fuss.

He sent that they had taken refuge in a burned-out house. I took the location from him. They were still close to the market.

"Are you sure it's safe?"

"Safer than on the street," Matthew sent fervently. "Besides, they'll never think I'd hide so close."

I hoped he was right. "Is Dragon all right?"

"She's unconscious," Matthew said. "How in Lud's name did you—?"

"You stay put, and I'll bring Gahltha," I interrupted.

I used the last of my reserve to drop a complete coercive cloak over Gahltha and myself, wishing I had time to rest. My diversionary tactics had obliterated my coercive suggestion that I was a boy. Even thickheaded soldierguards would work out that Matthew and I were the same gypsies wanted for the murders and sedition in Guanette.

By morning, the streets would be crawling with squads combing the city for us as the gate search surged inward.

The clouds cleared from the sky, and the sun shone properly for the first time in days. Everything in the sodden city steamed as we made our way in a wide arc around the market where Dragon had confronted the Herders, and into the next district.

Coming around a blind corner, I found my way

blocked by yet another of the small markets dotted throughout the city.

My first instinct was to circle it. I had had enough of markets. But it was not long until dusk, and I did not want to waste any more time. Dismounting, I took Gahltha's rein, leading him behind me.

Brushing along the aisles, my eye was caught by a table laden with swatches of colorful cloth. I stared, for I had never seen cloth dyed so brightly before.

"Sador dyes," I heard a stallholder tell a customer.

One of the pieces on the stall table was deep green, with a sheen as soft and yielding as the coat of a newborn pup. I ran a thumb over it, fascinated by the alien texture.

"Get yer dirty paws off it, ye halfbreed slattern."

I dropped the material in shock, feeling as if I had wakened from a drugged sleep. What in Lud's name had I been thinking of to stand about admiring a piece of cloth with half the city out looking for me? But I knew what was wrong: I was almost dazed with fatigue. It always happened when I used the strange power at the depth of my mind.

Now that the wretched trader had identified me as a girl, I could not make myself into a boy in his eyes, but I could stop anyone else from seeing me.

I began to back away, weaving a general coercive net, but the burly stallholder lumbered from behind his stand with unexpected speed and pushed me hard, sending me stumbling back against Gahltha's warm flank. Anger filled me, as hot and unreasoning as fire.

I choked it back, realizing too late that I had let my coercive cloak fall again. Since it worked by heightening and enhancing disinterest and inattention, there was no way I could reinstitute it with so many people goggling at me. Especially not with my energy so depleted.

"If you won't let a customer feel the cloth she might buy, I'll move on," I said pacifically, and backed away.

"Since when did halfbreeds buy when they could steal?" sneered another man, blocking the way from behind.

His skinny companion leered and stepped in my path when I tried to sidle by them. "And since when was a gypsy civil and honest at the same time?" he asked in a sinuous, high-pitched voice. "If you ask me, this one speaks too soft to be trusted. And why does a girl wear trousers, except for ease to run when she has stolen something?" He looked around at the gathering little crowd, seeking their support.

Several nodded, and I began to feel truly uneasy.

I let Gahltha's rein slip from my fingers.

"Shall I/Gahltha bolt/rear, ElspethInnle?"

"No!" Using the black horse as a diversion yet again would be as good as posting a sign saying the gypsies wanted for the market fracas were still close by. I dared not risk it with Matthew and Dragon in hiding so near.

"Find Matthew and Dragon and take them back to the safe house," I sent, giving Gahltha a mental map of their location.

"Gahltha must protect Innle," he protested.

"No! There are people here with knives and arrows, and they would think nothing of killing an equine. Obey me," I commanded. "I can take care of myself in this."

Reluctantly, Gahltha withdrew. Fortunately, no one noticed he was riderless and apparently ownerless, because all attention was riveted on me. "I think we ought to give her a good whipping just to teach her what we think of gypsy thieves," said the thin man who had stopped me from leaving. He unlaced a long whip from his belt with a practiced flick of his fingers.

Two louts cheered and offered to lay on the first stripes to show how it was done, and other people crowded nearer. I looked around and my skin broke into gooseflesh, for I had no alternative but to let myself be manhandled and whipped.

I clenched my teeth and steeled myself, invoking a coercive suggestion that the thin man should use the whip lightly. At the same time, I cursed and struggled as anyone would when the two louts grabbed me and ripped the gypsy shirt, baring my back.

"Now we'll see ye dance." The thin man laughed and flicked the whip. It whistled viciously through the air, and I screamed when it struck, though I felt nothing, for I had erected a mental barrier to postpone the pain.

I would experience the sting later, when there was no need to keep my wits about me.

The whip struck again.

"A weak blow," cried the cloth trader, and he strode out to commandeer the whip. I reached out a coercive probe to soften his blows, too, but, to my horror, he was naturally shielded.

I could not reach his mind without his knowing it—and maybe not at all in my weakened state.

"I'll show you how she dances to my music," he promised, and swung his arm as hard as he could.

The whip hissed, tearing into my skin. I felt no pain, but I screamed, writhing inwardly at the thought of the

166

agony I would have to endure when the barrier was dissolved.

He struck again and again, with no sign of stopping. Perhaps this was the death I had been promised. Maybe Maryon had misjudged the number of days or misread her vision. Maybe my time was already up.

"Dance, gypsy! Give us a show!" cried the trader as he lifted his arm again. His lips and eyes shone with lascivious pleasure. "I thought gypsies loved to dance."

"That is so," said a caressing masculine voice, and suddenly I was free, falling forward and grazing my knees on the cobbles.

Clutching my shredded clothing, I turned to see the dark-haired gypsy who had ridden after me the day before. This time he was on foot, and the two louts who had held me were sitting at his feet with dazed looks.

The trader gave a roar of anger and rushed forward. With lightning swiftness, the gypsy stepped aside and plucked him up by the scruff of the neck. The oaf must have weighed as much as Gahltha, yet the gypsy held him dangling in midair as if it were no effort at all.

"You have made a mistake, Littleman," he was saying to the dangling trader in a lecturing voice. "A gypsy dances as an expression of pleasure in movement or song, or for a lover. Not for moronish illbreds who would not know beauty nor grace if it bit them on the bum."

I was astounded that a lone gypsy would speak that way to Landfolk. Yet no one made a move to intervene. In fact, people began to edge away.

The stallholder was by now purple in the face and in imminent danger of suffocating, his jerkin screwed tight around his neck.

"What is that you say, Littleman?" the gypsy asked with exaggerated politeness.

"Erk!" the man squeaked, clawing at his collar.

I stifled an incredulous giggle as the gypsy put his ear to the trader's mouth. "Your pardon? You say you want to apologize to this girl? Do I hear you aright?"

The trader shook his head, then changed his mind and tried to nod.

"What was that?" The gypsy hauled him closer, drawing the cloth around the trader's neck even tighter.

"Ahhk," he gasped, batting his arms as if he were a bird about to fly away.

"You'd best put him down before you kill him," I said. The trader's eyes were rolling about in an alarming way, and his lips were blue.

The gypsy ignored me. "Ahh! Now I understand. You wish to apologize by gifting a piece of cloth to her."

"Ug," the trader said dully.

"A fine gesture," the gypsy said, opening his hand and letting the man fall in a gasping heap at his elegantly black-booted feet. "Now, what cloth was it that you wanted?"

I stared up into his bold, laughing eyes. "Uh. I don't think . . ."

"The green?" he said. "A good choice. It will suit you." He took up the cloth I had touched and held it up to my face. His knuckles brushed my cheek, and I flinched.

"You startle like an unbroken pony," he murmured.

The blood rushed to my cheeks, and he laughed, turning back to the trader, who had risen unsteadily to his feet. "The green it is. Now wrap it up, Littleman, and I will consider amends made and say nothing to the Councilmen."

The trader took the cloth in trembling fingers, rolled it up, and slid it into a paper sleeve. The gypsy took it and threw a few coins on the ground.

I was stunned at his audacity and thought the Twentyfamilies' tithe to the Council must be magnificent indeed to let him get away with such high-handedness.

Suddenly he reached forward, grasped my arm in a powerful grip, and propelled me behind the stall and down a side street. A few paces down the street, he thrust me into a shadowy doorway and pressed himself against me; I panicked and struggled.

"For Lud's sake and mine, girl, be still," he said in a hard urgent voice.

"Let me go!" I cried.

"Shut up," he hissed.

"Shut up, yourself!" I flared, temper overcoming fear. He pulled me against his chest and closed a hard hand over my mouth. "Shhh," he said quietly and distinctly into my ear.

Then I heard the sound of running feet on the cobbles and I froze.

"I tell you it was the girl from the other market. The one on the black horse that caused all that fuss," panted a man nearby. "The captain said there is a big reward for her or one of them other two who was with her."

Their footsteps receded. When the gypsy released me, I spun away from him angrily and rubbed my lips where his fingers had mashed them against my teeth.

"It would be polite for you to give your name to your rescuer," he said.

I glared at him. "I didn't need rescuing!"

"No? Then you wanted to be whipped? I apologize for intervening, but there are gentler pleasures." The wicked expression in his dark eyes made me step back involuntarily.

"I suppose you caused all that trouble over at the other market a little while ago as part of your quest to be whipped. It must have disappointed you to have escaped so easily. What have you done with your horse, though?"

My heart jumped. "I don't know about any other market or a horse."

"No?" He smiled. "Then I must have been mistaken in thinking you rode a black horse from the city just yesterday dressed as you are now, to appear as a boy."

I flushed. "All right. I ride a black horse and wear boyish trousers. So what? Why did you follow me yesterday? And why did you help me just now?"

"So I *did* help you, then?" he asked mockingly.

I scowled and gathered my will to give him a coercive mental jolt, hard enough to penetrate his mindshield, but, without warning, he stepped forward and kissed me full on the mouth.

Wit and breath fled at his audacity.

Releasing me, he spoke. "If I had known it was so easy to silence you, I would have done that sooner."

I scowled, mortified and furious that I had not pushed him away. Did he think because he was Twentyfamilies he could kiss anyone and they would like it? Childishly, I rubbed my hand across my mouth.

"Revulsion rendered me silent," I snapped. "Why did you do that?"

Heavy eyelids drooped secretively over his eyes. "Because I wanted to," he said.

I did not know what to say to the simplicity of such an answer.

His mouth shifted into a lazy, curving smile. "But what I want even more is to know this: Why are you pretending to be a gypsy?"

PART II

✦

THE TWENTYFAMILIES

· 16 ·

"WHAT ARE YOU talking about?" I demanded scornfully, gathering myself to run if he tried to catch hold of me again. "Of course I am a gypsy."

"Your back is bleeding," he said mildly. "You need treatment, and there is a gypsy rig nearby where you can clean up. I will take you there, if you wish. . . ."

I bit my lip, mistrusting his apparent indifference. Yet I dared not cross the city on foot in bloody disarray. Aside from that, here was the opportunity to learn why the man had followed me the previous day. Moreover, this might be my last chance to locate the gypsy woman's blood kin before Maryon's deadline.

"Very well," I said.

His lips twitched into a faintly ironic smile.

As we walked, I took good care to stay out of the reach of his long arms and a little behind him. I was shivering, but not from the cold. The pain from the whipping was locked behind the suppressing barrier I had set up, but there was no way to block the shock of it from myself.

True to his word, he led me to a rig set on a tiny green not far from the market. Alongside it, four horses grazed. One of them was Sendari, whom the gypsy had ridden the previous day. To my discomfort, he recognized me as we approached the rig and trotted over to push his soft muzzle against my hand. I could not reach his mind to ask him to withdraw, so I stroked him and pretended not to see the startled look the gypsy gave us. In some situations, it was safer to say nothing rather than to try explaining the inexplicable.

The rig itself was magnificent. Every panel of wood was intricately carved in an elaborate scene. It made our own poor wagon seem fit only for firewood. The carvings were unusual and reminded me vaguely of the stonework mural in the Reichler Clinic under Tor. Then again, they were also like the carvings that had once graced Obernewtyn's huge entrance doors.

"It is very beautiful," I said sincerely.

He nodded. "This is the skill of my family. It is a very ancient art." He caressed a ridge in the dark, smooth wood.

"This is *your* rig?" I asked, wishing that I could simply read his mind for the information I needed.

"Maire!" he called suddenly.

An extraordinarily ugly crone poked her head through the brocaded curtain. Her skin was much darker than the man's, and her snow-white hair hung to her waist in stark contrast, but she had the same black penetrating eyes. Squinting against the dusk light, she regarded him with disfavor. "What do you want?"

"This girl was whipped by some louts in the market. Her back needs treatment. Can you heal her?"

The old woman sniffed and raked me from crown to toe with her sharp eyes. "Can I? Yes. But should I? Will I?" She took up a battered box of woven reed, climbed from the wagon, and hobbled over to the smoldering remains of a fire. She was tiny and wore a bed dress of deeply embroidered silken material the color of the summerday sky. Setting the box on a log, she flicked a derisive glance at the man. "I suppose you rescued her. Your father would be delighted to hear what a hero has sprung from his loins."

When he made no response, she glared back at me. "Well? Are you going to show me your wounds, or do you want a body servant to strip you? I daresay your rescuer would oblige."

I felt myself redden but turned and shrugged to part the ripped shirt. She gave an exclamation that told me the wounds were as savage as I had feared. It also made me realize the weakness I was feeling might not just be due to overusing my Misfit powers.

"Am I a bird to fly up?" the old woman shrilled. "Kneel down, for Lud's sake!"

I did as she asked, thinking how much she reminded me of Louis Larkin, kindness hidden behind a shield of irascible carping. Tutting and muttering to herself, Maire bathed the flesh, then gently peeled away the cloth stuck to the wounds. Rummaging in her box again, she withdrew a bottle, and a moment later, the unmistakable odor of herbal preparations filled the air. The old crone was an herb lorist. I jumped at the feel of cold ointment on my bare skin. She slathered it on with a liberal hand, then stuck a dressing over my whole back.

"'Tis done," she said, slamming the box shut.

I thanked her and pulled my shirt about me as best I could.

She watched me with an odd expression on her aged face. "You are a tough one, girl. Not a flinch for all the nerves exposed and hurt. No Twentyfamilies would have done as well, for all their infernal pride."

I saw, too late, that I should have pretended discomfort when she was working on the open wounds, but the suppressing had prevented me feeling anything, and I had been too preoccupied to think of it.

I made myself shrug. "Halfbreeds are tougher than milky purebloods."

She snorted. "Except that you are neither."

I felt the blood drain from my cheeks.

"I am a gypsy halfbreed," I said faintly.

She cackled ironically. "So you say and so those rags you wear would have it, but it is not true. There is nothing in your face from Twentyfamilies stock. Not darkness of eye, not thickness of lips, nor any other physical characteristic that belongs to my people."

"I am a halfblood. I throw to my mother," I declared, watching the man from the corner of my eye. His expression had not changed, though the old woman's question exactly echoed his own accusation.

"Why were you whipped?" Maire asked.

"I touched some material, and the trader selling it objected."

I wondered why she did not reiterate her accusation. The gypsy man had changed the subject in exactly the same way, rather than demanding proof or arguing the point. It struck me that these gypsies were shifty folk who sidled about things rather than coming on them bluntly. I began to wonder if it had been such a good idea to come after all.

"Gypsies are not popular in these times," the man said in a neutral voice. "What is your name?"

"Elaria," I said. I felt as if there were undercurrents here concerning me, which I could not read.

The man shook his head. "That is not your true name."

Fear skittered along my backbone. How did he know that?

"Do Twentyfamilies know everything, then?" I sneered, drawing indignation from a little surge of anger. I did not like to be called a liar, even when it was true.

"Has no one told you that Twentyfamilies gypsies have the gift of truth?" he asked.

I licked my lips. "Truth?"

"Twentyfamilies know when a lie is being told."

My heart began to pound, for suddenly I remembered Domick's warning about making sure the gypsies did not guess I was an impostor.

Then I scowled, for how should he know if I spoke true or not? He was no Misfit coercer to read my mind—I would have sensed the intrusion if he was. He was guessing, or somehow I had given myself away.

The gypsy laughed suddenly. "You've spunk enough, for all your face reads like a book. Well, if you don't believe in gypsy powers, then let us say I know you lie because you lack the signs by which our kind know one another."

"What signs?"

His smile broadened. "That question marks you a liar even more than the absence of the signs."

"What signs?" I demanded, putting my hands on my hips.

In answer, he rolled up one sleeve.

I stared at the elaborate painting on the inside of his wrist and up his arm. Three birds were depicted flying in a spiral of black and green, shot through with red.

My mouth fell open with astonishment—it was the exact design Garth had shown me on the plast documents from the Reichler Clinic!

The arm painting was executed in greater detail, but there was no doubt that it was the same. But what on earth could it mean? How in Lud's name had a *gypsy* come to wear it? And could it possibly be coincidence that I, who had seen the design under Tor, should see it again so soon?

Both gypsies were looking at me so oddly that my heart skipped a beat. I searched my memory for the thread of the conversation. "I . . . What if I were to say I have no arm picture because it was washed off?"

The gypsy lifted his arm and spat on the painting; then he scrubbed hard at it. This had no effect and told me that the paint was indelible.

"All right." I shrugged, thrusting the monumental puzzle of the arm painting to the back of my mind. "So, I don't have one. What of it? Not all gypsies have them."

At least, the gypsy in the safe house did not bear any such markings.

"You did not let me finish before you rushed to tell me how your 'arm picture' washed off. This is a mark worn only by those of the Twentyfamilies and entitles us to pass through the gates of any city unsearched and untouched. No 'mongrel halfbreed' would wear it." There was a note of bitter self-mockery in his tone as if these words were someone else's, and this robbed them of offense.

He lifted the same sleeve higher to show me a metal

band around his upper arm. "This is what I meant to show you. All gypsies, full and halfbreed, wear these; yet, when I held you in the lane, I felt nothing. It tells anyone who might wish to know, whether you are bonded or promised or no."

I flushed, remembering the gypsy woman's metal band.

"And what of this?" He showed me a woven band on his thumb. "All gypsies wear these, too; weaved into the ring are signs telling the line of their descent. We bear these and other such things about us so that we may exchange knowledge about one another without the Landfolk hearing it. Do you still claim to be a gypsy?"

"Believe what you will," I told him stubbornly. "That is what my father told my mother, and he left in such a hurry, he did not have time to teach my mother the finer points of gypsy culture. Her family threw her out when it was learned she carried a halfbreed child, and so she brought me up alone in Rangorn. Then she died," I snarled, so carried away by the part I had imagined for myself that I felt bitter for the sake of my poor mother.

"The Twentyfamilies left without leaving his name, I take it," Maire asked, her eyes inscrutable.

I felt I had misspoken, but it was too late to change my story. "So my mother said."

She nodded and gathered up her box. "I will give you a shirt to wear in place of that." She hobbled back to the wagon.

"Well," said the gypsy man, "that is quite a story."

I did not know what to make of this, so I said nothing.

"Do you know that a girl fitting your description rescued a gypsy halfbreed from the Herder flames in the highlands?" he asked casually.

"That is nothing to do with me," I said.

"No?" He squatted down to poke at the fire, and the flames lit his face.

Only then did I register that the sun had fallen below the city skyline. The gypsy's sleek dark hair and hollowed cheeks gave him a devilish look as he fed the fire until it blazed high, sending showers of sparks into the sky. I stood awkwardly watching him and wishing the old woman would hurry up with the shirt. The sooner I got away, the better. But still I felt weak—my mind was taking longer than usual to recover.

"They say there is a rich reward for the wanted girl."

My heart began to bump.

"It is my guess that the girl who caused the ruckus in the market today and this Guanette gypsy are one and the same. What do you think?"

I shrugged, not trusting my voice to remain steady.

"Tell me, was it you or the boy you were traveling with who stuck a knife in the Herder in Guanette?" he asked casually.

"*We* didn't kill anybody. . . ."

I stopped, aghast that I had fallen into such a simple trap. I took a step backward, but at the same moment, the old woman appeared out of the dark and thrust a shirt into my hands.

"This is the girl from Guanette?" she asked the man.

He nodded and said lightly, "She rode a black horse then, though not the magnificent creature she outrode me on yesterday. The lad with her traveled in a false gypsy wagon."

The old woman turned to me, and I did not know whether to run or stay before the anguished intensity of her expression.

"Is she alive?" she whispered. "The woman you cut from the stake?"

I opened my mouth to say I didn't know what she was talking about, but the glint of tears in her old eyes stopped the lie.

"She lives," I said softly.

"Praise be." She grasped my hand.

"You . . . you know her?" I asked.

The crone nodded, mopping her eyes with the end of her bed dress. "Her name is Iriny, and she is . . . is very dear to me. I had feared her dead. Where is she? Is she in the city with your companion?"

Instantly, I regretted the impulse of pity that had made me tell the truth without thinking it through first. I could hardly lead them to the safe house. Yet this was the solution to my problem of what to do with the gypsy woman, for clearly these people knew who she was and cared for her.

"She is in Sutrium," I conceded, trying to decide how best to proceed. "She is very weak."

"Dying?" the man asked abruptly.

"Not now. But she almost did. She seemed to want to die."

"Ahh," the old woman moaned, rocking herself back and forth. "My poor girl." She fixed me with a sudden fierce stare. "Where is she? I must see her."

"She is in good and healing hands."

"You will take me to her now," the man said, advancing with a threatening air.

"No!" Maire said. She looked back to me with frank entreaty.

"I will bring her to you," I promised, ignoring the man and his threats.

"When?" he demanded.

"As soon as it is safe to bring her across the city," I told him coldly. "The soldierguards are looking for me—and her. Tomorrow it will be worse because of the business in the market today."

"That is so," he said darkly, his eyes troubled. "Yet we Twentyfamilies are to leave Sutrium in three days."

I blinked in wonder at him, for the Twentyfamilies' departure from Sutrium coincided exactly with the end of the sevenday deadline. Was this, then, the reason for the deadline Maryon had set?

The gypsy took my silence for a question. "On the reckoning of our history, we began our journey to the Land on that very day eons past. It is our custom to always leave Sutrium in the final hours of that day in remembrance and as a sign of good faith to the Council. You see, it was also on that day that we made the agreement of safe passage. We regard it as an auspicious day for journeys."

"Yet I will remain until Iriny comes," Maire said in a voice that brooked no argument.

He nodded. "And so shall I, if there is need. But the sooner we can get her out of the city the better, and it will be a simpler matter to get her out in a group than as a lone Twentyfamilies wagon leaving later than it should." He gave me a sharp look. "I will organize a rumor to say that you and your companion have left the city with Iriny. It will not take long for the soldier-guards to run after the scent and leave the city free. When this happens, bring her swiftly and safely to us, and I will reward you in good coin."

"I'm not interested in your coin," I snapped indignantly. "I did not save her life for coin, and I wouldn't bring her to you if I thought you meant her harm, no matter what you offered."

He looked genuinely taken aback, and indeed, I was surprised at the extent of my anger.

"He is a fool as all men are," Maire said dismissively. "Put on the shirt."

I did as she bid, turning my back to strip off the ripped shirt and don the other. When I was finished, she looked at me, then went to the wagon and brought back a bundle of clothing.

"What are these?" I asked as she put them into my arms.

"They are Twentyfamilies skirts and gewgaws. Wear them when you return, and no one will trouble you. But make sure it is night when you come. A dark night, if you can. And speak to no one, unless you cannot avoid it; especially avoid Twentyfamilies gypsies." The old woman gave me an imperious little push. "Go now," she said. "Walk safe and bring her with you when you come again to us."

A thought occurred to me like a burst of lightning on a dark night. "I don't want coin as a reward, but there is something I would ask. . . ."

"Of course," the gypsy said, his eyes flashing with triumphant cynicism.

"I want you to tell me all about Twentyfamilies gypsies and halfbreeds," I said. "I want you to tell me how you came to the Land and everything you can remember about where you came from before that. And I want you to paint that mark you wear on my arm and tell me what it means and how you came to use it."

The man looked at me in blank astonishment. "Only Twentyfamilies bear that mark. . . ."

Maire prodded his arm. "She knows that, fool. Can't you see she means to pass herself off as one?"

The man's eyes widened in disbelief. Then he gave me a narrow stare. "You would play a dangerous game, girl. Do you know that Twentyfamilies are by lore permitted to kill impostors?"

"How should anyone know me for an impostor with such marks and these clothes?"

He smiled. "I would know."

I ignored that. "There is another thing. I also want to know about 'swallow.'"

His brows shot up. "Who told you of Swallow? Did Iriny speak his name in her delirium?"

So Swallow was a person. I had not expected that. I ignored the question, because answering it would reveal the extent of my ignorance. Instead, I gave them both a challenging look. "Do you agree with my conditions?"

After a long tense moment, the man gave an unsmiling nod.

The old woman touched my hand. "Bring her safe to us and you shall have what you want. Better still, you shall meet Swallow if you wish it."

The man made a negating gesture, then shrugged. "So be it. But do not bring Iriny here when you come."

"Where, then?"

He frowned in thought. "Sometimes the best way to

186

hide a leaf is in a forest. Do you know the main gypsy green?"

I nodded.

"Bring her there, then. That is where we will wait for you."

I nodded and walked away down a lane without a backward glance. As soon as I was out of their sight, I threw a full coercive cloak about me and sent a farsense probe to detect anyone who followed.

Only then did I dare to relax and allow myself to feel relieved at having all but completed my appointed task.

With some effort, for I was not yet much recovered, I farsought Matthew using an attuned probe. It located him at the safe house, and I felt a surge of relief. Perhaps the streak of bad luck that had dogged us since leaving Obernewtyn was over.

· 17 ·

I ARRIVED BACK at the safe house to see the rebel Reuvan mounting a tan mare. I was taken aback to recognize the horse as one that had come to Obernewtyn for refuge the previous wintertime.

"Greetings, ElspethInnle," the mare sent, her dark-flecked eyes solemn.

"Greetings, Halda," I responded, concealing my surprise.

Ever since Brydda's beloved mount, Sallah, had chosen to remain with him after he set her free, animals would occasionally come to Obernewtyn claiming that Sallah had sent them and asking for Avra, mistress of the Beastguild. Most would remain only a short time, supposedly to be trained to live in the wild, before going out into the vast mountain wilderness.

Alad, the Beastspeaking guildmaster, was convinced that some were trained in a different sort of survival and sent back to Sallah. He believed she was the leader of a lowland arm of the Beastguild and a sort of animal network of spies, organizing their own rescues or sabotages.

I had thought this unlikely, but seeing Halda made me wonder, for she had been one of the equines who supposedly had gone into the wild.

Reuvan had not noticed my approach, so I coughed to get his attention. When he turned, the flesh was bloodless beneath his tan.

"What is it?" I demanded, wondering if there was ever to be a moment in Sutrium unmarred by disaster.

"Idris is missing," he answered in a hoarse voice. "Brydda sent me to see if he had come here."

"Was he sent here?"

The seaman shook his head and took up the rein. "I must go. There are other places he might have gone if he was injured. Brydda asked me to try them all."

"Can I help?" I asked.

Reuvan appeared not to hear me. He lifted his hand in a distracted farewell gesture and urged Halda on.

I hurried upstairs and into the kitchen.

"Where have you been?" Kella cried, jumping to her feet.

Matthew rose, too, his face pale and set. "Idris . . ."

I nodded wearily. "I know. I've just spoken to Reuvan. Did he ask you to farseek Idris?"

"It would ha' done no good fer him to ask me to farseek anyone here. Too many minds an' too much holocaust tainting."

"But he would not realize that," I said impatiently. "I suppose he was too distracted. I'll try."

I shaped a probe to Idris's mind-set, but since I had never farsought him before, I did not know his exact mind signature, which meant it was not a strongly defined probe. Forced to compete with the miasmic static rising from the sea and the river, and from various areas of the city, I had no great hopes of locating him.

I opened my eyes and shook my head. "I didn't find him, but I'm still weak from the business this afternoon."

In fact, though I did not say it, I felt as if all my energy were being siphoned away through some secret channel. I forced myself to concentrate.

"Did Reuvan say how Idris disappeared?"

"Apparently, he dinna come back two nights ago from some errand he had been sent on," Matthew said.

This puzzled me. Reuvan had seemed dreadfully upset considering Idris had been missing so short a time.

"Greetings, ElspethInnle," Maruman sent.

The old cat was curled on a blanket beside the hearth. I went to kneel beside him and warmed my hands at the fire. "I am tired," I sent.

He turned one flaring yellow eye to me, and for a fleeting moment, there was a mindless emptiness in it. Then his gaze sharpened. "You are tired because your body heals its hurts. This is a place/barud where there is much hurting. No matter. Soon we will leave."

I stared at him. "What?"

"Soon we/you will go far away. Very far . . ." His eye was cloudy again. I felt a surge of alarm at the thought that the old cat was on the verge of another fit of madness. Yet he had recently returned from a period of wandering madness, and the attacks did not usually happen in such quick succession. Perhaps he was simply tired. Lud knew that could make you a little mad.

"I/Maruman am weary," the cat sent as if to confirm my thoughts. "The H'rayka searches in the dream-trails of ElspethInnle, and I have fought many battles to guard the way."

Abruptly, I was wide awake.

"Maruman, who/what is H'rayka?"

"H'rayka is the one who brings destruction," the cat sent.

I felt a rush of pure terror. Atthis had told me that if I did not find the weaponmachines and disable them, another human, whose fate path twinned my own, would locate and activate them, raining a new doom on the world. She had called this person "the Destroyer."

And now Maruman said a Destroyer was searching my dreams.

I had never considered that the Destroyer might be someone I would have to confront. I had seen our search for the weaponmachines as a sort of parallel race. Surely Atthis would have warned me if this person was hunting me.

Another possibility occurred to me. What if Maruman was trying to tell me that the Destroyer had begun searching not for me but for the weaponmachines? This seemed far more likely.

Suddenly I was more angry than scared. If the Destroyer *was* searching for the weaponmachines, why was I wasting time in Sutrium?

Why hadn't Atthis called me?

"The oldOne called," Maruman answered my despairing thought. "You do her bidding here in barud-li."

I stared at him. "I do the bidding of Maryon/tallone."

"Maryon/tallone hears the ashling of the oldOne/speaks the oldOne's words to Innle."

I struggled to stay calm. "Are you . . . are you saying Atthis sent a dream to Maryon to make me come to Sutrium?"

"A path forms itself like snow in the high valley of

the barud," Maruman sent dreamily. "First there is this piece of coldwhite and that piece, and they are alone and nothing. But soon they join and cover the earth."

The obliqueness of his answer exasperated me, for past experience told me this was his way of indicating that he was sick of a subject. Any further questions would be met with increasingly obscure answers.

The old cat gave me a sly look, then curled to sleep.

I tried reading his subconscious thoughts but could not penetrate the drifting mists of distortion.

I sat back on my heels and stared into the fire.

Could it be true that Atthis has sent Maryon's visions? If so, then the need to return the gypsy to her people must be somehow connected to my secret quest to find and destroy the weaponmachines. Or perhaps the return of the gypsy had been nothing more than an excuse to get me to Sutrium. Yet the deadline Maryon had given fitted with the Twentyfamilies' departure, and I had learned, at least in part, what *Swallow* meant.

But why even bother to send messages through the futureteller instead of speaking to my mind directly? I had sworn to heed Atthis's direction, so it could not be through fear that I would refuse to obey.

Yet there was a precedent. The first time Atthis summoned me had been through Maruman's mind. In any case, if Maruman spoke the truth, I had no more cause to fret at leaving Obernewtyn or fear I would somehow miss a summons.

It struck me suddenly that rather than spending my time worrying about my destined quest, I should simply live and trust in the fates to bring me where I was needed.

I stared into the flames with a feeling of having perceived a tremendous truth.

For a moment, in spite of weariness and concern over Idris and the rebel alliance, I felt a sense of clarity and purpose such as I had not experienced since standing on the high peaks of the Agyllian Ken. It seemed that simply by existing, I fulfilled the purpose of my life.

"There is blood on your shirt," Kella said, sounding startled.

"Some louts in the market whipped me," I said.

"Let me see," she commanded.

I flapped my hand for her to leave me be. "It has already been cleaned and treated—by a gypsy herb lorist."

In a tired way, I enjoyed the amazement on their faces. I let them speculate a moment before telling them what had happened—leaving out the gypsy's kiss. It shamed me to think of it. Nor did I complicate matters by telling them about the triple Guanette bird design or the mysterious Swallow.

But what I did tell them was enough to have them all agog.

"When will ye take her to them?" Matthew asked.

"When Kella says it is safe for her to travel. After that business with Dragon in the market, all the eyes in every rat hole and cranny of the city will be peeled for gypsies, so even if she was able to move now, I'd wait a day or so. Unfortunately, neither of us will be able to move about too easily, Matthew, and certainly not together."

"Iriny," Kella said. "Strange to give her a name after

so long. She is sleeping naturally now, and her wounds have begun to knit nicely."

I nodded and looked around. "Where is Dragon?"

"Sleeping still," Kella said. "It's not surprising. You must have had to hit her hard to knock her out right through her shield. I didn't even know that was possible."

The stair door slammed and Domick came in. Kella recounted the day's events to him, but the coercer seemed more concerned about Idris than anything else.

"When did Reuvan say he was seen last?" he demanded.

"Last night. Or mayhap yestermorn," Matthew said.

"He has only been missing a day and a half," I pointed out as the coercer began to pace back and forth. "Surely this is a little soon for everyone to be panicking."

"Did ye try farseekin' him?" Domick demanded.

"I did, but I could not find him. It was an unfocused probe, though, and there's a lot of static in the city; he could be in a blank spot. Or he might just be sleeping. You know it is much harder to find a sleeping mind even with an attuned probe."

"He might also be dead," Domick murmured.

I glared at him. "Do you take pleasure in being so miserable and hopeless?"

His hard eyes met mine. "In suggesting Idris is dead, I offer hope. If he is not, he may very well wish he were."

"Wh-what?" Kella gasped faintly.

"None of you seems to have grasped what Idris's disappearance may mean," Domick said. "If someone has him and questions him, he will be made to tell all he knows. . . ."

"The safe house," Kella whispered, lifting a hand to her lips. "He knows where it is and all about us."

"He knows everything about Brydda and the rebels, too," Domick reminded us brusquely.

I groaned, seeing more than that. "Lud save us. He knows about Obernewtyn!"

"He'd nivver give us away," Matthew said stoutly.

Domick turned a bleak look on the Farseeker ward, and suddenly they seemed decades apart in age.

"You don't have any idea, do you? Faced with a skilled torturer, you or I, even Rushton, would tell all. And Idris is a boy. Make no mistakes—if those who have him want information, he will tell them everything he knows."

✦ 18 ✦

AFTER A HEATED discussion, we decided not to abandon the safe house immediately but to wait until first light in the hope that Idris would be found. At the coercer's urging, we spent the night packing Kella's precious store of herbs and her healing implements into woven boxes.

When we were almost finished, Kella went to wake Dragon so that she could apply the skin dye. After the incident at the market, we dared not let her remain undisguised.

Domick took out a city map, which showed the location of the nearest green.

"I wish you would reconsider," he said.

"I wish you would stop suggesting it," I snapped.

The coercer wanted us to go directly to Obernewtyn to alert Rushton and evacuate the valley. I had argued against doing anything so drastic before we had clarified exactly what the rebels knew of Idris's disappearance. After all, Reuvan had not suggested there was any danger to us or to the safe house.

Kella pointed out that he might have been too distraught to think of warning us. "He seemed almost dazed when he left the safe house."

I was sure that Brydda would have sent someone to

warn us if there was any need and had said so, arguing that we could lose ourselves quickly and easily in the morning bustle of traders moving into their places at the markets. If we stole away in the night, someone was certain to report it. We had agreed to go to the nearest green, where we would wait and watch. If there was no raid on the safe house, we would return to it after a while; if there was a raid or any suspicious activity at all, Matthew would ride at once to warn Obernewtyn, and the rest of us would follow in the rig.

"You must go back to Obernewtyn, too, if the safe house is lost to us," Domick told Kella as she rinsed dye from her fingers.

"What about you?"

"I will stay at an inn as Mika."

"I will stay with you," she said stubbornly.

"Mika has no bondmate, and I don't want you connected with him in case something goes wrong and he has to disappear."

Kella blinked hard at his peremptory tone, then turned away to pull the last of her dried herbs down from the wall racks. His words reminded me of something else.

"Domick, didn't your last report mention people just vanishing without a trace in Sutrium?"

The coercer nodded.

"Maybe, whatever happened to those other people is what happened to Idris. And since those disappearances have nothing to do with the Council, then surely we need not fear—"

"We don't know that the Council has anything to do with them," Domick interrupted.

"But your report—"

"Contained conjecture as well as facts. I simply said that I had heard nothing to make me think the Council was behind the disappearances. But I don't hear everything that goes on, and sometimes the very fact that I have not means only that people have been warned to hold their tongues." He shrugged. "There are so many factions within the Council and the soldierguard ranks, all with their own plots, and if I have learned one thing in the time I have spent here, it is that sooner or later, everything is linked to everything else."

There was something profound in his words, which struck a note of response in me, but it was swamped by a wrenching weariness.

"You remember when we went to see Brydda the first night you got here?" Domick went on. "Reuvan came in and spoke of Salamander."

I nodded. "You said he has something to do with the slave trade."

"He is its leader. Salamander buys the people who disappear, and the increase in disappearances corresponds with an increase in the demand for slaves."

"Buying them from whom?"

"The rumor is that the disappearances are the work of an organization that specializes in kidnapping or removing people for a price. I think it is likely that Salamander set it up to ensure his supply. No one in the slave trade knows what he looks like, because he is fanatical about keeping his face and identity secret. He delegates like a king to a whole herd of people and rarely appears in person. When he does, there is almost no prior warning. It has long been rumored that he is a Councilman or some other high official. No doubt he is well aware that the mystery surrounding his identity creates an atmosphere of terror and suspicion and keeps his people silent and obedient."

"I dinna know th' slave trade had a leader," Matthew said.

"It did not—until Salamander came on the scene. Once, it was only the odd ship that stole people from the Land and sold them to lands over the seas, which were supposed not to exist. Then a ship with a flag showing a flaming salamander began to attack and sink any vessel known to trade in slaves. Invariably, one crewmember would be kept alive, tortured, then cast ashore to tell the story of a ship with Beforetime weapons that spat fire. In no time, the trade virtually ceased, for no one wanted to make themselves a target for such a nemesis. It had seemed for a while that someone wanted to end the practice completely, but instead he was only ensuring he would have no competition."

I had a sudden vision of the hatred that had flared so unexpectedly in Idris's mild eyes when Reuvan had said Salamander was in Sutrium.

"Idris's family was taken by slavers, weren't they?"

"His father and his sisters," Kella said. Her shoulders were hunched forward, and there were dark shadows under her eyes. Whenever she looked at her bondmate, there was pain in her eyes.

Domick was oblivious. "If Idris has been taken by the slavers, he will be tortured for information that could be used, before he is sold. Blackmail is another of Salamander's specialties, and you can be sure he knows the value of a seditioner with inside knowledge of the rebel organization. He would sell it dearly to the Council. Perhaps he would even sell Idris himself. So we are back where we started."

It was a grim prospect, for Idris and for Obernewtyn, and we fell into a weary, staring sort of silence contemplating it. This was broken when Domick slammed a hand on the arm of his chair.

"Look at us sitting here and yawping into the fire like a herd of defectives! Don't you see that it doesn't matter who has Idris? If I am right, someone may be on their way here now! How will we escape with Dragon, and the gypsy unable to walk?"

He was right. I stood up and flung the dregs of the fement onto the fire. It gave a vicious hiss and belched a sullen cloud of smoke.

"All right," I said shortly. "Let's get everything down to the wagon."

Kella continued the last bit of packing while Domick and I transferred the boxes downstairs. Matthew took them from us and packed them into the cramped interior of the gypsy rig, sweating freely in spite of the chill air.

"If Idris is made to talk, won't he mention this room you keep?" I asked.

Domick shook his head and motioned for Matthew to take the other end of the box he carried. "He knows nothing about it."

"But he knows about you."

"He knows about Domick," the coercer corrected. "Not about the Council worker Mika. Even a physical description of me will fit a number of others. And if he does tell them of a spy in the Councilcourt, I will know they are seeking me long before they realize which one I am and will vanish."

He had it all worked out, and no doubt he was correct, but part of me wondered if this new Domick was not pleased for an excuse to hurry us all out of Sutrium.

"But why risk it at all?" Matthew demanded, shoving a box in place against the others.

The coercer's voice was curt with dismissal. "Because my position is too valuable to abandon lightly. Apart from that, if Idris is brought to the Councilcourt, I might be able to wipe his mind so he would be unable to speak of the rebels or of us."

The ease with which he proposed to erase the boy's mind shocked me. I stared at him for a moment, half tempted to loose a farseeking probe in case any surface thoughts drifted free of the coercer's mindshield. It would not be ethical to probe him, but if he was careless, I might learn what had so altered him. What stopped me asking him outright was the fear that whatever was wrong arose from his relationship with Kella. And no matter how it hurt her and chilled me to see him this way, the changes did not seem to be affecting his work for Obernewtyn and therefore were none of my business.

The sleepless night and the long day that had preceded it were taking their toll, and I thought longingly of my bed upstairs. It was hard and lumpy, and bits of straw poked into me in the night, but I could think of nothing more wonderful at that moment than to sink into it and pull the covers over my head while there were still a few hours of night left. Sometimes I longed fiercely to have only myself to worry about.

"After what happened with Dragon yesterday, all the gypsy greens will be under observation. It would be safer for you to go straight back to Obernewtyn,"

Domick went on relentlessly as we made our way back up to the kitchen.

I lost my temper. "Do you suggest we take the gypsy back with us to Obernewtyn? And if the greens are watched, then the gates will be watched, too, which means the risk of being identified as we leave will be doubled."

"Returning her to her people is surely less important than keeping Obernewtyn safe," Domick persisted. "As for the gates, you can coerce yourself past them, because you know who to coerce. In the city, you will have no idea who watches with hostile eyes, and if you are recognized, you will still have to pass the gates to escape."

I shook my head in exasperation and brushed past him to enter the kitchen again. Domick went on and on like water dripping on stone. Everything he said made sense—*if* Idris had been taken by someone who would ask about us.

"The gypsy cannot be taken on the trip back to the mountains just yet," Kella said, having heard my words. "After a couple days of rest and quiet—"

"I am sure she would prefer a little discomfort to being captured along with us and burned at the stake!" Domick interrupted coldly. He looked around the bare kitchen. "Surely everything must now be packed, Kella, or must you also bring such necessities as the bathing barrels?"

The healer's shoulders slumped as Domick turned on his heel and stalked out, and I wondered how long her love for the coercer could survive his insensitivity.

"He is rough in saying it but right," I said gently to her after a moment. "It will do the gypsy no good to be healthy if the soldierguards get hold of her. There are times when we must endure what comes and take our luck. Go and prepare her to be carried down to the wagon."

"A trip into the mountains might kill her."

"We are not taking her back to Obernewtyn. I will return her to her people. She must be back with them before we leave."

Kella's eyes widened; then she nodded soberly, remembering Maryon's deadline. Or Atthis's. It was possible I had already done enough to save myself and Obernewtyn in finding the gypsy's people and learning that Swallow was a person, but there was no way of telling.

Therefore, the gypsy must be taken to Maire. The trouble was that Kella and Matthew would have to come as well.

I was still trying to decide if it would be best to have them wait somewhere for me when Domick departed, saying he was expected at the Councilcourt.

Dragon trailed into the kitchen. In spite of the muddy dyes Kella had used to disguise her hair and skin, and a wan, woeful expression, she was lovelier than ever. She put her hand to her forehead and rubbed at it fretfully.

"Are you all right?" I asked.

She blinked at me, her blue eyes pink-rimmed. "Head hurts."

Small wonder after the ruthless jolt I had given her, I thought ruefully, drawing her to warm herself by the fire. It was not much of a reward for her courage in defending the woman and her children, yet what else could I have done?

Kella entered, frowning. "The sleepseal on the gypsy will hold only a little while longer. Seals are progressively less effective when applied in succession, and her mind is fighting it. It will hold for a few hours. No more."

"It will do. I'll get Matthew to help me bring her down in a minute." I nodded at Dragon. "Is she all right? She says her head hurts."

Kella examined the girl, looking intently into her eyes and touching her temple lightly. Rummaging in a basket, she made a soothing herbal mixture, and we both watched as Dragon drank it.

"She'll be fine once the herbs begin to work," the healer said softly. She glanced around the kitchen at the bare walls and sighed. "I suppose we might just as well go at once. I have sometimes longed for something that would send me back to Obernewtyn, yet now I am sad. I cannot imagine this place without me."

"Nor can I," said a gruff, familiar voice.

We both whirled to see Brydda Llewellyn standing in the kitchen doorway.

"Brydda!" Kella cried gladly, and flung herself into the rebel chief's arms. The big man hugged her, then gently put her away from him. His voice was grave.

"The soldierguards are searching the city for a gypsy girl and boy who freed a woman from a burning in Guanette. They are picking gypsies up all over the city and questioning them. The descriptions they are giving fit you and Matthew too well to be anyone else. They also tally with reports dozens of people gave after an incident in a city market where two gypsies and a red-haired Landgirl attacked Herder priests about their business."

I felt sick. Not only had they connected the market incident to the one in Guanette, but also Dragon's description was now being bandied about.

"Brydda—" I began, but he cut me off as if he had not heard me.

"I thought it must be you, so I came to . . . to warn you." There was an odd twitchiness in his manner.

"Has Idris come back yet?" I asked with sudden foreboding.

He shook his head.

"Then we must leave here at once in case the soldierguards come," I said firmly, and tried to propel him back toward the stairs. It was like trying to push a mountain sideways.

"The soldierguards won't be coming," he said.

Matthew came into the hallway behind us, but his welcoming smile faltered as he took in the strangeness of the older man.

"Something is wrong, but let him tell it how he will," I sent, forestalling his questions.

Dragon was staring up at the giant rebel in wonderment. Clearly, Kella's medicine had done its job. He stirred under her gaze and frowned down at her. "So it was you in the market, Dragon. What a little beauty you are. . . ."

"Bir-da," she said shyly.

The rebel's eyes lost their feverish look as he dropped to one knee to make himself her height, but she would not be coaxed nearer.

"Brydda, if the Council has Idris, they will force him to tell them about this place. . . ." I spoke more in an attempt to draw the rebel back to normality than in expectation of an answer.

205

"Idris will not talk," Brydda interrupted.

I bit my lip. After Domick's chilling assertion that a skilled torturer could make anyone talk, I did not understand Brydda's conviction that Idris would not be made to speak. Especially since a friend had once before been tortured to betray him.

Unless his suppressed Talent had told him something.

I was trying to decide how best to frame a query when the big rebel rose with catlike grace and moved past us to the dying fire. Kella and Matthew exchanged worried glances as he lowered himself onto a chair.

Dragon sidled gradually nearer until she came to lean against his knees and stare into his face. He did not appear to be aware of her at all.

"I am so tired . . . ," he said, rubbing his fingers in his eyes.

"Brydda, how can you know the soldierguards won't come here?" I asked, coming to stand by the fire, too.

The rebel did not answer, but, fascinatingly, Dragon's face twisted with the emotions she was receiving from the big man. Her ability to receive emotions had been slower to develop than her power to transmit them, but physical contact enhanced all Talent. Brydda had no idea of what was happening, because the empath-coercer's face was turned slightly away from him. It was disturbing and oddly grotesque to read the movement of a grown man's thought in Dragon's mobile young face.

First there was grief and guilt, then anger and frustration, and at last a sort of wretched despair.

"It does not matter how I know, only that I do," he answered at last, his face impassive.

"Do you know who has Idris?" I asked, keeping one eye on Dragon.

Her face again mirrored the rebel's inner turmoil, and I felt a deepening disquiet. Who could have taken Idris for Brydda to react so strongly?

The big man was staring into the red embers of the half-extinguished fire, still redolent with fement. "Idris was investigating something for me when he disappeared," he murmured at last. "He asked me to use him. But I should never have done it."

A terrible weary despair dragged at Dragon's youthful features forming a grotesque mask.

"You have heard of the disappearances in Sutrium?" Brydda asked.

"Yes. Do you think that is what happened to him, then?"

He gave a croaking laugh. "My curiosity is what happened to Idris. My infernal hunger for knowledge. I found the man Reuvan had told us about—a sot at an inn, boasting about knowing Salamander. I bought the fellow a drink, and it took me no longer than that to know he had lied. The slavemaster would never trust his face to such a ninnyhammer. I needled him a bit just for the sake of it, and he wound up telling me that his master knew Salamander. I had a feeling there was some truth in this, so I decided to have him watched. He shut up after a bit, as if he realized he had said too much. I did not want to frighten him off, so I played the gull for him. I got roaring drunk and let him rob me before I was thrown outside."

The rebel's eyes had grown as cold as sharpened icicles. "Idris volunteered to keep an eye on him while I organized a roster of watchers. The sot was lodging at the inn, and Idris had only to watch him and note the name of anyone who spoke with him while I was gone. I did not expect anything significant to happen."

He gave me a bitter look. "'Stay put and watch,' I said. But the sot went out about an hour after we left, and Idris followed. I was so busy gloating over having finally caught hold of Salamander's elusive tail that I took no account of the fact that Idris's passion to have the slave trade destroyed was far greater than mine. . . ."

"Do you think this man realized Idris was following and took him prisoner?"

"He was a drunk, and for all his smallness, Idris was strong and tough."

He fell silent.

"Then . . . what?" I asked.

Brydda did not answer. His face was as still as a carved image. Kella pinched me and pointed to Dragon. The flame-haired girl was staring out blindly, tears coursing down her cheeks.

A heavy dread settled in my stomach as I realized that Brydda had been speaking of Idris in the past tense.

Kella had reached the same awful conclusion. "Idris is dead, isn't he?" she whispered.

The big rebel jerked convulsively at her words. "Dead? Yes," he said flatly.

Dragon's face twisted, revealing the emotions the big man would not express, and she began to tremble. I signaled Kella to get her away from him.

"Are you sure?" I whispered.

The rebel turned dry eyes, hectic with self-hate and

grief, on me. "I am sure. His body was found this morning washed up on the banks of the Suggredoon."

Dragon let out an anguished howl, voicing the jagged spike of Kella's shock.

"We'll find whoever did it," Matthew vowed through gritted teeth.

I gave him a pointed look. The last thing we needed was high drama at such a moment. He rose and went out, muttering that he had to unpack the wagon. Kella went, too, taking Dragon out of the range of Brydda's searing anguish.

"Salamander killed him," he said when we were alone. "I have sworn I will crush the man and his foul trade once and for all, in the boy's name."

I bit my lip, but I knew I must say the unspeakable. "Brydda. Idris might . . . still . . . have been made to speak, before . . ."

The rebel shook his head emphatically. "His body did not show signs of torture. And he would never . . . never betray me willingly or easily." The last words were voiced in a savage rasp, and I blinked my own sudden tears away.

Brydda went on after he had regained control of himself. "No doubt the slavemaster killed Idris because the boy saw his face; killed him as a routine precaution, thinking him no more than a curious lad who had seen more than was good for him. If he had suspected Idris was a spy, Salamander would have had him tortured. That he didn't tells me Idris was killed as thoughtlessly as if he were a fly or an ant in the wrong place at the wrong time."

"How can you be so certain it was Salamander who did it?"

Brydda's face was grim with certainty. "A tiny lizard shape was carved into his forehead—Salamander's murderous trademark."

I felt a sick wave of horror. "I'm so sorry," I whispered, knowing there was no way to console the rebel for the loss of a boy he had loved like a son.

Brydda took a deep shuddering breath and seemed incredibly to compose himself to a bleak serenity. "I will not grieve while Idris's killer breathes. Salamander will pay for the boy's life with his own blood."

I shuddered inwardly at the mad, cold fire in his eyes, dismayed by the notion that one death could compensate for another. But I understood the guilt-driven anger that motivated him.

The rebel chief turned burning eyes on me. "That is the other reason I came tonight. You can help me to trap him."

I blinked, startled. "Salamander?"

He nodded grimly. "You can use your powers to lead me to him."

"When?" I asked warily.

"Now," the rebel said.

✦ 19 ✦

"*NOW?*" I ECHOED, incredulous.

Brydda inclined his head and rose slowly, as if his bones were stiff and pained him. Yet the ember glow from the dying fire rendered him mysteriously younger. "Come, I will explain as we go."

"I won't go without knowing what I'm getting myself into! You are my friend, but I have a responsibility to Obernewtyn."

He stared at me for a long moment, then sat back down, grief and fury extinguished with visible effort. "Listen well, then, for there is not much time. There was information on Idris's body about a meeting. . . ."

"Surely, Salamander would have found any message Idris carried? It must be some kind of trap."

The rebel shook his head emphatically. "It was not a message to any eyes but mine. Idris and I have a special code in case . . ." The momentary eagerness in his face faded to a grim recollection of his loss. "The message said that a Councilfarm overseer named Evan Bollange had approached the sot soon after I left the inn, offering five able-bodied Councilfarm workers whose deaths had been staged. The poor wretches had been smuggled into the city, drugged, and hidden under the boards of a manure cart. A time and place were named for a meeting between Bollange and the sot's master, a slaver in Salamander's employ, to discuss terms.

"The sot left the inn, and Idris followed. That's all I can say with certainty, for he wrote no more in his message. But it seems to me that the sot went to inform his master of the meeting date with Bollange. Salamander was either meeting with the slaver at the time or simply watching him, and Idris got too close. And he was not the only one.

"The sot was a minion, chosen precisely because he would boast—for an organization that is *too* secret will have no clients. Like all such, he was disposable. He was found yesterday with his throat cut. Such culling is not uncommon among Salamander's people. The sot had served his purpose for a time, but the slavemaster could not risk leaving so obvious a trail."

Brydda's eyes were hard and suddenly purposeful. "Yet, in his arrogance, he made a mistake. He let us find Idris's body, never knowing there was a message on it, telling the time and place of the rendezvous between Bollange and the slaver. They are to meet before dawn this day, in an inn on the other side of the city. If you will help me, we must leave at once."

"You are going to spy on the meeting?"

"I have no intention of spying," Brydda said, his eyes aglitter. "I intend to intercept Bollange and take his place."

"You would pass yourself off as a Councilfarm overseer?"

He shook his head. "There is every likelihood that the sot described Bollange to his master; therefore, I will be his brother, Arkold Bollange."

"You must be mad! The slaver will never believe such a far-fetched story!"

"I do not need to convince him for long," Brydda said calmly. "I doubt he would tell me anything even if he *did* believe me. But I only need to get close, because you will come with me as my assistant and read his mind. He must know enough about Salamander to reach him at need."

I gaped at his audacity. "And what if the slaver decides to just kill the overseer's unlikely brother and his gypsy assistant?"

"That is a risk," Brydda agreed, sounding as if he were admitting that it might rain. "But I doubt he will do that, even if he is extremely suspicious, because we offer something Salamander wants—slaves." He stood up suddenly. "Will you help me?"

I sighed, then stood.

"Rushton will be furious. He will like this no more than that I have decided to take your advice and meet with your rebel leaders."

Brydda's eyes widened. "Good on both accounts! Opportunities must be seized upon when they arise. We need leaders, truly, but sometimes decisions need to be made on the battlefield, in the heat of the moment. Without those capable of making such decisions, any force might founder. Rushton would appreciate the need and your ability to rise to it and make a decision without consultation."

"I wonder," I murmured dryly, pulling on my boots. I went to my chamber, donned a hooded cloak, and plaited my hair.

When we came down into the wagon-repair shed,

Gahltha stirred, sending a stern reminder of my promise not to go out without him.

"He insists I ride him," I told Brydda. "If there is trouble, he is a savage fighter. Jaygar has been trained to fight as well, and he offers to bear you."

Brydda shrugged. "I had thought to walk, but if we take the horses, we can get away fast if something goes awry." He signaled his thanks to Jaygar.

I was silent, impressed that the rebel did not simply accept Jaygar's offer as his rightful due. He genuinely regarded the horses as equals. Though he rode Sallah often, and in fact had stolen her from a Herder cloister, he never took her for granted. Sometimes I was convinced he had so easily accepted my Misfit powers solely because, through me, he had been able to devise a finger-signal language that enabled him to communicate with horses. He had been delighted when the Beastspeaking guildmaster, Alad, had asked to learn the language so it could be taught gradually to all at Obernewtyn who were not beastspeakers and to the beasts themselves.

As we rode out into the early morning, I wondered if Alad was right about Sallah being the lowland beast-leader and, if so, whether Brydda had any idea of it. It would not surprise me at all to find he had allied himself with the equines over his own kind.

The streets were all but deserted at this hour, and we did not see any soldierguards; nonetheless, I was unable to rid myself of the feeling that we were being watched. Certainly we made a strange enough couple, a gypsy boy on a magnificent, if dirty, black stallion and an enormous dark-haired man wrapped in an oil cloak and mounted on a stocky roan.

"I scent no funaga," Gahltha assured me.

I relaxed fractionally, reporting this to Brydda.

"Nor should there be," he said quietly. "I am taking us through parts of the city that are virtually deserted except during trading hours."

Brydda ceased his scrutiny of the streets to look at me for a moment. "As soon as we return, I will send birds off, to let the group leaders know about the meeting with you. It will take a few days for them to reply, though they have birds as well, because they will confer and scheme before responding."

"Is it wise to let the rebels know in advance that I am to come?" I asked.

"We must ensure that as many rebel leaders as possible come to hear you speak. Otherwise, the report they hear will depend upon the bias of the teller. And even if they were favorably inclined toward you, it is easier to dismiss secondhand reports as exaggeration. I will phrase my message so that every rebel leader feels they will miss out on something vital unless they attend. The rest will be up to you."

There was no sign of Brydda's earlier shattered disorientation; the big man was shielding himself from the pain of Idris's loss by concentrating on plans and schemes.

I said nothing, knowing he would have to deal with his pain eventually and that no words would ease it. I remembered how deep the hurt of Jik's death had cut into me. Words had not helped then—and sometimes I had longed for silence as much as forgetfulness. Time had abated the immediate wrenching sorrow I had felt at the boy's death, yet even now the thought of it sometimes made a dull ache in my chest, like a long-healed scar echoing its birth.

Suddenly Brydda signaled Jaygar to stop.

"Idris's message said Bollange had been told to seek out the street of five inns," the rebel said, looking about. "We are almost there, so we will wait here to intercept him."

"Do you know what he looks like?"

He shook his head. "I am confident he will come this way, and there will be few enough people about at this time. But you will know for sure when he comes," he added, touching his head to indicate that he meant me to use my farseeking powers.

It seemed a vague sort of plan. But then, Brydda had an uncanny intuition—he called it a "knack"—so I held my tongue and let him lead the way into a narrow lane between two high buildings. We dismounted, and the horses moved deeper into the lane to wait.

"What am I to do when I have him?"

"You must turn him back," Brydda said softly. "Can you do that so that he will not know what has happened?"

I sighed. "I will try, but his mind might be—"

"Someone/funaga comes," Gahltha sent urgently.

I froze, and at once we heard a quick, light step. It was a woman carrying a basket, and a few minutes later two boys ran by. Then, on the third sound of footsteps, I sent my mind flying out and breathed a sigh of incredulous relief to find the wiry little man coming down the street was indeed the very person we were waiting for. Best of all, his mind was wide open to me.

Gently, I riffled through his memories before coercing him into forgetting why he had come out. In the gap left by what was erased, I took an older memory of a rousing night's drinking from his memories and reestablished it as the memory of the previous night. I pinched a nerve and gave him a headache to match, then sent him around the next corner and back to his lodgings bewildered and disorientated.

"It's done," I said aloud. "He has forgotten everything about this meeting and believes he has been out carousing. I have made him forget about the slaves, too. He now thinks they really did die in an accident. You will have to free them, though."

"You know their location?"

"Of course."

"Good," Brydda said grimly. He cast a look at the sky. "We had better go on. The instructions said the overseer must stop at the public trough and drink, to identify himself."

We left the horses to wait and made our way onto the street of five inns. There was a dirty-looking trough about halfway along, and Brydda stopped at it and cupped his hands to scoop some of the brackish water to his mouth. I let my mind loose, but I could detect no watcher. It made my skin creep to think that Salamander might be somewhere about us, watching from a window or a pool of shadow.

A ragged boy stepped out of a doorway, and I gasped in startled fright. His lips were blue, and he was shivering violently. His eyes slid to me uneasily, then back to Brydda. "There was to be one man walking alone."

"It is none of your affair," Brydda growled. "What are the words you have been told to say to me?"

The boy seemed reassured by Brydda's roughness. "You are to go to the last inn on this street and ask for the man in the best room."

He turned and darted away down a lane.

"He was frightened," I murmured, but Brydda had begun to walk again.

The last inn proved to be a cheap roominghouse with a den attached for casual drinking. I grimaced, for the frowsy Good Egg had been positively luxurious in comparison. A rank smell assailed us at the door, rising from piles of stinking refuse to one side.

I gagged at the stench as Brydda knocked, wondering what had possessed me to agree to such a mad scheme. My powers would do us no good at the moment, because I could feel that the wretched place was constructed of rock lightly tainted with Beforetime poisons. Fortunately, this would not matter once we were inside the walls—as long as they did not lie between the slaver and ourselves.

"I/Gahltha am here. I will kick the wall down if you do not return," the black horse sent stoutly. I felt slightly less afraid, knowing the fierce equine meant exactly what he said.

A man with yellow-stained teeth opened the inn door a crack and squinted out at us. Brydda drew a little scrolled note from his pocket and handed it through the opening. "Give this to the man in your best room."

The innkeeper grunted in derision, but he took the note in his grimy fingers before slamming the door shut. "What was in it?" I asked.

"A note from my brother, Evan, introducing me as his proxy. And now we can do no more than wait and keep our sword hands free."

We waited in silence, and I spent the time adopting various creative ways of breathing in an effort to filter out the foul stench of the place.

The door opened again, and the man indicated that we were to enter. Brydda gave me an encouraging pinch as I preceded him. If possible, the smell inside was worse, and it was all I could do not to vomit. The rebel seemed completely impervious to it. I gulped and was glad I had an empty stomach.

The innkeeper brought us to a room with a brown door and held out a dirty paw. Brydda dropped a coin into it, then knocked, and the innkeeper scuttled away as if he did not want to be there when the occupant appeared.

This made me very nervous.

The door opened a slit.

"Enter," a papery voice rasped, and a shiver ran up my spine at the sound of it.

At first, I thought the chamber completely unlit, but it was simply that Brydda's bulk had blocked the light of a cheap lantern, which was shaded to throw its light toward us, leaving the rest of the room in darkness. The windows, if there were any, had been blacked out.

The only thing I could see clearly was the pitted surface of a wooden table and two enormous scarred hands with thick, powerful wrists resting on it. Between the hands was a curved dagger, carved with odd symbols, and the little scrolled note Brydda had sent in.

The atmosphere of threat in the room was almost palpable, and my heart began to gallop as Brydda stepped forward. "I am Arkold Bollange, sirrah. . . ."

"You do not resemble your brother," the man said, his skepticism patently obvious.

"Different fathers, sirrah," Brydda said, and it was all I could do not to goggle at him in astonishment. In the blink of an eye, without the benefit of even changing his shirt, the rebel had transformed himself into a self-important fool whose pompous facade barely concealed the sniveling coward lurking beneath.

I did my best to shape myself into the sort of cringing nitwit that I imagined such a man would choose as a servant. At the same time, I loosed a probe. It moved sluggishly because of the taint in the walls and floor. The first thing it told me was that the man seated behind the table was not alone. There were three others standing against the wall behind him.

I bent my mind upon one of them and learned that he and the man next to him were hired killers. The third was known to them only as the slaver's assistant. The two hirelings carried knives, unsheathed, and had instructions to kill instantly after a certain combination of words.

I tried the slaver's assistant, but his mind was shielded.

"Why did not your brother come himself as was arranged?" the slaver was asking Brydda.

"As he wrote in that note, sirrah, Evan feared he was being followed and sent me in his place. I am here only as an emissary to discuss, ah, price."

"Who is this gypsy?" The slaver's voice cracked out like a whip, and I jumped.

The two men with knives tensed, and so did I. "My servant," Brydda blustered. "You could not expect a man of my stature to go about in an area like this without even a body servant? I can't very well use my own people. You need not worry about him, though. He is defective except for a peculiar strength with his hands and feet that make him a useful guard in spite of his small stature."

Again the silence, and I prepared myself to coerce the two with knives if the slave supplier gave the signal to kill.

"Very well," he said at last in his sibilant voice. "But I do not want him brought again. I do not like gypsies, full or halfbloods. They are trouble and are carriers of disease."

"Of . . . of course, sirrah," Brydda babbled.

The slave supplier became businesslike as he spoke of the price he would pay for each slave and how this would increase with the number of slaves offered. The men in the shadows relaxed.

"How will I reach you if there is a problem before collection?" Brydda asked.

"There will be no problem," the slaver said with chilling finality.

"Of course not," Brydda babbled idiotically. "I understand perfectly."

The slave supplier stood, and even his hands were swallowed up by the shadows. A moment later, a bag of coins fell onto the table.

"This is an advance on the payment for the five. You will get the remainder when I get the slaves and make certain they are sound-limbed and not defectives."

"I assure you . . . ," Brydda blustered.

I swiftly summoned a coercive probe, realizing I had been so busy listening to the interchange that I had forgotten what I was there for. Sending the probe to the slave supplier, I was flabbergasted to find my way barred by another farseeking probe. Wrapped delicately around the slaver's mind, the alien probe had taken on the shape and feel of the host mind and in some places was indistinguishable from it.

Unwilling to disturb the probe until I knew its purpose, I cast about until I found its source. It was the man in the shadows whose mind I had been unable to read. The slaver's assistant was a Talented Misfit!

I hovered uncertainly, my mind reeling with shock. I had promised Brydda to get what information I could about Salamander, which meant getting past the othermind.

I clenched my teeth and readied myself to attack.

"Collection the slaves will take place in two days," the slave supplier was saying. "Here is a map. The shed where you are to bring the slaves is marked on it. When you hear a knock thus . . ." He rapped in a sequence. The movement brought him into the light for a fleeting second, and I glimpsed bad skin, dark-brown eyes, and a vicious slash of a mouth before he moved back into the shadows. "Then you will open the door. Do you understand?"

I braced myself for a battle and let an aggressive coercerprobe fly toward the slaver's assistant. To my complete astonishment, I met no resistance. The othermind opened to me—and I recognized it!

✦ 20 ✦

When we came outside, the sky arching above was a deep, icy blue, and there were few stars, for the sun was near to rising. We could only have been inside the inn a short while. I felt as if we had been in there for years.

Gahltha whinnied a welcome, and I stroked his neck in mute affection, realizing unexpectedly that whatever the enigmatic stallion felt for me, I loved him.

"What did you find?" Brydda asked as we mounted.

"Another mindprobe," I said. "Wrapped around the slaver's mind."

Brydda turned to stare at me. "Are you saying there was a Misfit among those who skulked in the shadows of that room? Protecting him?"

"Not just a Misfit. A Talent. And not protecting, though that is what I thought at first. *He* was trying to get into the slaver's mind, too. I traced the mindprobe back to its owner. Do you remember Daffyd, who brought Dragon to Obernewtyn when I was ill?"

"The Druid's armsman? The probe was his?"

I nodded; then we both fell quiet, for we had come to a lane where people were bustling about in preparation for the day's trading. In one tiny market square, a fire had been lit in a metal barrel, and cloaked men and women stooped over it, warming their fingers. They were busy and preoccupied with their own affairs, which made it easy to weave a coercive net that would make it difficult for anyone to keep their eyes on us. I wondered at the absence of soldierguards, given the events of the previous day.

I thought of my first meeting with Daffyd—a chance encounter, if such meetings were ever really chance. I had been waiting in the Councilcourt to undergo the Misfit trial that would see me sentenced to Obernewtyn. Daffyd and another man had been waiting to see about a trade permit for the high country. I could not recall what words had passed between us that day as we sat there, but somehow, Daffyd had given me the courage to hope.

I had never forgotten his brightness in that dark moment.

We had met a second time after I had been taken captive by the fanatical ex-Herder, Henry Druid. Daffyd had been one of his armsmen. It had been at the Druid's secret encampment in the White Valley that Daffyd and several others had been simultaneously awakened to their Misfit Talents and emotionally enslaved by a powerful Misfit baby, Lidgebaby; it was there that he had fallen in love with Gilaine—daughter of the Druid and despised by her father for her muteness.

I had shown them how to free themselves from Lidgebaby's powerful overmind in return for their help in escaping. When a firestorm razed the Druid camp to the ground, Daffyd alone had escaped.

Discovering the loss of his friends, he had been heartbroken, but he remained with us in the mountains for some time. He had left us during the last summerdays, after Maryon had dreamed of his friends. He had been convinced they had survived and was determined to find them. Maryon had told me the dream had been vague and the faces unclear, but Daffyd had not cared.

We had not seen nor heard from him since. Until now.

"Elspeth?" Brydda murmured with faint exasperation, and I realized we had entered an empty street.

"I'm sorry, I was thinking about Daffyd. Yes, it was his probe. I am sure that his working for the slaver has something to do with his friends from the Druid camp, though there was little time for him to explain. I farsent him the location of the safe house, and he said he would come when he could."

"It is a pity we did not know that he worked for the slaver all along. It would have spared you reading his mind. I doubt that was a pleasant experience."

I licked my lips. "Brydda, I didn't farseek the slaver. I couldn't. His mind is sensitive, and he would have felt me at once. Daffyd stopped me just in time. He has spent months trying and still has not managed it."

"If he has been working for the slaver for so long, he must have some notion of where Salamander is," Brydda said.

"I think not, since he is trying to get into his mind for that very reason: to find Salamander. That much he did tell me."

The rebel said nothing.

"I'm sorry, Brydda."

"I know you are not to blame, Elspeth," he said heavily. "But if Daffyd does not come by tomorrow night with the knowledge of Salamander's whereabouts, we will have lost the chance to stop him."

"But surely we can follow the slaver until he meets with—"

"You don't understand. Two nights hence, when I do not take the five slaves to the abandoned warehouse as agreed, Salamander will guess something is wrong. Knowing his reputation, there will be a short and savage bloodletting during which anyone with any connection to him will be slain. That slaver we met tonight will be one of the first to go if he knows what Salamander looks like or how to reach him. And perhaps Daffyd, too, though his ignorance might protect him. So you see, there will be no one to follow back to the source."

"Daffyd will come," I said, crossing my fingers.

The air was damp with the promise of more rain, and dark clouds obscured the waxing moon as we came in sight of the safe house. In the gaps between clouds, the sparse morning stars were winking out one by one.

We rode into the yard, dismounting to the squeak of leather and the jingle of metal buckles on the harness. When the horses were released into the grassy holding yard, Brydda bade them thanks with his finger signs, saying aloud to me that he would not come up. "Reuvan expects me back by sunrise, and it is moments away. Where are the drugged Councilfarm workers being kept?"

I told him the cellar's location that I had taken from the overseer's thoughts.

"I will return tomorrow night," the big man said as he strode away. "Let us hope Daffyd has come by then with some news for us."

Instinctively, I glanced up, seeking the pitted face of the moon. Maruman had always attributed his darkest foresight to it, and I had come to see it as a bad omen, too. As if summoned by my thoughts, the moon suddenly sailed clear of the clouds.

I felt a mindless rush of fright at the sight of it glaring down on me like the eye of some unearthly hunter. But even as I laughed at my melodramatic imagination, I felt oddly unsettled, and it took me a long time to sleep.

I woke just before midday.

Gray daylight streamed in through the sky windows of the sleeping chamber, but there was no warmth in it. I stretched under the covers, then sat up reluctantly, reaching for my robe. Ariel's face came into my mind, and I froze in the act of climbing out of bed, remembering that I had dreamed of him.

We had been in the stone tunnel again.

The stone tunnel was a recurrent image from my dreams, and once I had asked Maryon what it could mean. She had replied that it was either a place where I would one day go, or it represented me or some aspect of me.

I belted the robe, letting the dream flow back into my mind. This time, instead of pursuing me with a knife or some other horror, Ariel had been walking beside me, his hand nestled in mine, small but very cold. He had smiled up at me as we came to the part of the tunnel where the doors of Obernewtyn flamed.

With the strange logic of dreams, it had seemed perfectly reasonable to me that the doors, which I had commanded be burned, should exist here.

"Why did you burn them?" the dream Ariel had asked in his piping, eager voice. His eyes had seemed to bore into mine with hypnotic intensity.

"Because there was a map carved into the design," I had answered. "I did not want anyone to find it."

This was the truth. Everyone at Obernewtyn believed

the doors had been burned to free the inlaid gold in the design so that we could make guildleaders' armbands from it. But my true object had been to destroy the hidden map carved into the doors, which showed the location of the very Beforetime weaponmachines that I now knew I would one day seek.

Louis Larkin had once told me that he remembered, as a boy, Marisa Seraphim's purchase of the great doors. She was long dead now, but there was a painting of her at Obernewtyn. She had been very beautiful, but everything in the picture spoke of her brilliance and will and nothing of her heart. Her diaries had revealed a woman as clever and ruthless as a teknoguilder without soul.

In the dream, Ariel's face had possessed that same brilliant, soulless quality as he moved forward to peer at the doors.

Drawing on my slippers, I wondered what it meant that Ariel had asked such questions in my dreams. I had the powerful feeling that he had asked something more, but I could not recall what or if I had answered. The questions had ended when I had heard Gahltha's cool mental voice calling my name. He had emerged from the shadows behind me in the tunnel, dark and even more magnificent than in life.

"Ride on me," his mind spoke to mine.

I had responded instinctively, vaulting onto his back. We had ridden a road that led eerily up into the clouds and the sky, leaving Ariel and the dreamcave far below. We had ridden impossibly high, until Gahltha sent to me that he was unable to go farther. Before I could say it did not matter, he bucked violently, sending me flying up like a stone from a catapult.

I had screamed in fear, but all at once, an Agyllian

flew beneath me. I clutched convulsively at the warm feathers and thin bones.

I had thought the bird was Atthis, except the Elder was blind and would have been too small to bear me. This bird was enormous, but pure white rather than red like the Agyllians.

"Things bear their spirit shapes on the dreamtrails," a voice had whispered, but so faintly I could not tell whose it was. The bird bore me silently ever up and out, through a swirling rainbow of color and light that ended only when I awoke.

It had been a peculiar dream. Not an ashling, for all its vividness; perhaps no more than the distorted summation of a long day of turmoil. Even so, it was hard to throw off.

I took refuge in practicalities. A swift farseeking scan told me Matthew and Kella were busy shifting the last boxes from the rig back into the safe house. There was no sign yet of Daffyd. Or, for that matter, of Maruman.

I gathered up my clothing, careful not to wake Dragon, who was still sound asleep. I crept from the room and padded along the hallway to the bathing chamber to splash my face and neck before dressing.

My eyes looked out of the mirror at me, bloodshot but alert. That was when I realized with horror that I had done nothing about the mental barrier I had set up to catch the pain of the whipping in the market. I knew better than anyone the danger of allowing too much pain to build up, for when freed, it had an accumulative impact—the pain from a simple leg cramp, left for too long, could become a crippling agony.

My heart thumped with apprehension as I began

carefully to dismantle the barrier. I went very slowly, so as not to flood my senses with too much of the stock-piled pain at once. It was always difficult to regulate the flow.

To my surprise, nothing at all leaked out of the minute gap I had made. Puzzled, I removed the barrier completely, but there was not even a slight ache waiting to be endured.

My expression in the mirror was blank with aston-ishment. Stored pain could not be released without experiencing it, so what had happened? Had Maire's herbal ointment somehow absorbed or counteracted the pain? Or had I dismantled the barrier and endured the pain in my sleep? A suppressing barrier *could* split open of its own accord, but it was hard to imagine sleeping through it.

On the other hand, it might explain the queerness of my dreams and the sluggishness that had filled me on waking.

Well, I had no complaint if that had been the case. Relieved to have been let off so lightly, I decided not to push my luck and disturb Maire's bandages. Instead, I simply put on a clean shirt and went to the kitchen. Over a late firstmeal, I told Matthew and Kella what had happened in the meeting with the slaver.

Not unexpectedly, Kella disapproved. As a healer, she did not accept the notion of revenge. But to my sur-prise, Matthew also chided me.

"Ye know Rushton would nowt approve. An' ye should at least have let me know where ye was goin'."

This caution was so unlike the farseeker that I stared at him.

His eyes fell away from mine, but I caught a swiftly

shielded memory of Dragon with her arms about the two children in the market. This Dragon was not the dirty urchin Matthew usually saw when he looked at the empath-coercer. She was older, and her eyes shone with courage. In its own way, it was no more a true picture of her than the old one had been, but at least it was no longer derogatory.

Matthew had always peopled the world with villains and heroes, and his head was stuffed full of wild scenes of courage and drama. The fleeting and idealized memory of Dragon defending the children suggested her mad-headed bravery had forced a change in his attitude toward her. Clearly, he was finding that confusing enough to distort his other cherished attitudes.

Domick arrived during midmeal. He was unsurprised to hear about my encounter with Daffyd, saying only that he had expected the armsman to turn up sooner or later. He had come to tell me that the search for the renegade gypsies had been shifted to Rangorn. "There is a rumor that you were sighted up that way, and three troops of soldierguards have been dispatched to search the area." That explained the absence of soldierguards on the street that morning.

I was impressed. The gypsy who had rescued me from the whipping might be arrogant and conceited, but he had said he would get the soldierguards out of the city, and he had done it.

Even so, I could not help being puzzled by the scale of the search, and I said so.

"Th' Council mun have some reason fer orderin' such a sizable search," Matthew agreed.

The coercer shrugged. "If they even ordered it. The soldierguards may have done it on their own. They have the power, and given that some of their men were killed in Guanette, they might want revenge."

"But rank-and-file soldierguards are a mercenary lot," I said. "They fight for coin, not for justice or loyalty to their fellows. I cannot see it troubling them that a soldierguard or two died. They would simply give thanks to Lud that it had not been them."

"Well, then it may be the Herders' doing," Domick said impatiently. "The fact that gypsies killed one of their people would enrage them, and they might be putting pressure on the Council to strengthen the search."

Especially if they believed a Twentyfamilies gypsy was involved, I thought. If they could prove that, it might destroy the accord.

"I want you to find out for sure whose doing it is," I said firmly. "And where the coin is coming from to recruit all of these soldierguards. I heard a soldierguard say the Faction is going to fund a war against Sador. If the Herders are splashing bribe coin about, we must know from whence it comes."

Domick snorted scornfully. "How would the Faction have coin to finance wars? What coin they have is extorted from their congregations. It would not be enough to bribe one soldierguard, let alone a captain. You make too much of this and worry where there is no need. The search is concentrated on Rangorn, as I told you, so what does it matter? They will not find you there."

There was an arrogance to Domick's surmising that dismayed me. Yet he might be right that I was overreacting. After all, how much did they know that would hurt us? Only that there were a few audacious youths who had flouted Herder authority on two occasions—unlikely, but not impossible. I still was not completely convinced that this was the reason why a larger than usual number of soldierguards might be sent out. But since there had been no obvious use of Misfit powers on any of the three occasions, it must be seen as a mystery relating to gypsies, not Talented Misfits.

After the meal, the coercer returned to the Council-court, and Matthew accepted Kella's offer to learn how to bake bread.

I decided to spend the afternoon trimming the horses' hooves and reshoeing them. This was done whenever we came to the city, for it was the only time horses were forced to walk on stones and cobbles. In the mountains, they had no need of metal shoes.

The afternoon shadows were long, striping the yard, when I hammered the last nail into the last shoe and stretched the taut muscles in my back. I took a comb and began to smooth Jaygar's tangled mane, worrying at how this life had changed Domick.

I would let Rushton make the final decision whether to bring Domick in. Regardless of his usefulness as a spy, my own instinct said we ought to bring him back to Obernewtyn. Surely, with Domick's inside knowledge, someone else might be insinuated in his place. And it would be wise to have someone else trained, just in case something ever went wrong.

For a second, I had a remarkably vivid vision of the coercer lying slumped in a Councilcourt cell, his hair long and matted, his body covered in sores and filth. I thrust the revolting image from me and made the warding-off sign, for I believed, as Maryon did, that things could be made to happen by thinking of them too much.

I finished the roan's mane, acknowledged his thanks, and turned to Gahltha, my thoughts circling back to Maruman and the hazy look that had been in his eye when I'd last seen him. It had been more than a full day, and I had been unable to find him with a finely attuned farseek probe. I knew the cat's mind as well as my own, but if he had fallen into one of his mad states, his mind would change its shape, rendering him invisible to a probe that was specifically shaped to his sane mind.

Was he wandering, mindless, in Sutrium? I wondered if I should have restrained him for his own good. Since I loved him, hadn't I the right to stop him from harming himself?

With something of a shock, it occurred to me that this was the sort of thinking that had made Gahltha try to stop me from helping the little mare Faraf. And that had once caused Rushton to forbid me to go on dangerous expeditions.

I would never exchange freedom for safety, I thought, regardless of the danger. I had the right to risk my life as I chose.

"Truly, danger is part of freedom/freerunning," Gahltha sent unexpectedly. "It is easy to forget this when it is not us/me."

"It's easy to have one rule for others and another for myself, but there's no honor in such double standards," I sent mildly.

"Honor?" Gahltha snorted. "That is a little word for a great thing. Funaga have freerunning thoughts. But instead of admiring/joying in them, you would cage them with words. Some things will not be so tamed."

I smiled a little, thinking how Maryon and her futuretellers, or Dameon in his most reflective mood, delighted in such complex ethical and moral discussions as this. They never tried to come up with a final answer. For them, the reason for such a mental journey was in the wordy road traveled.

But it was not enough for me to admire words and ideas as beautiful abstractions. I had to see how they could be applied. And I knew only too well that what worked in words was often very different when you tried applying it to a real situation. In essence, freedom of choice sounded a fine and noble thing. But in reality?

Putting away hammer and brushes and heading back upstairs into the safe house, I admitted wryly that it was difficult to be philosophical about Maruman and his right to freedom when I only knew I loved him and wanted to protect him.

The kitchen was filled with the exquisite fragrance of freshly baked bread, and Kella and Matthew were so engrossed in examining the results of their afternoon's work that they did not notice my entry.

"That first one was like a lump of stone," Matthew laughed. "I will take it back to Obernewtyn and offer it to Gevan as a new kind of weapon."

I had crossed quietly to the fire when I caught a movement at the door. I turned to watch Dragon glide into the kitchen, hollow-eyed underneath her murky skin-stain. Her eyes swept the room, coming to rest inevitably on Matthew, but there was no vestige of the adoration that had hitherto marked her regard for him. She stared at the Farseeker ward as if he were a window opened on a barren landscape whose existence she had not before noticed.

Something in her bleak regard chilled me to the bone.

Matthew sensed her eyes, but the moment he looked up, she looked away. Kella gave an exclamation and hurried over to her.

"How do you feel, love? Does your head still hurt?" She rubbed her floury hands on her apron to clean them, then curled an arm around the empath-coercer's shoulders, drawing her close.

"Hurts," Dragon echoed dully, standing passively in the healer's embrace.

Kella's brow creased in thought, and she shifted to her bench and riffled through a disordered pile of herb parcels to mix another herbal infusion. Once Dragon had swallowed the last drop, the healer tried to get her to eat something, but the girl showed no interest. She said listlessly that she would rather go back to sleep, and the healer led her out.

Frowning, Matthew lay a damp cloth over two more loaves he had just kneaded. Only then did he notice me standing by the fire.

He flushed, and I wondered at his thoughts.

Kella came back and, noticing me, offered to slice some bread for supper. I nodded and moved to help her. "What will Brydda do if Daffyd doesn't come tonight?" she asked.

"He will come," I said firmly, refusing to give voice to my fears. "In the meantime, after we have eaten, I am taking our gypsy home."

✦ 21 ✦

Daffyd had not come by the time I was ready to leave, and resolutely I dismissed him from my mind.

"I am taking you to your people, Iriny," I told the gypsy.

She started at hearing her name, but her strange two-colored eyes were defiant and shuttered. "Do as you will," was all she would say.

I explained that we had given her a sleep drug so that she would not be able to tell where she had been kept, nor how long the journey had taken to the gypsy camp.

"I don't care if you give me poison," she said, and there was a flash of pain that told me her mind was on her bondmate. Her eyes closed as Kella imposed another sleepseal.

It was strange, watching her fall into a deeper sleep. The gypsy had been with us for almost three seven-days, yet we knew as little of her now as when she had come among us. There had been no true exchange. Now we would never know, for there was scant likelihood of our ever meeting again.

Matthew and Kella carried her between them down to the cart and installed her safely inside while I changed into the elaborate Twentyfamilies attire Maire had given me. The loose, wide-necked shirt was designed to slide off one shoulder, but it exposed the bandages on my back. The other shirt she had given me was stained with blood, so after a moment's debate, I unwound the bandages gingerly, reasoning that since there had been no pain, the wounds must be a good way to healing.

To my surprise, they had healed completely. I was unable to feel any scabbing. I would have to ask Maire about the ingredients she used in her miraculous ointment; Roland would give much to have such a recipe.

Buckling a thick belt with its dagger pouch about my waist and sliding a knife into it, I came down to the rig to find Kella packing blankets around the unconscious gypsy.

Matthew was in front of the wagon, holding out the leather harnessing so that Gahltha could back into it. The horse's skin twitched with loathing as the farseeker buckled the straps that bound him to the false gypsy rig.

"Well!" Kella said, her eyes widening as she noticed the elaborate gypsy clothing.

I laughed self-consciously and flipped the full Twentyfamilies skirt to reveal a multitude of red and green petticoats. "Elaria has never been so well dressed."

"If only Rushton could see you like that," she giggled; then she flushed at my astonished look and began to fuss with the blankets.

"Let us go," Gahltha sent tersely. "I/Gahltha do not like the feel of this funaga bond."

We departed, and though the moon had risen early, it was low on the horizon, and, as on the previous night, ragged drifts of dark cloud made the evening a matter of shifting ambiguities and anonymous shadow. I set about erecting a formidable coercive enhancement of the rig to make it seem more fitting as a transport for a Twentyfamilies gypsy. The last thing I wanted was to be stopped because the rig did not match the rest of me.

As it happened, this was hardly necessary, for there appeared to be no soldierguards about, and the few people hurrying along, huddled deep in their coats and cloaks, paid no attention to me. It was a freezing evening, and I shivered in the light gypsy attire. I had not worn a cloak, because I wanted the Twentyfamilies clothing to be completely visible. I dragged a blanket around my shoulders from the back.

With little to do but sit and shiver, my thoughts wheeled back to Kella's words and their meaning. The healer had long been aware that something lay between Rushton and myself, perhaps because of her empath abilities.

What *would* Rushton make of the gaudy Twentyfamilies clothes? He had told me once that gypsy clothes made me look like another person: wilder and more reckless. In truth, I did feel bolder in gypsy clothes, but the Twentyfamilies attire made me feel different again; more than Elspeth Gordie and more than Elaria the half-breed.

In my mind's eye, I saw Rushton standing in the misty mountain dawn, watching me ride away, his expression brooding. A waiting look, yes, but also a questioning look. And what sort of answer would Elaria of the Twentyfamilies give to that unspoken query, dressed as I was?

"Funaga play too many games/hide much," Gahltha sent. "Beasts have not so many faces for truth-hiding.

Why not say what is true, be what is true? Why hiding/ pretending/untruthtelling?"

"I don't know," I sent soberly. "Perhaps because the truth is sometimes frightening."

"Truth is fair/light/bright. Lies are darkness/ fear/ignorance."

"Sometimes it is hard to know what the truth is. And sometimes truth is pain. Easier to hide the truth and make a secret of it than to face it."

"Truespoken," Gahltha sent.

We came out from a narrow street, and I was glad to see before us the dark wilderness that was the largest of the city greens at night. Fires bloomed like orange flowers in the darkness, illuminating the side of a great shaggy tree and the edge of a wagon. The faces of the gypsies were pale blobs clustered about each separate campfire, hemmed about by ragged shadow, the spaces in between fires pitch dark. The green had seemed smaller when I had come there in the daylight, and more ordered.

As Gahltha picked his way down the uneven rows of gypsy wagons, parked in clusters with a little cooking fire at the center, the night was filled with spicy food smells and strains of music—singing and the languid strum of gitas, sprinkled with frequent bursts of laughter. At one campfire, I saw a girl and a boy dancing closely, spinning away and back to one another in graceful accord.

"Gypsies dance for a lover. . . ." The gypsy's words came to me like a caress. I thought of his kiss and flushed, thrusting the memory from me.

A warmth and a camaraderie filled the night around me. I squinted as we wove about, trying to distinguish the elaborately carven wooden rig that belonged to Maire. We passed several Twentyfamilies rigs, but none resembled hers.

After a time, I began to despair, for aside from the difficulties of seeing in the dark, the wagon rows were crooked and folded hither and thither about on themselves. This meant several times we found ourselves going the same way we had passed already.

"Gahltha/I can farseek Sendari?" Gahltha offered.

At the same moment, an older Twentyfamilies gypsy stepped from the darkness and called out to ask my name. I chose my words very carefully. "I . . . I call myself Elaria." This was true enough.

He came nearer, and I had the same sensation as I had with Maire, that he was looking not at me but somehow around me. Suddenly I was very glad of the darkness.

"I am seeking Maire, the healer," I said, tensing in case the name provoked a reaction.

The man nodded mildly. "Well, she is here, but that is all I can tell you. Usually, she sets her wagon over yonder."

I nodded my thanks. Even so, we needed directions from Sendari to find the wagon, which was parked under a tree that seemed to wrap its branches around the rig protectively. A fire had been lit, and thick cuts of wood were set on end around it as rough stools.

The gypsy man who had rescued me from the whipping was seated at the fire. Beside him sat a plump, dark-haired gypsy girl and opposite were two gypsy men. The three were clearly Twentyfamilies—richly clad and with a certain haughtiness in their bearing. I wondered if one of them was Swallow.

Hearing Gahltha whinny to the other horses as we drew closer, the gypsy man looked up casually; then his eyes widened. He jumped to his feet, dismissing his companions with an imperious flick of his fingers. The two men went at once, giving me impassive looks, but the girl glared, first at the man, then at me, before flouncing off into the darkness.

"You look better in these than in the boyish trousers you wore last," he said when we were alone.

If I had been Maruman, hackles would have risen on my neck. "I have brought Iriny," I said tartly, climbing down. "She is in the back of the wagon."

I moved to open the curtain and show him, but he caught my arm to stay me and looked about before letting me go. "Have a care. We do not want anyone seeing her."

"You could have said so without mauling me." I rubbed my arm, though in fact he had not held me tightly. I merely wanted to make the point that I did not want him grabbing at me.

He smiled, flashing white teeth, but before I could think of something cutting to say to wipe the leer from his mouth, he had crossed to Maire's wagon and hammered on the carved panel.

"Maire!"

The old gypsy emerged in a pale nightdress and woolly shawl, her white hair hanging long and loose like skeins of cloud about her neck and shoulders. Her expression sharpened when she caught sight of me. "You have brought her?" she asked eagerly, climbing down with sudden agility.

I nodded, and to my astonishment, she flung her

arms around me and pressed me to her withered bosom. "Lud keep you, girl!"

After another long look around, she and the man carefully lifted the unconscious woman from the cart, laying her gently on the ground by the fire. Maire knelt by her and opened her eyelids with a gnarled finger.

Finally, she looked up at me. "Is she drugged?"

"No," I said. "She is sleeping. Our healer said she would wake tomorrow."

Maire looked impressed. "She is so accurate at diagnosing?"

I shrugged, and let her make what she would of that as an answer. To my relief, she bent and continued to examine Iriny, paying special attention to the scarred inner forearms.

"These are healing well," she said approvingly.

I was gratified for Kella's sake. "I daresay they'll heal faster with your miraculous potions."

"Is she all right, then?" the man demanded, interrupting our courtesies in an impatient voice.

"Haven't I just said so, you idiot?" Maire snapped with a sudden return to her old manner. "Are you going to stand there huffing like a fool or get her into the wagon before she dies of cold?"

Obediently, he bent to lift Iriny gently in his arms, staring down at her with a tender expression far removed from his earlier supercilious haughtiness. He climbed into Maire's rig, and the old healer followed.

The dark grass and the flickering flames of the campfire bent beneath a cold wind that plucked hair from my plait and flapped the elaborate skirts about my knees. Suddenly I felt very alone.

"Not/never alone," Gahltha sent from the darkness with all the intensity of a vow.

The gypsy man climbed from the wagon, a glint in his eyes that I did not trust. "I suppose you want your reward now?"

"Since you will leave tomorrow, yes," I said. "First, I want to know who Swallow is. Maire said I could meet him."

"And so you have," the gypsy said. "Swallow is one of *my* names."

I tried to hide my surprise. "One of your names? What does that mean?"

"Nothing more than I said. 'Swallow' is one name, just as 'Elaria' is one name. But there might be others a person would wear in different circumstances."

I scowled. "What does 'Swallow' signify, then?"

"Swallow is the man you see before you."

"Then you will not keep your bargain?"

He crossed his arms over his chest. "You asked to meet Swallow. Here is Swallow."

I wanted to shout at him for playing words against me, but I was too busy wondering why knowing who he was could save my life. Regardless, I had surely fulfilled Maryon's quest.

I put my hands on my hips. "There was another part to this bargain, *Swallow*. You promised to paint onto my arm one of those pictures you have on yours. Unless you have found reason to renege on that promise now."

Instead of becoming angry at my implication that he was a cheat, his smile merely broadened. "Gypsies always keep their promises. But perhaps we should discuss it first. . . ."

"There's nothing to discuss," I snapped.

He gave me an amused look and shrugged. "Very well."

His tone was so meek that I was instantly suspicious. "Sit down and I will prepare what is needed," he murmured.

I sat, watching warily as he went over and reached into a trunk set on the side of Maire's rig. He came back with a woven box somewhat smaller than the healer's box of potions and sat opposite me. Opening it, he withdrew a series of sharp spikes and some little glass bulbs of color.

"Where are the brushes?" I demanded.

"Brushes?" The gypsy gave me an innocent look, but the flames reflected in his eyes danced.

"The . . . the brushes you use to paint the design on. And what are those?" I pointed to the sharp little skewers laid out neatly alongside the box.

"They are needles; I use them to apply the design," the gypsy said, attaching a spike deftly to the top of a bulb of color. "The picture is created by a series of tiny stabs, which allows the color to seep beneath the skin and set. First I prick out an outline of the design, and then I fill in the color. Usually the process is carried out over many days, but since you want the whole thing at once, it will take the entire night."

I felt foolish and angry. "You did not tell me—"

His eyebrows lifted. "No? It must be because you did not want to be told anything. Traditionally, the designs are marked onto Twentyfamilies gypsies when we are swaddled babes and too small to be afraid."

I bridled. "I'm not afraid. What are you doing?"

"Putting them away," he said calmly.

I took a deep, shaky breath and did not speak until I

was certain my voice would be steady. "Not before you keep your promise." I pulled up the sleeve on my shirt and held out my arm.

He stared at me, for once apparently bereft of witticisms.

"Well?" I snapped, angry because I was beginning to feel sick with apprehension. "If it is going to take all night, you had better get started."

"You want me to use these on you?" He held up one of the sharp spikes.

I nodded, not trusting to the firmness of my voice.

His eyes glimmered, and slowly he again took out the bottles and needles.

I swallowed a great lump of terror and looked away from the needles into flames that seemed to shudder with fear.

"In the Beforetime, it was called a *tattoo*," Swallow said. There was no mockery in his voice or his eyes now, but I would not have cared if he had sneered openly at me.

My arm felt as if it were on fire. Some obscure pride had made me endure the pain rather than sealing it away behind a mental net. The individual pricks had not been so terrible, but now my arm felt as if it had been savaged by a hive of virulent bees. Only the strange, long story he had told me as he worked had helped me bear it. Contrary to common gossip, Swallow said the gypsies had come from the sea, led by one who had vanished when they reached the Land. And though the story had taken hours to tell, I sensed there was much left unsaid.

Swallow passed his arm across his forehead, wiping away beads of sweat. For a moment, our eyes met; then he bent over his design again. I tensed involuntarily, expecting another endless series of needles, but he released me almost at once.

"It is done. Of course, you won't see the full effect until the scabs form and fall away."

Then he gave me such a queer, searching look that I felt uncomfortable. I glanced down for the first time, and a wave of nausea struck me at the sight of the raw and swollen welts.

What have I done? I thought in dismay.

"Maire!" Swallow called, dropping the needles into a pot of water suspended above the fire. I took a deep, steadying breath. The stars had faded. It was the second night in a row I had been awake to see the dawn.

He moved to the wagon again and rapped on its side. "Maire! Wake up. It is done."

The gypsy healer had called us a pair of fools before stumping off to her bed. "It offends her sense of fitness," Swallow had said, his eyes gleaming with mischief.

Maire emerged from the wagon, dressed in day clothes and wearing a full apron. She ignored my arm and looked critically into my face. After a moment, she shook her head.

"It is madness. Well, let me see."

I held my arm out obediently, hoping she would apply some more of her miraculous salve, but instead she only mixed me a foul potion to drink.

Swallow laughed at my expression. "The cure is worse than the ill when Maire is displeased."

She gave him a scathing look and bent to examine the tattoo. "It is a good job, though I would as soon not add to his conceit by saying so."

Swallow grinned, then his eyes turned back to me and narrowed into the same discomfortingly searching gaze. He rose. "And now to complete the process, an honorary toast offered by the D'rekta. I am not he, but I will do, as the heir apparent."

Maire gave him an astonished look as he crossed to the wagon and climbed inside. After a moment, she took a bottle from her basket and sprinkled a sweet-scented powder onto the tattoo; then she bandaged it carefully and instructed me to leave it untouched for some days.

"What is a D'rekta?" I asked when she was done.

Maire gave me a haughty stare, and for a minute her resemblance to Swallow was startling. "The leader of the Twentyfamilies. Each D'rekta is the eldest blood descendant of the first, who led our people from the lost lands. The present D'rekta is Swallow's father, but there is little love and much duty between them. . . ."

Swallow returned carrying a small box—not a woven container this time, but a box made from wood and carved in the same wondrously intricate style as the wagon itself.

"The making of the Twentyfamilies mark is generally toasted by the D'rekta," he said. He opened the box and removed a jeweled goblet from its velvety recess. It was the most exquisite thing I had ever seen, all streaked with iridescent green and purple and globs of shimmering gold. If this was a sample of Twentyfamilies tithe ware, I did not wonder that the Council would keep their pact.

He took out a small corked vial made of the same dazzling material, unstoppered it, poured a measure of the liquid it contained into the goblet, and raised it to me. "I am for you, as you are for me."

He drank, and I heard Maire's indrawn breath when he refilled the glass and offered it to me.

"No!" Maire said in an outraged voice. "You make mockery of the ancient promises."

He looked at her, his face deadly serious. "There is no mockery in what I do, Maire."

The old woman glared. "Have you gone mad? She is not Twentyfamilies. Nor is she even a gypsy despite all her talk. Indeed, we know nothing of her other than that she saved Iriny. For that I thank her, but she is no part of our destiny."

Swallow took the healer's withered hand with a tenderness that made a nonsense of their bickering. "Trust me, Maire. She may not be a gypsy, but she is part of the ancient promises."

Her face sagged with shock. "But how can this be . . . ?"

"What is all this?" I demanded, but they ignored me, seeming to commune or to pit their wills in some silent way.

The old woman broke away first. "So," she said in a subdued tone.

Again Swallow offered the goblet to me. "Drink."

I shook my head. "Not until I know what I am drinking and what it means. I won't be bound by something I don't understand."

The gypsy's dark eyes bored into mine, but I met his look, and at last he set the goblet down. "The toast I offered is an oath of fealty to the ancient Twentyfamilies promises, by those whose fate is bound up in them. As is yours."

"I know nothing of these promises. And, as you have said, I am no gypsy. What could they possibly have to do with me?"

"I will tell you," he said with a queer fierceness. "This night I have done a thing"—he gestured at my arm tattoo—"that, were it known to my father, would see me hunted to death by my own kind. Anyone seeing it on you and discovering you were an impostor will know a Twentyfamilies made it, for no other has the secret. That will end the truce between the Council and my people. If you are captured and tortured, you will speak of it and of me and Maire, and again our lives would be worth nothing. Nor the lives of my people, for we will be forced to settle and become part of this Land."

I shook my head impatiently. "If giving me this was such a terrible thing, why didn't you just refuse?"

"It was the reward you named for returning Iriny."

"Even so, you might have refused."

"It was a promise," he said sternly.

I shook my head. "I don't understand. Your people are supposed not to break Council lore or have anything to do with those who do. What is Iriny to you that you would risk so much for her?"

"She is my half sister," he answered flatly. "Before my father bonded with my mother, and before he was D'rekta, he loved a halfbreed gypsy. She who bore Iriny. It mattered not with whom he bonded, since he had an older sister who was to inherit the D'rektaship. But when she broke her neck in a fall, my father was forced by duty to set Iriny's mother aside and choose a Twentyfamilies woman so that he could have a pureblood child. He chose a Twentyfamilies cousin to Iriny's mother, and I am their son."

Again there was a flash of that deep bitterness in his eyes. "'Swallow' is not my formal name but a pet name I was given as a child by Iriny."

I blinked, suddenly convinced that Swallow was the Twentyfamilies gypsy the Herder in Guanette had wanted Iriny to name. I resisted the urge to warn him, for how would I explain knowing it? Let Iriny tell him when she woke.

"My daughter bonded with the D'rekta, but there was no love between them," Maire said.

I stared from one of them to the other. "He is your grandson, then?"

Maire wrinkled her nose, seeming to recover her equilibrium.

Swallow gave a hard-edged laugh. "There is too much division among our people. When I am D'rekta, I will dissolve the Great Divide. The answer to the half-breed problem is not to sunder ourselves from them but to make them understand why we must remain separate from Landfolk. When I am D'rekta, any gypsy who swears fealty to the ancient promises will be one of us, whether they be purebloods or no. But until that time, I must appear dutiful and seem to believe in tradition. It is only as Swallow that I am free to help Iriny and, through her, the halfbreeds."

"Swallow is the name you take on when you are among the halfbreeds!"

He nodded. "I help them as best I can. Unfortunately, my sister does not confine her good works to halfbreeds, hence her plight in Guanette. Landfolk are not overgrateful to those who aid them. I warned her, but Iriny does not care about her safety."

"You do?" retorted Maire. "And do not speak ill of Iriny. She is an angel."

"She was almost a dead angel," Swallow said.

"How did you know we had her? Iriny, I mean," I asked curiously.

Swallow's dark eyes glimmered with amusement. "The day you rescued her in Guanette, I was the archer in the trees."

My mouth fell open. "You! But Matthew said your hair was white. At least . . ."

He grinned. "A little flour ages a man dreadfully. I heard Iriny and Caldeko had been taken, and I came to help them as Swallow. I was too late for Caldeko, but I was determined to save Iriny, even at the cost of my identity or my very life—for, regardless of the Great Divide, she is blood kin and I love her. I was in the trees waiting for the chance to arrow that Herder when you walked out of nowhere claiming to be her sister."

I felt myself flush. "It was all I could think of. . . ."

"Do not mistake me. When you spirited Iriny from Guanette, you saved me having to reveal myself. That was the first debt I owed. Then you healed her and brought her here. Even the Twentyfamilies sacred mark did not seem too great a price for all of that."

Swallow's eyes shifted to where Gahltha stood in the wagon traces.

"That day in Guanette, I saw a horse come to you, though you made no sign, nor did you call to it that I could hear. It knelt at your side as if to pay you homage and received Iriny's body gently. And when you mounted and were struck by the knife, it traveled from the village without letting you or Iriny fall. That seemed surpassing strange and an omen of some force to me.

"I rode directly to Sutrium, for I had to be present at the Council tithe, and my absence would be cause for dangerous questions. I thought you would follow and let it be known about the greens that you had Iriny.

"When no one came, I began to wonder if you were a gypsy after all. In retrospect, there were discrepancies—the things you had said to the Herder and your behavior—but I could not begin to imagine who would choose to mask herself as one of the most despised creatures in all the Land, for so the unlucky halfbreeds style themselves."

I kept my expression still and polite.

"The only answer I could come up with was one who had a greater secret to hide," Swallow said.

✦ 22 ✦

"I GUESSED THAT you and your friends were seditioners or escapees from a Councilfarm," Swallow went on. "I do not ask you to tell me if I am right. Yet, when next we meet, there will be no lies between us."

"Next time . . . ?"

He held up a hand. "Let that rest for a moment." He lowered his hand and hesitated, as if trying to frame what he would say in words. "You asked why I include you in the ancient promises. Know that there are those among my people with the sight—an ancient power passed down from the first D'rekta—which sometimes allows those who possess it to see what will happen before it comes to pass."

Futuretelling? His eyes caught my involuntary movement, and he stopped, but I said nothing.

"This is a strange power and perhaps a fearsome thing. My people do not invoke it lightly, for if it were known, those possessing it would be burned. One of my people with such power told of Iriny's capture. When I returned from Guanette, the same seer told me that Iriny would be brought safe to Sutrium by those who held her, but he could not tell if she would return safely to us. So I waited and set those I trusted to watch for you and your wagon. They saw nothing.

"Then, one night, a voice spoke in my dreams, such as the first D'rekta heard, telling me that if I were to find Iriny, I must go at a certain moment to a certain market."

From the edge of my sight, I saw Maire gape at him and understood this was as much news to her as to me.

He looked at her. "You know I am no seer, Maire, and so it seemed madness to obey a dream voice. Yet there was such power in it that it was not in me to disobey. When I came where the voice had bidden me, I saw you, Elaria, dressed as a boy, with a Landgirl, buying birds. I meant to speak with you when I rode after you, but you outrode me."

The gypsy's face was pale and tense, his eyes looking inward, dark with wonder.

"The voice spoke again into my dreams that night, sending me to another market, lest all promises be broken. That is exactly the words I dreamed: 'lest all promises be broken.' What could it mean but the ancient Twentyfamilies promises? I obeyed and so came to find you being whipped. 'Save her,' the dream voice had told me. 'She is everything to you.'"

We stared at one another. I thought my expression must mirror his, pale and shocked. Two people, I thought, sent out by seers to find each other. There was a terrifying symmetry in it.

"I obeyed the voice because . . . such voices of power speak for higher reasons than to save the life of one man or a girl—even if horses do bend knee to her or become lame in her aid." I felt myself flush.

He nodded gravely, as if my silence was an answer to something. "I obeyed, too, because it ill behooved me to disobey; I, who must someday carry the weight of the ancient promises of the Twentyfamilies, for they are also matters of high destiny."

I wanted to laugh to bring us down from such heights, but his expression was deadly serious and forbade such cowardly evasion. And a voice inside asked me who I was, of all people, to sneer at his talk of destiny and high things. Was not my own life ruled by the very incomprehensible mystic forces he was striving to name?

"Last night, as I held your arm and made the tattoo, I knew that the time of the ancient promises foretold by the first D'rekta draws near." He looked to Maire.

The healer paled. "Can it be so?"

"I saw a vision," he said. "I saw this girl speak the words of the ancient promises in the place where first they were made."

"No," I whispered, backing away. *Not again*, I thought incredulously, fearfully. Not another mysterious fatebinding. First the Agyllians had bound me to their quests, and then the beastkindred claimed me for their legends. And now the gypsies wished to chain me with their ancient promises?

Surely it could only be Atthis's doing? Why had she seen fit to let Swallow believe I was connected to these ancient promises? So that she could use him, just as she used Gahltha and Maruman's belief in beastlegends to make them watch over me?

"Do not fear this," Swallow said. "I will stand by your side when that day comes. I feel the weight of that meeting across my soul and across the fatepath of the Twentyfamilies like a great, heavy shadow."

Something burned in the gypsy's face that frightened me, for it told that he truly believed his words, and believing a thing so passionately must bring it to pass.

"This is madness," I said, but even to my own ears the words lacked conviction.

"Do not fear it," Swallow said. "I will consult the seer again, and perhaps when next we meet, I will know better what is to come. And we will meet again—sooner than you think—and I will stand at your side in battle."

He glanced around. Here and there, people had begun to emerge from their wagons to stir their cooking fires, for the sun had risen, not bright and red as on the day before but wanly, veiled in gray cloud. I saw this as from a great distance.

"The green begins to stir though it is early, for this day we of the Twentyfamilies go from Sutrium. You should leave now, before full light. People are more inquisitive under the sun's honest glare." He took up the little jeweled cup and offered it. "Will you drink before we part?"

My skin rose into gooseflesh. Learn what *Swallow* means, Maryon had charged me. Or Atthis. Well, I had done that, and perhaps this toast was part of it. I felt powerless to resist the fey forces that seemed to drive this man as much as they drove me.

I shivered and reached out to take the cup, drinking a little sip of the bittersweet elixir. He took it from my cold fingers, leaning near. "Have courage, girl. Never did I dream that I would live in such a time and, even less, that I would be part of the ancient promises, yet so it must be. There is great honor in such a fate."

There was a wild joy in his eyes that frightened me as much as anything he had said. An exalted recklessness.

"Come," Maire said briskly. "Before you go, let me look at the whip marks to see how they are healing."

She had stood apart from us during the matter of

the drinks, as if she did not want to hear what passed between us. I was relieved at her words, for they brought me back to earth and freed me from the searing radiance of Swallow's face.

I rose to face the old woman, composing myself. "The scars are healed already, thanks to your salve."

Maire snorted, so I turned and lifted my shirt to show her. There was a long curious silence, and I craned my neck to see the tiny woman. My heart bumped against my rib cage at the look on her face.

"What . . . what is it?"

She let my shirt fall, her expression bland. "Nothing. You are right. The whip marks have healed."

I searched her face, but there was nothing of the amazement I had seen a moment before. I had imagined it, perhaps. After all, why would the mere sight of my back healed by her own potions give rise to such a look?

"I . . . I'd better go," I said to her. "I hope Iriny recovers completely." I turned to Swallow, forcing myself to meet his eyes, their black longing. "I do not think we will meet again, but I thank you for this." I touched my arm gingerly. "I swear that I will be careful and sparing in my use of it, and that no harm will come to you because of it. Goodbye."

He bowed. "I will say only this: ride safe, for whether you believe it or no, we will meet again."

Gahltha made no comment as I climbed into the wagon, though he had been privy to much of what had taken place. I had felt the light touch of his mind several times through the night.

Well, why would he object? I thought somewhat bitterly. He, too, believed I was part of higher matters and relished his own role in them. Too bad that I had no choice.

As we passed from the green, I glanced back through the forest of wagons to Maire's elaborate rig. Neither she nor Swallow were to be seen, and even as I watched, the last ragged flame from the fire, into which I had stared for so many hours, flickered and died in the rising wind.

Threading through the streets back to the safe house, I was certain that the voice that had summoned Swallow to my aid belonged to the Agyllian elder, Atthis. But did the birds always act in such secretive ways? Why not come to my mind and warn me? I thought of the tattoo I have been given and wondered if the Agyllians had any knowledge about the design since it featured them.

Only when Gahltha came to a halt did I start awake and realize we were back at the safe house. I was so fatigued that I had actually fallen asleep sitting up.

In fact, I still felt tired; this puzzled me. I always seemed to be tired lately, as if there was some hidden but constant drain on my energies.

Gahltha almost ran the wagon headlong into Matthew, who was coming out the gate at a breakneck pace mounted on Jaygar. I braked the wagon, and the rig slewed to a halt.

"Where have ye been?" Matthew cried, his accent thicker than usual. "I were about to go out lookin' fer ye."

I stared at him wearily, too tired to be bothered with his histrionics. "I have been with the gypsies. You knew that."

I brought the wagon properly into the yard and climbed down to release Gahltha from the harness. He did not trot away but turned to nuzzle at me.

"Elspeth, it's Dragon . . ." Matthew slid clumsily down from Jaygar's back.

"What is it?" I asked. "Has she run off again?"

"She . . . she were complainin' that her head hurt earlier. . . ." Matthew passed a shaking hand over his eyes as if to erase a nightmare.

Suddenly I was wide awake. "Tell me."

He opened his mouth, but before he could speak, tears spilled down his cheeks.

I swung around and ran into the shed and upstairs to the safe house.

"Dragon!" I yelled, slamming open the door. "Dragon, where are you?"

Kella emerged from the healing hall, her face grave and sorrowful. "Inside," she said.

Dragon lay on the mattress nearest the door. The gypsy had occupied the same bed, and it was as if one pale corpse had been exchanged for another. The empath-coercer's red-gold hair lay like frozen flames over the pillow.

"What happened to her?" I whispered.

Kella shook her head. "I don't know exactly. She and Matthew were arguing. I heard a thump; then Matthew burst out of the kitchen yelling that Dragon had fainted."

"She fainted?" I cried. "Is that all? You scared the living daylights out of me! Matthew met me at the gate as if someone had been killed."

"Elspeth, you don't understand," Kella said. "This is no ordinary sleep. Dragon has fallen into a coma. I can't reach her!"

◆ 23 ◆

"How LONG HAS she been like this?" I demanded.

"Not more than half an hour," Kella said. "It happened after firstmeal."

I felt sick. "A coma. I don't understand. How could it just happen like that for no reason?"

From the corner of my eye, I noticed Kella open her mouth and then close it again.

"What is it?"

The healer bit her lip. "It's possible that you . . . damaged the blocked part of her mind when you forced your way past her mindshield to—"

"Are you saying I caused the coma?"

"You go too far and too fast," Kella said, the softness of her tone a protest at my stridency. I resisted an urge to shout at her that it did not matter how loudly I talked—Dragon would not hear it. Kella pulled the covers around the empath-coercer's neck and gestured for me to follow as she left the room.

In the kitchen, the scent of food cooking only served to heighten my feeling of unreality. A fire blazed on the hearth, but it was some moments before my mind registered that Brydda was sitting in a chair before it.

He rose to greet me.

"I had gone out to the market to get some milk and

then bumped into Brydda downstairs," Kella explained. "We were coming up together when we heard them arguing. When we came into the kitchen, Dragon was lying on the ground."

"I struck too hard," I said.

The healer sighed. "There is no certainty of that. Damage to a blocked memory is not uncommon. Sometimes an eruption occurs spontaneously, and once disturbed, the memory inside will develop and shift until the block is shattered. Often that is the best thing, but Dragon's memory block is very deep-seated. The chances of her mind being able to deal with a flood of unresolved memories is slim. The whole healthy mind would typically be sucked into a sort of mental whirlpool revolving around whatever has been repressed. Eventually, all normal thought would be absorbed, and there would be nothing left in her mind but that single matter replaying itself again and again."

My skin prickled with horror as the meaning of her words sank in. "You mean she will be defective when she wakens?"

Kella held up her hands. "I said that *would* have happened, but Dragon's mind retreated, which is the best thing that could have happened under the circumstances."

"You call a coma the best outcome?"

"Everything is relative," the healer said firmly. "At some level, Dragon obviously sensed the block was damaged and likely to break open, and she willed herself inside it. This means that, right now, she is caught up in a loop of blocked memories: reliving over and over what she has repressed as she tries to resolve whatever caused her to block it out in the first place."

"Then she'll come out of it when she has sorted herself out?" Brydda asked, struggling with unfamiliar concepts.

Kella shook her head helplessly. "That is what we must hope. But there is no predicting how long it will take. It could take a year or a day or a minute."

I stared into the healer's face, seeing only my own culpability. With a flash of despair, I thought of Jik and Cameo and wondered if it would always be my fate to lead those around me to destruction.

"Elspeth, you blame yourself too much," Kella chided.

I glared at her. "Too much? How much should I blame myself, then? And who will take the rest of the blame? Dragon?"

"Perhaps," the healer said quietly. "It may be that this is indeed her own doing."

"It is *my* fault she's in a coma," Matthew said, hearing the last as he entered the kitchen.

Kella gave him a weary look. "I wish the pair of you would stop fighting over who is to blame and listen when I say the coma might be a natural development."

"Natural?" he murmured.

She nodded vigorously. "Exactly. This would have happened sooner or later, because Dragon never intended to forget her past. She didn't push her unwanted memory into her subconscious, the way the gypsy woman tried to do. Instead, she encysted it in her *conscious* mind—forgotten, yet not forgotten. She stored it as if whatever she has suppressed contained both something unbearable and something precious."

I tried to decide if her words offered hope or absolution, but my weariness had returned with redoubled force. I felt numbed.

"I have to get some sleep," I mumbled, but did not move.

"I am sorry for what has happened to Dragon. Truly I am," Brydda said, shifting forward to look into my face. "But life rarely permits us time to regroup or to mourn. I have come here because I need your help, and sad as this is, it does not change my need."

"Again?" I asked bleakly. "I could not help you last time. And I have been out all night. . . ."

The rebel shook his head. "I do not need you until tonight. You can sleep until then."

"What then?"

Brydda's expression hardened. "Daffyd has not come, and I am supposed to take the slaves to the warehouse for the slaver's people tonight. I mean to deliver them as agreed so that I can track them back to Salamander. Eventually, they will have to come to him. I cannot have them followed, because Salamander will certainly have someone watching. He would be a fool if he did not. But you could use your mind to track the slaves safely."

"I could," I said. "If they are not shielded and if they are not taken over tainted ground or water. And if a thousand other things that could go wrong don't."

Brydda looked taken aback at my fierceness.

I tried to explain. "It is difficult enough to farseek a Talented and a known mind in a city streaked with impenetrable tainted areas and among all these other mind patterns, let alone someone who is both unTalented and unknown."

Matthew sat forward, a flare of eagerness driving away the despairing guilt of moments before. "Th' slave you use as a marker need not be unknown or unTalented."

264

I stared at him, uncomprehending.

"I could take th' place of one of th' slaves," Matthew said.

I only stared at him.

"Ye'd have no trouble keepin' a probe on me. Ye could do it from here."

"No," I said. "The blind spots . . . I could lose contact with you—"

"Nowt fer long, if ye follow physically as well," Matthew interrupted. "Farther back than anyone would bother with but close enough to feel where I am, even if ye can't farseek me. I'd have my mind open to ye all th' time."

"It's out of the question," I said.

"Very well," Brydda said firmly, stopping Matthew's protest before it was uttered. "But you will trace the slaves?"

"If I lose them, they will be condemned to live as slaves."

The rebel's face hardened. "As they would have done had I not intercepted them. Perhaps they would think it fair odds, since I am trying to stop this foul trade altogether."

"The end justifies the means?" I asked cynically. "Have you given them a choice?"

The rebel frowned. "As far as they know, they are still captives held by slavers. They are resigned to their fates. This is the real world, Elspeth, and I am doing the best I can. I will not lose this chance," he said harshly.

I sighed. "I will track them. But I'll have to come to the warehouse so that I can get a fix on one of their minds."

Brydda rose and took a scrap of paper from his

pocket. "Here is a map showing where it is. The slaver said he would send his people to pick up the slaves before dawn, so I suggest you arrive well before that. I will be waiting for you."

"He also told you to get rid of me, so it will be better if I do not come inside."

Brydda frowned. "I doubt he will come in person, but perhaps you are right. We should not take the chance. You will have to get into position somewhere outside. Will that be close enough?"

I nodded and committed the route and warehouse location to memory before handing the paper back.

"You should assume you are being watched as soon as you get into the area."

"Am I nowt to come, then?" Matthew asked, caught between pleading and demanding.

Brydda looked at me.

"You had better come with me," I decided. "When we arrive, you will go inside the warehouse with Brydda and pretend to be his assistant. With different clothes and in the darkness, you can pass yourself as a seaman's lad. The skin stain has faded enough. With you inside, I can use your eyes to see what is going on there and communicate with Brydda even as I track the slaves."

The rebel nodded. "When you let us know where they have been taken, we will ride after them." He frowned. "No. On second thought, Salamander may have Matthew and me watched for some time after the slaves are taken to ensure we don't try to follow. I will have some rebels stationed nearby. Can you ride to them and tell them where the slaves are taken?"

I nodded, feeling incapable of more. Brydda stood

and squeezed my shoulder. "Get some sleep," he murmured.

"Ye should have let me do it," Matthew said sullenly after Brydda had gone. "There would have been no risk."

"There is risk in everything," I said, thinking of Dragon. I stood up.

"Wait!" Kella protested. "You haven't told us what happened with the gypsies. . . ."

Kella and Matthew both stared at me expectantly. I yawned and rubbed at my eyes. "I'm too tired to go into it all now, but I took her back." I looked at Kella. "The gypsy healer said you were a good healer."

She flushed with pleasure.

I stumbled down the hall and into my bedchamber, falling into the bedding fully clothed. Dimly, I wondered if it was possible that something was wrong with me. I felt incredibly fatigued, and this was not the first time. I had felt the same unnatural tiredness after the whipping. Perhaps this time it was because of the tattoo. Every time I was injured, my mind and body seemed to withdraw.

I flung my hand out, seeking the comfort of Maruman's rough, warm fur, but the place where he slept by my head was cold and empty. With an ache, I wondered where he was and if he was safe.

"Sleep the shortsleep. . . ." I heard Gahltha's voice in my mind. "I/Gahltha will guard the dreamtrails in place of Maruman/yelloweyes."

And sleep claimed me again.

⋅ 24 ⋅

THUNDER GROWLED IN the distance, and it began to rain.

I felt a prickle of unease, for a storm could play havoc with farseeking powers, and it would make retaining a link with one of the slaves that much more difficult.

Incredibly, I had slept all day, waking only when Matthew had roused me after dusk. But I was much refreshed; the numbing exhaustion was gone.

We had decided to ride together on Gahltha, for one horse would be far easier to cloak than two. As usual, Matthew's emotions impeded his ability to shield. This, combined with our close physical proximity, meant that I was shortly awash in his remorse over Dragon's coma.

Strengthening my shield to block his emanations, I felt a touch of anger that he would wallow in his guilt after having treated Dragon so shabbily.

"You should dismount here," I said. We were still several streets over from the warehouse, but I wanted to take no chances. "You had better get your mind fixed on what is ahead of us, rather than on what cannot be helped."

I ignored the farseeker's sudden rigidity and the

belated, mortified strengthening of his mental shield as he dismounted.

"You go on to the warehouse," I said, "and after a bit, I will follow. When I'm in place, I will farseek you to find out where Brydda's people are waiting."

Matthew nodded; then he shuddered violently.

"What is it?"

"I dinna know. I felt as if someone walked over me grave. Maybe ye should come inside, too. Anyone might spot ye in th' street."

Touched by his concern, my irritation at him faded.

"I will make sure no one sees me," I promised. "I have to stay out here so I can trail the slaves without being seen."

Matthew still hesitated.

"Go on," I urged, giving him a push. He turned to go. On impulse, I called, "Be careful."

"You be careful, too," he called in a low voice, and loped off.

I let a small farseeking probe drift with him. When he had gotten inside the warehouse, I signaled Gahltha, who turned into a lane a short way along the street. I dismounted, and he moved swiftly into the shadows at the end of the lane. It was a dead-end alley with no doors opening out into it, which meant no one could come up behind me. On one side, the sloping roof of an adjoining building had sagged into a dip at the center and thereby cast a deeper pool of shadow. This was where Gahltha positioned himself.

I stayed farther up the lane and leaned against the corner in the shadows. From this position I would be all but invisible even without coercion, and I could see both ways along the street leading to the warehouse. I set loose a general farsensing net, which would alert me to any movement in the streets, then shaped a probe to Matthew's mind signature and sent it flying in the direction of the warehouse.

As soon as he felt me, the farseeker opened his mind to permit me access to the synapses and nerves that would enable me to see through his eyes. I occupied these only passively for the moment, taking in the cavernous warehouse as Matthew looked around slowly for my benefit. The view was wavering and indistinct as if I were peering through a stream of water, but the image would sharpen if I took active use of his sight.

Dimly, I watched Brydda approach. The big man's face looked slightly less battered than usual, and it took me a moment to realize Matthew's hero worship of the older man was coloring his view. If I took over his sight, I would see Brydda clearly. Or rather, I would see him as I usually did. Intrigued with this thought, I wondered how much my own view was shaped by my emotions.

They spoke for some minutes, but I could not hear what they were saying; then they came down to the end of the warehouse.

"He is taking me to see the slaves," Matthew sent.

The five men stood passively in a little group, and I was puzzled by their stillness until Matthew sent to me worriedly that they had been drugged by Brydda to prevent their being questioned by whoever came for them, which could give the whole thing away.

I suppressed a surge of consternation at this news. I had not thought to warn Brydda that drugs would bar me from the slaves' minds.

Matthew and Brydda spoke again at some length.

Through the farseeker's eyes, I saw the rebel's look of surprise. Then he shrugged and nodded.

"What is he saying?" I asked Matthew curiously.

"He is saying the drug will take about three hours to wear off."

"I will have to—"

I broke off at the touch of Gahltha's soft muzzle against my shoulder. At the same time, I became aware of the warning tug of my farsensing net. I had been so engrossed in what was going on inside the warehouse that I had not felt a thing.

"Funagas come," Gahltha sent succinctly before moving back into the inky shadows at the end of the alley.

My senses told me there were two people walking swiftly along the street toward the warehouse, talking in low, intent voices. I poked my head out a fraction. They were some distance away, but I could see in the light of the single street lantern that they were both men; one was small and slender, while the other was at least twice his companion's size.

I shaped a probe and tried to enter the larger man. He was a Misfit but not Talented. His mind was buckled and distorted—hopelessly defective. I could pick up nothing more than a miasmic desire to cause pain, and I could not enter.

Shuddering, I withdrew and entered the smaller man's mind. It was something of a relief that he was neither defective nor naturally shielded. It was a moment's work to learn that he had been hired by Salamander, but there was no memory that would show me what the slavemaster looked like. He had simply been approached in an inn by a beautiful dark-haired woman bearing a note with Salamander's mark. It offered a relatively large amount of coin for what seemed to him a minor job. He had hired the defective because of his strength and brutish appetites, and because it never hurt to have a bit of muscle on one's side.

His thoughts showed that he admired Salamander's ruthless efficiency as much as he feared him. Apparently, the slavemaster had a reputation of being generous to those who performed their given tasks well and utterly vicious to those who failed.

He did not expect to fail, though.

His instructions were simple. Just before midnight, he was to go to the warehouse where he would find a man named Bollange waiting with five men. Though it had not been said, he understood that these men were to be sold as slaves. The woman had given him a bag of coin, which he was to give to Bollange once an examination of the slaves had proven them sound of limb. He was to bind and gag the slaves, then bring them outside where a wagon would collect them.

His final instruction was to kill anyone who tried to follow or stop the wagon.

I mouthed a curse at the realization that here was another dead end. He did not know who would come to collect the slaves, nor where they were to be taken. Withdrawing, I sent out a roving probe.

Several streets distant, I found what I was looking for—a man sitting in a closed wagon, waiting.

I was relieved, knowing there would be no need to track the slaves now. I could simply read their destination from the wagon driver's mind.

Unfortunately, when I tried to enter him, a strange buzzing vibration distorted his thoughts so that I could not negotiate them. I then tried to enter at his subconscious level; though this was also slightly distorted, I gained entry and rose up to his conscious mind. His thoughts at this level were chaotic, and only by chance did I encounter the driver's thought that he enjoyed the slightly hallucinogenic quality of the Sadorian spiceweed he was chewing. It had been gifted him by the same dark-haired emissary from Salamander. That explained the queerness of his mind.

Unable to gain a hold, my probe slithered loose before I could learn the slaves' destination. When I tried to reenter, his mind barred me even at the subconscious level. This suggested that the spiceweed produced a certain sensitivity to mental intrusion.

Glumly, I withdrew; if I could not gain a hold on the driver's mind when he was stationary, I had no hope of keeping track of him once he began to move.

The only solution now was to track the wagon physically, using my coercive powers to hide myself and Gahltha from any watchers. There would be no time to inform Brydda's waiting rebels.

To my consternation, the two men stopped right in front of the lane where I was concealed. I drew back slightly into the shadows. At first I thought they had spotted me, but I soon realized they had simply stopped to confer.

A slight coercive enhancement of my hearing enabled me to make out their words.

"I want you to stay out here and keep watch," said the smaller of the pair. "I'll go inside and see Bollange. If anyone comes along, kill them."

"Kill," the hulk echoed.

"Exactly. Now, when I come out with the slaves, you

stay where you are. Understand? Stay and watch for a while. That way we'll see if this fellow has traitoring on his mind. If he has, we'll get a bonus for putting him out of the picture. You got that into your skull, Lill? You stay and watch until I come back for you."

"Lill watch?"

The second man nodded. "Yeah. And if anyone so much as pokes their nose out the door, you know what to do."

"Stay?"

"No, stupid! You kill. Get it? If anyone comes out, kill them."

"Wait. Watch. Kill." The brute repeated the words lugubriously.

"Right. Now go and hide. That alley looks like a good spot."

He pointed straight toward the lane where I was hidden!

Frantically, I tried to coerce the shambling giant against the idea, forgetting that he was defective and therefore impenetrable. By the time I thought of coercing the second man to change his instructions, he had already gone striding off toward the warehouse, his mind on other matters.

There was nothing I could do but remain utterly still as Lill bore down on me. I dared not even shift back to where Gahltha was.

For a minute, we were literally face to face, and I thought my heart would batter its way right through my chest. Fortunately, he barely glanced down the dark end of the lane, turning instead to face the street and the warehouse. "Stay. Watch. Kill," he muttered to himself.

Behind him in the shadows, a bare handspan away,

I could feel sweat crawl down my back. Trying to stay calm, I shaped a probe and sent it to Matthew to warn him that I was trapped in an alley by a man whom I could not coerce and dared not confront physically—especially since any confrontation would alert Salamander that his network had been contaminated, setting off the very bloodbath we were at pains to avoid. I told him swiftly about the second man approaching the warehouse and about the carriage driver.

Dimly, I registered the sound of knocking at the warehouse door.

"Tell Brydda not to send the slaves, because I have no way of tracking them. Have him quibble about the coin," I sent urgently, knowing Matthew would have to speak to Brydda before the hired thug was inside the warehouse.

I slid along my probe and into Matthew's waiting mind. The interior of the shed swam dimly into focus. I was startled to find that Matthew seemed to be standing behind the Councilfarm workers. Was he trying to keep himself out of sight?

"What is happening? Did you tell Brydda?"

"Everything is fine," Matthew sent with admirable calmness, and my panic subsided slightly. "Are you all right out there?"

"I am as long as I don't move a muscle or make a sound."

"Lucky ye've no need to move with a farseekin' probe."

My heart began to thump again. Could he have possibly misunderstood me? "Matthew, I told you I can't farseek the carriage driver any more than I can farseek the slaves."

"You can now," the farseeker sent. "I've taken th' place of one of th' slaves. Ye need nowt blame Brydda— I told him ye'd changed yer mind. As things transpire, it's lucky I did."

I could not deny that entirely, but I was filled with a terrible foreboding.

"Matthew, if something goes wrong . . ."

"Nothin' will go wrong. Ye'll trace me, an' when ye can move, ye'll lead Brydda to me an' th' others."

I bit my lip. It sounded simple, but life seldom went according to plan. On the other hand, we had no choice now. The slaver's hired thug was inside the warehouse, and Matthew was committed to his course of action. It was not the time to tell him that sacrificing himself was no way of atoning for his treatment of Dragon.

The slaver's man was now examining the slaves, feeling their limbs and making them walk about to ensure they were not lame. Matthew's eyes did not look at him directly, and this annoyed me until I realized he was deliberately letting his gaze wander as if he was drugged like the others.

I had a single clear glimpse of the squat fellow and his mouthful of blackened teeth as he peered right into Matthew's face. As his lips moved, I wished I could hear through Matthew's ears as well, but we had not yet found a way to achieve that.

"What is happening?" I asked Matthew.

"He's claimin' we're all defectives. Brydda is arguin' that we are drugged," Matthew sent. "Now th' slaver is sayin' he has no instruction to say we're meant to be drugged."

There was a pause.

"Brydda's makin' th' fellow think he's a coward. He

said he was nowt takin' any chances on us tryin' to run away or fight him. It looks as if he's bought it. Yes, he's givin' Brydda the bag of coin."

Abruptly, I withdrew from the farseeker's mind, conscious of a warning tug on my senses. At once, I became aware of the clatter of carriage wheels on the cobbled street.

The carriage driver had come for his passengers.

In front of me, Lill flattened himself to the wall as the wagon rattled past the lane opening. It was a closed rig without windows; once Matthew was inside, there would be no using his eyes to orientate myself.

I crossed my fingers hard that nothing would go wrong.

I returned to Matthew's mind and found he had now been bound and gagged along with the other four. "The man has told Brydda to stay inside the warehouse until daylight. If he comes out before that, Salamander will have him killed."

My heart sank at the thought of being forced to stay perfectly still in the lane all night.

"Now he's bringing us outside. . . ."

Through the farseeker's eyes, I saw the wagon and the surly carriage driver. He said nothing as he climbed down and unbarred the back of the carriage. The slaver's hired man loaded in the five, including Matthew, and slammed the door shut, plunging the interior of the wagon into darkness.

I left a probe with Matthew and withdrew to my own mind to watch the carriage trundle past again.

The hired thug strode off down the street, and Lill shifted forward stealthily to watch the warehouse. I waited with my ears peeled for any sound in the street.

"Wait," the brute muttered in a disgruntled tone after some time, and he relaxed slightly. Only then did I relax, too, realizing Brydda must know not to come out. There was nothing more to do but wait until the other man came back for Lill.

My probe was still securely locked into Matthew's mind, and I tested it for the thousandth time.

"Dinna hold on so tight," he protested with a mental wriggle.

Apologizing, I loosened my grip.

"I think we're stoppin'," the farseeker sent suddenly. "Perhaps—"

The carriage door was flung open, and I could see nothing as he was blinded by the brightness of a lamp. Matthew blinked rapidly, trying to restore our vision.

As his eyes adjusted, I saw the face of the man holding the lamp. A feeling of terror assailed me, for it was the very same soldierguard captain who had seemed to recognize Dragon in the market!

"Who's there?"

The surly grunt dragged me instantly back to my own body as the hulking Lill turned to peer into the shadowy lane. I realized with dawning horror that I had gasped aloud!

He dropped a great paw to his belt and withdrew a long-bladed knife, squinting to see more clearly as he took a careful step forward.

One more step and he would literally fall over me, but his eyes were on the end of the lane. He had no idea how close I was. I was paralyzed with terror.

"Move/shift," Gahltha sent sharply. A split second later, he gave a shrill whinny and charged the thug.

The man issued a bellow of fright and stumbled backward, dropping the knife as the black horse leapt at him and over into the street. He turned his head to watch Gahltha gallop away into the night, and as he did so, I sprinted lightly to the sagging roof above the alley and hauled myself up. The sound of hooves on the cobblestones drowned out any noise I had made, and I lay completely still.

There was a long silence as the thug got to his feet and retrieved his knife. He turned and came down the lane, brandishing it purposefully. Fortunately, it did not occur to him to look up, and when he found no one, he shrugged in bafflement, muttering to himself about abandoned horses as he returned to his position at the head of the lane.

I lay for some moments shivering before I realized that I had lost contact with Matthew.

I remembered the soldierguard captain with renewed shock and sent out an attuned probe to find Matthew, wondering what on earth a soldierguard was doing with slavers.

The probe would not connect.

With burgeoning fear, I tried again and again, concentrating fiercely on Matthew's mental signature.

It would not locate.

On the verge of panic, I swept the entire area surrounding the place where I had last had contact with the farseeker.

Nothing.

✦ 25 ✦

THE GIANT, LILL, abandoned his post several hours short of daylight after a sudden downpour. Drenched to the skin, I hurried into the warehouse to tell Brydda what had happened. The cloudburst had ended by the time we came out, and Gahltha emerged from his own hiding place to carry us to where Brydda's people were still waiting for me in an abandoned house. The rebel leader gave them instructions to scour the area where I had lost contact with Matthew.

I went back and forth in the area, riding Gahltha farther than a carriage could have traveled in any direction. I farsought Matthew until the heavens opened up again, the season showing its claws. I stopped only when torrential rain fell so heavily that it obscured the surrounding streets like a gauze curtain, and the storm rendered me all but mindbound.

There was nothing to do but return to the safe house and break the news about Matthew. Brydda and Reuvan had come with me, leaving their people to continue searching.

We huddled over a fire lit hastily by Kella. The noise of rain on the tin roof was thunderous, and water ran in a gurgling torrent along the roof guttering.

"Maybe you couldn't farseek Matthew because he is asleep," Kella offered timidly.

I coughed and pulled a blanket closer about me. "I was inside his mind when he saw that soldierguard captain, Kella. Matthew recognized him just as I did. There would be no way he could just drop off to sleep after that. Not in such a short time. I was out of touch for a couple of minutes at most."

"I meant he might have been *put* to sleep," the healer persisted. "If he was drugged or knocked unconscious . . ."

"I would not be able to communicate with him, but if I was close, I would have felt his presence when Gahltha and I combed the area."

"Maybe you made a mistake about where they were when you lost touch."

I shook my head.

"All right," Brydda said. "Then maybe more time passed than you reckoned. The Suggredoon is not far from where you lost them. If they put him on a boat while you were out of contact, you could not have reached him, because, as you said, the water has been tainted."

Reuvan disagreed. "A boat could not have come up to the river wharf, because it would have been low tide and there is a barrier of exposed mudflats."

I said nothing, numbed by so much catastrophe. My throat ached with despair. I looked down at my hands clasped together in my lap, feeling a strong urge to weep.

Matthew's image floated before my eyes, alternating eerily with the thin limping boy I had first met and the young man he had become.

"It is as if he was just snuffed out of existence," I murmured, then was aghast at what I had said.

The slavers had killed Idris. Why not Matthew as well? I blinked away a horrid vision of the farseeker's body washed up on the tide.

"What if the soldierguard captain recognized Matthew from the market? He would know straightaway something was wrong. Maybe he suspected a trap and just . . . just . . ." I could not speak my worst fear.

I found I was weeping after all.

Brydda clasped me in his big arms. "If this soldierguard had known the lad, killing him outright would be the last thing he would do. Salamander would want to question him, wouldn't he?"

My eyes widened as an incredible thought occurred to me. "Brydda . . . what if the soldierguard *was* Salamander!"

I broke off in a savage fit of coughing that scratched my throat and made Kella eye me sternly. But she was distracted by Domick's arrival. As the coercer divested himself of his sodden cloak, Brydda told him what had been happening.

Domick maintained his calm. "I think you are right in guessing he is not far from where you lost contact with him. Salamander would not risk the wagon being stopped and searched by soldierguards, even with some of them in his employ. He would have instructed his people to get the slaves somewhere safe until he was ready to take them by boat."

Brydda nodded. "Domick is right. Salamander does nothing in haste, and he never exposes himself or trusts anyone. He would have the slaves taken somewhere so he can watch and make sure it is not a trap. That's the way he works. Slave ships depart from Morganna, so Matthew and the others will have to be taken over the Suggredoon. That means they must travel by the ferry or by a hired riverboat. Since we cannot find where they have been hidden, we will set a watch on the Suggredoon."

"It might be wise to watch all the city gates," Reuvan said. "They might be taken inland first and across the river at the Ford of Rangorn. Salamander will have to figure out the least dangerous way to get five drugged and bound men out of Sutrium. That rules out the ferry, since the slaves would have to walk on board if they were to journey that way. Drugged slaves would be obvious at once."

"Not necessarily," Domick said. "With some drugs, the five slaves would simply obey instructions to walk onto a ferry or out of Sutrium and be rounded up outside by their masters later."

Reuvan and Brydda looked thoughtful.

"I have never heard of such drugs," I said.

"They are brought in from Sador," Brydda said. "They are a by-product of the spice groves."

"I have not had the chance to make a report about them to Rushton yet," Domick said. "They enable you to function normally in every way except that you are utterly docile and suggestible. It is much simpler to deal with obedient puppets than with unconscious bodies or men and women who have been drugged into a shambling idiocy. This soldierguard captain would certainly know of them well enough, since the Council have them using it on prisoners."

"But it doesn't make sense that he would drug them," Kella objected. "You said the other four slaves were already drugged and that Matthew was pretending. Why would the soldierguard bother doing it again?"

"How would this soldierguard know they had been drugged?" Reuvan demanded. "You said there was no conversation between the man Salamander had hired and the carriage driver when the slaves were transferred from the warehouse to the wagon. And there would be no way of telling, with the slaves gagged and bound, who was drugged."

"A drug would not stop me from sensing Matthew," I insisted.

"Would you have even recognized him?" Domick asked. "If Matthew was given such a drug, even if your probe touched his mind, it would read it as the mind of a stranger."

"All right," Brydda said, sitting forward in his seat. "Now we are getting somewhere. If we assume the carriage driver was instructed to take them to a certain place and then this soldierguard, who might or might not be Salamander, met him and administered a Sadorian drug, what then?"

"They were moved indoors?" Kella suggested.

Brydda nodded his head slowly. "Salamander has done everything in a roundabout way. That is part of the secret of his success. The obvious thing would be to have the carriage brought to its destination, but maybe they are kept here for some time, drugged as a further safeguard. But no matter where they are or how they got there, the slaves will have to be moved from the city to Morganna. I think we ought to concentrate on that and forget trying to find them in the city."

I felt hope stir in me. "But if Matthew is drugged, as soon as it wears off, I'll be able to farseek him."

Domick sighed heavily. "I am sorry to be a doom-crow, but whoever has them might not let the drug wear off. And even if they give it a break, which they would be wise to do if they do not want to damage their slaves, then you would need to be farseeking at the right moment to reach Matthew. Even you cannot farseek indefinitely."

"It will not hurt to try. How soon before a single dose of this Sadorian drug wears off?" Brydda asked him.

"Several hours, more or less," the coercer said after some thought. "It might have worn off already. The drugs react differently with each person. Weight and how much has been eaten and drunk need to be taken into account for even an approximation. But the other thing we have to consider is that the soldierguard may have got a good look at Matthew—his dark skin would stand out in the daylight—and if he did not recognize him before, he might have done so now."

Brydda thumped the table in excitement. "But don't you see, that will work for us! If this soldierguard recognized him from the market, he would definitely let the drug wear off so that he can be questioned."

For the first time, Domick looked convinced. "You are right. They would be fools not to interrogate him." A darkness flickered in his eyes.

"How frequently can you farseek in a day?" Brydda demanded, looking at me.

"If I was fresh, every hour or so." I turned to Kella. "Can you drain the fatigue from me?"

The healer stood up and put her hands on her hips. "Are you mad?"

"I am not planning to scan the whole of Sutrium," I snapped. "I will be using an attuned probe, and it will only take a few minutes to send it out. Either it will find Matthew or it won't. It may be our only chance to save him."

Kella's ire faded. "I can only drain your fatigue the once. You have not eaten all night, and it would be better if you slept a little. Later—"

"Later may be too late," I interrupted her grimly.

The healer sighed and held out her hand. I gave her mine and relaxed completely as her Talent hummed through my body. Gradually, the night's tensions drained from me into the healer, and with them the chilly stiffness from all the hours of waiting motionless on the roof and the queer light-headedness I had begun to feel.

When I opened my eyes, I felt as if I had just woken from a sound night's slumber. Kella's eyes were closed as she dissipated the fatigue poisons she had drained from me.

I closed my own eyes again and concentrated on shaping a probe tuned to Matthew's mental signature. Sending it out, I kept my fingers crossed, but before long it was obvious I would not locate him that way.

On impulse, I sent out a farsense searcher probe. Starting at the place where I had lost touch with Matthew, I let my mind fly out in ever-widening circles, dipping fleetingly into every mind I encountered just in case I happened upon a mind or group of minds that were oddly distorted. If that happened, Brydda could check to see if it was Matthew and the four slaves.

I moved gracefully in a spiraling mental dance, because awkwardness would waste energy. I kept fanning out until I felt my little store of energy fading; then I withdrew into my own mind and opened my eyes.

The others were all staring at me hopefully. I shook

my head, not trusting the steadiness of my voice. Brydda began to pluck agitatedly and absently at the beard hairs beneath his jutting chin as I described the many tainted areas in Sutrium.

"That is only your first try," Reuvan said. "It is quite likely this drug has not even had a chance to wear off yet. And we can search the areas you can't farseek in."

"That is true," Domick said, getting to his feet and pulling on his coat. "I must go back to the Council-court," he added, in answer to our questioning glances.

"But you've been there all night," Kella protested. "And you have eaten nothing."

He glanced about and took up one of the loaves Matthew and Kella had baked together. "This will do. I have no time for more."

The healer stared at the loaf as if she wanted to cry.

"Is something happening at the Councilcourt?" Brydda asked. "Surely you do not always work such long hours."

Domick shrugged on his sodden cloak. "The Council is shifting us about at random to see who moves easily and who resists. It is a thing they do occasionally. A security measure. In fact, I have been thinking I might stay at an inn for the next few nights, just in case I am under investigation. That is what I came to tell you."

He did not look at Kella when he spoke, and her expression told me this was the first she had heard of it.

Reuvan rose, saying he must leave, too. Kella stood up swiftly, saying she would walk them both out. Her face was pale and set.

· 26 ·

"He is so cold," I said to Brydda when we were alone.

The rebel gave me a stern look. "Do not blame Domick for being good at what you and your people have asked him to do, Elspeth."

I shook my head. "Does being good at spying mean he has to be so cold and remote? So hard?"

"Of course it does," Brydda said sharply. "Spying requires a person to turn themselves inside out in their efforts to pretend to be what they are not. In a sense, Domick has had to become the enemy, and that means he must work against the very things he believes in most passionately. He must do and witness things that are abhorrent to him, and yet pretend to approve. And he is in constant peril. Of course it has changed him. How could it not? If he had not hardened, what he does would have destroyed him."

Chilled, I thought of Domick's knowledge of torture methods and his certainty that anyone exposed to them would talk, and I remembered the rumor of his presence in the torture chamber. "Sometimes you have to endure a lesser evil in dealing with a greater one," he had said.

Oh, Domick, I thought. He had said he was not a torturer. But of course he must have seen terrible things—

torture and death and executions, experimentation with new drugs. He was spying in the Councilcourt, for Lud's sake. What sort of naive idiot had I been to think he would simply sweep floors and gather up the odd secret?

Brydda rose and threw a knot of wood on the fire. "I have received replies from almost all the rebels as to whether or no they will attend your meeting."

I nodded without enthusiasm. A meeting with the rebel leaders was just one more possible disaster in the making.

Brydda gave me a level look. "You are going to meet with them still, I trust?"

I nodded again. "I'll go, but I just don't see that it will change anything."

"Not if you go with that attitude," he said shortly. "It will be held in Rangorn. I will not tell the others the location until the day of the meeting. Less chance of a leaking mouth."

I was startled out of my dejection. "But Rangorn is thick with soldierguards scouring the place for me!"

"Exactly why it will be the safest place to hold a meeting. By the time we get there, they will have given up searching and left." He smiled disarmingly. "There are plenty of good reasons for choosing Rangorn, but in truth, I have an urge to see the trees I climbed as a boy."

"What am I supposed to do at this meeting?"

"Answer their questions as best you can and remember that the aim is to make them see you as a Talented human rather than a Misfit," Brydda said. "When the question of your abilities arises, I would speak of farseeking as the power to communicate over long distances with others who possess the same power. Say nothing of mind reading or coercing unTalents. You might explain beastspeaking since that is unlikely to frighten them, and they have already heard mention of it. And empathy since it is fairly harmless. But I would not mention futuretelling at all. Also don't let yourself be pressured into demonstrations."

"You want me to impress them without scaring them."

"In a sense," Brydda agreed with all seriousness. "The main thing is that you establish yourself as normal and human in their eyes. And I think it would be best for now to let the rebels believe you are truly gypsies. If they knew the truth, they would want to know the whereabouts of your stronghold. It would not occur to them to ask about a gypsy stronghold because of the safe-passage agreement."

"But you'll be there, won't you?" I asked, puzzled at the advance instructions.

"Of course," Brydda said. "But if I appear too much on your side, they will feel threatened. It would cause them to see me as a rival, and ultimately that would endanger the rebellion. Certainly, it would not serve you. That is why I chose to have the meeting in Rangorn—it is neutral territory, because no rebel leader controls it."

I frowned. "Why would your rebels need neutral territory when they are allies?"

"An ally is not a friend. At best, these are reluctant allies. You must remember that these rebel chiefs are working toward smashing the established order."

"Yes?" I said blankly.

"Well, think about it. What happens when the current power structure of Herder Faction, Council, and soldierguards is obliterated? Who will run things?"

"You mean they're worried about which of them will be in charge when it's all over?" I asked incredulously.

"It is something that must be considered," Brydda said. "This is not a fairy tale where everyone lives happily ever after. Following the rebellion, there will be chaos and, in the midst of it, a struggle to decide who will have power over whom in the Land. Many of those who rule the various rebel groups are prepared for that and are determined to come out on top. For that reason, there is great rivalry between the most powerful groups. Indeed, some of the leaders hate one another more than they hate the Council or the soldierguards!"

"But that is stupid," I said.

He smiled sadly. "Stupid, yes, but it seems it is the nature of humankind to want control over one another. Why do you think I prefer the company of horses? Of course, in some ways, the rivalry is my fault. Before I brought them all together with the notion of revolution, there was no competition, because no one imagined it would be possible to get rid of the Council. No one thought further than simple survival. Now, of course, they think of afterward. . . ."

"Is that what the man you have joined wants? The Sutrium leader?"

"Bodera? No. There would be no point. And his son, Dardelan, is too young to be regarded by the rest as any sort of competition. That is what gives Bodera his neutrality and his best advantage." Brydda fixed me with a hard look. "It is because of this that I have been able to set the rebellion in motion. As to this meeting with you, make no mistake, they come more to keep an eye on one another than to give you a hearing. But they will hear you."

With a faint chill of apprehension, I wondered if the future of Talented Misfits lay only in changing one set of oppressors for another. What if someone like Tardis or Malik came out on top?

As if he had read my thoughts, Brydda said, "I have not heard yet from Malik. Bodera predicts he will send his refusal at the last moment to be difficult."

"Your Bodera sounds like a wise man," I said. "I would like to meet him."

The big rebel smiled with affection. "Truly he is worth meeting, but the rotting sickness has distorted his features dreadfully, and he dislikes being looked at. You will meet his son, Dardelan, though, and he is very like his father. He will attend the meeting in Bodera's stead."

"To remind the other rebels that he, and not you, is his father's chosen successor?"

Brydda nodded. "The rebel leaders are a suspicious lot, and it will not hurt to reassure them."

"Who else will come?"

"Tardis will send an emissary. That is not good, but it is better than nothing at all. There are few responses from the upper lowlands seditioner groups, because Malik has a strong following in the region and he has yet to respond. They will vote as he does, and only after he does.

"Malik sees Tardis as his most serious rival, because the Murmroth group is the largest next to his own. The west-coast bloc has the numbers to rival them, but they have been unable to amalgamate. The bloc is made up of rebel groups from Port Oran, Halfmoon Bay, and Morganna, each with its own leader. The trouble is that none of the three wants to step down. They have promised to send representation, but if one comes, I daresay all will come. None will want the others to gain an advantage.

"Naturally, the other major groups encourage the discord, for they have a vested interest in keeping the situation as it is, though for the sake of the rebellion it would be best if one leader took control of the bloc."

On one level, I listened with fascination to the internal machinery of the rebel network, but on another I was conscious that Brydda was talking as much to take my mind away from thinking of Matthew as anything else. "Elii of Kinraide is a strong leader, but his numbers are small . . . ," Brydda was saying.

I stared at him, wondering if this could possibly be the same Elii who had guided me and other orphans from the Kinraide orphan home to harvest whitestick. Then again, Elii was not an uncommon name.

" . . . as well as Bram and Jakoby of Sador."

"Sadorians!" I was startled out of my lethargic drift. "I don't understand. What do the Sadorians care about our struggles? The Council has no jurisdiction over them."

"Not yet it doesn't," Brydda said darkly.

Abruptly, all the gossip I had heard of the distant region coalesced in my mind. "They support the rebellion because they don't want to be absorbed by the Land and ruled by the Council!"

"Exactly. It is inevitable that this will happen if the

Council's might is not curtailed, and the Sadorians are too intelligent not to see it. I approached them, but—"

"You went to Sador?" I interrupted.

The rebel nodded, smiling reminiscently. "It is a strange place—nothing at all like the Land. There they worship the earth, and human life is seen as short and unimportant. Ever since the road opened to Sador, the Sadorians have had to endure Faction missionaries. Interestingly, like the gypsies, Sadorians are nomadic.

"Bram and Jakoby are simply two of the wisest of the tribal leaders. There is little strife among the tribes mainly, or so it seems to me, because they do not own the desert they call Sador. They shift about constantly, so there are no boundary disputes or territorial struggles. And when there are disputes, I believe they have devised some sort of ritual to mediate."

"How did you get them into the rebel alliance?"

"I simply pointed out to them that overthrowing the Council would ensure their autonomy." He shrugged. "But I think they had already worked that out. They are a very practical people."

"I wonder what they will make of me?"

Brydda's expression was unexpectedly wry. "I doubt they will come. I have asked them more out of courtesy than anything else. At present, we are allies only in principle—not in practice. But we will see."

For a moment, his eyes were distant and distracted. Then he sighed and suggested I try farseeking Matthew again.

The probe returned without locating him.

Three times before midmeal, and then three more times in the afternoon that long, gray day, I farsought

Matthew, each time to no avail. Rain fell intermittently, and Reuvan came with progressive reports as the rebels scoured the tainted areas I had named. They found no trace of Matthew or the others. Brydda remained with me, talking when I was not trying to farseek. By dark, I felt exhausted and strangely hot.

Drawing up a mental probe for the eighth time, I shaped it to fit Matthew's mind with difficulty. When I sent it out, the probe felt heavy and unwieldy. It did not surprise me that such an uninspired search did not find him.

Opening my eyes, I seemed to see the flames on the hearth through a gray haze, and even shaking my head required a tremendous effort of will. I felt dizzy, and it seemed that I must be too close to the fire, but I had no energy to pull myself away.

"Elspeth?" Brydda said from a long way off.

The room began to sway and dim, and there was the sound of voices, but it was too hard to understand what they were saying. I closed my eyes, and it seemed the flames were inside my skin. For a terrifying moment, I thought I was burning at the stake.

"Damn you! Where is it?" cried a disembodied voice.

"Elspeth!"

I dragged my eyes open and looked up to see Brydda's bearded face hovering above me. The world rocked. It took a moment for me to understand that the rebel was carrying me down the hall in his massive arms.

"Must . . . keep trying . . . ," I said, struggling feebly, though I could not for the life of me recall what was so urgent.

"Sleep," Brydda said with gentle insistence. "Sleep . . ."

I dreamed again of the dark tunnel. This time I was being pursued. Something huge and savage was pounding along the tunnel after me, closing the gap between us with impossible speed.

"Be gone!" Gahltha sent, leaping out of the darkness behind me. I whirled as he reared in the tunnel, blocking the way. But in the dream, there was something different about him. Before I could understand what it was, I found myself again on the threshold of the flaming doors. Incredibly, the Teknoguildmaster was beside me.

"It's amazing, isn't it," Garth demanded, "what can be concealed when it is right in the open?" He looked at me. "Of course, you realize what it means?"

I shook my head.

"It means that you are really a gypsy."

His words seemed to come from a long way off.

The gypsies keep the signs, someone whispered.

I knew the voice and tried to sit up. "Atthis! Why don't you speak to me?"

Hands pushed at me, and I fought against them.

"Atthis?"

"Sleep," said a familiar voice. "Sleep and heal."

"Who?" I croaked.

"Sleep . . ."

I woke, groggy and lethargic. Staggering to the bathing room, I plunged myself entirely into a barrel of icy water. The cold took my breath away, and I washed swiftly, aching and gasping before getting out and rubbing myself hard enough to make my skin tingle.

In the kitchen, Kella was nursing a cup of spiced milk. There were dark shadows under her eyes when she looked up, but an amazement in her expression startled me.

"What is it?" I asked.

"You . . . you're all right?" she stammered.

I stared at her, bemused. "Of course I am. Why shouldn't I be?"

"Last night you had a terrible fever. You were delirious and pouring with perspiration. After everything that has happened, I was afraid . . ." She shook her head. "I can't believe you look so well!"

"It must have appeared worse than it was—or I'm tougher than I look," I said. "Where is Brydda now?"

"He left before first light." The healer frowned and answered my unvoiced question. "None of his people has found any trace of Matthew."

Depression fell over me like a blanket. "And Dragon?" I stared into the fire as I spoke and tried to keep my voice even.

"No change," Kella said quietly.

She poured some milk and sat it near my hand, but I pushed it away. She shoved it firmly back. To my surprise, the warm, creamy liquid tasted delicious.

"Have you seen Maruman?" I said.

"No. I suppose he has gone exploring. You know how he is. Almost as bad as a teknoguilder."

"I hope you're right. I'm going to try again for Matthew." I closed my eyes and shaped a probe, letting it fly with a prayer. I cast it far, right to the edge of the Suggredoon and the sea rim, but there was no response.

I opened my eyes and saw my own despair writ large on the healer's face.

"What are we going to do?" she asked in a frightened voice. "Brydda says you must leave Sutrium in a few days to meet with the rebels. Will you go if Matthew has not been found?"

"I have agreed to this meeting, and I have no choice but to go. We'll find him." I looked at the healer levelly. "Kella, there is something else. I want you to come with me when I go back to Obernewtyn."

"What about Domick?"

"We need him here for the time being," I said.

"Why shouldn't I stay with him?" Kella's voice was defensive, truculent.

"Your face is becoming too well known to people who dwell hereabouts. This is a good safe house, and we don't want to endanger it by overusing it. Domick can keep an eye on it, but he will be staying at an inn for the time being."

I gave her a quick look and saw that she was unconvinced. "Aside from that, I need you to look after Dragon."

The protestations died on her lips. Sipping at my warm milk, I watched the healer over the rim of the cup.

"It need not be forever," I said softly when the silence had gone on for too long.

"Everything is going wrong," Kella announced in sudden despair.

Hearing her voice my own thoughts had an unexpected effect—I felt a sudden surge of stubborn optimism.

"No," I said.

The healer looked startled at my sudden belligerence.

"We have to have hope. It is the least we can do. Matthew is missing, but wherever he is, he will trust that we have not given up on him. He will believe that we are searching, and he will be doing his best to find a way to reach us. We Misfits are hard to kill."

Kella smiled, a quick genuine twitch of her lips. "You are proof of that."

I smiled back. "We have all proven it."

Hope ignited in her eyes, and I was surprised to feel my own heart lift fractionally.

"You really think everything will be all right?"

She sounded suddenly very young. I smothered a resurgence of doubt. "Of course. You'll see. It's only hopeless when we've given up hope."

"And Domick?" she asked after a minute.

I looked at her quickly; the animation had died from her face.

"You know something is wrong with him and so do I," she said. "I have tried to get him to talk to me, but bit by bit he has withdrawn. Now we are like strangers. If I leave now . . ." Her eyes shone with tears, but pride kept her from shedding them.

"Whatever is the matter with him has something to do with his spying," I said, considering my words carefully. "It is something he needs to work out on his own, or I am sure he would have told you what was wrong. But he still loves you."

"Then I should not leave," Kella said quickly.

"That is exactly what you should do!"

I hesitated, then decided she needed some hard words to stiffen her backbone. "Why do you suppose he has been spending so much time away from the safe house if not to be alone—to get away from you? Perhaps he feels smothered by your worrying about him so much."

I did not believe this. But Kella needed to come

home, and Domick wanted her to go. Perhaps her presence was a strain he could not bear on top of everything else. Kella looked stricken, and I wondered if I had misread her, but after a moment, her face settled into determined lines. "Maybe you're right," she said at last. She was silent for a time, her brow furrowed in thought. "All right, I will come back to Obernewtyn. Domick will know where to find me when he wants me."

"Good girl," I said, heartened by her courage. I wondered if I would have had as much in similar circumstances. "Now all we need to do to complete the day is find Matthew."

"*I know where he is*," came a familiar farseeking voice.

◆ 27 ◆

I JUMPED TO my feet, knocking the chair to the ground. Kella gaped at me in amazement. "What is it?"

"Daffyd is in the yard below!" I cried aloud to her. "He's just farsent that he knows where Matthew is!"

Her eyes widened in joy, and we hurried down-stairs.

I stopped dead at the sight of the ex-Druid armsman as Kella let him into the repair shed. He was wearing an oiled cloak that glistened with rain.

At the inn, Daffyd had been concealed by the dark-ness, and before that, I had not seen him for an age. Like Domick and Brydda, I saw now that time and whatever straits he had undergone had altered him. He had lost none of his tan, which suggested he still lived an outdoor life, but there was a new intensity and a depth of pain in his dark-brown eyes that made me wonder what he had been doing since he left us. He was taller than I remembered and thinner, the skin on his bones so scant that he looked frail. But when he em-braced me, I felt his indomitable will in the sinewy strength of his arms and was reassured.

"I am sorry I did not come sooner, but they are very watchful," he said. "Even now I dare not be gone too long, or they will become suspicious."

"You said you know where Matthew is," I said eagerly.

Daffyd gave me an assessing look. "I do, but before I tell you where he is, you must make me a promise."

I stared at him, bemused. "What?"

"I have spent much time working my way painstakingly into the slaver's organization, waiting for a time when Salamander would expose himself. That time is near, and I can't let you do anything that would stop him appearing."

"Is Matthew with Salamander?"

"The slaver you and Brydda met, Ayle, has Matthew and the other slaves, but Salamander will come for them. If you free them, you must do it at the last minute. You don't have any idea how fanatically suspicious Salamander is. If he gets the slightest notion that something is wrong, there will be a lot of dead people and dead ends, believe me, Matthew and I are likely to be among the cold ones."

"I'll be guided by you," I said quickly. "We will not act until you give the word."

"Do you speak for Brydda as well?"

I paused. "I can't speak for him," I said at last. "But he has also been searching for Salamander, because the slavemaster killed Idris. He won't want to frighten him away any more than you do."

"Salamander kills like other people breathe. I suppose Brydda wants revenge."

"He wants to smash the slave trade," Kella said.

"That is a fine desire," Daffyd said. "But this is a trade that brings a river of coin into the hands of slavers. Killing Salamander will not end it altogether. But I wish him luck. My quest is somewhat more personal." There was something unbending in his face now.

"You are still looking for Gilaine and the others?" I temporized.

"Always," he said, the terse word a vow.

"Then Salamander has them?"

"Not now. But he had them, and he is my sole link to them." He frowned, seeming to weigh things in his mind. Finally, he spoke again. "Matthew is being held with a whole lot of other slaves in a warehouse on the banks of the Suggredoon."

"One of the river wharfs?" Kella asked eagerly.

Daffyd nodded, but his eyes did not leave mine.

"Then we were right. He means to use the Suggredoon to get them out of Sutrium," the healer said.

"Matthew is drugged, then?" I asked.

"He was, though he did not appear to be," Daffyd said. "I near died when I spotted him among the others. When I could touch him, I tried to farseek him to find out what he was up to. That was when I discovered that he had been drugged.

"I managed to get the job of redosing the slaves, and I let Matthew's dribble onto the ground and kept my fingers crossed that he would not give me away before his mind was clear. Eventually, we were able to exchange stories. I promised to come and find you, but it took all night to think of an excuse that would not cause suspicion." He glanced outside where it had begun to rain again.

"I don't understand," I broke in. "I farsought Matthew all day yesterday. If he was free of the drugs,

303

how is it that I couldn't locate him? Is he on tainted ground?"

Daffyd shook his head. "The place where he and the other slaves are being held is built to extend over the Suggredoon. I think there is something tainted in the water, because sometimes the fish glow at night or they are grotesquely deformed."

I opened my mouth and huffed a sigh of relief. That explained everything. Probably whatever was tainting the river had also affected the sea along the shore. And from Daffyd's description of Matthew, it looked as if Domick had been right about the slave suppliers using Sadorian drugs. The only mystery was why the soldier-guard had stopped the wagon partway to administer the drug dose.

"How does the soldierguard captain fit into the whole thing?"

Daffyd gave me a blank stare. "What soldierguard captain?"

I did not want to divert Daffyd when we had so little time, so I shrugged dismissively. "How did Gilaine and Lidgebaby end up in Salamander's hands?"

Daffyd's eyes gleamed with obsessive fire. "Well you might ask, for it is a strange and dark story. And long. Too long for these few moments. Suffice it to say that they were sold to him as slaves. I have infiltrated the slave trade specifically to reach Salamander so that I can learn where they were sold and to whom."

He looked around again, as if he feared someone might have followed him. Taking me by the arm, he drew me deeper into the shed and out of sight of the yard gate.

"There is to be a change in the way things are done.

A streamlining, Ayle called it. Moving forward, all slaves are to be brought to a single spot in Sutrium—this will be regularly changed. The slaves are to be picked up by boat and taken over the seas to be sold."

"Straight to sea from Sutrium? No more routing them through Morganna?" I asked, my mouth dry.

"Ayle said nothing of that, but I would guess this slave boat will stop at Morganna as well. He is to manage the sorting house in Sutrium, and I suppose there will be another sorting house and another Ayle in Morganna—maybe one in every coastal town." Daffyd's eyes narrowed. "What I know for sure is that Salamander will come in person, and that means I have the chance I've been waiting for."

"Chance?" Kella murmured, voicing the question shaping in my own mind.

The armsman flicked a look at her. "I mean to farseek Salamander to learn where he has taken Gilaine and Lidgebaby. If that does not work, I will force him to recall by cruder means. If he has truly forgotten, he will pay for his amnesia with his life."

"Hard to believe that Salamander would come to pick the slaves up himself," I said. "It seems so out of character for him to expose himself like that."

Daffyd shrugged. "He is setting a new aspect of the slave trade in place, and he does not trust any other to do it properly. In any case, while he is aboard the ship, he will be in no danger. I daresay he will not come ashore longer than it takes to load the slaves, and it is likely he will be masked. But a mask will not keep me from his mind. And I will have some time; it will take more than a little while to board so many slaves."

"So many slaves?" I was puzzled.

Daffyd laughed bitterly. "I told you, Ayle's warehouse is to be the new sorting house. Every day, more slaves are brought in to await Salamander's ship. There are more than one hundred already waiting for collection."

"One hundred!" I echoed, astounded.

"It is nothing to what will be coming, according to Ayle. These are early days."

"How long before this ship comes to take the slaves?" I asked with sudden foreboding.

"Ayle said tomorrow."

"Tomorrow!"

Daffyd nodded grimly. "Remember, you must not act until the last moment."

I nodded back, thinking this *was* the last moment. We would be lucky to get anything set up in such a short time. "Does Matthew have any ideas how we might get him free?"

Daffyd gave a rare, crooked half smile. "I think Matthew thought you and Brydda would come up with those minor details."

I shook my head in exasperation.

Daffyd looked again from the repair-shed door into the driving rain. "I must go back now. Is there anything you want me to tell Matthew?"

"Tell him to be ready," I said decisively.

"I will." He pulled up the hood on his cloak and turned to face me, his eyes shadowed. "Remember your promise."

He strode away without waiting for a response and was lost behind the curtain of rain even before he had reached the gates to the repair yard.

I turned back to look at Kella.

"He is so full of hatred," she said. "I have only slight empath Talent, and yet it burned me."

"He loves Gilaine, and he is emotionally linked with Lidgebaby. And his brother was in the camp, too. I wonder how they got into Salamander's hands in the first place. And how they escaped the firestorm that destroyed the Druid camp."

"What are you going to tell Brydda?"

"Yes, what?" Brydda asked, stepping out of the shadows behind us.

We both whirled to face the rebel.

"It seems I do not have to decide that question," I said coolly, not liking that he had deliberately hidden himself and listened to words that had not been intended for his ears.

"Perhaps it is lucky for us both that you do not," Brydda said with equal coolness. He shook his head, and the harshness melted from his expression. "I did not mean to overhear. I did not recognize Daffyd and so I hid. Only when you spoke did I realize who he was, and by then it was clear he would not welcome my presence."

"What will you do, then?" I asked.

"What would you have me do?"

"You heard what Daffyd said. He wants to find out where Salamander took Gilaine and the others. I would ask, as he did, that we do not get in his way."

The rebel's eyes were somber. "Perhaps I have given you some cause to doubt me, but I tell you now, on my life, you can trust me. Daffyd wants Salamander alive so he can milk him for information, and I want him dead. Both our wishes can be met."

"What did you have in mind?"

Brydda gave a feral smile. "Rescuing Matthew and taking Salamander captive so that we can question him to our heart's content. And when he has no more to tell us, then I will deal with him."

I shuddered and wondered if there was ever any other way of dealing with hatred and violence.

"Well?" Brydda prompted. "Shall we see how a sly Salamander deals with the Black Dog's teeth?"

I looked at the rebel steadily. "If I don't agree?"

He frowned. "You gave your word. I was not meant to hear what I heard, and we are friends. Therefore, by virtue of that friendship, I will abide by your decision."

I felt ashamed of my doubts. "You are a better friend than I am," I said. "I will say yes, but I must let Daffyd know that this has become a rebel operation."

"Let us go there tonight. I will need to have a look at this warehouse and the river wharfs in order to formulate a plan, and we will find a way to communicate it to Daffyd."

I nodded. "Come by at dusk, then. Did you come for anything in particular?" I added as the big man turned to go.

He slapped his head. "Of course. All of this drove it from my mind. I came to tell you that Malik has agreed to meet you but that he refuses to come unless the location of the meeting is changed."

"But you said they did not know where—"

"They don't. But he proposes his own location. He says the meeting should occur on truly neutral territory and has named Bodera's home in Sutrium."

"Oh Lud," I said uncertainly.

"Malik sent his letter directly to Bodera, which

suggests that, in spite of all my efforts, he has begun to see me as a rival."

"What did Bodera say?"

Brydda scowled. "Unfortunately, he thought it was a good idea. He is proud to think that his home is neutral territory."

"Then what is the problem? If he is not troubled . . ."

The big rebel ran an agitated hand over his unruly thatch. "It is dangerous to have these sort of meetings in a permanent place that we use. And, apart from that, the location of the meeting will be known in advance of the day, which increases the chance of treachery."

"How much danger will there be?"

He shrugged. "Not so much as all that, I suppose, since none of the leaders would risk giving away a secret meeting at which they themselves might be taken prisoner or slain. The other thing, of course, is that the rebels do want the rebellion to occur, and a raid at Bodera's house would immediately put an end to it." Brydda shook his head. "I don't know. Maybe I am worrying over nothing, but I think it sets a bad precedent. And I don't like putting Bodera in danger."

"I suppose I must accept the risk if you and the others do. When will the meeting take place?"

"Within the sevenday," Brydda said. "And the sooner it is over, the better I'll feel."

◆ 28 ◆

I SPENT MOST of the day sitting by Dragon's bed, holding her hand.

I had brought her out of a different kind of solitude to Obernewtyn, and now she was lost to us again, locked behind the fortress of her own mind.

In the late afternoon, the rain clouds parted to reveal a watery sun. I donned fur-lined boots and a thick cloak just the same, determined not to freeze as I had the last time I kept a midnight vigil outside a warehouse.

I went down to ask if Gahltha wanted a blanket.

"I/Gahltha am not cold," he sent.

"Maruman/yelloweyes has been gone longlong days," I sent, wondering as always why the beasts called a one-eyed cat "yelloweyes." Although, I did it just as unthinkingly. Perhaps because, like Dameon, the old cat often saw better than those of us with two eyes.

Gahltha gave me a level look. "He does what he/yelloweyes must."

I frowned into his dark eyes. "Do you/Gahltha know where he/Maruman is?"

"The voices of his chaos/madness call him when they will, and he/Maruman must hear them. The strain of guardianship caused the voices to call."

I frowned, confused. "Guardianship?"

"Of the dreamtrails. I/Gahltha know that it is not easy. Yet I have sworn to Maruman/yelloweyes that I would take his place. I did not know how until he/yelloweyes showed me. The dreamtrails are strange/dangerous. On them are beasts like none that walk the earth and shapes that hide/conceal other shapes, yet one grows better at it."

I wondered if I was understanding him correctly. In my mind's eye, I saw the black horse leap into the tunnel of my dreams, urging me to run while he fought off whatever it was that followed me. Maruman's H'rayka? A dark unease filled me at the thought that somehow those nightmares were real.

"Are you/Gahltha saying that Maruman/yelloweyes asked you to look after me . . . my mind or my dreams, and then went away in his madness/mindchaos?"

"Did I not say so?"

Was it possible I was being somehow stalked in my dreams? Impossible as it seemed, I shivered, for if the H'rayka was my mirror image, wouldn't he possess the same powers as me?

"Sallah comes," Jaygar sent.

I turned to see Brydda ride into the yard on the white mare Sallah. The golden afternoon sunlight gave her a dazzling regality. I was surprised Brydda did not try to hide her beauty as I did Gahltha's. But perhaps his size was enough to dissuade thieves.

"Greeting and hail, ElspethInnle," Sallah sent formally.

"Greetings," I returned, embarrassed at the thought that the white horse might have communicated to

311

Brydda her belief that I was the incarnation of a savior figure in beastlegend.

"Beastsecrets are not for the funaga," Sallah sent with clear reproof.

"Am I not funaga?"

"You are Innle," Sallah sent.

"Are you ready?" Brydda asked.

I nodded, and Gahltha came forward so that I could mount him. Wordlessly, we rode out into the yard where Kella waited by the gate to say goodbye.

"Be careful," Jaygar sent after us.

"Always," Gahltha returned.

It was chilly already, and I was glad of my cloak. Gladder still that the rain had stopped. With luck, it would remain clear until we were safely back at the repair shed.

"We had better dismount," Brydda said when we neared the river piers. "I have a few rebels in a house close by. They have been watching the place all day. We can leave the horses there and go the rest of the way on foot."

I gave him a quick look, disturbed that he had already set his people in place.

"Just in case of trouble," he promised, sensing my disquiet. "I wanted to have some idea of the movement of traffic about these river piers. I had no particular knowledge of them."

The house turned out to be yet another of the city's burned-out hovels. I was glad to find that only three rebels awaited us in the yard behind it. Reuvan was one of them. Beside him was a tall, lanky fellow I had not seen before, with woolly brown hair and a beard to match. The third was the blond woman with the plague-scarred face whom I had met at The Good Egg. I searched my memory for her name—Oria. Fortunately, she was engrossed in the examination of a map and had not seen me arrive. For Domick's sake, I swiftly erased my face from her memory. When Brydda introduced us, she gave me a searching look, but there was no recognition in it.

"What have you found out?" Brydda asked her briskly.

She flicked her fingers at the bearded man, who had a steady, seasoned look about him, and drew us into a room whose windows had been blackened. He lit a small lantern and unrolled the piece of paper Oria had been studying.

"Here is the sea," he rasped, stabbing a brown-stained finger at the paper. "There are four pier warehouses that traders lease privately from the Herder Faction. They are spread apart a little so that carts can draw up between them. As you see, there are the same number of piers. Each warehouse has its own, and here, opposite, there are sheds for storage—one for each warehouse. They are quite often leased out separately. A rough road runs between them."

"The Faction owns the pier sheds, too?" I asked.

Oria nodded. "They bought them recently from the Council, and the wharfs. They use the river to travel straight from their cloister on the edge of the Suggredoon to Morganna and Aborium and then to Herder Isle. The Council controls all of the main sea wharfs and warehouses, as well as the ferry that checks the riverboats, but they leave the river to the Herders now. Of course, other boats use the wharfs to ship wares in or out, and they pay the Herders for it. Small vessels mostly. The Herder ships are the largest that use the wharfs."

I nodded but felt chilled at the thought of being on property controlled by the fanatical Faction.

"The pier manifest says there are only two ships due in tomorrow. One of them must be the slave ship," the bearded rebel put in. "Unless it comes in unscheduled."

"Is the pier empty now? Can we get any closer?" Brydda asked.

Reuvan shook his head. "A Faction boat docked about an hour back, and there are at least a dozen burlymen and seamen roving about. We'll have to wait until they're done, but it should not be too long—they are loading straightaway."

Oria touched Brydda's arm, and there was a clear look of devotion in her eyes, though her voice was brisk and businesslike. "The other thing is that troops of soldierguards have spent the day running some sort of training exercise on the banks of the river right by the warehouse that juts out over the water. Their camp is not far from here. Once it is dark, they will certainly be leaving, too."

"I wonder if the soldierguards are making Ayle nervous," I murmured.

"No doubt he is thanking his lucky stars that the exercise was run today rather than tomorrow," Brydda said with sharp humor. "Imagine them trying to shift a hundred slaves under the noses of the soldierguards."

"A hundred," Oria murmured. "It is hard to believe how brazen this is."

"Since we have to wait anyway, I might try to reach

Daffyd," I said, sitting on an upturned box to make myself comfortable.

"I doubt he will be out in the open with so much going on," Brydda said. He looked at Reuvan. "Do you have any food? I have not eaten all day and . . ."

His voice faded as I closed my eyes and shaped an attuned probe to Daffyd's mind signature. The mental static was very strong this close to the water, which meant I had to concentrate fiercely to keep my mindprobe intact. Given Brydda's warning, I was shocked when the probe not only reached its target but elicited a strong reaction from Daffyd—as if I had thrust a brand into his mind.

The intensity of his response was blistering.

"I have prayed and prayed you would reach me," he sent frantically. "Elspeth, it was a ruse! They're loading the slaves aboard a ship right now! They're going to leave as soon as it's done!"

✦ 29 ✦

"WE DARE NOT go any closer," Reuvan whispered from our hiding spot behind a pile of crates. "The soldierguards are still there, marching back and forth like a lot of fools. I can't imagine what they are doing, but they will have to go when it gets dark. We should wait until then to get nearer."

"This is madness," Brydda said softly. "Burlymen and soldierguards all milling about while the slavers openly load an illicit cargo of drugged slaves."

"Daffyd didn't sound as if he was making a mistake," I said softly. "He sounded panic-stricken and deadly serious."

"Keep your voices down," Oria warned. "Sound carries far and easily by the water."

"We have to get closer," Brydda said, frustrated. "Ask Daffyd if he can—"

I shook my head. "I can't reach him. He must have gone back into the warehouse, and the static from the tainted water is like a stone wall."

"Luddamn it!" the rebel chief hissed.

"I don't understand," said the brown-bearded rebel. "The only ship on the manifest for tonight is *The Calor Lady*, and like I said, that is a Herder ship."

"That is the least strange thing about this whole

affair. Herder ships are for hire at the right price, like any other," Brydda said. He looked at me. "Can you hide us somehow? We need to get closer."

I glanced instinctively at Oria and the other rebel. Their faces showed slight curiosity but nothing more, and I wondered how much Brydda had told them of me.

"I can cloak two of us," I said.

"Wait here," Brydda instructed the others.

"Just a minute," I said quickly. "I can feel Daffyd again."

I closed my eyes, and the general probe I had left in case the farseeker emerged sharpened into an attuned probe. Like Matthew, his farseeking power was too weak to combat the static from the Suggredoon on its own, but I could make up the difference.

"You'd better do something now if you are going to, Elspeth," he sent urgently. "Matthew is in the last lot, and they are going to load them shortly. Once he is on the ship, you will have no hope of helping him unless you brought an army."

"What about Salamander?" I sent. "Have you managed to farseek him?"

"No!" Daffyd's mental voice was savage with disappointment and rage. "He has not come ashore, and I cannot reach him over the damn water!"

"Ask him about the soldierguards and the Herders," Brydda hissed into my ear.

I shook my head angrily, for he had distracted me, and it was difficult enough to focus in the static.

"Daffyd?" I sent. "Why are they boarding them on a Herder ship?"

There was no answer.

"He's gone, but he said they're going to load Matthew any minute."

"What about Salamander?"

"He hasn't left the ship."

Brydda scowled. "The man has the instincts of a fang-cat. It is almost as if he knew we were waiting for him." He took a deep, steadying breath. "Well, let's get nearer."

He led the way, and I concentrated on cloaking us coercively as we emerged from behind the crates and made our way through a narrow lane toward the water. I could smell the faintly brackish scent of the Suggredoon and hear its rush before I saw it. The static from the tainting was incredibly strong, and I wondered what had caused it. Certainly the upper reaches of the river, which fed the lake beneath Tor, were clean.

The row of sheds came into view, and through the gaps between them, I could see they were separated from the river by a stone walkway. Right on the bank were the warehouses, facing away from the river. The warehouse jutting out over the water was farthest away from us and set back a little from the rest. People were moving about in front of it, and even from this distance, I could see the huge front door stood ajar.

Tied up alongside it was a ship, its three masts and a small part of its bow visible behind the bulk of the warehouse. Judging from the movement of people about it, the gangplank lay on the warehouse side of the ship.

Brydda pressed my arm and pointed past the warehouse to an open field, where fifty or so soldierguards in full regalia were marching in formation. They were paying no mind whatsoever to the ship.

The whole scene was bathed in the ever-deepening

pinkish gold light of the predusk. In less than an hour, the sun would set.

"It can be no coincidence that the soldierguards are here," Brydda whispered.

"Do you think they were hired by the slavers?"

"Not this many," Brydda said. "Too much risk of someone talking." He gave me a searing look. "Of course, a soldierguard captain might have some hidden reason for ordering his troops to perform their exercises here."

I bit my lip and wondered again about the soldierguard captain.

"Can you get us any closer?" the rebel prompted.

I shook my head decisively. "There are burlymen loading a wagon from that shed just up there. You can't see them from here, but I felt them with my probe. Too many to coerce into blindness."

Brydda and I stared at one another, and with dawning horror, I saw resignation shape itself in his eyes.

"We have to help Matthew," I cried.

"Shh," he said sternly. "I know how you feel, but it is impossible to attack openly. If he is to be rescued, it can only be by stealth and wit. Between the seamen, the slaver's hirelings, the burlymen . . . Even with your powers, there are only five of us, six counting Daffyd, and Matthew makes seven—if he is in any state to fight."

"There are nine—if you count the equines as two more," Gahltha sent sternly, and I turned to see that the black horse had followed us.

"I/Gahltha hid myself," he sent imperturbably. "Sallah watches over the other funaga."

"Hell!" Brydda started in fright when he noticed the horse. "What in the name of . . . ?"

I shook my head impatiently, knowing two horses would not tilt the balance in our favor in an open battle. Then I spotted Daffyd coming from the warehouse with a small group of shuffling slaves. He led them along the pier and then vanished between the building and the ship.

"Elspeth!" Daffyd sent as soon as he felt my probe. "I'm taking this group to the ship, and Matthew is in the next lot. It doesn't matter if you cause a fuss, because Salamander is out of my reach anyway. Help Matthew . . ."

His voice faded, and the contact dissolved. I guessed he had stepped onto the gangplank and out over the water.

I sent a swift command to Gahltha and pulled myself up on his back. At once he started forward, evading Brydda's grasp.

"Elspeth!" the rebel hissed, not daring to come out in the open after us.

"Stay still and no one will see you," I said over my shoulder as I urged Gahltha forward.

"Elspeth, there is nothing you can do!" he said. "For Lud's sake, come back."

Gahltha's hooves clattered on the pier boards, drowning out Brydda's frantic whisperings.

"Go along the pier/ride slowly," I sent to the equine. Then I turned my mind to the warehouse. "Matthew!" I sent. "Matthew!"

But, of course, there was no answer.

Closer to the warehouse, I could see *The Calor Lady* properly. It was an elegant vessel with slender lines and its name stamped in red on the bow. Underneath was the distinctive Herder insignia. Given what Brydda had said, it had probably been hired for the occasion to encourage people to mind their own business. Though I could not see why, since they were brazenly loading slaves in public with soldierguards paying no mind to them at all.

The vessel rested low in the water, underlining Daffyd's warning that most of the slaves had already been boarded. No doubt the armsman had contrived as best he could to put Matthew's boarding off to the last moment. If this was imminent, it meant the ship's departure also loomed, as well it must if they meant to catch the out tide, cross the sandbars at the river mouth, and reach open sea by nightfall.

I came level with the burlymen I had sensed. They had been loading bales of wool onto a wagon from a shed opposite the first of the four warehouses. But they had ceased their labors to watch the loading of the slaves. I felt dizzy with confusion. They were watching as if it was nothing out of the ordinary. There had to be more going on than officials turning a blind eye.

"Good riddance, I say," said one of the two.

His thickset companion nodded, and I could not stop myself staring at them. Since when had slavery gained such general approval?

"Reckon the Herders should have rounded 'em up a long time ago. Waste of space they are," the first man said.

His silent companion nodded again.

"Can't see them succeedin' in healin' this lot, though, no matter that they say Lud'll help 'em. Even if they do have skilled healers on Herder Isle. Once a defective always a defective, I say."

I struggled to keep my face expressionless, but

suddenly I understood what was going on. No one knew these people were slaves! Those watching thought that Herders were taking a load of defectives to their Isle for treatment. That was why the soldier-guards were doing nothing and why the whole thing could be done in broad daylight without fear. And the new Sadorian drugs meant none of the slaves behaved as if they were drugged.

My heartbeat quickened as the two burlymen turned to stare at me.

"Gypsy slut. Ought to round *them* up, too," said one.

This time the other was prevailed upon to grunt his assent. I felt sick. I had been so concerned about Matthew that I had forgotten to maintain my coercive enhancement of my boyish apparel. At any minute, I was sure to be recognized by the soldierguards. I inserted a sharp coercive command to the burlymen to get back to their work, and they reacted as if galvanized. They would remember me later, but in the face of everything else, this seemed a minor problem.

Then I coerced an image of myself as a sun-browned seaman's lad. It took a steady surge of power to hold the image, and this, along with trying to combat the sea static, was proving a frightening drain on my mental energies. Soon I would have no reserve of power.

Yet what else could I do?

I sent to Gahltha to slow down as we came level with the warehouse from which the slaves were being led. At the same moment, a man brought a small knot of people outside, and I slowed to let them go before me, glad of a reason to delay.

"Elspeth!" Matthew sent.

I stiffened, for if the farseeker could reach me, it

meant he was among those who had just been brought out.

"Matthew!" I sent gladly, urging Gahltha up beside them.

"Ride on past fer Obernewtyn's sake!" he sent urgently.

Startled by the intensity of his command, I obeyed.

As I passed around the little clutch of people, I glanced down at them casually. The farseeker was less than a handspan from me, his expression carefully blank.

"Go slowly/be lame," I sent, and Gahltha began to affect an exaggerated limp.

After a few steps, I pulled him up and slid off his back, pretending to examine a hoof. With a careful eye, I measured the distance between myself and the little group of slaves. Matthew was only three or four steps away.

"It's no good," the farseeker sent suddenly. "This time I've got myself in a fix ye can't get me out of."

"What are you saying?" Fear made my mental voice strident. I pretended to pick a rock from Gahltha's hoof.

The man who had brought out Matthew and the others went back to close the doors, leaving the slaves standing alone. Matthew turned his head to look at me.

"Elspeth, ye know ye mun let 'em take me," he sent. "Ye can't fight them all yerself."

"Brydda is with me, and Sallah, and there are three rebels besides."

"Against dozens of soldierguards and burlymen, not to mention the ship's seamen?"

"Then I'll create a diversion, and you can run for it. I'll pick you up, and we'll ride clear on Gahltha."

"How? I'm shackled to these other slaves, ankle to

ankle an' wrist to wrist. There's no time to do anythin' about that. Right now, these slavers think I'm nothin', an' I'd as soon keep it that way."

"Then I'll make a fuss to stop them boarding. I'll pretend to recognize one of the others. I'll say you're not defectives—that's what everyone watching thinks. Better to be taken to the Councilcourt by the soldier-guards than spirited away to Lud knows where on a slave ship. And maybe then Domick . . ."

"Listen to me," Matthew sent. "Th' soldierguards are mixed up in this somehow. I dinna think they would take us to th' Councilcourt if you made a fuss. I think they'd just bundle us aboard, an' then you an' Brydda would be caught too."

"Matthew, they'll take you away!"

"I know," he sent calmly. "An' ye'll let 'em, because we both know that this time we're outnumbered. Look, I'm nowt afraid. Wherever this ship goes an' whatever happens, there'll be other ships. An' I'll be comin' back on one of them. I swear it. Tell Daffyd I'll keep a look-out for his Gilaine."

"Get a shift on, lad," said a surly voice right behind me.

I froze, recognizing it as the voice of the slaver Ayle. I did not dare turn around. I knew I could not coerce him, because he was mind-sensitive. I tangled clumsy fingers in Gahltha's mane and, without turning, hauled myself onto his back.

"Go," I sent, and the black equine moved forward.

Daffyd appeared right in front of me. He paled at the sight of me, but my whole mind was too tightly focused on maintaining contact with Matthew to let me communicate with him.

"What's wrong with you?" I heard Ayle demand of Daffyd. I held my breath for his answer, slowing Gahltha.

"Seasick . . . ," Daffyd muttered, passing me.

Ayle bellowed with laughter. "Well, here's the last lot. You can kiss the ground when yer done." There was a little pause; then the slaver's voice reached out to me. "You hear me, boy? Get a move on. You've no business here."

"Go!" Matthew sent.

I heard Ayle's purposeful tread behind me.

"Please!"

With a heart as heavy as a stone anvil, I signaled Gahltha, and he moved forward. After a few steps, I glanced back and saw Ayle retracing his steps, shaking his head and muttering about half-wit gypsies. At the same time, I saw Daffyd take up the leading chain of the last little group of shackled slaves and move toward the gangplank of *The Calor Lady*.

"I love ye, Elspeth," Matthew sent fiercely, meeting my eyes. "I'm sorry about Dragon an' all . . ."

His mental voice faded as he reached the gangplank and walked out over the water.

Every instinct in my body rebelled against riding away, yet I knew Matthew was right. There was nothing I could do to help him.

Almost at once, the gangplank was withdrawn. The seaman standing ashore threw off the ship's mooring knots and leapt aboard. *The Calor Lady* drifted from the shore, borne by the swift-flowing tide that would take it to the sea, its sails snapping and fluttering as they were unfurled slightly to turn the ship.

Matthew was no longer visible. He had been taken

below like the other slaves, but I could not take my eyes off the receding vessel. I was stricken by the feeling that I had failed the Farseeker ward and would never see him again.

I watched as a tall youth with white-blond hair and a great flapping black cloak came out on deck and leaned against the rail, staring back at the shore.

He was extraordinarily beautiful, long boned and slender, probably younger than me by a few years, with skin so pale it seemed to gleam in the fading sunset. My eyes lingered as I mused on how uncommon that sort of fairness is in men.

As I watched, he ran his fingers through his hair.

My mouth fell open in shock, and I stared at the blond youth with incredulity, remembering where I had seen that languid hand drawn through fair hair before.

The mannerism was Ariel's.

I had only ever thought of Ariel as a young boy, but I had not set eyes on him for years. Of course, he would be grown near to manhood now. I told myself it was impossible, that this was another blond youth. Ariel had traveled to Herder Isle to become a priest.

But this is a Herder ship! I remembered with utter dread.

My eyes hurt with the effort of trying to see more clearly, but the light was fading to a golden dimness, and the distance had grown too great. I could see no more than the white blob of the youth's face turned toward the river's mouth. But even as I watched, I saw his head turn until it seemed that he was looking straight at me.

PART III

◆

THE SADORIAN BATTLEGAMES

✦ 30 ✦

I CONCENTRATED ON walking, putting one foot in front of the other and keeping up with Brydda. It required all my energy. Listening to his words was more than I could manage.

It was early morning and the dismal start of a chilly and miserable day. Five days had passed since Matthew had been lost to us. The streets were blurred with a light drizzle of the sort that penetrates as damply and effectively as heavy rain.

We were making our way across the city for the long-planned meeting with the rebels at Bodera's home. Since leaving the safe house, the rebel had offered a monologue of advice and warnings, but somehow I could not make myself care about the meeting enough to hear what he was saying. Matthew's loss meant much more to me than any political alliance.

"Malik arrived with Brocade of Sawlney and with letters of authority that allow him to represent and vote on behalf of the Saithwold and Darthnor groups. And Tardis has sent a man called Gwynedd," Brydda was saying.

I nodded absently. Matthew's face seemed to float before my eyes, borne on a tide of grief and regret. My mind circled back for the hundredth time to our abortive rescue attempt. Not once had I imagined we would fail.

It was useless to wish now that I had thought it out more carefully and had been less certain of outwitting the ruthless, clever Salamander.

Since then, I had thought of a dozen perfectly good ways to get the Farseeker ward from his captors that had not occurred to me at the time, and somehow that made it all the worse.

"Elii of Kinraide has come, too, but the real surprise is that Cassell has come on behalf of the entire western bloc. You will recall I told you of the three rebel groups that have been unable to choose a single leader?" Brydda's eyes sought mine.

Did I remember? Yes, I nodded.

Reassured, Brydda brought his brown eyes back to the way ahead. "Well, then, his presence alone may mean that Cassell has gained control of the group and that it has at last been welded into a unit—in any event, it will give Malik cause for concern."

I pulled my cloak tighter to stop water dripping from the saturated tendrils of hair down my neck and glanced up at the heavy gray sky. Matthew had always disliked the Days of Rain, saying they drowned a man's spirit and dragged at his soul.

Ariel's face came to me then, his lips tilted in a mocking smile. I imagined him exactly as he had been when I met him: sweet-mouthed, with soft white skin and a golden nimbus of fair hair floating like a halo around his head. He had been as beautiful as an angel, but the radiant exterior had concealed a heart that was rotten and black to the core. And then his image changed, aging and altering until the face that mocked me was that of the dazzling blond youth on the deck of *The Calor Lady*.

I was tormented by endless imagined scenarios in

which Ariel came face to face with Matthew, whom he had known when they were both orphans in the old days at Obernewtyn. What would happen when Matthew, who had wanted to kill Ariel for torturing little Cameo to death, learned he was on the same ship as his most hated foe?

I could only pray that with so many slaves, Matthew's face would be lost in a sea of others; in spite of the farseeker's courage and strength, he was no match for Ariel's vicious subtleties.

"The biggest surprise, of course, is that Jakoby has come. . . ."

The odd name slipped through my haze of despair. "Jakoby?" I said aloud. "Isn't that one of the Sadorian tribe leaders?"

The rebel nodded approvingly. "Jakoby came by ship. From what I can make out, the Sadorians had no intention of attending this meeting until one of their Temple guardians had some sort of significant dream, and so they decided at the last minute to send someone. There was not time enough for a land journey, so it was a ship or nothing."

"Because of a dream?" I asked warily.

"Some matter of smoke shapes and feathers burning." Brydda dismissed this with a flick of his fingers. "The sort of ritual whose outcome can be read to mean anything—I expect the Temple guardians wanted to get our measure, so they came up with a guiding dream."

I swallowed, my mouth dry at the thought of such dreams.

"Anyway, Jakoby has come. Other than that, Dardelan of Sutrium will stand in for his father as I told you. . . ."

My mind began to drift again. Jakoby had come by sea, and Matthew had been stolen away by the waves.

Brydda stopped suddenly, swinging around to look into my face. I met his searching gaze with composure, but then, without the slightest warning, my eyes filled with tears. Fortunately, the street we were walking along was empty, for, within seconds, I was sobbing my heart out into the rebel's chest.

"Elspeth, girl," Brydda said, patting my back with awkward gentleness and drawing me into a doorway. "I am truly sorry about Matthew, and I know his loss is a mortal blow to you," he said.

"You don't understand. It's all my fault," I choked. "First Dragon and now this. And last time I came to the lowlands, it was Jik. I'm not fit to lead an expedition. Everyone I care about dies or is hurt terribly."

Brydda put me from him and looked into my face with stern sadness. "I know how it is to feel responsible for the death of a friend," he said. "But we are their leaders as well as their friends, and leadership often means putting people we care deeply for into danger."

"But that's wrong," I said in a hoarse voice.

"Which is more wrong? That a leader risks those he cares for or that he cares nothing for whom he risks? And those who follow us are their own people; they make a choice to follow us, and we must honor it. As we love them, we must accept that their tragedies come from their choices—not ours, else we are no more than moon-fair puppeteers, and they, sawdust dolls."

Involuntarily, I shivered, but Brydda seemed as oblivious to the cold as he was to the rain.

"Matthew chose to join Rushton's cause," he continued. "You do him no honor to grieve and put on funeral weeds. He has powers that will stand him in good stead wherever he goes." He gave me a slight shake. "Now dry your eyes, Elspeth, and take hold of your will. Let Daffyd discover what he can. Until then, put what has happened from you. There is work to be done, and this meeting is important to all of us. Prepare yourself for it."

"How?" I asked miserably.

"The same way we all do at such times," Brydda said harshly, the calmness suddenly drawn aside from his eyes as if it were a veil, revealing raw pain. "Do you think I have forgotten Idris already? Of course I have not. I fear some part of me will always be grieving for him. But I cannot let grief get in the way of a cause that both Idris and I believed in. So I act. I pretend. And some of the time I am able to forget that it is a pretense, and for that little period, I forget my pain."

"Act?" I echoed blankly.

He shook me again. "Pretend, Elspeth. Pretend that you are clever, wise, brave, calm, courageous—in the same way that you pretend to be Elaria the gypsy."

A man and a woman came out of a nearby door with a child between them. The parents ignored us, but the little girl looked deeply into my eyes, seeming to search for something.

"We are almost there," Brydda said when they were out of earshot. "They are expecting you to be a fumbling half-wit, and I have made no attempt to question their misconceptions. Their surprise will give you an advantage. For Obernewtyn's sake, you must show your best and most impressive face, as well as your most human one. This is not the time to be cold and withdrawn. You must give them something to warm to. Once we are in there, I cannot be seen to instruct or direct you—

especially since Malik already suspects that you are my pawn."

I took a deep shuddering breath; then I drew on an expression of determined calmness and turned it to the big man.

"Hmmph." Brydda's lips twitched in a faint smile. "Well, that is not so good, but it will do to be going on with." The rebel turned a corner into a lane that was too narrow for me to walk alongside him, and I fell behind. At once, the false smile fell from my lips and eyes. If he wanted acting, then acting he would have—but I would not pretend to myself.

As we walked, I tried to recall Brydda's warnings about subjects to be avoided and what I must and must not say, his advice on how to behave if this or that happened. My mind seemed to whirl with a tempest of words that would not connect.

"We are here," Brydda said suddenly. His tone was light, but his eyes betrayed tension. He flung his hand to indicate a tall cream wall in which was set a heavily carved wooden door. He paused, his hand poised over the gate latch, to look at me. "Are you all right?"

I nodded resolutely, though in truth I felt like sitting on the footpath and howling.

Brydda merely nodded and pushed the gate open. Beyond it was a little lush wilderness in miniature, open to the sky. It reminded me with painful insistence of a leafy glade where, during breaks from the summertime harvest on the farms, Matthew, Cameo, Dameon, and I had often gone to sit before Rushton took over Obernewtyn. Matthew and I used to lie flat on our backs, searching the clouds for images of the future, of our hopes and our dreams. My eyes misted, but

I blinked savagely as a thin boy a few years older than me came through the trees to meet us. Either he had been waiting, or the door had given him some silent warning of our approach. He had a long serious face, flyaway gingerish hair, and sad blue eyes that were unchanged by his smile.

"Welcome, my friend," he said in a warm, unexpectedly deep voice, clasping the rebel's hand. Then he bowed formally to me.

"You are Dardelan?" I guessed.

He nodded. "I suppose it is not hard to guess. Brydda probably told you that I am by far the youngest rebel you will meet today. A fact that Malik has seen fit to mention in at least a dozen ways since his arrival," he added ruefully to the big rebel.

"I am Elspeth Gordie," I said, holding my hand out to him.

He shook it solemnly, then led the way along a little winding path to the terrace of a graceful-looking residence.

"This is a wonderful idea," I said, waving my hand behind us as we passed into an overheated hallway. "Much better than building up against the street. Far more private."

"The Beforetimers used to have many such walled gardens—one to each residence, or so my father says," Dardelan murmured, ushering us inside. "They were very keen on privacy. I must apologize for the heating. I know it is too hot, but my father's illness makes him very susceptible to chills."

"It is nice to be warm," I said politely, though in fact I felt stifled by the hot, closed atmosphere of the house. "Brydda told me of your father's illness," I said on impulse, thinking of the teknoguilder Pavo. "I had a friend die of it. I am sorry."

Dardelan nodded acknowledgment, and his eyes held a measure of speculation that indicated I was not what he had expected. He led us through the house via a dark hall into a huge sunken room. It was windowless, being at the center of the dwelling, as near as I could make out. Two lanterns cast a murky light over the room's occupants.

A subdued hum of conversation fell into silence as they became aware of us, and I felt myself suddenly to be the cynosure of all eyes. I bore the visual dissection in dignified silence, blinking and waiting for my eyes to adjust to the dimness.

After a long pause, a handsome older man, with smooth gray hair and eyes the same shade, rose and stepped forward into the lantern light. "So, the Misfit," he said in a sneering voice. There was an arrogance in the way he eyed me from head to toe. I waited for him to introduce himself, but when he did not, taking into account his deliberate discourtesy and arrogant bearing, I guessed he was Malik.

I lifted my eyebrows and stepped farther into the room. "I will move closer to the light so that you may get a better view, should you wish to count my teeth and toes."

An astounded silence met my words; then an elderly man gave a startled bark of laughter.

But Malik was too experienced a player to let this pinprick upset him. "You are even younger than the stripling," he said disparagingly, as if my words had been callow rather than clever. And, in addition, he had managed to turn the words into a sideways jab at Dardelan.

"To be young is not necessarily to be weak," Brydda said pleasantly. "Whereas to be old . . . but you know what it is to be old, don't you, Malik. It renders the mind resistant to anything new." As he spoke, he moved to stand near Dardelan, symbolically allying himself with the youth rather than with me. I was, I realized suddenly, truly alone.

Malik gave Brydda a stiff smile. "I am older, true, but I am proud of my years, for age brings caution and experience and wisdom, and these things are well in one who would command. But perhaps that is why you surround yourself with children and freaks, Brydda. With such an obedient and malleable following, you would have no need of age or its virtues."

Dardelan colored slightly but wisely he held his tongue.

"I am no leader," Brydda said mildly.

Malik snorted, and it must have been obvious to the others in the room that he regarded Brydda as a rival. His eyes came swiftly back to me. "Does it speak, we wonder?" he inquired brightly. "Or has your parrot exhausted its meager repertoire, Brydda? Perhaps you should have toiled harder to gift your little pet more words to play with."

I had to bite my tongue to keep from showing anger before I spoke. "I speak when I have something to say, not to admire the sound of my voice," I said flatly.

The rebel's eyes glittered with malice, but his smile did not falter.

"Malik, this is Elspeth Gordie," Dardelan said. "It is

impolite for us to speak to a guest without using her name."

"She is no guest of mine, boy," Malik snapped. "I have higher standards. She is a gypsy halfbreed and a Misfit to boot."

The man who had laughed earlier leaned forward in his seat, and I realized that prematurely gray hair made him appear older than he was. His face was unlined, and I guessed his age to lie between Brydda's and Malik's. He was far less robust in appearance than either of them, yet there was a craftiness in his eyes that suggested the muscle he used to reign was one of brain rather than brawn.

"There is not much to you but skin and bones, child," he murmured. "Are they all like you, these warriors Brydda says you would bring to strengthen us?"

I saw then the part I was meant to play at this gathering. I was to be a pawn for these men to score against one another. Anger drove away my dreary sadness. I would be no one's pawn. I made myself smile.

"Do you measure your followers by their mass, sirrah?" I asked sweetly. "We Talented Misfits measure ourselves by our deeds, and surely you of all people would concede that size does not always indicate courage or cunning or even strength." I let my eyes fall momentarily to his own slender frame.

It was difficult to tell in the half-light, but I thought his pale cheeks flushed slightly. "I am Cassell," he said at last. "And talk is cheap."

"That may be so of rebel talk, sirrah," I rejoined promptly. "But my words bear my honor; therefore, they are valuable indeed."

This time his brows raised. "Well, you can talk a good fight."

I sensed I had won a slight victory but did not press the point. A movement on the other side of the room caught my eye. When the man who had made it rose, it was all I could do not to gape. It was the Elii I had known as a girl at the Kinraide orphan home. The orphanage guardians there had always predicted that Elii would die of the rotting sickness as his father had, for he had led orphans questing for whitestick. But he showed no sign of ill health. Nor did he show by word or gesture that he remembered me.

For that I was grateful, since he had not known me as a gypsy but as an orphan. And perhaps the simple answer to that was that I had changed, too.

He shook my hand and looked into my face, and I remembered that he had always been prone to judge by instinct rather than by the words people offered. The man alongside him had a stern, ascetic face and disdainful eyes, and wore his yellow hair in two flaxen plaits. Dardelan introduced him as Tardis's representative, Gwynedd.

Dardelan moved me past the silent Murmrothian to a hugely obese man named Brocade, who did not trouble himself to rise. He might have been brother to the Teknoguildmaster, except that where much of Garth's bulk was muscle, Brocade was like a plump, overstuffed powder puff. He was dressed in as much lace and silk as any maiden would wear on her bonding day. From Brydda's lecture, I remembered this man was a staunch ally of Malik's and resisted the temptation to ask Cassell if this was the sort of size he liked behind him.

Brocade had a haughty, self-important air as his eyes swept over me disparagingly. "The creature is very badly dressed considering the importance of this meeting," he said in an affected tone. "Are all your Misfits the same color as you? I am not fond of that darkish skin color, for as a rule, such belongs to people of inferior mentality."

I was too dumbfounded by this absurdity to respond.

A drawling and unusually accented female voice arose from the darkest corner of the room. "This is a very interesting observation, Brocade. I must be sure to mention it to Bram and the tribes when next we speak."

I turned with the rest to see a woman unfold herself from a couch as gracefully as a cat. Standing, she was at least a head taller than any man in the room and possessed of considerable exotic beauty. Her skin was a striking yellow-gold, and her tawny eyes were slanted up at the outer edges. Her hair was as straight and black as combed silk and cut perfectly level at her jaw and across her brow. The hair and eyes and graceful movements made her appear almost catlike, and the impression deepened as she displayed an amused, feline smile.

Yet the look she bent on Brocade was anything but amused, and he swallowed convulsively, numerous chins wobbling in alarm as her fingers slipped casually to the hilt of an ornate knife in her belt.

"I did not mean to insult your people," he bleated. "Your color is not the same as this creature's."

"What has color to do with anything?" Jakoby asked, for I knew it must be her. She wore voluminous trousers, a long tunic belted at the hip, and flat sandals.

Her fingers caressed the hilt of her knife absently, and Brocade followed the movement with bulging eyes. "I meant no offense," he said.

"None taken," Jakoby said pleasantly. "Provided you retract your statement. But if you wish to stand by. it, then I must demand a bout to see whether your pale skin really reflects greater wit than other colors."

"A . . . bout? You can't mean I should wrestle you? A woman?"

Her brows arched. "Is my gender also cause to think me inferior?"

"No! I—I—I retract!" Brocade stammered, mopping his damp brow with a scrap of silk.

Jakoby gave a throaty laugh of derision; then she turned to me and held out her long hand. I put mine into it, expecting her to shake it, but instead she seemed to weigh it in hers thoughtfully as she stared into my eyes. Then she turned my hand over and examined the palm minutely. After a long moment, she closed my hand into a fist but kept it in her own hard grip, looking again into my eyes.

"A good hand, girl. One that must grasp many threads of destiny. A hand whose owner is at once open and true, and yet who is the keeper of terrible secrets and a seeker of them."

Before I could wrench my hand away, Jakoby released it and turned to face the rest of the room.

"I vote for an alliance with this girl's people," she announced.

♦ 31 ♦

THERE WAS A moment of astonished silence before Malik leapt to his feet with a snarl of fury.

"I do not know how things are done in Sador, madam, but here we talk before deciding such issues as whether to ally ourselves with the likes of this creature."

"You talk. I have decided," Jakoby pronounced imperiously.

If the moment had not been so fraught, the look of baffled and impotent fury on Malik's face would have been comical.

"Jakoby, we honor you and know that your ways are different," Brydda interposed smoothly. "Were we in your land, we would abide by your customs. But this is our land, and here decisions among allies are made by a majority decision through a vote, taken from all participants after everyone has had their say."

The Sadorian grunted and flung herself into a seat with feline grace. "Very well. Talk," she said in an openly bored tone.

Malik looked perfectly furious, and the other rebels were clearly discomforted by her contempt. I tried to imagine this domineering gold-skinned woman at a guildmerge, where everything was decided by consensus, and failed utterly.

"Lady," Dardelan said, "you are a chief in your land. This, my father told me, is the Sadorian way, to choose the best and brightest by means of ritual challenges and then to allow them to lead without interference. But this is not Sador, nor is it Sadorians whom you will battle. The Council, the soldierguards, and the Herder Faction are Landfolk, and perhaps in this light you may concede that there will be times when we will know better how to deal with them. Maybe you will learn something useful from observing our ways, just as we will learn from you. Isn't that the advantage of an alliance?"

Jakoby made no response to this speech, but she had lost her bored expression.

"On behalf of the western bloc, I would like to say—" Cassell began, but Malik cut him off by snorting rudely.

"'On behalf,' Cassell? Do you have signatures over letters from Radek and Madellin explaining their absence and entitling you to represent them?" Malik demanded.

"We have come to an understanding—" Cassell began, but Malik interrupted him again with a loud laugh.

"An understanding—a very vague and useful term, is it not?"

Cassell flushed with anger, but he was not quick enough to compose a cutting rejoinder.

I glanced at the Sadorian, wondering how she felt about their petty bickering. It was no great advertisement for Land ways.

Elii rose to speak. "I want to know what these Misfits can do," he said in his gruff accent. "I thought that was what we were here for."

"That is what I was trying to say earlier when I was

343

interrupted," Cassell interposed with a dark look at Malik.

"I am not concerned with her tricks," Malik said flatly.

"I would like to hear what Elspeth has to offer," Dardelan said diffidently.

Brocade laughed coarsely. "No doubt you would, but we speak of war, boy, not bedsports."

Dardelan flushed bright red, and I felt the blood from my own cheeks.

"If you would conduct a war the way you conduct this meeting, then I think it *best* if you stick to bedsports," I snapped.

Brydda's eyes warned me to be careful; a display of temper would undo any favorable impression I had managed to make.

"I suppose Misfits know better than human beings how to run a meeting," Malik sneered.

Anger surged through me. Malik's continued attempts to label me and his implication that we were neither normal nor human would not stop until I had answered him decisively. Yet I would remain calm and dignified if it killed me, I vowed.

The effort of keeping my temper leached all emotion from my voice, and when I spoke, it sounded curiously toneless. "We do not consider ourselves abnormal but only possessed of certain additional abilities. We lack nothing that any other human being has in the Land, excepting perhaps a place in the order of things. It is the Council who names us Misfit, along with dreamers and defectives. I do not know whether we conduct meetings better, but do I know that our aim when we meet is not to use words as sly daggers but to exchange information."

Sensing I had their undivided attention for the moment, I shifted to address the room rather than Malik.

"I came here today to offer you the opportunity to find out how my people can help you win your rebellion against the Council. Yet I am treated with as little courtesy as if I were your enemy. You insult me and sneer, and from this, I might judge that you wish me to depart."

Malik's eyes sparkled with triumph, and anticipation of his disappointment enabled me to infuse a sweetness I did not feel into my words. "Yet, in case not all who are in this room share Malik's opinions and attitudes, I will speak my piece in spite of all his efforts to stop me." I hurried on before the furious rebel could cut in. "I have told you that we have additional abilities, and that is so. There are among us those who can communicate mind to mind over some distance. These we call *farseekers*. In a rebellion, with one such at your side, you could constantly exchange information and intelligence among yourselves and seek advice without leaving battle posts."

I sensed I was speaking well, for all but Brocade and Malik had lost their skeptical looks and were listening intently—even the stern, silent Gwynedd.

"Others among us have the ability to empathise— that is, to receive or transmit feelings. Such an ability at your command would enable you to strike fear or doubt into a soldierguard captain at the crucial moment in a battle, or even to send love and friendship into the hearts of attacking forces to confuse and distract them."

Malik laughed, but no one paid any attention to him. I felt a wild thrill. I had them!

"Some of us can communicate with beasts, which would enable us to project instructions and conflicting commands to enemy horses, thereby defusing a mounted charge."

"That fingertalk of Brydda's," Malik sneered.

I shook my head, refusing to let him shake my confidence or control. "Brydda's success at his fingerspeaking is admirable, but communicating with beasts, for those who have the Talent, is generally done via the mind as with farseeking. Were I nearby or even some distance away, I could reach out a voice from my mind to the horse on which a soldierguard is mounted and, provided my request was polite and reasonable—"

"Polite!" Cassell sounded startled and amused.

I looked at him gravely. "I find courtesy serves in any situation. Don't you?"

He looked faintly abashed.

"Of course," Malik jeered, drowning out whatever answer Cassell might have made. "We could all take a lesson from this and curtsy to our dogs and goats before breakfast."

Brocade guffawed loudly. "I think I can conduct my forces without advice from my horse."

I resisted the urge to suggest his horse could probably do a better job of it and went on to point out that, apart from our additional abilities, there were others among our number who had trained themselves as warriors and who were prepared to stand beside the rebels and fight.

"Are there other abilities?" Jakoby asked.

I glanced at her but did not let her catch my eyes. "Some of us have herb lore and are healers," I said, keeping my fingers crossed that she would not persist. "All of our abilities we would place at your disposal if we were allied, in the hope that by defeating our common enemies, the Land will become a place where we can all live in peace, without persecution or slavery."

"A pretty speech," Malik sneered. "But the heart of the matter is that you wish to trade your dubious and unproven additional abilities for acceptance among normal humans." He turned his burning eyes to the others. "We oppose the Council because of its misuse of power, not for its attempt to clean the human race of holocaust poisons and mutations. If we were to accept aid from these Misfits, we would have to give up trying to cleanse our race of deformity and mutation. Such a move would say that, hereafter, we will permit any freak or defective obscenity not only to live, but also to exist alongside us, to share our Land, our food, our crops; to bond with our sons and daughters."

There was a charged silence, and I felt frozen by the hostility in the faces that turned to me.

"She is a Misfit, and I see no monster," Dardelan said softly. "Is she the kind you mean when you speak of freaks and mutants, Malik?"

The boy had formidable subtlety, and I wondered what the father must be like, to have such a son.

"She is not visibly deformed," Malik conceded with ill grace. "But what of those she represents? No doubt they have sent her precisely because she was the most comely among them. After all, they would not send a monster, would they?"

"There are none among us whom you would see in a crowd and know as Misfits," I said. "None of us is physically deformed."

I stopped, for this speech soured my mouth. I could not compromise what I believed, not even to win these people.

I looked directly into Malik's eyes. "But were such a one to come among us, grossly deformed or not, we would not turn them away excepting that they were deformed of spirit or soul."

From the corner of my eye, I saw the Sadorian shift involuntarily as if the words held some goad, but when I looked, her face was impassive.

"See!" Malik declared. "She has said that she and her kind would accept grossly deformed mutants, as long as they possess these Talents. And with such a philosophy, how many generations before we would be reduced to a herd of howling beasts? Rather the Council should continue to prevail than that. The thought of allowing mutants to exist alongside normal, decent Landfolk is an obscenity to me and one I could never condone.

"But," he went on quickly, striding to the center of the room, "if your own values and decency are not enough to let you see what the ultimate outcome of this alliance must be, then think on this: These Misfits are little more than children, despite all the abilities they claim. Is that not so?"

He shot me a look of icy interrogation.

"The majority of us are young, that's true, but—"

"There you are. Condemned out of her own mouth," Malik cried. "Are we to act as wet nurses to monstrous children in the very midst of battle? Is it not a burden rather than an asset that we would gain in shackling ourselves to her people?"

"Youth means nothing," Elii said sharply. "I was a youth when I set up my rebel group. It's guts and brains that count, not age—and this girl sounds to me as if she has enough of both. I've no love for mutants, but she is no freak. And if her people can do what she says they can, then they would give us an advantage the Council and the soldierguards could never counteract."

There was a moment in which I thought Elii had actually won them over for me.

"Your brain is surely addled from whitestick," Malik snarled. "Oh yes, by all means, invite these freaks to fight alongside you, Elii. And while you are at it, employ the cripples and the scum that clog the lanes of every city street and would as soon cut our throats as guard our backs. But in the remote chance that you would win with such a force, remember that you will not easily set them aside when war is done.

"I will seek out instead the best and worthiest to fight behind me, and though my force be less in number, it will prevail, for it will be made up of true humans, not distorted copies and ghastly shadow creatures. Every one of my force shall know what they are and be proud of it."

"Your instinct for drama never ceases to enliven our meetings," Brydda said, as if the whole of Malik's impassioned diatribe had been nothing more than a puppet show for the rebels' amusement. "However, it might be as well to point out that this meeting is not to decide the future of the human race but merely to ascertain if this girl's people can aid us when we rise against the Council."

His dry businesslike tones diminished the effect of Malik's wild rhetoric, but the gray-eyed rebel was not done yet.

He stepped up to Brydda, his eyes narrowed. "I am not a fool," he hissed. "You want these Misfits to join us, and you connive with soft words and wiles to this end for some secret purpose of your own that eludes my reasoning." He swung to face the others. "Ask yourselves that, too, my comrades. Why does Brydda Llewellyn support an alliance with them? Is it that he seeks control of the rebel forces with their help?"

"My father also favors an alliance," Dardelan said coldly. "Do you also claim Bodera has secret purposes?"

Malik gave him a startled look, as if a duck had suddenly defended itself against a vicious dog.

"Do we need them?" Cassell asked, and the others turned to stare at the older man. "I ask if we need these Misfits, regardless of how useful they will be. Can we win without them? It seems to me that is a question we ought to be addressing."

"There are more soldierguards than there are of our people," Brydda said. "The simple answer is that we need everyone we can get."

"No!" Brocade shrieked. "I say we dare not take them among us, no matter how great is our need. Misfits are despised by Lud. If we accept them, it is the same as rejecting Lud, and we will be punished with another plague or some worse thing than that. Lud will visit disaster on us, and perhaps because of their eldritch aid, we will lose when we would have won."

I cast a look around the room and saw that all the rebels, even Elii, were looking thoughtful. I had underestimated fat Brocade badly.

I swallowed, and found my mouth dry with fear and tension and too many empty words. In that moment, I glanced at Malik. His eyes looked straight into mine, filled with naked loathing. His eyelids fell like shutters over the expression, but the hatred was burned irrevocably into my mind. In that instant, I understood that there would be no winning Malik's vote and no compromise. Not ever.

"Cassell was right in asking if we need them. I say we do not! This is a war we will wage, and to win it, we need only good armor and weapons and the warriors to use them—strong, committed adults. But most of all, we need strong centralized leadership."

The others were all nodding approval, the question of alliance shunted neatly aside.

"I say we strike soon, before the new intake of soldier-guards is fully trained," Malik went on forcefully, and I realized he was on the verge of taking over the meeting and perhaps the rebellion. With his smooth, handsome face and eyes that glowed with confidence, he looked the picture of a leader of men. I knew then, as if by futuretell vision, that if Malik assumed the mantle of leadership now, Misfits would be doomed after the rebellion. He and his people would hunt us down and destroy us.

The rebels had begun to argue and discuss the merits and disadvantages of different seasons to mount a successful rebellion. I glanced at Brydda, but his face was blank and unhelpful. Well, he had warned me that I could not expect his aid—especially not when Malik had practically accused him of using us to seize leadership.

I noticed that alone of all those in the room, the Sadorian woman was watching me from her shadowy corner, her yellow eyes glinting. This reminded me vividly of Maruman and, oddly, gave me the courage to do what I did next.

"The question of alliance has not yet been voted upon," I said loudly and firmly.

Malik gave me an irritated look. "Children should be at play, not meddling in the affairs of their elders and betters."

"Then let us speak plainly as children are wont to

do," I said, still loudly. "You, Malik, wish to set yourself up as the leader of the rebellion and of all these others sitting here, because you think you are better than them and because you desire the power that would accrue to such a position after the battles are over."

Malik flushed, then whitened, to hear me name his ambitions so nakedly and shorn of all softening or justification. Even Brydda looked aghast. It seemed that in the world of men and battles, only the truth was too shocking to be mentioned aloud.

But Malik was caught, because, without looking like a fool or a liar, he could not deny what I had said, when every person in the room knew it must be true.

"Each person has their expertise," he said at last through clenched teeth. "Mine is to lead."

For a moment, the capricious balance of power was tilted in my favor. I looked into Gwynedd's blue eyes. "What of Tardis? Does he also not possess the ability to lead? What of"—I stretched my memory—"what of Yavok, and indeed of any one of you in this room? Are you not all leaders of your groups because you possess exactly that same expertise to lead as Malik? And, in that case, why should he be set above you?"

"*One* must rule in wartime," Malik snapped. "In the end, a single person must be put above the rest. A rebellion must have a commander to whom all intelligence is sent. Once the battle begins, only one person can direct its course, can have the power to say go or stay, fight or retreat. A horse cannot have two heads or ten, and if it must have one, then give it the one who knows the trail best. I am a warrior. I know tactics, and I know the feel of battle."

"Malik is right. Sooner or later, we must choose

one to lead us in battle, and that is his strength," Elii said.

It was well said, but I had a final card to play in this game of words, and Elii had brought me neatly to it.

"Why choose at all when, with my people by your side, each of you may lead your own forces and confer whenever you need? With farseekers to link you, there is no need for one warlord! Why not go on as you have begun—each ruling your own people and conferring through mine when there is need? And then, when the war is won, choose one among you whose gift is peacetime rule, if you decide it is necessary."

"It makes sense," said Elii. "If each of us conducts our own share of the war, then what need have we of a leader in the aftermath of the rebellion? Could we not continue to rule our own provinces?"

"Bodera sent Brydda here to convince us with his silver tongue to join together, because divided we were nothing more than thorns in the Council's side. With great eloquence, he spoke of the need for us to be welded into a single unit with a single aim. Remember those words? And now he would have us splinter into tiny groups. Do you not wonder why? Could it be that divided we will be easier for him and his mutants to conquer?" Malik demanded.

Brydda stood up, his face showing anger for the first time. "I did not know Misfits like Elspeth existed when this began. But since they do, it seems to be wise to look at what they can offer us. But the decision is not mine to make, whatever Malik implies. It is yours, and I am nothing more than Bodera's and Dardelan's man."

"All I am offering is the means for you to retain independence," I said.

"I, for one, know my master would prefer to retain control of our people," said Gwynedd in a thin, sardonic voice. "It would surprise me if any rebel leader would say they wished someone to rule over them."

"Without having to decide who is going to run things, we might better concentrate on winning our battle," Dardelan put in.

"So speaks the wisdom of the ages," Malik sneered.

"I speak for my father," the young man said quietly.

"Again, I offer an alliance with my people," I said. "We will allow ourselves to be dispersed among you—"

"No!" Malik snapped, banging his hand on the table. "Who is this girl to offer alliance to us? Is she the ruler of her people? I think not. Why does not her master come among us, or is he so grossly distorted that he cannot be seen?"

"Some of us have met him," Cassell said mildly. "He is not a Misfit at all."

"Well, what sort of man is he who chooses to rule freaks? And I ask you again, how do we know that these mutated brats can do what she claims? I want more than children who can whisper to one another across the land, in exchange for accepting this girl and her freakish kin as comrades. I want warriors who can fight."

Jakoby rose, and so great was her natural presence, we all looked up at her. "You wish to see if she and hers can match your people in battle, Malik? Is that it? And if they could, what then? Would you accept them as allies and equals?"

"I would accept a cow if it could prove itself my equal," he snapped.

The others laughed, and though I kept my face still and calm, I seethed inwardly.

"Then there is a way to solve this matter," Jakoby spoke above the laughter. "In Sador, we have the Battlegames. It is a series of ritual contests that run between dawn and dusk on a single day. I offer you this as a way of solving this deadlock. By it, you will learn if this girl and her people can turn their talents to winning war." She turned her glowing golden eyes on me. "And your people will have the chance to prove yourselves and gain the alliance you seek. If you fail, then it is as well that this alliance does not come to pass."

"You said contests. Who would be contesting with whom?" I asked, my mind reeling at this new possibility.

Jakoby shrugged. "An equal number of yours and those who would test you. His people." Her eyes flicked to Malik.

"Where would these Battlegames be held? And when?" I asked.

"I do not see the point of playing games," Brocade interpolated.

I did not take my eyes from the Sadorian woman.

"A trial of honor is fitting at such an impasse," she said calmly, glancing at Brocade. "As to when and where, I offer Sador on behalf of my people. And whatever the conclusion of the Battlegames, the occasion may well be used to decide our own final strategy in dealing with the Council and its soldierguards."

That rendered all of them silent and thoughtful.

After a long minute, Malik nodded, his eyes glittering with triumph. Perhaps he was seeing that, as a victor of this mock battle, he would naturally assume leadership of the rebels. I had probably played right into his hands.

"Then it is agreed that your two peoples shall meet

at the Battlegames and that the fate of the alliance between you shall rest upon the outcome?" Jakoby asked.

"Done," Malik said savagely.

I stared at him helplessly, wanting to ask for time to
think, yet knowing I must not hesitate. If I refused the
contest now, Malik would win by default. Yet to agree
without consulting the others went against everything
that guildmerge stood for.

I thought of Malik's eyes, filled with open hatred, and
knew there would be no other way to get him to agree to
an alliance. And so, truly, there was no choice after all.

"All right," I said softly.

There was a momentary hiatus, then a babble of talk.

"I do not think fighting among ourselves is . . . ,"
Dardelan began.

"My master would agree that this is fair, I
think . . . ," Gwynedd said.

"It solves one thing, certainly," Cassell said mus-
ingly. "The need for us to meet together to plan the rebellion has been pressing for some time. Can it be
organized for all of the rebel leaders to come to Sador?"
Here he looked to Brydda.

Jaw clenched ominously, the big rebel nodded. "I
will send birds out, and the groups who have their own
will send replies by the morrow as to whether they will
journey to Sador or be guided by those who will go
and, in the latter case, whether they will assign their
vote to another or go with the majority on decisions."

"How long would such a journey take?" Cassell
asked. "I do not like the idea of being away from the
Land for too many days."

"Isn't Sador very far and the road to it dangerously
close to the Blacklands?" Brocade asked.

"By road it is far, but by sea it is two or three days only," Jakoby said.

"By sea!" Dardelan murmured, his eyes wide.

"We should think about this," Brydda cautioned.

"I have thought it through, and it seems to me that this is a good idea," Elii said decisively. "I have no love for sea travel, but it is a journey of two days that we talk of. If these Misfits beat Malik at this contest, it is worth whatever the bother afterward to let them stand with us. If they fail, then it does not matter. More importantly, to my mind, we will be able to organize the rebellion once and for all."

The others nodded at this blunt pronouncement with varying degrees of enthusiasm.

"Well, then, it seems we are to journey to Sador together—let us hope the ship does not sink, or the rebellion will be scuttled before it begins. At least this mock battle should be amusing," Cassell said, as if I had volunteered to bring a troop of clowns or tumblers to perform for them.

"What is to keep Sador from treachery when we are all in their hands?" Brocade asked querulously.

Jakoby gave him a look of scathing violence. "Were you not a barbarian, I would cut your tongue out for that insult," she hissed. "Sadorians do not betray allies."

Brocade stared up at her like a stunned rabbit.

"You do not have any honor," she said, leaning toward him like a snake readying to strike. "Yet you understand fear too well, for I think you are old friends." She stared into his eyes, and he grew so pale I wondered that he had not fainted.

At last she withdrew a fraction.

"You have no reason to fear, for since we of the

plains desire none of your squalid little Land, there would be no point in our hostaging or slaying those of you who would choose to come." Her eyes flicked contemptuously around the room, finally coming to settle with less fury on Brydda. Then she frowned, seeming to have some unexpected thought.

"It comes to me that I am at fault in this," she said at last. Her voice was calmer now, but colder than the sound of the Brildane howling in the icy wastes of the highest mountains. "I should not have expected you to recognize honor. As a token of faith that you will understand, I will leave my own daughter in this city, and I shall not come for her until you are returned from Sador. Is this acceptable?"

Dardelan stepped forward and bowed to the Sadorian chief. "Lady, I need no proof of your goodwill. But I offer my father's house where your daughter may stay in fitting comfort. She will be guarded as carefully as if she were my own sister," he said earnestly.

I blinked back sudden tears; this was the sort of romantic gesture Matthew would have made under the circumstances.

The cold light in Jakoby's eyes softened. "I think you will find a daughter of Sador does not need much protecting."

Dardelan bowed. "I will speak with my father, and preparations will be made at once."

"So it begins," Gwynedd said, and there was a curious finality in his voice.

"I am ready," Malik said; then he laid his head back and laughed wolfishly.

Brydda closed his eyes and sank into a chair.

◆ 32 ◆

WALKING BACK TO the safe house very late that night, the difficulties of what had been agreed to preyed on my mind.

Madness, Brydda had called it, and he was right. But I did not see what else I could have done. He had wanted me to impress the rebels with my normality, but right from the start, it had been only too clear that most of them could not and never would see us as normal.

And whether Brydda admitted it or not, Malik had been on the verge of taking control of the rebellion. If that had happened, we would then have had to start regarding them as deadly enemies.

I had to make guildmerge see that the Battlegames could not possibly alienate the rebels from us further. Nothing would be lost.

I sighed.

Not quite nothing. We must lose our innocence, for to agree to the contest meant literally casting aside all of our dreams of peaceful coexistence and gradual friendship. It meant accepting that we would only ever be tolerated, and even that must be fought for. Well, they would have to face that unpleasant truth sooner or later. It was only too clear to me now that we had been naive to think we could win the rebels by offering our help. We had wanted to believe that opposing the same enemies made us allies, but that was not so.

I tried to anticipate how guildmerge would respond to my suggestion that we use the Battlegames to teach the rebels to respect us—even to fear us—so that they would think twice before turning on us, no matter what happened in the rebellion. What other choice had we but to play by their rules?

Rushton would understand that—his whole life had been one of compromise to obtain his birthright. But I could imagine how Roland and Maryon would take it.

Under their leadership, the Healer and Futureteller guilds had opposed the Coercer's Talent contests when the idea was first mooted in guildmerge, claiming that competition promoted aggression. They had been narrowly outvoted, and the contests had since become an important event during our mountain moon fair.

There had been unexpected benefits. Mindmelds had increased in coordination, and individual skills had been honed and strengthened with the competitions as a goad. In addition, the stress of competition occasionally revealed unsuspected secondary and even tertiary abilities.

Though there was rather more at stake than a crown of flowers, the Battlegames was still a contest.

Of course, Roland would point out that what had begun as competition between guilders had swiftly metamorphosed into stylized displays of skill, with both competitors playing to the audience rather than trying to outdo each other; it was as much a team effort as anything else.

I would answer that it might be so with the Battlegames.

But that would expose the main weakness of my argument: I did not know what the Battlegames entailed, any more than Malik or Brydda did. Jakoby had refused to elaborate, saying only that they were not for the fainthearted and would test our ability in battle decisively. She would give no hint about what qualities and abilities might be needed. All we knew was that each side should muster a team of ten and must reach Sador within five days, for Jakoby had explained that Battlegames were held only on full-moon days during the Days of Rain.

I had come to Sutrium galvanized by an impossible deadline, and now I would leave the same way. Life seemed to resound in echoes and oblique reflections.

I could still hear Malik's malicious laughter ringing in my ears, as jagged as pieces of broken glass falling through the night. He had laughed, I thought, because he imagined I had played right into his hands in agreeing to the contest. That might have been expected from Malik, but it had shocked me a little to think that Brydda felt the same.

"How can your people win against Malik and his warriors?" he had demanded just before our parting. "He is the best strategist among us. He will win these Battlegames, no matter what they involve. It was madness for you to agree, for in doing so, you have made an alliance with Misfits conditional on a win. I don't know what possessed you."

"You said there could be no rebellion without Malik," I had pointed out. "I tell you, he would never have agreed to an alliance any other way than this. Now, at least Malik has committed himself to accepting us if we beat him, and Gwynedd seems to think Tardis will agree, too."

Brydda had only shaken his head and insisted I tell Rushton that the whole matter could be dismissed as a mistake if he would send a message quickly, saying I had overstepped my authority. He had even promised to send Reuvan to the safe house with a bird that might be loosed from Obernewtyn with this message.

Out of honor, I would have to convey Brydda's words and the doubts that fueled them. I wondered if Rushton would take the rebel's advice or mine.

Coming through the repair-yard gate, absorbed by my thoughts, I was utterly unprepared to see the object of them leaning against the side of a small gypsy wagon.

I stopped dead, a fist of reaction clenching in my gut. Rushton's arms were folded across his chest, and he was clearly deep in thought, a closed, brooding look on his face.

Though I had not spoken nor made a sound, he must have sensed he was no longer alone. He turned his head toward me. His green eyes seemed to reach across the yard with all the force of a jet of flame.

"Elspeth."

Just that: He spoke my name flatly, almost coldly. He straightened and walked across the yard, and I felt the blood rise in my cheeks. I made myself walk to meet him, to show I was not disconcerted, only to find that this brought us too close for my comfort. Before I could prevent myself, I stepped back.

Rushton's face sharpened to a kind of ironic enjoyment at my awkwardness. He stopped and made a little bow, as if something had been agreed to between us.

"I have been waiting for you. Kella said you had gone to meet with the rebels."

I nodded, my thoughts chaotic, but on the heels of my reaction to Rushton's presence was a rising fear. "How . . . why are you here? What has happened?" I demanded.

"Nothing. Not yet, at least. We are here because Maryon sent us."

I was about to ask who else had come when it struck me, with some force, that there was only one explanation for this expedition. Maryon had foreseen the journey to Sador.

Could it be that need would be answered so gracefully after all the misfortune that had haunted our time on the coast?

Rushton nodded. "So it's true, then. She said you would understand."

"Understand?"

"Maryon futuretold us coming here, but she did not know why. She said you would."

And again that awful, swirling, helpless feeling of being a leaf borne on some impossibly strong tide. Maryon had known that I would know. It was too much.

"You just came without knowing why, because . . ."

"Because Maryon said it was vital for Obernewtyn. Yes." Rushton nodded, a faint challenge in his green eyes. "It would be a little late to be deciding now that we would not live our lives by the whimsical wisdoms of futuretellers, don't you think?"

"But that was . . ."

"Dangerous, foolhardy, rash? Of course." He spread his fingers into a gesture of acceptance. Then his expression hardened, and the mockery in it died. "Why are we here, Elspeth?"

I took a deep breath. "I think because of something that happened at my meeting with the rebels."

"Do you think you might manage to be a little less cryptic?"

"You were right when you said they regard us as freaks. The meeting did not change that, in spite of Brydda's hopes. That was why Brydda had not contacted us—he was trying to make them change their mind," I said. "The two main rebel leaders in particular wanted nothing to do with us. . . ."

I told him everything then, about Brydda's intention in bringing me to the meeting, about Malik and Tardis and the power struggle between them, and finally about the Battlegames.

It was impossible to know if he was angry. He was too good at keeping his thoughts and emotions hidden.

At last he sighed. "We had better go and tell the others to prepare themselves for a sea journey."

Maryon had named the members of the expedition herself, Rushton told me. My heart sank when I saw whom she had sent. No wonder Rushton had sighed when I told him of the Battlegames.

The young Empath guilden, twins Miky and Angina, were sitting across from each other at the table sorting herbs. Receptive Miky intercepted my astonishment and swung around, her face creased in a welcoming smile tinged with mischief. "I bet we are the last people you imagined seeing here."

"That is saying it mildly," I said.

The stocky Coercer guilden, Miryum, was seated by the hearth with a pile of toasting forks on her knees. She had been rubbing the points over a whetstone as we entered, but hearing Miky, she threw them down and strode across the room to thump me on the back with painful enthusiasm.

"It is good to see you, Guildmistress. This is a queer business, is it not?"

I was distracted from answering by the sight of an unfamiliar plain-faced girl with yellow hair.

"Greetings, Guildmistress Elspeth," she said. "I am Freya. I believe you left Obernewtyn a sevenday or so before I arrived." She gave me a sweet smile that lit serene gray eyes, and I realized I had been wrong. She was not plain at all.

"Greetings," I said faintly.

The enormous, soft-spoken coercer Hannay was helping Kella to slice cheese and bread. "Greetings, Guildmistress," he rumbled, and went on slicing.

Beside him was the Teknoguild ward, Fian. "Kella told us about Matthew. I am sorry," he said gently, and his highland accent hurt because it reminded me vividly of the farseeker.

"And Dragon," Miky murmured, her face falling. "Poor little Dragon. If only Maryon would have let the others come and get her."

I stared at the empath. "What do you mean, if Maryon had let the others come?"

"She foresaw Dragon following you," Rushton said briskly. "We wanted to come after you to get her—you had only been gone a few hours. But Maryon said you needed to have her with you, that it was necessary." His eyes met my growing fury with bleak resignation. I remembered the words he had just said to me, about living by the whims of futuretellers.

I shook my head, anger making my eyes burn and

my head hurt. Did we have no will to exert? No choice? I remembered, with a kind of sickness, that it was Maryon's futuretelling that had sent Jik with me to the lowlands and to his death. "Did she dream of Dragon falling into a coma as well, when she stopped you bringing her back?" I snarled.

"Maryon foresaw Dragon following you, Elspeth," Rushton said wearily. "But Dragon chose to come after you of her own will. And you cannot have it both ways. If Maryon was right in predicting that Dragon would follow, then it must be that she was also right when she predicted the necessity of it happening."

I wanted to scream at him. If Maryon saw me walking off a cliff, would he not try to prevent my death? Might there not be moments when a futuretelling was shown as a *warning*? Would so much have been altered had Maryon defied her vision? What difference would it make if Dragon had not come to Sutrium, other than that she might not now be comatose?

A great deal, I realized with a queer chill. I might just as well ask how many ripples a single fallen leaf would cause in a stream and how far they might spread.

"Dragon's not dead. She's just asleep," Angina said softly, his empath Talent swirling out to enfold me in hope and compassion.

I sat down. "I know . . . I know. I'm sorry."

There was a moment of silence, and then the others began to talk, filling the void with words to give me time to recover myself.

"It was awful on the road, Elspeth," Miky murmured presently. "We were searched at the gate, and when they started to check our papers against a birth register, I near died."

"Miryum and Hannay had to coerce us through," Angina said eagerly, taking up his sister's lead, his face a masculine echo of hers. "Even so, we were lucky, because the second gate guard had a natural shield. A good thing he wasn't the one checking."

"I can't believe we're really here in Sutrium!" Miky said. "When Rushton came to firstmeal an' told us that Maryon had futuretold another expedition to follow you here, we never guessed for a minute we'd be on it."

Angina took up the story without missing a beat. "We thought there would be a guildmerge and a voting, but Rushton said Maryon already knew who was to come."

Why these Misfits, Maryon? I wondered with sudden suspicion. *What are you up to now?*

"She said it was vital for Obernewtyn," Miky went on.

Doesn't she always? I thought bitterly. Hannay's inclusion made sense, as much because of his deep patience as for his utter reliability. And Miryum's coercive powers were formidable. But why choose Miky, who had great empathic Talent but no secondary ability and no physical strength; and Rushton, who could not reach his powers; or this Freya, who, no matter what her Talent, was a newcomer to Obernewtyn?

"She would nowt say more'n that," Fian spoke with all the disgruntlement of a thwarted teknoguilder, interrupting the dual flow of the twins' story.

"She didn't know any more than that," Miky said quickly.

"But Elspeth knows," Angina chimed.

The others looked at me expectantly, but I realized I did not know why they had come. Not them in particular. And there were only seven of them.

Then all at once, it occurred to me there might be more of them. There must be.

"Who else came?" I asked with a shimmer of uneasy premonition.

Rushton gave me a queer, lopsided smile, anticipating my reaction.

"One other. Dameon."

I stared at him incredulously. Maryon had sent Dameon, the gentle and blind Empath guildmaster, to do battle with Malik and the rebels for the future of Obernewtyn!

◆ 33 ◆

DAMEON WAS SITTING by Dragon's bed, holding her hand. She was oblivious of his presence, though some foolish bit of me had hoped he might have reached her. But, no, she was locked in a sleep that must be close to the equines' longsleep, suspended in some netherworld between life and death.

I could have wept for the sadness in his face and the bowed shape of his shoulders. I felt a rush of love at the sight of him that was nearly painful.

Of course, he sensed the surge of emotions. I saw it in his sudden stillness.

"Elspeth," he murmured in his gentle voice.

Only then did he turn his face to me, his white-blind eyes gleaming in the light of a single candle guttering low in a wall sconce behind me.

"I could bear everything, if only she would wake," I murmured, coming to stand beside him.

He rose to meet me, letting go of Dragon's fingers to take mine.

"She will wake," he said. His words were a promise, but how could he know? He was no futureteller.

"Oh, Dameon," I sighed.

"There was a Beforetime story in one of the books you brought back from the underground library, which told the tale of a sleeping princess," he said, drawing me to sit by him.

"A story," I said flatly.

He smiled, and the compassion in his expression was like a slap, for what right did I have to expect him to comfort me? Was Dragon not his charge, as a member of his guild? Had he not known Matthew longer?

"The story tells of a beautiful princess who may or may not had red hair and who, cursed, pricked her hand on a poisoned needle," Dameon went on. "She fell into an enchanted sleep from which none could wake her."

I looked down at Dragon and shivered.

"She slept long, until a prince came who was her truest love, and the enchantment between them allowed him to break the spell."

"How?" I breathed, drawn into the story in spite of myself. "What did he do to wake her?"

"He woke her"—Dameon took Dragon's pale hand again and lifted it to his lips—"with a kiss."

I thought of Matthew—the only love Dragon had ever known, and an unwilling one at that. Would that love ever return to kiss her awake?

"It is a . . . lovely story," I said huskily.

Dameon nodded. "It is. Miky and Angina have made it into a song, and they will sing it to you."

"Dameon . . ."

He shook his head and gathered me into his long arms. "I know."

He patted my back as if I were a very young child or a frightened animal, his empathic Talent wrapping me in a warm blanket of affection and reassurance. I was dimly surprised to find he had erected an empathic barrier between us. He must have sensed I would not want my emotions bared to him.

"Matthew has been taken," he said gently. "But no slaver or shackle will hold him for long. He will return, just as he swore he would. As full of gossip and wild stories as ever."

Listening to his soft accent, I felt for the first time that it might truly be so.

"Well, this is touching," Rushton said from the door. "When you have finished the tender reconciliations, perhaps you will spare us a moment."

Sitting in the kitchen with the rain pattering against night-dark windows, Rushton told me for the first time what Maryon had futuretold.

"She said she saw eight of us journeying to Sutrium and your face, Elspeth, at the end of the journey. There was more—something about thirteen going over water." He hesitated, and I sensed there was something here he kept back. "She said it had something to do with Obernewtyn and figuring out what to do next." He frowned, as if this was not exactly right. "Something about finding the right road to tread."

He made a gesture indicating that I was to go on from there, and so I did, telling the group all that I'd told Rushton.

"I do not understand why this Jakoby woman would make such an offer," Miryum said suspiciously when I had finished. "What does she get out of helping us?"

"She wouldn't see it as helping us or the rebels," I said. "There was a problem, and she simply offered a Sadorian solution. Sadorians are . . . are not like

Landfolk, and I don't think you can judge them by our values. But honor is very important to them, so I don't think they would cheat or lie."

"Are you so sure this woman's offer of the Battlegames is what Maryon's futuretelling concerned?" Dameon asked softly. "She said nothing about battles."

"It would be too much of a coincidence for it not to mean Sador," Hannay said. "Where else would we go on a journey over water? Across the Suggredoon? Maryon said Elspeth would know, and she knows about the trip to Sador and the Battlegames."

"Could it have meant something about rescuing the Farseeker ward?" Freya asked. "He has been taken over water, after all."

"Where would we search for him, and how?" Rushton asked. He shook his head regretfully. "I wish we were going to find Matthew, but my instincts say the journey foreseen by Maryon is the one offered by this Jakoby. It fits too neatly. Why else would so many of us come, if not to take part in these Battlegames and win the alliance we need?"

"But there are not enough anyway," Miky said. "Maryon said thirteen of us would go over the water."

"It is possible this battle will not happen. Perhaps we must go to Sador for some other reason that has yet to be revealed," Dameon said slowly. "Maybe we will have the chance of proving to this Malik and the other rebels that we are human."

I hesitated, then shook my head, not wanting to give anyone false hope.

"There is no point in us going into this imagining we can all be friends afterward. We will never be accepted by the rebels. But the Battlegames are at least an opportunity for a temporary alliance. And they will also provide us with a chance to show the Maliks of the Land that we can defend ourselves from them!"

"A show of strength," Miryum said approvingly.

"If you like. Or maybe just revealing ourselves for what we are."

"And what are we?" Dameon asked, his voice threaded with sadness. "Warriors? Misfits? That is part of our trouble. We do not know what we are, and so we are constantly reacting to things, rather than taking the initiative."

"Maryon said we would find the road to tread on this journey over water," Rushton said pensively. "We have to see what happens."

"There is another thing you should know," I said, remembering. "After the contest, the rebels plan to meet and to decide once and for all when and how the rebellion will be staged."

Rushton's eyes flared with an unholy green fire. "Well, that puts it in a very different light. By winning, we would have gained the right to take part in their councils."

"And of course we will win," Miryum said. "Whatever the nature of these games, I do not think we need be frightened of ten unTalents. Hannay, Elspeth, and I could deal with them between us."

It was late the following day before we stood on the deck of a ship bound for Sador.

Contrary to Maryon's futuretelling of thirteen, there were only eleven of us, counting Dragon. We could not leave without her, and Kella had assured us that the journey would not hurt her. Domick had embarked on a Council errand to Morganna, and he wouldn't be back for day. And we were forced to leave the horses behind in Sutrium—much as Gahltha disapproved—for fear that the travel and the climate would do them harm.

No amount of searching had located Maruman. I couldn't help worrying, though I knew the old cat could fend for himself. He had made his own way to Obernewtyn before; he could do it again.

Reuvan, calling to drop off a homing bird at Brydda's instruction, had learned we meant to travel to Sador at once. Advising that we leave it to him to organize a ship, he arranged passage to Sador's Templeport with a seafaring friend and longtime rebel supporter.

Powyrs turned out to be a jolly, bold, brown-faced man with twinkling eyes and a habit of winking that startled us somewhat until we were accustomed to it. He had no qualms about carrying gypsies. I had the feeling he would not have given a damn if we told him we were Misfits.

I was standing on the deck of Powyrs's sturdy little ship, *The Cutter*, waiting for the Council inspectors to give final clearance to sail, when Kella pinched my arm to get my attention. Leaning close, she whispered into my ear in an absurdly furtive way that Reuvan was coming. I was not surprised that he had come to see us off, but I was startled to see that Dardelan was with him, as was a long-limbed, exotic girl with yellow, almond-shaped eyes and a satiric smile. She could only be Jakoby's daughter. If anything, she was more beautiful than her mother.

"You are the first to leave, but the rest of us will not be far behind," Reuvan said as they approached us.

"Malik and his cronies are traveling tomorrow, and I will travel with Jakoby and the rest on the Sadorian ship, the *Zephyr*, on the next day."

"Am I to be presented, or shall I stand like a nameless dolt?" the dark Sadorian girl asked haughtily.

Dardelan flushed and apologized. "This is Jakoby's daughter, Bruna; Bruna, this is Elspeth."

"I am pleased to know you," I said.

"Ah. I-am-pleased-to-know-you," Bruna said, exactly mimicking my intonation.

Unnerved a little by this and by her frank scrutiny, I busied myself introducing the others. When Dardelan and Rushton shook hands, they exchanged a measuring look and seemed satisfied by what they saw.

"You will like my land, of course," Bruna said haughtily. "Your people are welcome there, for like the tribes, they have no need to mark the ground where they have been, like a rutting beast marking its territory. Unlike these Landfolk." Her eyes ran over our halfbreed gypsy attire approvingly, but she gave poor Dardelan a look of amused contempt.

"In Sador, there is room to run with the wind and ride the kamuli," she went on, seeming to address all of us now. Wearing little, despite the gray, chilly weather, she was as oblivious to the cold as she was to the stares of passersby. No wonder Jakoby had looked amused when she said Sadorian women needed scant looking after.

The girl waved an imperious finger under Dardelan's nose. "And now you will guide me to the place of many trees. The forest. These I do not see in my own desert, and there might be some beauty in them worthy of a song."

"Of . . . of course," Dardelan stammered, and she bore him away.

"A pup watching over a bear," Reuvan said.

"A bear cub," I corrected, thinking that for all her imperiousness, Bruna lacked her mother's subtlety and dangerous grace.

It began to rain lightly as the inspectors arrived and set about searching the ship from top to bottom, seeking any Landgoods that were being exported without tax being paid to the Council. When Powyrs suggested we go inside, I was glad enough to do so. The fishy smell of the ship's oiled deck and the movement of it running up and down the swelling waves were making me feel distinctly queasy.

"I will want to cast off as soon as this is over to catch the out tides. Go into the main salon," Powyrs said. He looked at Reuvan. "I will come there and warn you before we are to depart."

As we trooped along the deck, I could not help but think of Matthew being led onto *The Calor Lady*'s gangplank in chains. Had he felt this strange, unsettling nausea? Was he somewhere out over the ocean being rained on, too?

I glanced back and noticed an old beggar in filthy brown robes come up to Powyrs and speak with him. At first the seaman shook his head decisively, but then he stopped and seemed to be listening intently. I was curious enough to farseek, but the queer static from whatever had tainted the sea about Sutrium's shores prevented this.

"Come on," Miky said, tugging at me.

The salon turned out to be spacious and light,

despite dark wood paneling and floor-to-ceiling book-shelves. This was due to three enormous box windows along the outside wall, crisscrossed by wide-spaced metal grilles. Cushioned seats were built into the windows, and a table, chairs, and various other pieces of furniture were fixed to the floor. The salon adjoined the galley, and Kella's eyes lit up as she surveyed its miniature neatness.

Rushton dropped into a window seat and gestured to Reuvan, Miryum, and Hannay to sit beside him. They talked in low, serious voices while Angina and his twin began to tune their instruments. Kella came out of the galley and stood at a window. Her eyes looked out to the sea, but I was sure she saw nothing but the face of her bondmate.

Powyrs had taken Dameon below to a cabin with Dragon. I moved to the door with the thought of going to sit with him, but Powyrs returned, blocking my way.

"Casting off!" he warned in a stentorian bellow. "All who will not sail should get ashore."

Reuvan rose. "I'd better move. A seaman is ruled by the tides, and if catching the tide means an unwilling passenger or two, then so be it."

The ship lurched suddenly, and all of us pitched sideways save Reuvan, who was accustomed to walking on a shifting deck.

He smiled somewhat wistfully. "You must learn to dance with the sea—not tread on her toes."

We went out on deck to bid him farewell. The rain had ceased, and the clouds had parted to reveal the sun sinking toward the horizon.

As the ropes were cast away by Powyrs's crew and

the shore began to slip away, a curious but definite feeling of loss assailed me, a feeling that I had somehow cast off from my life and was sailing toward a new one.

From the look of those gathered along the edge of the deck, I was not alone in this feeling. The others gazed back to the shore, their faces reflecting their unease. This was the first time any of us had left the Land. There were numerous disaster stories Landfolk told about the perils of the seas, and suddenly the wildest tales seemed to gain substance.

The sun sank into the sea, becoming increasingly large and orange as it did so, staining the gray-edged clouds that framed it a livid pink. I was intrigued to feel the taint in the water fading. That meant whatever had caused it was confined to the shore area. Perhaps some Beforetime container had broken under the sea, spilling its poisons.

"That's that, then," Kella said huskily when the sun finally vanished and Sutrium fell into a purple haze that merged with the horizon. "I feel as if I'm leaving a part of myself here."

I forbore pointing out the obvious.

"To Sador," Miky sighed dreamily on the other side of me.

"I feel sick," Miryum said, and I was startled to see that she looked bright green about the face and lips.

"I do not feel so well myself," I murmured.

✦ 34 ✦

KELLA SET ABOUT adjusting our senses to the movement of *The Cutter*, but some of us responded better to her treatment than others.

The empaths were only mildly affected by the motion of the waves and were quickly eased. I was less fortunate.

Because of the instinctive blocking ability I appeared to have developed as a response to intrusion, I had to hold my mind open to the healer. This was not easy, and when she was done, the wooden decks continued to pitch, rendering me queasy and disoriented.

Disappointed, I asked Powyrs if there was not some seaman's remedy that would settle my stomach.

He looked at me intently for a moment, then shook his head. "Your illness is not physical. It is a matter of the will. You resist the ocean as if it were an opponent. But you cannot defeat the sea—it is too great and too uncaring. You can only surrender to its power. While you fight, you will suffer."

I laughed and said he talked as if the sea were alive. He only shrugged. "Laugh, but it is true. All things that exist live, though maybe they do not measure life as we do."

I thought this absurd. The fish in the sea lived, but

not the sea itself. It was just water. But seafolk were as notoriously superstitious as highlanders, and I liked Powyrs too much to make fun of his beliefs.

The coercers suffered worst of us. That was not un-expected, for coercers were always disturbed by any-thing that altered their balance or perceptions. Roland believed this had something to do with the nature of coercing and how the deep probe was shaped to serve their Talent. The more powerful the coercer, the more severe the response. Accordingly, Hannay was nau-seous but Miryum violently ill. All Kella could do was render her unconscious with a sleepseal.

Like me, Hannay resigned himself to an uncomfort-able few days.

That first night, my stomach churned at the thought of food, and I sat a little apart as many of the others ate a mushroom stew and regaled Kella with news from Obernewtyn.

Turning to a window, I looked through the reflec-tion of the room and its ghostly occupants to the dark sea beyond.

I shook my head at the sudden melancholy that as-sailed me. Perhaps it was that I had grown accustomed, these last two sevendays, to strife and activity and ur-gency. Sea travel was not like travel on land where there were always things to be done, if only to break camp and set up bedding at night. We journeyed, and yet we went nowhere.

I sighed, wishing it was not my nature to see life as if it were the reflection in a window. I could never just accept it. I had to be squinting my eyes and looking to see what was underneath it, tormenting myself with doubts and questions. And it was worse when I had nothing to distract me.

The moon penetrated the clouds for a moment, lighting up a small cluster of rock spikes. Powyrs had said these were good shoals because you could see them. But there were many more such shoals hiding just below the surface that could tear the bottom from a boat if the seamen were not vigilant. The ocean's teeth, he had named them, winking.

I was like a wary seafarer, never trusting the smooth, glimmering surface of life for fear of the hidden teeth. Perhaps that was why I could not settle as the others had and enjoy the enforced idleness. Even when there was no need, I watched for the teeth.

I scowled at my own face in the glass, telling myself again that I should be content. After all, Maryon's dream had solved my immediate problems.

I bit my lip, understanding that this was what lay at the root of my strange discontent. I had left Obernewtyn driven by Maryon's dreams. But once away, I had done as I chose. I made decisions and acted on them and felt as if I owned my life. Now Maryon and her dreams had reached out to wrest control from me again. I was not the wary seaman after all. I was a ship, floating on the tides and eddies of capricious fate just as *The Cutter* was driven by the sea. But at least the ship had a captain. Who was the captain of my voyage? Atthis? Maryon? Certainly not me.

I thought of the futureteller. How did Maryon feel to know that she had only to speak of her dreams to be obeyed? It was true power. But Maryon did not control her dreams, so, in a sense, the power was not hers. The dreams controlled her, pulling this way and that, demanding to be told or acted upon. Was the self-knowledge she and all her fellow futuretellers sought worth this slavery to their dreams?

The salon door banged open, and I turned to see Rushton enter.

Of us all, Rushton had adapted most easily to the movement of the ship. From almost his first steps on deck, he had mastered the graceful rolling walk affected by Powyrs and his crew. His cheeks were red, his hair wildly tangled, and his eyes bright as they swept the room. He was clearly finding his first sea journey exhilarating.

"I am ravenous," he said.

The door behind him burst open again to reveal the old beggar who had been speaking to Powyrs at the bottom of the gangplank just before we departed.

"You can't come in here . . . ," Hannay began firmly.

The beggar threw off the hood of his brown robe to reveal a familiar tanned face in the candlelight.

"Daffyd!" I murmured. There were cries as the others recognized him, too.

He ignored them, his eyes sweeping the room to settle on me. I gasped, for only when he faced me properly could I see that his left eye socket was swollen to twice its size, his lip split, and his cheek marked with bloody striations.

"What in Lud's name has happened to you?"

"I escaped from Ayle," he said hoarsely.

"Sit down, man," Rushton said, steering him to a window seat beside me.

"He found you out?" I asked.

"Ayle found nothing out. Salamander told him I was a spy."

I was confused. "He can't have returned already?" My heart rose. "Unless the slaves have only been taken to Morganna or Aborium . . ."

Daffyd shook his head. "Salamander told Ayle, the day he came to take the slaves, that I was to be locked up until he got back." He shuddered. "Lud knows how he learned I was a spy or what he planned to do to me when he returned. As soon as I got a chance, I broke out and fought my way free. I headed straight for the city gates, but Ayle was quicker. I spotted his people just in time. I would never have made it, and I knew if they were watching one gate, they would be watching them all."

"You went to the safe house?"

He nodded. "It was all locked up. I had no choice but to try sending out an attuned probe to you. It near killed me to hold it together when it got near the sea, but it locked on to your mind a split second before the static got the better of me. That was long enough for me to learn that you were sailing at dusk for Sador. I told your captain that I was a friend. I hope you do not object to another traveling companion."

"We are glad to have you," Rushton said, but he spoke as if his mind was elsewhere.

"That's twelve of us," Miky breathed beside me.

"Elspeth believes she saw Ariel on board the Herder ship that took Matthew away," Rushton said. "Did you see him?"

Though I would not have thought it possible, Daffyd paled further.

"It seems unlikely, since there is no connection between Ariel and this Salamander . . . ," Rushton said.

Daffyd stood up abruptly and stared down at him.
"You are wrong." His face was clenched in misery, and
he began to pace. "I said at the safe house that there
was not enough time to tell my story. Now I wish I had
taken the time."

"It would be a simple matter if lives were lived by
hindsight," Rushton said. "There is much we would
not begin if we could see how it would end."

Daffyd would not be consoled. "Matthew was my
friend, and I ought to have done something. If Ariel
was aboard . . ."

"From what Elspeth said, there was nothing you
could have done," Rushton said firmly. He pulled
Daffyd back down and motioned to Kella to wash his
wounds. When the healer was settled and bathing the
gashes, Rushton asked Daffyd what connection there
was between Salamander and Ariel.

"I will tell you," Daffyd said, "but I must start at the
beginning. After leaving Obernewtyn with Kella and
Domick last summerdays, I traveled to the White
Valley and the site of the Druid encampment. My plan
was to see if I could find any clue as to what direction
the survivors might have taken." His eyes were distant,
as if he truly gazed into the past and saw the events he
described unscrolling before his eyes.

"I left the valley without any sign to give me hope
and tracked all through and around the Gelfort Range.
I found some few scattered camping places, but there
was never any way of knowing whose they had been. I
went about small settlements in the highlands and in
the upper lowlands, talking and asking questions. I

sometimes pretended to be a Councilman and at other times a Herder agent.

"Then one night at a dingy inn in a tiny settlement, I came face to face with one of the Druid armsmen from the camp."

Daffyd's face reflected the elation he must have felt at this first breakthrough in his long search. But the smile faded at once. "He told me that shortly before the firestorm destroyed the camp—mere days—Ariel came to see the Druid."

I seemed to see that pale, impossibly fair face turning to me on the deck of *The Calor Lady*.

"As you know," Daffyd went on, "Ariel was working as an agent for the Herder Faction back then, and for the Council, while at the same time styling himself a secret friend to Henry Druid. On this last visit, he told the Druid that the Council had learned the location of his secret camp and that soldierguards were being dispatched to clean it out. He advised the Druid to prepare his people for battle, insisting that they would be able to defend the fortified camp, and he suggested sending the young, the frail, and the elderly out of harm's way up into the foothills of the Gelfort Range. Ariel claimed he dared not remain to help drive off the soldierguards, since it would betray his identity and put an end to his usefulness as a spy. But he offered to lead those who would not fight to a safe place in the hills until it was over."

Daffyd's face twisted in a spasm of uncontrollable rage. "The Druid thanked him for his friendship and loyalty and did as he suggested. When Ariel had gone, Henry Druid decided to send out a small advance party to give warning of the soldierguards' approach. The three scouts rode out a bare hour before the firestorm razed the camp to the ground—the man who told this story to me was, of course, one of the three. They saw the storm and returned when it was over to find nothing remained of their camp. They looked for Ariel and those who had been led away, but there was no trace of them. Nor, in the days that followed, did any soldierguard force materialize."

It took a moment to understand what this must mean. "Ariel lied!" I said incredulously.

Daffyd nodded, his eyes bleak. "What other answer could there be? I suppose he true-dreamed the firestorm and saw it as a natural and anonymous way to end a potentially embarrassing and no longer necessary connection with an outlawed priest. The visit was simply to ensure that the Druid and his armsmen were in the camp when it burned." His voice was choked with rage and despair.

I saw that Rushton had grown pale. At first I thought he was experiencing the same shock as I, at this suggestion that Ariel had powers like ours. But then I remembered that, long ago, the Druid had befriended Rushton and treated him as a son. He had not seemed terribly affected when the firestorm destroyed the camp, but there was a difference between being killed in a firestorm from nature's random arsenal and being lured into a deadly trap. Ariel had even found a way to use nature for his perverted ends.

"What of the people he led out?" Kella murmured.

I could guess what was to be told next—the answer was threaded through all that had happened.

"When the three surviving armsmen could not find them, they split up. Two went to the west coast. The third man remained, and it was he who I met. For a time, we traveled together, but we found no trace of the others. He began to fear that taking them from the camp had simply been Ariel's means of getting out before the firestorm struck, a ruse, and that he had killed them after. But I could not accept they were dead. So we parted, too. Gilbert went to join the other two armsmen, and I—"

"Gilbert?" I said, remembering vividly the red-haired armsman who had befriended me when I was captive in the Druid camp.

First Daffyd, then Elii, and now Gilbert. Who else would I meet out of the past, circling back to merge their lifepaths with mine? Did it mean anything or nothing?

Daffyd frowned. "You remember him? Strange that you should recall one face out of all the Druid's men. He spoke of you but thought you were dead. Of course, I did not enlighten him."

I nodded. The last time I had seen Gilbert had been on the banks of the upper Suggredoon, a look of helpless anguish on his face as my raft was swept away by flood-swollen waters into the depths of Tor.

The armsman went on. "Well, we parted as I said. I came to Sutrium, and it was there that I met another from the Druid camp, a woman. She was calling herself by another name and tried at first to pretend I was mistaken, but eventually she admitted the truth. She told me she had been a slave fleetingly but had escaped being transported and sold with the help of a seaman who had fallen in love with her. He threw her clothes overboard and pretended she had drowned herself, but he warned her never to speak of it, for if the truth was known, they would both be killed.

"I asked how she had been taken by the slavers in the first place. 'Taken'? she mocked me. 'I was *given* to the slavers. Betrayed and sold with no chance to run or fight. My bondmate saved me, but he could not save all of us. The others have gone over the waves, wherever slaves are taken.'"

Kella gasped aloud. "Oh Lud. Ariel sold those he had taken from the camp to the slavers!"

Daffyd nodded. "I was a fool not to have seen it sooner. The woman told me they saw the camp burn and could do nothing. There had been men and women, hired thugs, waiting in the hills to bind them and lead them away. Ariel had sold them to Salamander."

Daffyd ran his hands through his hair. "You know, the thing that gnaws at me is that I had been only a little distance from their camp the day they were taken out of the mountains by the slavers. If only I had been able to farseek Gilaine as soon as the storm ended."

There was such anguish in his voice. The static thrown up by the firestorm would have prevented his farseeking, but that he had not gone looking for them at once was my fault. I had been injured terribly, and we had just found Jik's charred body. I had begged Daffyd to take Dragon to Obernewtyn before the pass to the mountains was closed by snow.

"I felt . . . helpless. Hopeless," he went on in a barely audible voice. "It had been months since they had been sold, and they were long gone on the slave ships. For the first time, I felt they were truly lost to me. I wanted revenge on Ariel. You cannot imagine how badly. But he had gone by then to Herder Isle.

"So I turned my mind to the slave trade with the idea that perhaps I could inveigle myself a job and learn where they had been taken. It is madness of a kind to be so persistent, yet somehow I felt that if they lived, I must find them."

Daffyd's eyes burned with near-fanatical hatred; the search for Gilaine, Jow, and Lidgebaby defined his existence now. Truly, he was not so far from madness.

"I suppose this woman from the camp did not actually see Salamander?" Hannay asked.

Daffyd laughed harshly. "No. No one has ever seen Salamander's face—except perhaps Ariel. It was only after the sale of the Druid's people that Salamander moved in properly on the slave trade, killing anyone who stood against him, terrorizing the rest, and streamlining the operation into one smooth, efficient monopoly. I thought Ariel's connection with him was a passing thing, but if he was aboard the ship with him, perhaps there is more to it."

"I wonder what Ariel got out of the bargain. Coin?" Rushton murmured. "He would not aid the slaver for nothing."

Daffyd's expression hardened. "Perhaps. They are as like to one another as two buds from the same plant. Both are secretive. Both love pain and desire power."

The desperation returned to his face.

I laid a hand on his arm. "What will you do now?"

"Survive," he said harshly. "If Salamander wants me dead, I will live to spite him. He will have the city scoured for me when he returns, and it pleases me to think that he will be thwarted. We will have our day of reckoning. And when I am done with the slavemaster, I will find Ariel."

· 35 ·

It DID NOT take much persuasion for Daffyd to let himself be shown to a bed. He was clearly exhausted far beyond his endurance.

I felt too nauseous to sleep and decided to go out on deck. Perhaps some fresh air would make me feel better.

The wind had risen, and it fluttered my clothing and snapped the sailcloth. The sea was higher, too, and slapped against the wooden hull in a broken rhythm. I shivered and pulled my cloak about me, trying to imagine what it would be like to do as Powyrs suggested and give myself to the sea.

"Wet, doubtless," a voice clove into my thoughts.

I started violently, for draped languidly on a mast strut right in front of me, licking one paw, was Maruman!

"How in Lud's name did you manage to get aboard?" I demanded. "And where have you been?"

For once, my questions did not rouse his ire. He stretched with slow and infuriating feline grace and jumped lightly to the deck to rub against my leg.

"There you are!" Powyrs bellowed, and swooped over to scoop him up.

I froze, but instead of scratching the seaman, the bedraggled feline lay quiescently in his arms, an alarming mixture of complacence and thwarted mischief in his single gleaming eye.

"I wondered where he had been hiding," Powyrs said, pretending severity. He looked at me and winked hugely. "The fools I have working for me think he is a bad omen, but he is too smart for them to catch and throw over the edge as they would like. He torments them, the naughty thing. Darting out and scaring them. Twice he has made seamen fall overboard." He beamed at Maruman with paternal pride, and I could barely stop myself laughing aloud.

I stood up and reached out to pat him. Powyrs's muscles tightened as mine had done moments before, but he relaxed as the cat allowed himself to be petted.

"Well, you are honored. Usually he will suffer no one to touch him but me," he said, sounding astonished.

"He is magnificent," I said, repressing a grin at how utterly Maruman had beguiled the burly seaman.

"Of course," Maruman sent haughtily.

"He can be savage," Powyrs warned. "You'd best leave him be, except when I'm holding him. He's used to me. Reminds me of the sea, he does. My father said to me when he advised me against being a seaman; 'The sea is a wild beast that eats the lives of those who would try to tame it.'"

"You didn't listen, then?" I smiled.

He shrugged. "I never liked tame things, even as a boy." He glanced over and noticed one of his seamen mending a sail. Snorting in derision, he set Maruman down gently before stomping over to instruct the seaman on his deficiencies.

"Well, I see how you managed to get yourself aboard," I sent, grinning at him.

Maruman made no response. He leapt up onto a box beside me, and I felt a surge of pure happiness as he climbed onto my arm and clawed his way up to my shoulders to drape himself about my neck. I breathed deeply, taking in the slightly fishy smell of his coarse fur, as if it were the scent of fresh flowers. Oddly, I no longer felt sick.

I yawned and decided I would go to bed. For the first time in many days, I felt content.

"I am glad to see/carry/smell you," I sent, repressing my usual instinct to cuddle him close and tell him I loved him.

"I am glad also," Maruman sent with rare sweetness.

The tiny cabin I had chosen contained only a bed and was no more than a closet. Its virtues were that it was situated on the main deck, which meant there was no need to grope my way down ladders in the darkness, and I would have some privacy. In a short time, I was leaning down to let Maruman jump onto the narrow bed, which was fixed to the wall under a small round window looking out to sea. The moon slid out of its envelope of cloud, and the old cat sniffed suspiciously at the pillow where its silvery light fell. Then he turned to me, his eye filled with moonlight.

I froze in the act of taking off my sandals.

"The oldOne sent ashling to Maruman/yelloweyes. Say come. Maruman coming. Say: tell Innle. Maruman tells," he sent.

"Tell me what?" My heart pounded.

"Maruman flew the dreamtrails with the oldOnes. Saw Innle on blackdeathroad. Going to the endmost means end of barud. Obernewtyn finished and all gone for Innle."

I stared at him. Atthis had sometimes called my quest a black road. Maruman seemed to be saying that if I completed my quest, Obernewtyn would not be there anymore. But what did that mean? That it would be abandoned? Destroyed? And why would Atthis want him to tell me this now?

I took my sandals off and climbed into the bed, shifting Maruman to make room for myself. Maybe I was misunderstanding him. After all, beastspeaking obeyed no rules. Communications were entirely idiosyncratic, dependent on how much Talent a beast possessed, their mood at the time of communication, their relationship to the human with whom they communed, and, sometimes, even on what was to be told. Beasts interchangeably used their own odd dialect, human words, and imagepictures enhanced by empathised emotions. And Maruman was harder than most because of the distortions of his mind.

Maybe Maruman had not meant that Obernewtyn would fall but that it would be lost to me. The Agyllians had warned me that my quest would lead me away from my friends. But I had always assumed that, when that quest was over, my life would be my own. It disheartened me to think this might not be so.

I remembered Ariel saying in my dream, "Do what you wish, and you do my bidding." Was that my mind's way of warning me that free will was an illusion and that my life would never be mine to command?

"It would be a little late now to decide that we would not live our lives by the whimsical wisdoms of futuretellers, don't you think?" Rushton had asked the previous day.

And it was too late. My sworn quest was the central and defining truth of my life now. Just as Daffyd's long search for Gilaine shaped him, so my quest shaped me. If there was a black road, then I was on it already and had been all the days of my life. And I would walk it to the end—no matter where it led me. Even if it meant I could not go back to Obernewtyn.

Then it came to me. Perhaps Atthis had sent Maruman to test my resolve.

"Rest/sleep," Maruman sent insistently. "All things seem dark under the whiteface." He curled against my chest, and we slept.

I dreamed I was on land, walking through country as Ludforsaken and desolate as the drear vista of the Blacklands I had once seen from the top of the high mountains. The road beneath me was black, and I saw that its darkness had climbed into my limbs, staining them a sickly purplish yellow—the livid shades of advanced rotting sickness that told me the road was poisoning me.

I wondered then if Maruman had meant that I would not be able to return to Obernewtyn because I would be dead.

I woke to unexpected stillness.

It felt as if the ship were not moving at all, and I wondered if at last my senses had realigned to shipboard life. There was a weight against my arm, and I opened my eyes to find Maruman sprawled alongside me, his head resting on my elbow. I eased myself out from under him and turned on my side to watch him sleep. Poor, dear muddled Maruman filling me up with his garbled thoughts and gloomy predictions. In the daylight, such cryptic nonsense did not seem so terrible.

I leaned forward and kissed him very softly, knowing he would be furious if he caught me.

Kella poked her head in the door.

"Oh good, you're awake, Elspeth. Come and see this."

I put a hasty finger to my lips and pointed to Maruman. The healer's eyes widened at the sight of the cat asleep in the rumpled bedclothes, and she backed out of the room. I climbed from the bed, ran my fingers through my hair, and laced on my sandals.

Kella was waiting for me outside. "How in Lud's name did he get here?" she demanded.

"He must have had a true dream. He got aboard even before we did and settled himself to wait. He's got old Powyrs twisted round his paw."

Kella's eyes shone. "I'm so glad he's all right. Oh, Elspeth, maybe it's true what Powyrs says about them being good luck."

"'Them'?" I asked, baffled. "Cats?"

She shook her head and beckoned, and I followed her to the edge of *The Cutter*. "Look out there," she said, pointing.

I looked and was startled to see that the ocean was utterly still, stretching away like a mirror on all sides of us. Now I understood why my nausea had abated. Not a breath of air stirred the sagging canvas sails or rippled the glassy sea. We were so completely becalmed that a reflection of the ship and my face stared back with perfect clarity from the water. There was no sign of the coast, but Powyrs had explained to us the previous night that he would have to set a course directly away from land to begin with, in order to avoid the shoal beds clustered thickly in the sea between the Land and the Sadorian plains.

And then I saw three sleek, satiny, silver-gray fish, as big as grown men, propelling themselves high into the air, somersaulting, and plunging back into the water.

I gaped, astounded at their strength and agility.

"They have been known to save the lives of humans who fall from the deck," Kella murmured.

"Good luck is right," I said. "Good luck for the drowning seaman."

I watched the strange fish leap out of the water as if they were moon-fair acrobats. They must be incredibly strong to lift themselves out of the sea like that, I thought. I had never tried to communicate with fish before, but some instinct told me these might be capable of beastspeaking. The sea was utterly clear of tainting, and I could have tried, yet I found I did not want to. These lovely creatures were oblivious to the humans watching them, and I was content to have it so. Humans had caused so much sorrow for the beast-world; let these remain untouched.

"Ah, ship fish. They are nowt truly fish, you know," Fian said, coming to stand beside me.

I jumped, for I had not heard him approach.

"Of course they are," Kella said.

"They are warm-blooded, an' they suckle their babes on milk after bearin' them whole as humans do. An' they need air." He held up a thick book with a mot-tled green cover. "This book tells all about them. Ship fish are much like humans."

"Are they descended from the merpeople?" Kella

asked. She had become fascinated with accounts in Beforetime books of a race of humans with gills and fishtails who had dwelt under the sea.

Fian frowned. "I dinna know. This books says nowt of them, other than that ship fish were sometimes mistaken for them. It does say that Beforetimers had boats that would go under water."

"Where the merpeople lived?"

Fian frowned at the healer. "I told ye, it doesn't say. Perhaps this was written after they became extinct. Apparently, there were ruined cities under th' sea. . . ." He looked down at the tome in his hand. "Powyrs has even more books in a trunk in his room, an' he has told me I may look through them."

"So many books," the healer murmured.

"And all about th' sea," Fian said. "Enough for a lifetime's study, and I have only a few days." He cast a final long look at the ship fish and turned to hurry back into the salon.

Kella shook her head. "Teknoguilders," she said with faint disparagement. "How can he think of books when there is this to see?"

But a little later she grew tired of the ship-fish antics and went in.

I decided to climb up to the small upper deck, for it would give me a better view. It was piled with boxes, and I sat on top of one, dangling my legs and looking out at the sea. I had never known such stillness. It seemed to accentuate the vastness of the world and, in contrast, my own insignificance, but it was not an unpleasant feeling. In the face of this endless sea, I was no more than one of the ship fish, jumping in my bit of the ocean, making my little waves. There was a queer peace to be found in the thought, and I tried to draw the immense calmness into my heart to erase fear and anger and sadness.

My concentration was shattered by a muffled explosion of laughter.

"It tickles," I heard a female voice giggle. I recognized Freya's melodic voice and smiled, wondering whom she was with.

A moment later, I saw Rushton stroll to the rail, and my amusement evaporated.

Even as I watched, Freya stepped up beside him and shook her head, the springing golden curls catching and diffusing the morning sunlight into a pale halo.

Rushton appeared to be doing most of the speaking. Then he grasped Freya's hands in his and stared into her face intently as if waiting for some response. Freya's head was sunk as if in thought.

At last she nodded.

Rushton's face suffused with joy. He flung his arms around her and hugged her tightly.

A terrible, savage pain clawed into my chest.

"You don't know how much this means to me," I heard Rushton saying as they moved toward the steep little stairs leading down to the main deck, obscured now by the sail. "I don't want to tell anyone just yet. Let it remain our secret for now. . . ."

Their voices faded, and the pain in my chest intensified, spreading through my body like some exotic plague germ. The image of Rushton holding Freya in his arms seemed to have seared itself onto the inside of my eyelids so that I could see it even when my eyes were squeezed shut. I pulled my knees up to my chest and held them tightly, making myself into a ball.

"Rushton," I whispered.

And who is she? I thought bitterly. *Where did she come from, to steal him while my back was turned?*

I clenched my teeth, resisting sour envy. While my back was turned? No, Freya had taken nothing that belonged to me. What could it possibly matter that he had turned to her? There was no room for anything in my life but my quest to destroy the weaponmachines.

Perhaps that was what Maruman had been trying to say the previous night—that there would be nothing for me at Obernewtyn when my quest was over. Maybe this was the price I must pay—not just Obernewtyn, but Rushton's love.

I took a deep, shaky breath and made myself look into the gray calmness of the sea all around me. The ship fish had departed.

I had not wanted Rushton's affections or encouraged them. So why did it hurt so much to learn that they were lost to me?

It does not matter, I thought fiercely. *My feet are already on the black road. It is too late to choose another, and this one I must walk alone.*

✦ 36 ✦

WE WERE BECALMED for two days, but by early afternoon of the third day, *The Cutter* was making up lost time, running before a stiff wind.

We were sitting in the salon, and Fian was describing the discovery of the Reichler Clinic to Daffyd.

Maruman stirred restively on my knee but did not waken. The others had taken his appearance with some equanimity, since they had only the day before learned of his loss. But I felt it was nearly miraculous to have him with me. It was Angina who pointed out that Maruman made us the thirteen that Maryon had predicted.

"Hard to believe you just stumbled on it," Daffyd was saying.

"In a city so big? No, it was more than chance. I believe we were *meant* to find it."

"After all, Hannah Seraphim was Rushton's ancestor," Kella added, her eyes shining. "Some things are meant to be."

And some are not, I thought, and was unable to stop my eyes from going to the table at the far end of the chamber where Rushton was talking with Hannay.

Why was it so hard not to look at him all of a sudden? Before this journey, I had done anything I could to avoid his gaze and his attention. I had refused his every overture, convinced that the force that sometimes crackled between us arose from him, that my own feelings were no more than reactions to it.

But in this new life of pain, the knowledge that Rushton no longer loved me seemed to have released a tempest of conflicting emotions all my own. I could not believe he had endured what I now felt—this hard, painful burning in the chest, this ache in the belly and throat. How could this be love?

If it was, it was as bad as ever I had imagined it must be. I should think myself fortunate that Rushton had turned from me before what simmered between us had burst into flame.

I focused my eyes on Fian, wondering how soon I could reasonably retreat to my chamber again. Then his words caught my attention.

"It wasn't until we had read a lot of the plasts that we realized what we had found wasn't the Reichler Clinic after all," he said.

"But we saw the name carved on the wall," I protested.

He nodded. "We misinterpreted it. What we found was exactly what the sign said—a *reception center* for th' Reichler Clinic. Nowt th' place itself. Th' real Reichler Clinic was where Garth always thought it mun be—in th' mountains."

"At Obernewtyn?" Kella asked breathlessly.

The teknoguilder shook his head. "Obernewtyn, or th' building that stood there before *our* Obernewtyn, was likely th' main residence for the Misfits. Th' actual Reichler Clinic labs were almost certainly sited where the cave of the Zebkrahn now stands. We have long known some Beforetime building once stood there, but we little dreamed which building or that it—"

"Labs? For experimentation on the Misfits?" I interrupted with real horror.

"I dinna think the experiments run by the Reichler Clinic would have been harmful or dangerous," Fian said. "Better to call them tests, as the plasts do. Hannah Seraphim would nowt have stood fer anything wrong. Fact is, we're pretty certain she was what th' Beforetimers called telepathic. In short, a Talented Misfit."

I was surprised, though it was the obvious answer to why she had opened the clinic in the first place.

"This were kept a secret, along wi' th' names of those who came to be tested. Ye might say th' Reichler Clinic we saw under Tor were a front fer an operation very like ours, or, I should say, it became so after Govamen began to stalk Talents."

"I still don't understand what they did with them," Angina grumbled.

"There are indications, as Garth explained last guildmerge, that—"

"I know, they were trying to use them somehow for war-making. But how?" Angina asked.

"As to that . . . ," Fian began with some heat, but he stopped again and shook his head fractionally. "Well. We will know more of that when we unearth th' clinic."

"Unearth it?" I asked sharply. "Then the clinic was buried by the holocaust like the city under Tor?"

"No," Fian said. "And nor was the city under Tor. Both were *originally* built under the earth."

He let us clamor for a moment before going on with a rather smug expression. "Th' upheavals are to blame for th' flood waters, but no more."

"But why?" I asked. "Why would anyone want to build a city under the ground?"

"Because of the whiteface." Maruman's sleepy thought drifted into my mind. I looked down at him, startled. When he snored, I decided he must have been sending in his sleep.

"I suspect the Reichler Clinic was built under th' earth so that it would be hidden. But we will know more once we have got into th' lower levels of th' caves."

I thought of the tattoo on my arm, still hidden from the others in its bandage. Perhaps the Teknoguild had learned something more of what it meant. I would ask Fian about it when I had a moment alone with him.

Freya came into the salon, and I felt a wave of despair. Was this how it was to be? Every time I had begun to build a wall of calmness, it was to be shattered by the smallest thing? I half expected her to sit with Rushton, but she crossed to the galley and set about making up a tray of food.

On impulse, I touched Angina's arm. "What is Freya's story? How did she come to Obernewtyn?"

"She ought to tell you herself," he said, and before I could stop him, he called out to her. I forced myself to smile as she approached, wishing passionately that I had kept my mouth shut.

She was very small and dainty and, like Rushton, had adapted gracefully to the ship's movements. I felt myself to be as long and gangling as a string bean beside her.

"I have wished for the chance to speak with you, Guildmistress," Freya said. "Rushton spoke of you on our journey here, and truly, your life has been one of danger and marvels. My own story is nothing to yours."

My heart bumped against my chest in a sort of frightened leap, and all my hard-won composure vanished at the thought that Rushton might have confided that he had once loved me.

"Tell her," Angina prompted Freya.

She flushed prettily. "Rushton rescued me."

Of course.

"I had come to Darthnor with my father. He is . . . was . . . a horse trader." A fleeting unhappiness showed in her eyes. "Along with his horses, there came a day that he offered his daughter for sale. . . ." She swallowed as if her throat hurt. "Rushton offered to buy me and the horses as a lot. He seemed a great man when he rode up on his white horse and threw a fortune in coin at my father's feet."

What sort of life had she led to be flattered that a man offered to buy her as a lot with horses? If Rushton had done that to me, I would have just as likely picked the coin up and thrown it back at him! Though probably he had meant it to be a gesture of contempt for Freya's father.

"I did not know until later that Alad was with Rushton and that the horses had told him I was . . . a Misfit," she went on. "But he said he would have bid whether I was Talented or not, for people should not be sold any more than beasts. He told me about Obernewtyn, though not where it was, and offered to bring me there, where I could stay and commune all I wished with horses, or I might have a bag of coin and go where I willed."

Her lashes tilted secretively, and I saw that she had

not needed much convincing to choose Obernewtyn. I felt a rush of savage jealousy and was astonished. Was this violent, pointless rage part of love, too?

"You are a beastspeaker, then?" I asked, and was horrified to hear how cold I sounded.

"Not exactly," Freya laughed, obviously taking my sharpness for a joke. "I am an empath, I suppose, but am not able to receive anything much."

Thank Lud for that!

"She may not be much good at receiving emotions," Angina said cheerfully, "but she has a unique variation of projective empathy."

"Unique," I echoed.

Angina gave me a frankly puzzled stare.

"Dameon calls her an enhancer," he said. "She can enhance another's Talent. Her ability seems to be closest to what I do when I amplify Miky's projected emotions. Only Freya can do it to whomever she chooses or switch it off altogether."

Freya's remarkably expressive eyes darkened. "I cannot reach everyone. Never my father. There was a wall in him—a natural mindshield, Dameon called it. And since I saw no one but him, I scarcely knew I had a Talent before I came here. I lived in terror of my father, for he was violent and angry much of the time. He kept me with him only because I could calm even the most uncontrollable horses."

"The interesting thing is that her empathic Talent works with animals as well," Angina said eagerly.

"Sometimes it made people furious when they sold a wild horse for a few coins, only to see me riding it a little later," Freya went on. "Several times we had to leave moon fairs quickly because someone claimed I had used the black arts on their horse. My father feared he would be called up by the Herders to explain.

"In Guanette, we had to leave before my father had completed his bargains. That is what made him drink and decide to sell me in Darthnor. I wonder, now that he is sober, if he thinks the price for me was fair," she added sadly.

The clear hurt in her face robbed me of bitterness. I could imagine how little joy there had been in her life. My head ached with the effort of trying to bring order to the whirl of my emotions.

"All that's over now," Fian said. "Freya's in great demand with the novices, because whenever she's around, they're all smarter and quicker than usual."

"Unfortunately, my ability to enhance is only an illusory sort of boosting," she said diffidently. "It lets me show them what they could do, and so they strive harder."

"Which means they learn better and faster," Miky said, wandering over to join us.

"I am still learning myself," she disclaimed, flushing. "Speaking of which, Dameon is waiting to give me a lesson as soon as he has eaten." She smiled at me again, her eyes revealing, of all things—the most painful to me just then—shy admiration. "Rushton told me you are a beastspeaker and might easily have led that guild instead of Alad, if you had wanted it. I wish I could speak to the horses the way you do, rather than simply feeling at them, but I am learning to use signals with them."

She turned to retrieve the tray of food and went out of the salon with it.

"She's nice, isn't she?" Miky asked.

"Yes," I said bleakly.

I looked over at Rushton and found him watching me. I dropped my eyes quickly, feeling dizzy and heartsore.

A little later, he crossed the salon to look out the window where I was seated. Flustered by his nearness, I looked out, too, and watched a lone seabird spiraling on the winds.

"I think I could love this life," Rushton said softly. "It is very peaceful."

Something in me trembled in fury. How easily he used the word *love*. I wanted to ask if his love for the sea would be more enduring than his love for me, but I bit my tongue and swallowed the salty taste of blood.

"We are very different," I said icily.

His hands tightened where they rested on the sill. They were brown and strong, and the thought came to me of how they would feel against my skin. Ruthlessly, I pushed the vision away, mortified at my lack of control.

To my relief, Powyrs came in to convey a request from his men that the twins play them a few songs. They had played a great deal to while away the anxious hours as we waited for the wind.

The empaths obliged and collected their instruments. Powyrs made to follow them out, but Rushton stopped him to ask about Templeport.

Powyrs glanced wistfully at the door as the strains of music drifted in, but, obligingly, he set down his jug.

"It is the only real settlement in all of Sador. The tribes are nomadic and move constantly about the desert, living in tents. They believe they should not leave any sign of their passing. The only permanent construction in all of Sador is their Earthtemple, and that is in Templeport. They regard the port itself as a necessary evil, because it is the only place along the Sador coast where boats can put in. All the rest is murderous high cliffs."

"What else is there besides a temple?" Rushton asked curiously.

Powyrs shrugged. "There are lots of people from the Land, and maybe from other places, but they are not allowed to build huts or houses. They have to set up tents, like Sadorians. Being nomadic is part of their religion, and it is terribly important to them."

"What *is* their religion?" asked Fian, abandoning his books to listen.

"It is not easy to tell such a thing simply. Central to it is their love of the land. By that, I mean the earth itself. To a Sadorian, nothing is more important. All life rises from it and returns to it. They think humans are no more important than any other creature. They don't believe in Lud at all. They think the land is infused with an earth goddess. They don't have priests, but some Sadorians are sent from birth to be Temple guardians. It is a great honor. Everything in Sador occurs under the guidance of the Temple and its guardians."

"It sounds very different to Herder lore," Daffyd murmured.

"Truly," Powyrs said. "Where a Herder believes humans are made by Lud to rule over the world, the Sadorians believe they are important only as part of the harmonious whole. The Herders claim everybody has to think their way or Lud will send the Great White again. In Sador, belief is a matter of personal choice." He leaned forward, his blue eyes twinkling sardonically.

"Funny thing is, Sadorians are a lot more devout by choice than Landfolk bound by Herder lore."

"I gather you don't like the Herders," Rushton said.

Powyrs winked angrily, a peculiar combination. "What's to like? I admire the Sadorians, though I don't go for putting land before people. Now if it was the sea . . ."

"How can these Sadorians live off a desert?" Hannay wondered.

"Most of their needs come from the spice groves inland at the foot of the mountains. Sadorians weave cloth from a fiber they get from the trees' bark, and they get sugar and medicines from its leaves and sap, and a potent fement from its berries. Most importantly, they get spice from its flowers, and they trade that for everything else the trees cannot offer."

"What about water?" Fian asked.

"There are natural springs all around the perimeter of the desert that water the groves, and in the desert there are isis pools. The Sadorians call them the tears of the goddess."

"What of the slave trade?" Rushton asked. "Do the Sadorians involve themselves in it?"

Powyrs chuckled. "Oh yes. The Sadorians involve themselves, all right. They send slavers and anyone proven to have dealt with them out into the desert without water. If the slavers make it to the other side, they are freed."

"Do many survive?" Kella asked.

The seaman grinned wolfishly. "One that I've heard of, and he was stark raving mad. The Temple looks after him, though, just as it does anyone who is sick or aged or who can't keep up the pace of the kar-avans."

"Kar-avans?" Kella echoed.

"They are what a group of Sadorians on the move call themselves. And Sadorians are always on the move."

The ship listed slightly, wiping the smile from his face. "Got to watch these fools who call themselves seamen or they'll run my *Cutter* up on a shoal," he muttered, hurrying outside.

"I have to get a look at that Temple," Fian said with all the fanatical determination of a teknoguilder on the trail of new information. "Garth will kill me if I don't."

"And I'll kill you if you start any fuss," Rushton said with perfect seriousness. "We're not here to tread on Sadorian toes. There's every likelihood that this Temple will be out of bounds to Landfolk."

Fian subsided, looking chastened; then, at Rushton's request, he and Kella went to retrieve the twins, Dameon, and Freya.

When we had all gathered, Rushton squared his shoulders in the way he did when conducting guildmerge. "Tomorrow we will reach Sador," he said. "I have no doubt we can win these Battlegames, but this is the first time we will pit ourselves against unTalents who know what we can do, and this will season us and allow us to see how we function under stress. I want you all to store up impressions about the battle, thoughts and suggestions that can be shared during guildmerge when we return to Obernewtyn.

"One warning. Under no circumstances are you to use your Talents on anyone in Sador, except during the games. No farseeking or coercing, no empathising. Although these rebels will be our opponents in the Battlegames, we hope to fight beside them in the future as allies. We must be able to offer a code they will trust and assure them they will not be violated by our abilities."

He glanced once about the salon to emphasize this point. The others nodded, but I thought of Malik's cold laughter and doubted any code Rushton could promise would impress him. Everything would hinge on winning.

"Daffyd has agreed to fight with us," Rushton went on. "Dragon cannot take part, and we should assume that Dameon will be unable to participate as well. That makes us ten if we include Daffyd and myself. And though I have no usable Talent to offer, I have battle skills, and there may be need for these."

His green eyes shifted to me, but I looked away quickly, afraid of what he might see in my face.

"I do not feel that I will disadvantage us," he added pointedly, and I realized he thought my refusal to meet his eyes indicated my disapproval of his inclusion.

At the end of his speech, Rushton asked me coldly to see him in his chamber after the nightmeal.

⋆ 37 ⋆

I DID NOT go.

In time, I would be able to face Rushton calmly, but not yet. I could not trust myself. What if somehow I betrayed my feelings? Perhaps I already had by speaking so stiffly to Freya. My thoughts ran wild. What if Rushton wanted to see me alone so that he could apologize for not loving me any longer? What if he tried to explain his attachment to Freya?

These were stupid thoughts, and it was the fear of making a fool of myself that made me cast about desperately after the nightmeal for some plausible excuse not to go to Rushton's chamber. I found myself plucking nervously at the bandage covering the tattoo Swallow had given me, and this produced an idea.

I would go and see Fian about the Govamen mark. He was ensconced in Powyrs's chamber, and I doubted anyone would think of looking for me there. The tattoo was reason enough to have forgotten Rushton's summons. I would tell Rushton of the tattoo—and I imagined the apologetic and slightly flippant smile I would wear as I said it—and explain how it had come about. I would casually mention that the gypsy had kissed me. Just as if people were always kissing me, so that I hardly even bothered about it.

Let him dare try to pity me then!

Having worked myself into a fury, I marched off to Powyrs's cabin, taking good care to let no one see me enter.

"Elspeth," Fian said, sounding surprised. He had to flatten himself against the wall to get the door to the tiny chamber open, but there was hardly enough room even when it was closed. He waved me to the only seat that would fit and propped himself on the corner of the rickety wooden table piled high with books.

"I'm glad ye've come. Ye know there are actually some Beforetime maps amongst these papers? I am tryin' to . . ." He stopped. "Lud, I do blather on. It is a teknoguild failing, I know, to imagine th' world revolves around us. Did ye want somethin' in particular?"

I bit my lip, suddenly unsure of how much I wanted to tell.

"I did," I said slowly. "Do you remember the mark on the Govamen plasts we saw beneath Tor?"

Fian wagged his head impatiently. "Yes, yes. Three Guanette birds goin' round one another?"

"Was there anyone else who might have used the same mark other than Govamen?"

"Unlikely," Fian said. "It appears on every single piece of research an' plast from Govamen, an' I think it was especially devised fer them. In fact, th' plasts appear to have been stolen from Govamen—we think the Reichler Clinic had a spy working there. It would have to be one of th' scientists—that's what th' Beforetimers called teknoguilders."

"You think this scientist wanted to help Misfits stay hidden?" I asked curiously.

"Or help them to escape, if Govamen had them already. Why do ye ask about th' mark anyway?"

I took a deep breath. "Do you have any idea what gypsies were before the holocaust? Where they come from?"

"There were people called gypsies in the Beforetime, but they were swallowed up into other races long afore the Great White. Our gypsies are just people who took on some of their philosophies—there's no true connection." Fian's puzzled expression deepened. "What is this all about, Elspeth?"

I went on to explain much of what Swallow had told me.

"Amazin'," Fian said after some time. "You must write this down for our records. I had no idea gypsy society was so complex. But what has any of it to do with th' Govamen mark?"

"The purebloods wear it on their inner forearms."

"That is odd. Why would a gypsy wear th' mark of a long-dead Beforetime organization?"

"Exactly what I am wondering," I said. "And how do you explain that the gypsies regard it as a sacred mark?"

"Perhaps their mark only *looked* like th' Govamen symbol," Fian suggested.

I rolled up my sleeve to reveal the grubby bandage around my arm and gestured for Fian to pass over a jug of water sitting on a tray.

He stared as I dipped my arm in it and let the water penetrate. "A Twentyfamilies gypsy gave the mark to me," I said. "You will see if it is exact or merely alike."

Fian listened, horrified, to my description of the tattoo procedure.

"Let's keep our fingers crossed it is healed properly,"

I said, carefully separating the sodden bandages. When I lifted the last layer away, we both stared.

"Is this a joke?" Fian demanded crossly.

I was mute with astonishment, for other than the crisscross reddening left by the bandage, my skin was utterly without mark or discoloration.

The tattoo had vanished!

Leaving Fian's tiny room, I dismissed his suggestion that I had been tricked into thinking I had been given the tattoo. If Swallow had intended to rook me, why would he have told me so much about himself? Besides, I had seen the needles and felt them pierce my skin.

But I could hardly blame the teknoguilder for his doubts. Unfortunately, only Swallow could answer what had happened.

I sighed and decided to relieve Miky, who was sitting with Dragon. Maruman was sleeping curled up at the foot of the mattress, but he woke as I entered.

When the Empath guilden had gone off yawning to her bed, I sat on the floor and took Dragon's small, limp hand in mine. Maruman rose, stretched, and came to curl himself into my lap. We made no attempt to communicate, and I was grateful for his silent companionship. It had been a long, confusing, painful day, and I just wanted to lay my head on the bed and be still.

I put my cheek against Dragon's hand and stared out the small circular window at the sky. Almost at once I slept.

I dreamed of walking along a black road. Rushton was behind me, calling. "Wait. I will come with you."

I walked faster, thinking of him holding Freya. "Elspeth . . ."

But his voice faded. I was crying, but I walked faster still.

I fell then into a deeper dream: a chaotic tumult of images that made no sense.

There was a chair, red and bulging with carvings of grotesque faces. One moment the faces appeared to convulse with mirth, and the next, they seemed to shriek with agony.

I saw a tall, beautiful woman smile.

"All the women in my family have it," she said in a soft, musical voice.

Then the same woman was slumped in the carved chair. Her hair was red like Dragon's, and her breast, too, for she had been stabbed there, and the knife still protruded from the gaping wound. Bending over her was a bald man with a pale, greasy face and a bloody hand. "Who will ever know it was my hand that struck the killing blow?" he whispered with feral glee.

The vision changed, and I was aboard a ship going over the waves. Then I was in the sea, and the water about me was tinged with the red-haired woman's blood, for she was beside me in the water. I tried to keep her afloat, but the waves were violent and kept tearing us apart.

"My daughter," she rasped. "You are . . . you must . . ."

"Templeport ho!" a voice called, and I woke with a start to a blazing hot day, my head aching abominably.

I got up stiffly, disentangling myself from Dragon. I rubbed at my stiff back, ignoring Maruman's grumbles at being disturbed.

The others were outside already when I got there, all pressed up against the side of the ship and staring out through the goldshot salt haze at Sador. I was astounded to see how high the sun was. I had slept near through to midday! The air outside was dry and hot, and breathing seemed to burn the inside of my nostrils.

The soaring sea cliffs lay before us, running as far as I could see in both directions. They were sheer and utterly inaccessible. But right ahead of us, the cliff was cracked as if split by a giant axe, and sand from the desert beyond had trickled out to form a spit, pointing out into the dark sea like a white finger. This, Powyrs said, was Templeport.

As we came closer to the tip of the peninsula, we could see a cluster of tents fluttering white like scattered blossoms, but there were no buildings and no greenery at all. Little wonder. The spit would be barren, saturated as it was with salt from the sea, and the pitiless heat would scorch anything that tried to grow. The shore wavered and danced through shimmering waves of heat, appearing as insubstantial as an illusion.

"How can anyone live here?" Miky said. This had been directed at Angina, but her twin was busy murmuring softly into Dameon's ear, describing the scene.

I kept a tight shield around my mind, for Dameon always seemed to sense my darkest moods. The image of Freya and Rushton was still fresh in my mind, and I had no wish to confide my feelings to the empath, for all that I loved him dearly. Some pains were not to be shared.

"It is too hot," Miryum grumbled, her voice slurred by her long sleep.

"You'd best get used to it," Hannay said. "The ship will be cool compared to the land."

"Hmm," Miryum grunted. "Well, at least the ground will stand still under my feet."

"There is the Earthtemple," Powyrs said, pointing.

I scanned the spit for a building but could see nothing.

"Oh Lud," Daffyd murmured suddenly. "There. In the cliff. No wonder it is called an Earthtemple."

The Temple was part of the cliff and visible only because the cliff exterior was carved from top to bottom. Closer, I could make out windows in the carving. From the number of them, the Temple must be enormous.

I felt someone at my side.

It was Rushton, and his eyes were accusing. "I asked you to come and see me last night."

"I . . . I had to see Fian," I stammered. "He . . ."

Rushton's eyes blazed with such fury, I faltered. He turned on his heel without a word and went to stand with Freya and Hannay.

"What in Lud's name are those?" Angina exclaimed once we had disembarked.

He was pointing at a group of great, shaggy, dun-colored beasts with four legs and a lump of flesh pouting up from their backs.

"They are kamuli," Powyrs said, looking over his shoulder with a grin. "The Sadorians use them rather than horses, and they are not mutants, however much they might look it. They existed in the Beforetime and were called 'desert ships' because they traverse the sands effortlessly with their soft, splayed hooves."

"Sadorians do not use horses, then?" Freya asked curiously.

"Inland they do," the seaman said. "Where the spice groves are, the ground is hard and there is thick forestation that makes horses more suitable as transport."

I noticed Kella watching me and made an effort to look interested.

"Act," Brydda had once advised me. "Pretend that you are clever, wise, brave, calm, courageous." Pretend, and some of the time you can forget it is pretense.

It was incredibly noisy on the spit. Everyone seemed to shout at the top of their voice—a great deal of bartering took place literally from ship decks—and there was a tremendous bustle as people carried boxes and bundles to and from the ships. Yet the scene was, for all its loudness, curiously colorless. The savage blaze of the sun seemed to bleach everything to a blinding bone-whiteness that made my head pound and my eyes water. More than anything else, I longed to sit in a bit of shade and drink a cold mug of water.

Unfortunately, the only shade available was that cast by the towering Sadorian cliffs, looming on both sides of the sloping pass that led up to the desert, and that was a goodly step away.

Powyrs pointed out a spot farther up the spit where it widened at the base of the cliffs. "About halfway to the cliffs, there is a place where visitors set up their tents. Can you see them? Nearby are stalls where you can purchase food, and at the very base of the cliffs there is a freshwater spring. The water will cost you nothing, but you will have to change your coins for barter tokens at the Earthtemple if you want to buy food."

Watching us go, the plump seaman gave Maruman, who was draped around my neck, a long look of bewildered wistfulness that spoke of the strength of his attachment. I had coerced all memory of their brief association from his mind, but clearly the impression had been deep and some residue remained.

✦ 38 ✦

RUSHTON, HANNAY, AND Miryum cleared the rough shale and, with the twins' aid, set about erecting the tents we had bought in Sutrium at Jakoby's suggestion. Daffyd and Freya were charged with getting water, and Fian and I were to exchange our small store of coin for Temple barter tokens. Dameon elected to walk with us, and since the spring was on the way to the Temple, we went that far together.

I was relieved to find that Freya's presence no longer disturbed me nearly as much as Rushton's. Not that we did much talking. The heat beating down on our heads and thrown back as a reflection from the dazzling white sand was terrific. By the time we reached the cliffs, we were all gasping for breath.

We threw ourselves down at the edge of the icy spring and drank deeply before retreating into the dense shade cast by the cliffs.

"Incredible," croaked Daffyd in a low voice.

"Where does such heat come from?" Freya asked weakly, fanning her face with her skirts.

"Ugh," Fian groaned. "I've just realized we'll have to climb up th' rest of th' spit to change th' coins. Powyrs told me th' Temple entrance can only be got to from th' top of the cliffs."

I would have groaned, too, if I had been able to spare the energy. The first impression of coolness in the shade had begun to abate, and already I was hot again. We sat a good while before I could bring myself to move.

Standing up reluctantly, I noticed two halfbreed gypsies among the throng of Sadorians. They stood out as much as we must in this land of tall, gold-skinned people in their flowing robes. Powyrs had said gypsies were treated well here. That being so, I had no doubt more would avail themselves of the coast road when the poisons had receded a little farther.

"Uh-oh," Fian murmured.

He had risen, too, and was gazing back down the spit. I turned to see what had caught his attention. A number of gray-clad Landsmen stood talking, yellow cloaks fluttering at their shoulders—senior-ranking soldierguards.

I had known there were soldierguards in Sador, yet still it was a shock to see them. Even more so were the two Herders with them, clad in white robes and arrogance. I was astounded to see a number of Sadorians clustered about the priests. Could these possibly be converts?

Even as I watched, the taller Herder lifted his pale face to the Earthtemple, his lip curling in scorn. Letting my eyes follow the same direction, I was startled to discover that what I had thought randomly carved patterns on the cliff were, in fact, a multitudinous swirl of faces.

"You'd better get on," Daffyd advised.

"Perhaps you should not go," Freya told Dameon when I offered him my arm. The Empath guildmaster smiled unerringly down at her. "I am not ill. I am only blind."

She flushed.

"I am going to have another drink before we start," Fian announced.

Daffyd caught his arm. "Don't be a fool. You will be sick if you fill your belly with water, then walk in this heat. Drink when you return."

It was a steep walk up to the top of the cliffs, but Fian found breath enough to describe what he was seeing to Dameon. I was glad of his monologue, for it freed me of the need to speak and kept the Empath guildmaster's attention from me. Before long, though, we were all trudging along in silence again.

"The sun is like a hammer on my head," Fian panted when we stopped to rest halfway. "It did not look so far from the camp. At this rate, it will be dusk before we are back."

My own head was pounding, yet the heat in the desert running back from the cliffs must be a thousand times worse. Still the Sadorians spent their lives sailing the sea of sand on their desert ships. Strange how differently humans could live and still be human.

The Earthtemple had two facades.

The grandest was the one it presented to the sea and to the spitroad. We had been sitting literally with our backs against the base of it when we were by the spring. The road from the spit had risen gradually to the height of the clifftop, where a small rocky path had peeled off to the left, running down into a deep fissure. A man had told us this would bring us to the entrance of the Earthtemple.

After making our way carefully and with some relief down the shaded path running along a deep sloping cleft, we discovered the second facade of the Temple. It was neither gilded nor carved, and there were no windows. A single, rough-hewn portal served as the doorway, while a great, plain slab of stone, set upon a smaller pivoting stone, served as its door. Its simplicity seemed far more in keeping with the Sadorians' philosophy as expounded by Powyrs than the ornate, carved facade of faces it presented to the sea.

The stone door was currently tilted to allow a slender opening on either side, and beyond, the darkness was so complete that it was impossible to say what lay within.

There were at least thirty people lined up outside in five separate queues. One line seemed to consist of very elderly people, worried-looking adults with sickly children or babes, and others with rough bandages or hacking coughs.

A young man with wild eyes, held tightly between two plump, distressed-looking women, lashed about babbling and shuddering. Clearly, he was undergoing some sort of seizure.

This, then, must be the line for supplicants seeking healing.

The line next to it had more animals than people, therefore, this must be where beasts were brought to be examined for disease before they could be sold. The animals were all small, so the larger beasts, such as horses, must be dealt with at some other point.

In the third line, there were Sadorians carrying sacks. An acrid odor suggested they were the spice gatherers Powyrs had mentioned, bringing in their tribe's quota to exchange for barter tokens.

At first I wondered why the queues were not

advancing; then I noticed a number of barefooted men and women clad in hooded linen tunics moving along the lines.

"The Temple guardians," Fian murmured. "Looks as if all of the ministerin' is done outside." He sounded disappointed.

I waved him back and moved closer to listen to an exchange between one of the hooded guardians and a Sadorian woman of middle years.

"What do you seek of the earth?" the Temple guardian asked. His voice and shape proclaimed him a man, but I could not see his face. As with the other Temple guardians, this was concealed by the drooping hood.

The woman launched into a detailed litany of physical ills to which he listened with great patience. When she could find nothing more to complain about, he rummaged in a small pouch bag tied at his waist and removed a twig. Pressing it into her hand, he bade her in a gentle voice to soak it in boiled water, then drink the fluid.

Fian poked me in the ribs, his eyes bright with suppressed laughter. "It's no more than a wee bit of relaxin' herb he's given her. A sop."

I nodded absently, wondering what the fourth line was for. Its people did not look sick, nor did they lead beasts or carry spice.

A smaller guardian approached a man in this line. "What do you seek of the earth?" asked a girl, her voice muffled slightly by the hood.

"Wisdom, Guardian. My son desires to bond, but he has yet to make his first spice gather." He seemed undaunted by the fact that the voice could not belong to a girl much older than his son.

"Is the girl he would take worthy in your eyes?" she asked.

"Yes, it is only his youth that troubles me," the man answered. "In truth, it may be that *he* is not worthy of *her.*"

The diminutive guardian nodded sagely. "Say to the father of the girl that he must set the boy a quest to determine his worthiness. If he fails, then he must wait another season. If he succeeds, then he shall have her."

The father nodded and went away.

"That's no more'n a bit of common sense. Th' man's a fool nowt to have thought of it fer hisself," Fian muttered.

"Perhaps he had thought of it but needed reassurance," Dameon murmured.

Another Temple guardian came out of the shadowy doorway with two clinking bags slung about her waist. She passed briskly along the farthest line, exchanging coin for tokens.

"Wait here," I said, and took my place at the end of the line. When the guardian reached me, she asked, from the depths of her hood, "What do you seek of the earth?"

"I . . . We have come to pay our respects to the earth goddess and to get some barter tokens," I said politely.

She nodded and counted the coin I offered into one bag at her waist before giving me a handful of small, pale metal discs from another. She lifted her hand to my forehead and made a sign, but the words were drowned out by a scream.

I turned swiftly to find the frenzied youth had broken free of the women and was rushing toward me.

I thought he meant to attack me and flung up my hands, but to my astonishment, he threw himself at my feet. "Do you bring the Moonwatcher?" he whispered fiercely.

The two women had hurried forward and pulled him away from me, apologizing profusely. "When these fits come on him, it is as if he is possessed by demons," one said.

The Temple guardian who had been attending to me waved the women and the now-silent boy back to their place in the line, then turned to me.

"Who are you?" she asked in a strangely tense voice.

My heart began to gallop. "I . . . I am a visitor from the Land."

"Whom do you visit?"

I did not know what to answer, so I told the truth. "Jakoby has invited me. She is—"

"I know of Jakoby," the woman said shortly, and now her tone was indifferent. She lifted her hand and made the same mark on my forehead. "May you nurture the earth and find harmony."

She moved to the man behind me, and I returned to Dameon and Fian, feeling somewhat bewildered.

"What happened?" Fian demanded.

"I'm damned if I know," I said.

As Fian had predicted, the day was indeed drawing to a close by the time we returned to the spit. The shadows were lengthening, and people were lighting cooking fires and lamps. Already the moon had risen, and it hung like a great coppery disc, low on the skyline—a full moon.

As we reached the trade area, Fian suggested we get some food to take back to the camp. The atmosphere surrounding the selling tents was as familiar as the rest of Sador was strange. In the mill and jostle, there was a similarity to markets in Sutrium and Kinraide and Morganna, which reassured me in some deep way. Well, that was not so surprising. After all, people had to eat and drink and trade and speak.

All about us, men and women were involved in the mundane business of haggling with traders. Here, at least, there were almost as many Landfolk as Sadorians.

"Got any silver to sell?" demanded a squint-eyed jack. Dameon smiled in the direction of the voice and shook his head. The man recoiled as if his blindness might be contagious.

"Need flints or salt?" a woman in the tent alongside him asked.

"Maybe later," I said.

She spat on the ground in disgust. "Filthy gypsies."

"Like a girl, pretty boy?" whispered a woman with lustrous painted eyes, peering at Fian from the shadowy interior of another tent.

He shuddered and backed away with comical haste into one of the odorous desert ships sitting with its legs folded queerly beneath its body. The creature snorted fiercely and eyed him with pouting ire.

"Greetings," I sent, wondering if its mind would accept me. It regarded me for a long moment, but either could not or would not understand.

"You want to buy this fine animal?" a Sadorian

trader asked, appearing from nowhere at the beast's side.

"I don't think he likes the color of my eyes," I said, and walked on, leaving him to stare after me.

"How can they live in this heat?" Fian panted as we reached our camp at last. "It's practically dusk. Doesn't it ever cool down?"

"I suspect the night will be cold," Dameon said.

Fian snorted as if coolness here was something no sane person would believe in. "They are surely mad to live in such a place."

"Perhaps so," said a familiar voice.

I whirled to find myself staring at a tall woman, clad in a flowing cloak of beaten animal hides atop a thin shift of some golden material that matched her eyes and bared the full, dark muscular length of her legs and arms. Her hair was woven into tight, metal-beaded braids, which clinked whenever she moved.

"Jakoby," I said.

Rushton approached us and bowed. "I am pleased to greet you. Elspeth has told us much about you. We feared you might have been becalmed, as we were."

"The winds were good to us." Jakoby smiled enigmatically, her face illuminated fitfully by the fire that had been kindled in the angled embrace of the tents. The others stared at the Sadorian woman in wonder. She looked about at them, taking time to examine each of the faces carefully.

"Your chosen warriors are young indeed," she said at last. "But age does not always signify, as the Landman Elii said. Will you come now? The two of you," Jakoby asked.

I faltered under Rushton's green glare.

"We will be glad to accompany you," he told Jakoby tersely. "Where do we go?"

"To meet Bram, who is to judge the Battlegames, and the Temple's overguardian, who shall preside."

"Are all of the rebels here?" Rushton asked.

"Not all, but all who will come. More, I think, than Brydda expected."

We were turning to leave when I heard Miryum's voice ring out angrily and the sound of a blow.

Hurrying around behind one of the tents, we discovered the stolid Coercer guilden standing over a Sadorian man, who sat in the dust, his nose running with blood.

"What happened?" Rushton demanded.

"Him," Miryum said fiercely, glaring at the man as he got to his feet.

"What did he do?" I asked.

Miryum looked over to me. "He . . . this fellow was making fun of me," she muttered wrathfully.

"This is not so," the man said carefully. He bowed low to her and then to Jakoby. "I am sorry if I have given offense. I spoke ravek. I did not mean to insult her. Do you wish me to kill myself?"

Miryum gaped.

"Well?" Jakoby asked her mildly. "Do you want him to kill himself for insulting you?"

"But surely you can't mean he would . . . would . . ." The coercer looked more disturbed than I had ever seen her. "Of course he mustn't . . . kill himself. Not for a joke."

"Very well, you may leave," Jakoby told the man indifferently.

"It was not a joke I made," the man said gravely. He

bowed to Miryum and then again to Jakoby before backing away.

"What on earth did he say to you?" I asked.

Miryum reddened. "I will not say."

Jakoby walked slowly, adapting her long stride courteously to our pace.

"What is a ravek?" I asked her.

Her teeth flashed in the darkness of her face. "It is an endearment between those who are heartfasted. It means 'you who have my heart beneath your foot.' The man your friend struck offered to make her his ravek. That is a formal proposal of bonding in Sador."

In spite of everything, I smiled. Obviously, Miryum had caught some of his meaning but hadn't known how to take a compliment.

Jakoby stopped before a large tent.

She lifted the tent flap, and the muted sounds of laughter and the clink of plates and knives spilled out into the dusk. She gestured for us to enter.

Inside, a fire burned in a ground hearth lined in stone. Three trestle tables were set around it in a U-shape and piled high with all manner of food and drink. Seated at the tables were both familiar and unfamiliar faces.

At the central table on a raised dais was a wizened Sadorian man with skin the shade of old bronze and hair as white and tight-coiled as the fleece of wild mountain goats. He wore a cloak of what appeared to be animal pelts sewn together about his skinny shoulders, as Jakoby did.

It was not difficult to guess that this was Bram.

I ran my eyes swiftly around the rest of those seated.

Plump Brocade was at one end, seated beside Tardis's yellow-haired emissary, Gwynedd. Brocade was wearing a jewel-encrusted vest stretched tight across his wide belly. A little farther along sat a tall, fair, proud-looking woman. She wore no jewelry, and her hair hung white and unbraided and perfectly straight about her shoulders like a snowy veil. She sat with Brydda and Dardelan.

Also next to Brydda was a stooped man who smiled faintly in greeting when our eyes met. I guessed this was Yavok, who had taken over for him in Aborium. Brydda had called him trustworthy.

On the other side of Bram, among a great number of strangers, were white-haired Cassell and Elii. It seemed Brydda's recruiting journey had borne fruit. But I had no doubt they were here first for a war council, rather than to see whether we were fit allies.

Last of all was Malik.

When our eyes met, his lips curved into a sneering smile that made me instantly conscious of my sweaty, dust-smeared face and clothes.

"It is the Misfit and its master," he told the dark-eyed man on his right, just loudly enough for us to hear.

I felt Rushton tense with anger beside me.

"As you see, this master is but a stripling himself," Malik went on scornfully, not bothering to pretend to be speaking in an aside. Rushton's silence had made him bold, for he took it as weakness.

Jakoby said nothing, and I sensed she was waiting to see how Rushton would deal with this.

The Master of Obernewtyn merely settled a long, impassive stare on the rebel, whose smirk faltered, then faded altogether.

"What are you looking at, boy?" he growled.

"I am not sure," Rushton said. "It might be a man, but then it might be a kind of performing ape. It is hard to tell in the firelight."

Malik stared at him incredulously. Then he rose with a curse, pulling out a knife.

"Enough," Jakoby said imperiously. "The Battlegames do not commence until the morrow, and it is unseemly to sour our feasting with such behavior before then. All things in their right time."

Malik resumed his seat, though he was pale with fury, and Jakoby ushered us up to Bram. I was surprised to see one of the hooded Temple guardians in the seat beside him. The hood gave no sign of its wearer's sex, but I thought it must be a wizened old creature, for it was very small. No doubt the over-guardian Jakoby had mentioned.

"Bram, this is Elspeth Gordie of whom I have spoken," Jakoby said. "And Rushton Seraphim, who styles himself the leader of these Misfit gypsies."

"Seraphim," Bram echoed. "An old name, I think."

Rushton bowed. "I do not know if your name is old or not. I have heard only a little about the Sadorian people, but it has made me curious to know more, and I am pleased at this chance to speak with you."

Bram chuckled fruitily. "Yet I think this is not an occasion for speeches. I hope you do not think to win the Battlegames with words alone."

"We are prepared to meet whatever challenge is offered," Rushton responded smoothly.

"Good." Bram's dark eyes shimmered in the fire-light. "I have heard from those among my people who watched for your arrival that your force contains war-riors who are even younger than you. And though you may count yourself a man, you are too young to be seasoned properly to battle. Have you hope of win-ning against such men as Malik, whose prowess is leg-endary?"

"I would not have come otherwise."

The old man cackled. "No? But sometimes battles must be faced whether or not there is a hope of winning them. This is a truth known to men and women of honor."

"No battle is lost until it is lost. Men and women of courage know this."

Bram nodded in appreciation. "True enough! You speak well, lad. I regret that you are not yet a sworn ally and therefore have no place at this table. Yet, if your people acquit themselves well and survive the testing tomorrow, we might yet sup together and have this speech you desire."

"Survive?" Rushton echoed carefully. "Surely there is no question of not surviving since this is only a con-test."

The overguardian stirred.

"These are the Battlegames, lad, where matters large and small may be decided without massive bloodshed," said Bram. "It is war in miniature. If death was not possible, there would be no true testing. Of course, death is not the aim, nor is injury inevitable."

There was a silence, broken by Malik's cutting laughter. "Look. The boy is nearly unmanned with fear at the thought that death might wait for him."

"The morrow will bring what it brings," Rushton said softly. He turned his eyes back to Bram. "If it is permitted, I would like to know something more of the Battlegames."

Bram's smile died, and for a moment, he looked like a weary old man. "Are you in such a hurry for war, lad? You were more handsome when you spoke of talking and learning." He sighed weightily. "Malik asked the same question, and I told him what I now tell you. The Battlegames designed by my people are many, but the earth goddess will decide which of these may be played." He drew himself up and summoned a formal and ceremonious air. "Once, among the tribes who were much sundered during the time that followed what you Landfolk call the holocaust, there were wars occasioning great bloodshed among our people, and harm was done to the earth. Then came one among us who heard the voice of the earth goddess. She commanded us to build the Earthtemple, that others might come there and learn to hear the voice of the land as well. And so it came to pass. Through her disciples, the earth goddess forbade war forever. But still there were disputes, great and small, which needed mediation. Hence were the Battlegames devised, both to decide issues and to expiate the violent urges that are the plague of humanity.

"Each of the games is designed to test some specific quality in a competitor—courage or wit or charm or honesty or fitness. In your case, the games will test fitness for battle. But the earth goddess alone knows which of the many games will be selected, for they will be chosen at random using a tool we call *dice*. Some games are short and others long, so there is no way of telling how many will take place at a single contest. The games commence at sunrise and end at sunset, for these are moments of power."

"Are all ten of a team to play each game?" Rushton asked. I guessed he was thinking of Dameon.

Bram shook his head. "Not necessarily. The number of participants for each game will again be randomly selected by a further throw of the dice, but it is up to the two leaders to choose who will fill the places. For each Battlegame completed, there will be a spoken assessment, and then when the day ends, the winner shall be named."

Bram reached for a piece of bread. This appeared to mark the end of the discussion. All along the trestles, men and women reached for goblets or turned to whisper to one another.

"There is just one thing more," Rushton said.

"And that is?" Bram inquired through a mouthful of bread.

"I want you to understand that we intend to use all of our powers in these Battlegames, but outside this contest, we would never use those abilities on allies."

Bram chewed and swallowed. "You should return to your camp now. Eat well and rest. You will be brought to the field of battle before dawn."

Jakoby escorted us outside. "If you can, forget about the Battlegames tonight. Worrying and wondering about what will come will not avail you. Rest well."

She turned and went back into the tent, leaving Rushton and me alone in the dark.

◆ 39 ◆

"WE'D BETTER GET back," Rushton said. "The others will be waiting to hear what happened."

I shivered, though it was not cold, and followed him back across the spit.

"I am . . . sorry," I said at last, with stiff formality. "I did not know there would be danger. Jakoby didn't tell me that when she offered the Battlegames."

"You think she meant to deceive you?" He did not look at me when he spoke.

I shook my head. "I do not think it would have occurred to her that it would matter there was danger."

"Then there is no blame to be laid."

Rushton's voice was remote, and I knew he was still angry with me. I had never felt further from him. I had the urge to say something that would restore even the old uneasy comradeship between us, but his silence daunted me.

We walked without speaking the rest of the way back to the camp.

Angina saw us approach as he stirred the cooking fire, and he alerted the others with a cry. In moments, they were clustered around us. In swift, unemotive words, Rushton told them what had happened.

"The Battlegames are more than a contest, then,"

Miryum said dourly, but without fear. "Is it possible that one or more of us may die?"

"Possible," Rushton said calmly. "But certainly not inevitable. We will know more when we know which games are to be played."

"I do not like the sound of this Malik," Hannay said.

"He is a hard, strong man," Rushton said. "A bitter man and a tough fighter by all accounts. I do not relish the thought of being his opponent, but if we fare well tomorrow, that strength will be at our side when we fight the Council. Wars make for strange bedfellows. We need the rebels, and it seems this is the only way to win them."

"I wonder if such a victory as this will truly win us anything worth having," Dameon said as Kella handed him a mug of mulled fement.

"It will win us the aid we need against the Council," Rushton snapped. "We cannot afford the indulgence of philosophizing about what constitutes victory. Save that for when the fighting is over."

He took a long deep breath, then shook his head. "I am sorry. I did not mean to snap, my friend. I am . . . tired." He sat down on the ground, facing the fire, and invited us all to do the same. "Let us not talk about the morrow anymore. It will come all too soon. We will nourish our bodies with food and rest, and our souls with a song."

Miky's face lit up and she went to get her gita. Freya brought us plates of stew, then settled herself beside Rushton. Watching the smile that she gave him, I found I had no appetite.

I longed to comfort Rushton, but what could I truly offer him? Even if he had loved me still, I could not say

437

that I would never leave him, because I would. I could not speak of undying love, because I was not certain this bitter, painful emotion his embrace with Freya had roused in me was love.

A great sadness filled me as I stared into the red heart of the flames and listened to the lovely, haunting song the Empath guilden had made from the Oldtime story of the sleeping princess wakened by a kiss. As it rippled out into the night, I could not help but think again of Dragon, locked in her secret, internal battle with her past, trapped in a fortress of her own mind's making.

Powyrs had agreed that the comatose empath might remain aboard the ship, for he was to bring us back to the Land when the Battlegames were over. He thought we were to perform at a bonding of one of the tribal chiefs. Little as we had liked leaving Dragon, she was safer on *The Cutter* than with us.

"In this long sleep, in this fortress of dreams, I live a shadow life and in it dream of one who will come . . . ," Miky sang softly, and Angina took up the harmony in his deeper voice, at the same time elaborating the melody with tiny bells and empathising it delicately with his Talent.

I rose quietly and slipped away from the fire to crawl into one of the tents. Removing only my sandals, I stretched out fully clothed.

"Greetings, ElspethInnle," Maruman sent, and I looked up to see him enter the tent. I made a place for him beside me. The red glow of the fire through the tent opening made his fur appear bloody and discolored. He slept at once, but my mind was too active to let me sleep. On impulse, I shaped a probe and let it soar away from the spit and over the dunes like a nightbird.

I did not try to direct its flight but let the music take me where it would.

Here and there, I encountered the silvery shimmer of other minds—small nocturnal creatures foraging. Once, I was drawn to a brighter shimmer and held for a moment by a deep mind that was clearly intelligent and just as clearly nonhuman.

I flew until my mind was calm.

At long last I returned to my body. The fire outside had died, and the music had stopped. I fell asleep.

It seemed only a moment later when someone shook my shoulder.

"Elspeth, wake up," Miky said. "The Sadorians have come to take us to the Battlegames."

I opened my eyes, unable to believe it was morning already. Maruman had vanished, but a warmth by my head said he had not been gone long.

"They said to hurry," Miky urged. "We have to be there before the sun comes up, or the whole thing will be called off."

I sat up, pulled on boots instead of sandals, and crawled out of the tent. It was still dark, and the air was cool and pleasant. The moon had set, but a few stars still pricked the darkness. Wordlessly, Kella pressed some of the bread and cheese I had purchased the previous day into my hands as Rushton announced to the two Sadorians that we were ready.

We were conducted quietly through the sleeping camp to the road where a host of shaggy kamuli and several other long-legged Sadorians waited. As we mounted the seated beasts and settled ourselves in the wooden contraptions that served as saddles, I far-sought Maruman with an attuned probe. He was prowling about the cliffs in search of eggs.

"If there is any trouble, go aboard *The Cutter* with Dragon and Powyrs," I sent. He did not deign to respond, but I knew he had heard me.

When we were all mounted, one Sadorian perched precariously behind each of us, they made a clicking noise with their tongues and the kamuli rose with a great drunken lurching. They walked with a slow, rolling lope that reminded me horribly of the pitching movement of *The Cutter*. No wonder they were called ships of the desert.

"Oh no," Fian moaned as the kamuli made their ponderous way up the spit slope toward the cliffs. "We're headed out into th' desert."

"It was the obvious place," Hannay said mildly. "We'd better start praying to Lud for a cloudy day, or the sun will fry us."

"The rebels will find it just as hard as us," Angina pointed out cheerfully.

We had traveled for about an hour into the trackless desert, and the sky was empty of stars when the Sadorians pulled their beasts to a halt. I looked around, but there was nothing on all sides but featureless dunes. Were these Battlegames to take place here in the middle of nowhere where there was no shelter and no water? If so, where were the rebels and the Sadorians? I looked up at the sky again. In the east, there was a lightness that heralded the dawn.

One of the Sadorians rode up to Rushton and said something I couldn't hear. Then he pointed.

I could see nothing but sand dunes.

"He said the place where the games will be held is there," Ruston said loudly, sounding puzzled.

The Sadorians clicked their tongues and the kamuli continued.

"I can smell flowers," Kella said, and a moment later, we found ourselves riding along a long, narrow crack in the ground. Past its edges, we could see that it opened up into a great cave under the earth. It was too dim to see much, but I could smell greenery and flowers, and at the very bottom of the hidden chasm, I could see the glimmer of water.

"This mun be one of their isis pools," Fian said in sudden excitement.

"So this is where their goddess weeps her tears," Kella said dreamily. "No wonder they can spend so much time out here."

"You'd never find it if you didn't know exactly how to get to it," Daffyd murmured.

Miky described the valley to Dameon as the Sadorians turned the kamuli onto a narrow track that wended its way downward. Powyrs had said there were a number of isis pools in the desert, and I had imagined wells. I wondered if they were all like this. Clearly, the wave of earth and rock almost covering the chasm protected it from the sun but let in enough light to allow growth. The combination of heat and water produced humidity that generated a luxuriant growth of plant life. The air became increasingly moist as we descended.

By the time we reached the bottom, sunrise was only moments away. From a distance, Jakoby emerged from what I had taken as a mass of greenery but now saw were row upon row of Sadorian men and women.

We dismounted, and she brought us to Bram, who sat cross-legged on a raised dais under a gigantic drooping tree with coiling, pale green leaves and long, creamy pods. The overguardian of the Temple sat at his feet. The rebels stood in a cluster to one side, and the ranks of Sadorians were arrayed behind them.

Malik and his chosen nine stood ramrod straight in two disciplined lines facing Bram. Jakoby indicated that we were to take our place alongside them. The rebel I stood beside was almost twice my height, his muscular arms scarred. I knew those looking at us must see the contest between us as absurdly unequal.

Jakoby took her place at Bram's side and looked expectantly at the sky. She stood that way until we saw the sun rise through the crack where the sky was visible, casting pink and orange rays that stained the few straggles of cloud. I realized they had been literally waiting for sunrise to begin the Battlegames.

"Are you prepared?" Jakoby asked, and I jumped at the loudness of her voice in the still dawn.

"I am," Malik intoned.

"We are," Rushton said.

Jakoby looked to Bram, who inclined his head, then clapped her hands. The little hooded overguardian rose and offered the dice—two small cubes with a different number of markings on each face. Bram leaned forward with a grunt to take them up and mumbled a few inaudible words before flinging them high.

All eyes turned up to watch the two gleaming cubes

whirl in the air, and then down to see what number of marks they offered to the sky.

"Six," Bram said. "The Pit, then."

Wordlessly, the overguardian gathered the dice and passed them back to Bram. He threw them again, and this time they fell showing four marks between them.

"Each leader will choose four from among his number to contend in the first Battlegame," Jakoby announced in a ringing voice.

"Choose," Bram said.

There was a momentary hiatus; then Rushton took a half step forward. "Is it permitted for me to speak?"

The old Sadorian lifted straggling white brows at him. "I told you last night this is not a battle that can be won with words."

"I only wanted to ask how you expect us to choose well without knowing more about this Pit."

"I will answer your question with another. How do warriors face lack of knowledge in a battle?"

Rushton bowed and returned to face us, beckoning us to gather close.

"You must choose for diversity," Miryum advised him.

"Maybe we can take some sort of clue from the name," Dameon suggested.

"The Pit," Angina murmured.

"I suppose it will be in the ground. Another of these rifts. Therefore, climbing may be needed, or lifting." Rushton swept his eyes over us. "Hannay is strongest physically."

"Powyrs told me th' Sadorians sometimes use pits to catch fangcats," Fian said. "There may be beasts, therefore."

Rushton nodded. "Freya," he said at last. He did not look at me and, hurt, I did not suggest myself.

"Maybe th' pit is worked by some mechanics," Fian continued.

Rushton frowned for a long moment. "Yes. You, then, Fian. And Miryum, because she is a powerful co-ercer as well as strong physically."

Neither he nor Miryum looked at me, although they both knew I also possessed coercive abilities. But nei-ther of them knew how strong I was, because I had al-ways tried to downplay my powers.

Sweat beaded Rushton's lip as the four Misfits were led away with Malik's rebels. I guessed it had been hard for him not to name himself. I felt a surge of admi-ration for the strength of his will. Malik had not named himself either, but it seemed to cost him nothing.

"They are permitted to choose a single implement each from the armament," Jakoby explained. She pointed as she spoke, and we watched as the eight con-testants vanished into a small gray tent billowing in the freshening dawn breeze that swirled through the gap in the earth and stirred the heavy air.

"How can they choose without knowing what they need?" Angina asked Rushton indignantly. "This is madness."

"Perhaps not," Miky disagreed with her twin. "After all, Malik is in the same position, as you said."

It was growing steadily hotter, and I shuddered to think of what the surface temperature must be. Looking up, I saw that the roof of the cavern was moss covered and wondered how often there were rock-falls.

The eight returned. The rebels had chosen between

them a double-edged sword, a huge axe, a long knife with a frill of jagged spikes about its tip, and a net. The Misfits had taken a coil of rope, a wide flat shield, a tapered stave of wood, and a knife.

Bram clapped his hands again, and we were led toward another pit—almost a miniature copy of the rift we were standing in and, like the larger chasm, invisible until you were almost upon it.

When we were standing on the edge, I saw that a cage had been set into the rift, neatly dividing it. Inside the cage were two bears. The larger was lumbering slowly back and forth, while the smaller sat in a corner of the cage, its paws clasped around the bars.

"Let the first Battlegame commence," Jakoby's voice rang out.

The Sadorian servitors immediately lowered the Misfits into one end of the pit by rope and the rebels into the other.

"I do not like the look of this," Miky murmured uneasily.

"Shh," Angina hissed. "Watch."

The servitors shifted to other ropes, and the cage was hoisted up, removing all dividers. The bears seemed more bewildered than angry at this turn of events. They appeared not to have noticed the people at either end of the chasm.

For a long moment, no one moved; then the smaller bear noticed the Misfits. It stood up and lumbered toward them, growling slightly.

Without hesitation, Freya stepped forward in front of the others, her face serene.

"She is empathising it," Miky murmured, her face absorbed.

Without warning, two of the servitors at the sides of the pit lifted long, thin pipes to their lips and blew.

Both bears started violently as the darts found their mark. The larger gave a tremendous roar of fury and reared up onto its hind legs, clutching at its back.

Both Misfits and rebels in the pit froze.

I could tell from the dawning despair on Freya's face that she had lost touch with the bear. That she could not regain a hold suggested that the darts had been drugged.

The larger bear turned to stare at Freya, its eyes red with fury. With a low growl, it advanced on her. The smaller bear seemed confused, staring from its companion to the girl and back.

Hannay and Fian stepped forward to stand on either side of Freya, lifting stick and shield to fend off the beast. Freya did not move. Her eyes were fixed on the smaller bear.

"She is sending calmness and compassion," Dameon murmured.

The smaller bear stared back at her, plucking fretfully at the dart lodged in its fur, and even the larger beast seemed to hesitate.

It shook its head slightly.

"She's getting to them," Miky whispered.

On the other side of the pit, there was a sudden and unprovoked movement. The rebel with the sword ran forward and drove the blade deeply into the smaller bear's side.

I watched in impotent horror as the bear fell without a cry and lay utterly still.

Freya shrieked horribly and fell into a faint, for her

mind had been linked empathically to the bear's. If Freya had been a farseeker or a coercer, she would be dead.

I reached out my mind, seeking the bear's life force, but there was nothing. Thoughts swirled out from the larger beast, revealing that the smaller bear had been its cub.

I felt Kella trembling violently at my elbow.

The female bear approached her cub's body and prodded at it. Then she put back her head and howled with such anguish that it rent my heart in two. While she was thus distracted, the four rebels moved forward in a solid phalanx.

I poised my mind to drive them back, then realized I must not interfere for fear of a forfeit.

I looked to the Misfits in the pit. Hannay had dragged the unconscious Freya to one side, and Miryum had slipped past the grief-stricken bear, raising her knife to the rebels. She was trying to keep them away from the bear!

The creature looked up from its cub's corpse, focusing on the coercer's back. It rose slowly, eyes blood-red, and growled with chilling hatred.

Fian ran around to its side, waving his shield to draw the bear's attention from Miryum. I wondered in horror what he was trying to do.

All at once, it snarled and shambled toward Fian, raising massive paws to strike. Even from a distance, I could see the wicked sharpness of its talons. Fian leapt out of the way as the bear swiped at him, and Miryum jumped to one side, leaving three rebels face to face with the enraged creature.

It growled again, and the rebels hastily backed away. Miryum and Fian stood perfectly still, faces set and grim.

I looked back to where Hannay was trying to revive Freya and saw the fourth rebel creeping behind him with a knife. My mind flew back to a dark cavern and the Zebkrahn machine, and Madam Vega with her knife poised above Rushton's throat.

I felt the inimical force in the depths of my mind coalesce, and knew that I could not sit back and watch Hannay die simply to win a contest

Before I could act, Freya opened her eyes. Something in her expression must have warned the big coercer, because Hannay reacted instantly, spinning and using the force of the turn to drive his elbow savagely into the rebel's groin.

"Oh no!" Kella whispered beside me, and my eyes flew to where the rebel with the bloody sword and the other with the ax had driven the bear back toward Miryum. The third joined them, grinning triumphantly.

But his smile faltered, and a moment later, he flung down his net and began to execute a frenzied dance, slapping bare arms and legs as if they were on fire. His two companions gaped at him incredulously. Then a second rebel abandoned his sword and seemed to be trying to throttle himself. The she bear appeared baffled and had ceased her growls.

"Miryum is coercing them," Miky murmured.

The remaining rebel, realizing that whatever ailed his companions arose from the stolid coercer, slammed his fist into her temple. She fell to the ground, leaving Fian standing alone.

Again, the rebels began to harry the bear back

toward him. Abruptly, the rebel with the axe stopped and clawed at his eyes.

Hannay was coercing now, but he had nowhere near Miryum's strength. The rebel with the knife ran at him, and he was forced to release the other man's mind to defend himself.

"Lud, if only they had nowt struck Miryum down. A little more time and she could have held 'em all in thrall!" Daffyd muttered.

All at once, the bear seemed to go mad. It howled and clutched at its head, raking the air with its razor claws.

"The drug must have progressive effects," Kella murmured.

The servitors at the pit worked another set of ropes, and a hidden passage appeared in the side of the rift wall. The three rebels ran for it, and the bear snarled, charging after them, but the gap was too narrow. Thwarted, it turned.

Freya, whey-pale, worked frantically to revive Miryum. Hannay and Fian positioned themselves in front of them, shield and stave raised.

The fourth rebel, now recovered from Hannay's blows, climbed stiffly to his feet. Seeing no one was watching him, he caught up his knife and rushed at Hannay, his face a mask of hatred. The motion caught the eyes of the crazed bear, and it turned and charged.

Freya staggered out to set herself in the bear's path. The beast stopped, and its wild eyes focused their madness on her.

"No!" I whispered.

Step by step, Freya approached the bear, drawing

gradually within reach of the lethal claws and killing embrace. The bear made a crooning sound.

"She has it," Miky whispered.

Indeed the bear seemed mesmerized. Then it groaned, clutched at its back, and keeled over.

"No!" Freya screamed, flinging herself beside the creature. It did not move, and she looked up out of the pit with a face that streamed with tears. "You bastards! It is dead."

"Poisoned," Kella breathed.

"The first game is ended," Jakoby announced.

• 40 •

"INTERESTING," BRAM SAID.

We had returned to the side of the isis pool. In the light flooding through the crack, the water was as blue as a summerdays sky. Miryum had been laid on the grass beside Bram's dais, and Kella was tending her. Jakoby had warned us that if the coercer failed to resume her position before the third game commenced, she would be disqualified, reducing our number to nine. That would not happen, because, if necessary, Kella could heal her quickly. But this would drain her energy, so we had decided to wait to the last minute and hope the coercer would revive naturally.

Jakoby had not mentioned Freya's cry, and the blond girl stood beside me, pale but defiant. Malik's mocking smile said all too clearly that we had fared badly in the first Battlegame. But the day was young, I thought, gritting my teeth.

"Interesting to note what each group saw as the object of the Battlegame," Bram said. "The rebels sought to slay the bears and, if possible, to have the bears slay their opponents. Failing that, to get away alive. Would you concur?"

Jakoby nodded.

"In attempting to attain these objectives, the rebels

were swift, aggressive, and sure. They worked well together when it was useful, never hesitating to cut their losses at need."

Jakoby nodded again.

"The Misfits' behavior, on the other hand, appeared primarily defensive to my eye. They sought to protect both themselves and the bears. Since the female was trying to kill them, this was a confused and somewhat sentimental strategy to adopt. The Misfits' mental powers are clearly considerable, but they didn't use them in any decisive way in this instance. If they can control the bears, why not have them attack the rebels? Why not have the rebels turn on one another?"

Bram closed his eyes and seemed to sink into a small trance after this speech. After a moment, he roused himself and announced that the second game would begin.

The dice were thrown again, and this time their number indicated a Battlegame Jakoby called "the Wall." A second casting gave two players to each team.

Rushton chose Angina, because he was agile and we thought the wall might have to be scaled, and Hannay again, because he was strong and a coercer, in case the wall had to be shifted or broken down.

We had not lost heart despite the first battle, for we were confident that we would perform better now that we had some idea of what the games might entail. The most important thing we had learned was that we must define our objectives when they were not specifically named.

When Angina and Hannay were taken off with the two rebels, Rushton frowned after them. "I hope we do better than in the first game."

Miky gave him a swift, startled look. "You can't mean you think they should have killed that bear."

"Of course not," he said. "I do not see what else they could have done. However"—he looked at me—"do you think Malik instructed his men to kill us if they got the chance? Or were their attacks in the pit instinctive?"

I let him see the answer in my eyes, and his frown deepened.

Angina and Hannay returned, now clad in loincloths, and they seemed to be arguing furiously. None of the four contestants bore any weapons. They were ushered past Bram's dais and over to the bottom of the rift wall, where Sadorian servitors bound Angina's wrists and ankles. One of the rebels was similarly bound.

"What on earth can they be expected to do tied up like that?" Miky said worriedly.

The servitors now turned their attention to Hannay and the second rebel, buckling each of them into stout leather jerkins and swathing their bare limbs in what appeared to be bandages. Boots reaching to the knee were strapped on their legs, and long heavy gauntlets were pulled over their hands.

"The climber must scale the rift wall to the summit," Jakoby said.

Miky frowned. "But how can Angina climb with his arms like that?"

"A strong cord will attach the climber to the burden," Jakoby went on.

We listened, aghast, as she explained that one in each doublet was to drag the other with him as a helpless bundle. The arms, legs, and hands of the climbers were bound in cloth to protect them from the cliffs, which were impregnated with streaks of holocaust poison. The burden had no such protection and must rely entirely on the skill of the climber.

"But . . . coercers are no good off solid ground," Miky reminded us, ashen cheeked.

"They had to let Hannay climb. Angina could never lift him," Rushton snapped.

Miky looked sick.

"At least it's not Miryum. Hannay won't be as badly affected as she would," Kella said stoutly. She did not say what she must have been thinking—what we were all thinking—that Miky's twin's life was in the hands of a man who could not bear heights.

The bout would be over, Jakoby announced, when both pairs reached the desert above.

"Climb," Bram shouted.

We watched with bated breath as the game began.

To begin with, the rebels were at an obvious disadvantage, because they were both of equal height and weight. This gave the climber an arduous task. But Hannay climbed with agonizing slowness. Soon, the rebels were some distance above.

Then, all at once, Hannay began to climb swiftly, his hands and feet sure. Gradually, he closed the gap between himself and the rebel pair.

"Angina's helping him not to be afraid," Miky said with a flare of pride.

Now the pairs were level. But the climber in the rebel team had reached a small ledge that allowed him to stand and free his hands. He began to take chunks of rock and hurl them at Hannay.

"He's trying to dislodge them!" Daffyd cried.

The big coercer paid no attention and had soon risen above the rebel climber. The rebel turned his attention to Angina and went on hurling stones and abuse.

Suddenly Hannay stopped climbing.

We stared, straining our eyes to figure out what had happened.

"Angina's been knocked out by the rebel's stone," Miky said.

"Oh Lud," I whispered, knowing that, unconscious, the empath could not send courage to the big coercer. And if Hannay fell now, he would kill them both.

The rebel climber began to ascend again.

For a long time, the coercer did not move, but at last he began to climb again, too.

"Has Angina . . . ?" I began, but incredibly Miky shook her head.

That meant Hannay was going it alone. He went very slowly, testing handholds and creeping over the face of the cliff like an ant in a windstorm.

By contrast, the rebel climber rose with exultant speed, uncaring that his partner was being dragged and bumped against the poisoned rock wall. When he reached the top, he hauled up his trussed partner and gave a great shout of triumph.

This was echoed by the rebels below.

It was more than a half hour later when an utterly exhausted Hannay dragged himself onto the platform and pulled Angina up after him.

They were brought back down on kamuli. Angina had regained consciousness, though he had a lump on his forehead the size of a hen's egg and claimed to be seeing double. Kella drew the slight concussion out of him, and Miky went to where Hannay sat heavily on a boulder, staring at the ground.

"That was brave," she told him softly. "I know co-ercers hate heights. Are you all right?"

"That was the hardest thing I have ever done. But it was not bravery that moved me, Miky. It was blind terror."

"Not so blind," Miky whispered, pressing a kiss to his cheek.

A faint color rose in his face, just as Jakoby approached to summon us back to the dais. Miryum had wakened and joined us as we took our places. Bram looked closely at the stocky coercer before agreeing that she was fit to continue. Now we were ten again, but Malik had lost one player. The man who had been trussed and borne up the ridge wall had touched the walls too often, and he was seriously ill. There would be no question of his returning within two games.

"The rebel climbers clearly saw the object of the game as speed," Bram said. "Having identified their objective, they lost no time in pursuing it. It is also clear that the rebels have a second objective—that is, to destroy or harm their opponents. They have been equally single-minded in their efforts to fulfill this objective but so far have failed. Oddly, this does not appear to have excited a desire to retaliate on the part of the Misfits. They have done no more than use their unusual Talents to protect themselves when they were under attack.

"Neither did they use their powers to inhibit their opponents' progress up the wall," Bram continued, tugging at his earlobe. "They might have caused their opponents to jump from the cliff under some delusion. But they did not. They only appear able to use their abilities to help themselves or to defend themselves. There does not seem to be any capacity for aggression in them."

He straightened and the overguardian brought the dice again.

At the first throw, twelve marks faced up.

"The Pole," Bram intoned.

On the second throw, three marks faced the sky, and we gathered around Rushton to decide which three should represent us.

"I have some skill with the pole as a weapon, but twice I have failed," Hannay said despondently. "I am not afraid, but I think you should not choose me."

"You did not fail," Angina said. "I made you brave, and when I was hurt, you made yourself brave."

The coercer smiled wanly and ruffled the empath's hair. "Let us say you showed me the knack of it."

"I will do it," Miryum said stoutly. "Pole fighting is my specialty, and if it is aggression they want, I am the person to give it to them."

Rushton nodded. "I name myself as well to this, for I, too, have some skill at the pole."

"We need three," Miryum reminded him.

"I have not learned the pole, but I am strong," Daffyd offered diffidently.

"Why not," Rushton agreed, sounding almost cheerful. I guessed he was glad to be involved rather than watching.

"What if they are not to fight with the poles?" Dameon murmured, but Jakoby had called for Rushton to nominate his team for the third game. Malik spoke, and the chosen six were marched off to the armoring tent.

When Jakoby explained this game, my heart sank; we had misjudged yet again, for the game did not involve the common sport of pole fighting. The title referred instead to a long, slender piece of wood run between two high stands. Two of these scant bridges were erected before our eyes, to stand less than an arm's width apart.

The object, Jakoby said, was for the members of each trio to cross the pole from end to end, one at a time.

Hannay groaned. "Badly as we have done already, we cannot hope to succeed now. No coercer fears heights more than Miryum."

Our only consolation was that the rebel team seemed no happier. I kept my fingers crossed that at least one of their people would also be afraid of heights.

The six returned carrying short staves, which were clearly to be used for balance. Even at a distance, I could see Miryum was white and tense, as Jakoby told them each team must begin at opposite ends and proceed at their own pace.

"Begin," Bram shouted.

Rushton went first, crossing with an obvious lack of fear and the grace and balance that had served him so well aboard *The Cutter.* The first rebel had no hope of matching him and made his own crossing slowly and carefully, sweating and swearing at every step. By the time he reached the other side, Daffyd had already taken Rushton's place and was making his way carefully across the pole.

The second rebel was far more agile. He swarmed up the ladder and stepped out onto the pole with confidence. He looked across at Daffyd and smiled.

My heart pounded uneasily as he came level with the grimly concentrating Daffyd.

The rebel swung his stave out without warning and dealt Daffyd's a hard thump.

Panicking, the farseeker dropped his stave and swayed. The rebel laughed, holding up his own stave for another blow. But he stepped forward, failing to notice Daffyd's stave had fallen to straddle the two poles, just beneath the rebel's feet. He lost his footing and fell with a terrified scream.

"Lud help him," Miky whispered, but my eyes were riveted to Daffyd, who was still swaying dangerously.

"Use your arms!" Rushton cried.

Slowly, Daffyd lifted his arms, and after a long, tense moment, he stepped forward again, only to misjudge.

Kella screamed as he fell but, at the last second, he caught hold of the pole. He hung there for a long moment before beginning to make his way hand over hand to the other side.

There was dead silence as he climbed down the ladder and crossed to where the second rebel lay in the red-stained sand, motionless.

He looked up at the two rebels, who had made no move toward their fallen comrade.

"He's dead."

"Go!" snarled the first rebel to the third, shoving him. The red-haired man licked his lips, then began to mount the stand.

I looked across at Miryum.

She was trembling violently, her face paper white, her eyes fixed on the dead rebel.

Rushton cursed audibly and set his hands on the ladder at the finishing end.

"Look at me, Miryum," he urged from across the sandpit.

She lifted her head.

"Put your hands on the ladder. We'll climb up together. Do exactly as I do, and don't look down."

Seeming half mesmerized by his fierceness, she obeyed, putting her hands around the first rung.

And so they climbed.

The third rebel was halfway across now, but moving very slowly. The first rebel shouted and jeered at Miryum, calling her a great stupid sow, but her entire attention was focused on Rushton.

They had reached the top of the ladder and were facing one another. "Come," Rushton invited softly. "Walk across to me. Come as slowly as you wish and don't look down. Don't think. Just step out."

She did not move.

I closed my eyes, unable to bear the tension.

"Lud save us. She's doing it!" Hannay whispered incredulously.

I took a deep breath and opened my eyes to see Miryum had indeed taken up a balancing stave and stepped out onto the narrow pole. She walked forward, step by slow step, her eyes fixed on Rushton's as if they were her lifeline. She reached the center of the pole. The exact center.

Then I saw her eyes sweep down to where the rebel lay.

She stopped.

"Come on," Rushton urged. "You've come this far." But she was like a statue, frozen with terror.

"Come on," Daffyd shouted from below. "Reach down and swing the rest of the way like I did."

"She can't," Hannay murmured, his own brow beaded with sweat.

"I'm strong!" Miryum cried in an agonized voice. "I'm strong!"

For one dreadful moment, I thought she was going to jump.

There was a cry of anger from the rebels, and I saw that Rushton had come out from the other end using his hands outstretched to balance himself. In moments, he and Miryum were facing one another. He spoke too softly for us to hear what he said, but it was clear that he was coaxing her. The third rebel had reached the end and was jeering and exhorting the coercer to join the dead rebel on the ground.

Miryum shook her head at Rushton.

He reached out, talking all the while, until he was also grasping Miryum's balancing stave.

"No!" Miryum moaned as he pulled her gently toward him.

"Yes," Rushton said calmly, firmly. "For Obernewtyn. Walk, Miryum."

And, incredibly, she did. He walked backward, leading her slowly, feeling his way with his feet and instinct.

When they were safe, I cheered myself hoarse with the others, blinded by tears of pride. Miky and Angina were nearly crushed to death by an elated Hannay, and there was not a dry eye among us.

The rebels roared, too, hissing that it was a cheat.

"How so?" Jakoby inquired of Malik, who had made the charge formal.

"He helped that fat cow. She would not have made it without him."

"That is true," Jakoby said, and for a moment her golden eyes were full of irony.

"The Misfits show great courage and great devotion to one another," Bram said. "Perhaps too much, for if the girl had fallen, she would undoubtedly have taken their leader with her. A wise leader does not risk himself in this way. Not for a lone warrior."

He went on to praise the single-mindedness of the rebels in trying to thwart their opponents but suggested they needed to temper zeal with thought, since they had lost another player and were now down to eight.

"There must be some warriors left in case a battle is only one of many in a war." He expressed regret at the dead rebel as the body was carried away, but none of the other rebels seemed overly disturbed by what had happened to their companion.

The next game to be played was called "the Ride."

✦ 41 ✦

"I AM FOR this," I told Rushton, for a swift probing had told me there were horses in a corral just behind a clump of trees.

For a moment, our eyes met.

"Yes," he said. "But, Elspeth, we have to do more than win this with speed and grace. We won the last game, I am sure, but we have to show some aggression. It sounds as if these Sadorians value that in the rebels, and we're losing because of it."

"I'll try," I said.

When Rushton named me to Bram, Malik named himself.

We were brought to the small herd of beasts I had farsensed and bade to choose our mounts. Malik immediately selected a huge gray gelding with intelligent eyes. He had clearly chosen the most powerful beast, but a race among horses sometimes had more to do with endurance than strength. I paused for a moment and swung myself into the corral to walk among the other horses.

I beastspoke at random, asking who was stronger and faster than all the rest. Suddenly I found myself face to face with the little mare Faraf, whom I had aided at the city gate the day I arrived at Sutrium.

"Greetings ElspethInnle," she sent. "It seems our paths are twined. As you see/discover, my escape did not bring me to the freerunning barud."

"You were captured?"

"Yes, and sold to these. As funaga go, they are not bad/evil. Yet I dream of the freerunning."

"Choose," Malik snarled impatiently.

Ignoring him, I explained my need to the mare.

"The other/funaga has taken the strongest among us. But you had better choose me, for I am small and not strong," she advised.

"Why? Will the strong/wise other let us win? My need is very great."

"He would if I ask it, Innle, for he knows what you are. But they will feed us a garrug/a leaf that some call *prickleberry*. It causes a madness that infects/burns the brain. Better to ride a weak mad horse than a strong one."

I bit my lip to keep a smile of triumph from my mouth as I led Faraf out.

Malik looked down at the slender mare incredulously, but a servitor merely offered us a choice of saddles. The rebel chose a great solid armored thing with sharp metal spurs. On Faraf's advice, I took one that was light and deep-seated. I chose the simplest bridle but removed the metal bit.

When we were brought back to the isis pool, a space had been cleared, and Jakoby explained what Faraf had already told me. We would get onto the horses, and they would be fed the prickleberry, which would madden them temporarily. We would sit on them until the drug took effect. When one of us was unseated, the game would be ended.

"This weed will not kill the horses as it did the bear?" I asked, trying to recall what I knew of prickleberry.

Jakoby's brows lifted. "The bear did not die from the garrug. Its heart was weak and burst under the strain of battle."

The shadows were long now, and I prayed this game would end the day. If we won, it would leave both sides equal, and perhaps that was the best way to win this fight.

"Courage," Faraf sent as I mounted her. The saddle felt stiff and hard against my backside, and the metal stirrups pressed my feet uncomfortably. A servitor brought a nosebag, and as Faraf ate, a thought came to me of how we might further impress the rebels.

"Faraf/littlesistermind, if you will let me into your thoughts/open to me, I can block the effect of this leaf so that it will not madden you."

"I will open, but already it begins to affect me."

This was true, for her whole body was already twitching. I sent a probe into her mind and examined the effect of the prickleberry. It moved swiftly, but I was faster, blocking nerve paths and sending it by innocent trails to the bowel, where it would be voided. Still, some of the drug remained in her system, so I took control of her nerves and immobilized her completely.

Gradually, the trembling faded, and she stood quietly.

Malik's horse, meanwhile, was pacing about, shuddering and shying at nothing. The rebel's face was pale, and he held the rein cruelly tight, ready to saw on the horse's mouth the minute it tried anything.

Without warning, the animal gave a shrill whinnying shriek and reared up.

The sound tore at me, and I tried to get to Malik's horse to ease him off. But the drug had taken hold, and his mind was inaccessible. The horse plunged and bucked violently, but the rebel kept his seat. He was a superb rider.

He gave me a look of patent fury, and I read his intention a moment before he kicked his horse into a maddened run—straight at me!

I could do nothing to move Faraf out of the way, because I had shut down her nerves. As Malik thundered past, the saddle spikes cut her neck and my leg deeply.

The horse bucked in a circle as Malik fought to bring him around. Then he charged again.

"Stop!" I screamed as this time the metal spur tore open the little mare's flank. I was trying frantically to restore her motor responses, but the drug was preventing me.

Again Malik fought his mount to turn it, and as he bore down on me, I saw that he meant to kill me if he could or to cut Faraf to pieces under me. The spikes missed, but he dug the horse with his heels and it kicked out, catching Faraf on the side of her head.

Blood streamed down her face, and she staggered sideways in a hideous parody of the first time I had seen her. He turned again.

"No!" I screamed, and threw my leg over her to slide to the ground. "I forfeit!"

There was a roaring sound in my ears, and my leg felt oddly numb, but I turned to slide my arms around the mare's bloody neck.

"I am sorry, ElspethInnle. I have failed you," she sent humbly.

"Never," I whispered, looking into her eyes. I kissed

her soft nose and limped with her back to the pens. I did not look at Malik, who had jumped clear of his horse.

"There is nothing to be said since this game was forfeited," Bram said when we were all assembled again.

"Ye did th' right thing," Fian whispered angrily when I returned to them. Freya nodded and squeezed my arm. But I was not comforted. If only I had possessed the presence of mind, I might have coerced Malik, but fear for Faraf had stopped me thinking clearly.

I dared not look at Rushton.

Bram rose to throw again. The fifth game was named "Song," and the number of players from each team was two. We could not lose, and yet it was now impossible for us to win.

"A song! This is a joke," Malik snarled.

"I told you, the Battlegames test many qualities. Proceed, unless you would forfeit," Bram said tranquilly.

The two red-faced rebels Malik chose sang a bawdy battle song, probably the only one they knew.

In contrast, Miky and Angina's song dealt not with the glory of war but with the tragedy of it. It was an old song that told of two boys—brothers separated at birth and sent to war against each other. Only when one had killed the other did they understand what had come to pass. The song was supposedly a dirge, sung by the surviving man over his brother's body.

I had heard the song before, but never like this— never with such rending sorrow. Empathised, it became something greater and deeper than a song about two brothers. It became a song about all wars. I wept for the pity of two brothers, lost to each other until it was too late. But I also wept for my own brother, Jes; for Jik, Matthew, and Dragon; for the gypsy Caldeko; and for the nameless rebel who had broken his back on the pole. For all the victims of hatred and war.

And I was not alone. Kella and Freya and Dameon wept, but many of the Sadorians wept, too. Even some of the rebels wiped their eyes surreptitiously as Miky sang the final words: "Will there ever be a time when war does not kill the babes and the dreams of the world?"

When the final notes faded, the sun set in a dazzling golden haze, and it seemed to me that the radiant sky itself paid homage to their voices. Malik stood dry-eyed and contemptuous as Bram rose to speak, dabbing at his eyes.

"The rebel song offered humor, and this is a fine thing to bolster a warrior's courage," he said. "But the Misfit song is greater, for it reaches into the very soul of a warrior and causes him to question himself."

"What does it matter that a song brings tears to the eyes of the weak and the womanish? Will it win a battle?" Malik demanded.

"A song will not wield a sword of metal, my friend," Bram said softly. "But it can put a sword into the heart that will never rust or blunt. It can cause warriors to fight when good sense bids them surrender, raise an army, or quell the tears of a babe."

He rose and lifted his arms.

"The sun has gone, and the Battlegames are ended."

"Who won, then?" Malik demanded.

Bram cast a cool eye on the rebel.

"Impatience is not the least of your faults, Malik. It is a kind of greed, and someday it may see you undone."

He cast his eyes about to take in rebels, Sadorians, and Misfits alike.

"I have been asked to judge these Battlegames. I tell you now that this is not merely a matter of tallying points but of examining how each game was played. Sometimes this makes the judging difficult, for what seems a simple victory may be deemed less of one in light of our purpose."

My heart swelled in sudden hope.

"In this case, however, the judging is a simple matter," he went on. "The games were staged to determine who were the greater warriors and whether the Misfits and their unusual powers were worthy of alliance. The answer is that the rebels are clearly far more fitted to warfare than the Misfits. They have shaped their souls for aggression and quicken to violence as a gravid mare quickens with new life. The rebel legions, if they are truly represented by these men, are made for battle. No instinct of mercy would restrain them, no compassion stay their hand, no love of beauty keep them from destruction. The Battlegames have shown them to be swift, decisive, ruthless, and resourceful. They are filled with the warrior's desire to dominate and subdue.

"As for the Misfits, if they are truly represented by these before me, they are no warriors. They care too much for life and for one another. They are not stirred by the glories of war, and the shedding of lifeblood brings them sorrow, whether it be of beast or human, friend or foe. All their instincts are for defense, and so their great powers are all but useless in the cause of war. They are not cowardly or weak, but their minds appear incapable of allowing their great powers to serve them as weapons.

"Witness that they used the incredible ability that they call *empathy* to its greatest effect in a song, rather than to turn their enemies' hearts to terror. They will never have the rebels' single-mindedness of purpose, nor, therefore, their driving force, because they cannot see things in terms of simple goals."

He turned in the dead silence wrought by his oratory and faced the rebels. "We here in Sador value the earth above all life—humans and beasts alike are short-lived and unimportant. This you know. We have thought that Landfolk valued their own lives too much, regarding themselves as the chosen of their Lud. But these Misfits seem to value all life, and this is strange for us to contemplate. But think you this: You rebels opposed alliance with the Misfits, because you thought them monsters and inhuman. Ask yourselves now which team has this day shown the keenest humanity and which has shown itself to be more monstrous."

The old man paused; then he said in a voice drained of all vitality, "I declare the rebels the victors of the Battlegames."

The rebels cheered, but there was a puzzled, half-hearted edge to the sound. Malik's face was thunderous as he moved to join the other rebel leaders and receive their congratulations.

Rushton turned to us, looking much older in that moment than I had ever seen him.

"The old man's judging was fair," he said.

I stepped forward to tell him that if I must be like Malik to be a warrior, then I would not be a warrior, but my leg buckled under me. As I fell forward, Rushton opened his arms to catch me, but I slipped through them into the abyss.

I dreamed I was bound to the Zebkrahn machine and my legs were on fire.

I dreamed of the Agyllian healer, Nerat, telling me she would teach my body to heal itself.

I dreamed of a red-haired woman drowning in an ocean of blood, of Swallow raising a sword to salute me, of Ariel searching for me down long tunnels.

I dreamed of Maruman telling me I would lead the beasts to freedom, and of walking on the deck of *The Cutter,* watching the ship fish dance.

I dreamed of Rushton waiting at the doors of Obernewtyn and of Freya in his arms.

I dreamed of a shining river that called my name.

"Do not go into the stream, ElspethInnle."

"Atthis!" I sent. "At last you speak to me."

"I have spoken often through the yelloweyes and the dreamingwoman you call Maryonfutureteller."

"Why did you never speak to me?"

"Because the H'rayka would hear. He flies the dream-trails. He listens to hear what I will say so that he may thwart me/us/you."

"Can he not hear us now?"

"He would not dare come so close to the death/dreaming river for fear that it would swallow him. And so it might, for you are perilously close. You must come back from the edge now. I am holding you, but my strength fades."

"I like it here. There is no pain, and it sings to me."

"It is not yet your time to hear this song."

"Then why am I here?"

"A bloodpath in your leg was severed during this testing called Battlegames. You bled near to death. They have stopped this, but you are too close to the stream. Your body has learned to heal itself, but it cannot do so when you are so close to the stream. You must draw back if you would live."

I felt a great wrenching pull to return, but I fought it. I was not sure I wanted to live.

"What you feel is the spiritcall of one who would have you live, ElspethInnle. Go back and let yourself heal, for the world has need of you. Go back, or the H'rayka wins. Go back, or the beasts will never be free."

I felt the pulling again and wondered whose spirit held me so tightly. Curious, I let myself be drawn away from the stream by it.

"Who are you?" I called, but there was nothing, only a roaring sound in my ears. There was a long rushing darkness, and then I opened my eyes.

A monster peered at me. I screamed and fled back to the darkness.

I opened my eyes and Kella smiled at me.

I opened my eyes and Dameon touched my cheek.

I opened my eyes.

I was lying in bed in a dark, cold room. Beside me sat the hooded overguardian.

"You are in the Earthtemple, Elspeth Gordie," said the voice from within the hood. "You have slept long."

᛫ 42 ᛫

"COME," THE TEMPLE guardian murmured, his voice shuddering and whispering along the damp, echo-ridden stone tunnels that honeycombed the Sadorian cliffs.

"Where are you taking me?" I demanded, exasperated. "And when can I see my friends?"

"Soon," he answered. The same thing he had said for days in the same queer, breathy voice.

"I am no longer sick, and you are keeping me prisoner!" I snapped. "I know they were in here before, so why can't I see them now?"

He did not answer.

I glared at the damp walls resentfully. Maybe Rushton and the others had not come in to see me because they had left Sador. After all, I had been unconscious for five days and awake for three. Eight days in all since the Battlegames had ended. The Temple guardians had cared for me when I woke, weak and disoriented, and I was grateful for that. But I was fully recovered now. If the place had not been such an impossible warren of tunnels, I should have long since walked out myself.

I was about to repeat my question when we rounded a bend. Set into the side of the tunnel was a huge panel carved of wood; I had not come across it in my wanderings.

I stopped and gaped at it in amazement, for there was no doubt in my mind that whoever had executed it had also carved the doors to Obernewtyn! The chisel work on the doors possessed a precision in angling that could not be mistaken, as individualistic as the markings on a person's palm.

"Come," the guardian prompted.

Dazed, I did not move. "Who did this?"

He came back a few steps, reluctantly. "Kasanda. Now will you come?"

I followed him. "Who is Kasanda?"

He did not answer, and my temper rose again. I wrestled it down.

"When can I see the overguardian?" I asked sweetly. Again he did not respond.

I ground my teeth and searched my mind, but before I could come up with something rude enough to fracture even a guardian's phenomenal composure, he stopped before a stone doorway.

"Go in. The overguardian will come to you here."

I opened my mouth to speak but thought better of it and went through the door. Behind it was an enormous lantern-lit chamber. Like most of the caverns, it was devoid of furnishings. The temple was, in fact, a natural labyrinth, and the guardians inhabited only a fraction of the chambers and tunnels. But unlike the other empty chambers, every bit of wall space in this one was taken up with huge panels of carved stone. I could see at a glance that they had been created by the same hand that had executed the wood carving in the hall.

"The sequence begins here," the guardian said, pointing to the panel nearest the door.

I nodded absently and moved to the first panel.

It was part carved, part daubed with mud and fiber to raise up shapes, and tinted with darker and lighter tones. Little enough with which to create a world, let alone a lost world of unimaginable wonders, and yet the panel showed one of the Beforetime cities. I was reminded inevitably of the city under Tor, but the city depicted in the panel was vibrantly alive. The constructions were magnificent, reaching to the skies and embodying the greatness of their makers. The panel was a paean of praise to the Beforetimers.

I shivered, for surely such a vision could only come from one who had seen the cities of the Beforetime in all their glory.

After a long while, I tore myself from the first panel. The next also featured the towering Beforetime structures, but they were subtly different. After only a moment of admiration, I noticed not the buildings but the way they crushed and smothered the earth. I saw the caged and stunted trees devoid of sunlight. I realized that this panel spoke not of greatness but of soaring, overweening pride and, most of all, oppression. The Beforetimers had gouged and yoked and reshaped the very earth to their creations.

I shifted to the third panel. Here again were Beforetime structures. Above lay a pall of blackness such as rose chokingly from the smithy's forge. I did not know what purpose these buildings served, for no smith would need so much space, but the message was clear. Not content to despoil the earth, the Beforetimers had smeared the skies with their messes.

One after another, the panels depicted similar scenes—rivers clogged and poisoned, forests hewn down and transformed into salted deserts, mountains leveled to rubble. The Beforetimers had been masters of wanton destruction, and they had built their world regardless of the cost.

I moved to another panel and here at last were scenes of the Great White. Seen thus, it seemed to me that the holocaust had been inevitable, given the nature of the Beforetimers. How else could their story have ended, but with men and women and beasts and birds fleeing in terror from the huge fiery mushrooms that rose in the skies behind them? And when the whiteness faded, there were panels of utter desolation—sere deserts and poisoned waters: the Blacklands.

"Truly this is a place of sorrows," a boy's voice said.

I whirled to see the tiny hooded figure who had sat at Bram's feet during the Battlegames. The over-guardian's hands lifted and removed the hood.

I recoiled involuntarily, for the face revealed was grossly deformed. In stark, dreadful contrast, his eyes were the color of isis pools, sad and beautiful.

"I am sorry," I said. "I did not expect . . ."

He smiled, a grotesque twisting of his lips. "I am the overguardian of the Earthtemple. That which poisoned the earth also poisoned my mother. It is so with all of the guardians here."

I took a deep breath, hiding my surprise at his age as much as at the fact that he was a Misfit. "I am glad to meet you. Thank you for healing me. . . ."

"I did not heal you. Your body healed itself. We do not know how."

His words evoked a memory of my dream and

Atthis telling me my body could heal itself. Had it really been the old bird or a feverish delusion? Yet if it was true, it would explain so many things. Perhaps even the disappearance of Swallow's tattoo.

"There is a story," the boy said dreamily. "It tells of one who will come from across the sea in search of the fifth sign of Kasanda."

I frowned, drawn from my despair by curiosity. "The same Kasanda who carved these?"

He seemed not to hear. "There are many born with Kasanda's gift, here and even in your own Land. And it is said that when one comes in search of the signs, three companions will come also, one of whom shall be of true Kasanda blood."

"Why are you telling me this?" I demanded coldly. His talk of seeking and signs chilled me.

The boy shrugged. "Perhaps I dreamed that you would come and that I must say these words. I have Kasanda's gift of true dreaming, and so I am sometimes called a kasanda. But the first Kasanda is the one who dreamed of the Seeker."

"The . . . Seeker?"

He nodded. "After the signs. Kasanda told my people that the Seeker would bear the Moonwatcher and be borne by the Daywatcher, who is the color of shadows. You see the beauty and intricacy of the images? The Moonwatcher's daylight eye and the Daywatcher's shadow hue are complementary. Two sides of the spinning coin. The implication is that one may emulate the other in times of need. The interesting thing is that there is no information about the Seeker—as if that was too dangerous to be left."

I shivered, unnerved by his use of the name Atthis

had given me. I thought of the disturbed youth outside the Earthtemple flinging himself at my feet. He, too, had spoken of the Moonwatcher. But the threads of my quest could not stretch this far, surely.

"It is said Kasanda took the signs from her dreams and strewed them across the lands so that they should not be found except by the Seeker. There are rumors that they lead to the deepest treasures of the Beforetimers. Still others say they are the key to a power that is great enough to shift the stars, and even to quench them."

Power again, I thought bleakly. That was what had brought about the holocaust. "Do you know what the signs are?"

He smiled enigmatically. "I know many things. I know that the Herders come bearing lethal gifts of disease and that they must be watched constantly to prevent them harming the earth or our people. I know that when the Seeker journeys forth with the Daywatcher and Moonwatcher, and with one of Kasanda blood, they will be looking for the final sign. Then may the kasanda, who is the overguardian, aid them."

I shook my head angrily. "This is nothing to do with me. I want to get out of here." I glanced around at the panels with loathing.

The boy sighed and resumed his hood. "Very well. Tomorrow your friends will come to the Temple for you."

He went out, and when I followed, he had vanished.

Left alone in my chamber, I sat on the edge of the bed. My mind was filled with pictures—the Herder torturing Iriny's bondmate, my parents killed for their beliefs, Malik's eyes filled with hatred, and the dark dreadful visions in stone left by the mysterious Kasanda for the Seeker.

Well, the Seeker had seen them.

I thought of the transcendent beauty of the first panel and tried to understand how the ability to create such wondrous beauty could have become so perverted, so destructive.

With power, my mind whispered.

I felt desperately confused and lay down, longing to be in the mountains. I closed my eyes and sent my mind out into the desert. It was night, and the pale changeless dunes undulated beneath the night sky, going on as far as the eye could behold without a sign of human life. So must the world have looked before the Beforetime and the demon-angels we named Oldtimers. The Great White now seemed the least of their evils. Perhaps not evil at all, for if it had not come, then what would they have done next? Shaken by this thought, I tried to draw the calm grace of the desert into me, but the despair was too strong.

Again I felt a fierce longing for the clean coldness of the mountains.

"Then seek them," Maruman's voice whispered into my mind.

"Where are you?" I sent, trying to decide if his voice was real or imagined.

"Maruman/yelloweyes flies the dreamtrails. Fly to the mountains if you need them."

I sighed. "It is too far. You know I cannot send my mind over Blacklands."

"You can if/when you farsense you seek the dreamtrails. Come."

I let him take hold of me, but almost immediately I

felt claws. Before I could summon the wit to struggle or fight, I had the uncanny sensation of hurtling through the air as if hurled from a catapult.

"Fly/seek!" Maruman's mindcry faded behind me.

"ElspethInnle. Come ride with me. . . ." Gahltha's mindvoice came to me.

I opened my eyes and was amazed to find myself sitting in my turret chamber at Obernewtyn.

Dazed, I crossed to the window and looked out. The black equine was standing in the moonlit garden below. I felt a surge of joy at the sight of him.

"I'm coming," I sent, and turned from the window to drag on riding boots and a cloak.

This can't be happening, I thought, hurrying down.

"It has happened, and anything that has happened can happen again. Life is filled with circlings," Gahltha sent as I mounted. He wheeled to trot down the drive. The air was cold and thin, and I shivered.

"Is this real?"

"What is real? You are here and I am here, but we are also far from here. Who knows which existence is more real?"

Which was no sort of answer, but as Gahltha traveled gently out of Obernewtyn's gate and along the road with its whispering green sentinels looming darkly above, it did not seem to matter very much. When the trail ran out, he broke into a wild gallop, crossing the long grassy plain like a creature possessed. His tail and mane streamed out behind as we sped through the gap in the foothills and climbed the narrow way into the valley above, and the one above that.

At last we reached the valley that lay at the feet of the highest mountains. Though it was not yet wintertime, the ground was hard, and snow lay spattered on the ground like ash. The peaks were already white.

We rested by a hot spring, and as I sat on a rock, warming myself, Gahltha grazed on the sweet grass that grew about the edge of the simmering water. "I will eat the grass and you will nourish yourself on the mountains," he sent, as if it were no more than biting into an apple.

Giving myself to the dream, I lay my mind wide open, seeking the detachment and clarity the mountains enabled. Their wild beauty always seemed to make a gentle mockery of brief human woes and lives. Had not these jutting bones of the world survived a thousand eons of human life? Could anything I or any human do really matter in the face of that?

But for once, I could not comfort myself and answer no. I had stood in the Earthtemple, and I had seen the panels made by Kasanda. In my mind's eye, I saw again the smothered and abused earth, the befouled waters and blackened skies. I saw again the desolation that lay on the other side of the mountains—the endless bleared deadness of the Blacklands—and I knew that even mountains could be killed.

It seemed to me then that I felt the earth's life, the cold sweetness of its breathing winds, the deep beat of its stone heart, and I understood the Sadorians' devotion to the earth. Everything lives, Powyrs had told me, and I realized he was right.

For the first time, it seemed to me that I knew the true evil of human wars and their instinct to dominate and oppress and subdue, for hadn't the Beforetimers poisoned great tracts of the earth with the holocaust? And if the Destroyer reached the hellish slumbering weaponmachines first, would not the task be finished for always? If mountains could die, and vast plains, then why not a world? Humans would perish, and perhaps it was no more than they deserved, but so would equines and bears and the Brildane. If the earth died, not a single blade of grass nor a cat with one eye would survive.

The moon rose, a thin sliver now, and shone its eldritch light through a haze of cloud and onto the mountain peaks, silvering their snowy mantles and transforming them into shimmering ghosts.

I clenched my teeth.

My resolve, shattered and confused for so long, became, all at once, blessedly strong. When the Agyllians called, I would leave Obernewtyn as I had promised. I would obey the prophecy the birds claimed I had been born to fulfill and all the strange strands of fate that sent me here and there seeking signs and ways; I would follow the sinuous, difficult, puzzling manywindings of my quest, whether they led me into the deserts of Sador, or over the vast dark seas, or into the very fires of hell—I would complete my quest so that what had been could not come again.

I would walk the dark road to its end and never return, for nothing was too great a price to pay for the earth and all its life. Not love or my own little life.

My quest was greater than fear or love, and it was greater than Obernewtyn and the fate of the Talented Misfits there, and nothing would ever make me question that again.

I slept then, dreamlessly, and when I woke, I was in the hard little Earthtemple bed. The terrible draining tide of sorrow that seemed to have defined my whole life had ebbed, along with the fears and murky apprehensions that had haunted me for as long as I could remember.

I felt as clear and light and pure as a glass of sunlit rainwater as the guardian led me through the tunnels to the outside. As I blinked into the fierce sunlight, I felt as if it pierced me and filled me up.

"Elspeth!" Kella cried.

She and Dameon had come to meet me. I let them hold me but felt a great distance had come between us. I had seen too much and flown too high.

"I am glad you are well," Dameon said gravely.

"The rebels have decided on their rebellion," Kella said, and a shadow passed over her features. "It is to be after wintertime."

I did not want to hear about rebels or rebellions. "Is Maruman all right?"

Dameon chuckled. "He has made himself at home again on Powyrs's ship. The old man dotes on him."

"Dragon?"

The healer sighed and shook her head. "There is no change in her condition. Maybe when we get back to Obernewtyn . . ."

I wondered suddenly if I *should* go back. There was nothing there for me now. I could just as well wait to hear from Atthis in Sador.

When we reached the tents, the others crowded around to greet me.

"Where is Rushton?" I asked, noticing abruptly that he was not with them.

A silence fell, and in spite of my new detachment, it made me uncomfortable.

I turned to Dameon and touched his arm. "Is he . . . he is not hurt?"

Kella looked exasperated. "Oh, Elspeth. Rushton has been odd ever since the Battlegames. He blames himself for our defeat."

"He walks alone and hardly eats," Miryum said. "He refuses to lead us."

As they settled back into their tasks, I looked around at the others. At Miryum brooding over our loss of the games as Hannay worked to cheer her; at Fian and Kella grinding leaves for herb paste; at Freya and Dameon, settling in to listen as Angina and Miky sat side by side, practicing a new song. Angina still bore the great bruised lump on his forehead from the Battlegames, but their faces were serene.

I thought of the song they had chosen for the Battlegames, and in a flash, I understood the power it had possessed. The empaths had sung it before, never knowing why the soldier sang. But now they understood. No wonder it had reached even the hardened hearts of warriors, for there was truth in it.

I stared wildly about me, and the icy wall of detachment that had risen around me came crashing down.

Atthis had told me once that I should go to Obernewtyn and aid the Misfits in their struggle because it was worthy. I had gone and I had worked alongside the others, but I had always felt myself to be marking time, waiting for my true quest to begin. Now I saw that the two quests were parts of the same purpose. One without the other was meaningless.

Bram had been right to judge us unfit warriors. And perhaps in a world without threat of extinction from the weapons of the past, Obernewtyn would be free to usher in a new breed of humanity that would not take the same terrible path to destruction as the Beforetimers.

"What is it?" Kella asked, and I realized I had begun to grin like a fool.

I looked around and found they were all watching me. I took a deep breath.

Rushton had said we would learn about ourselves by taking part in the Battlegames and competing with the rebels. Well, we had learned all right. We had learned what it truly cost to be warriors. We had learned that the price was too high.

Losing the Battlegames had been the best thing that could have happened to us.

◆ 43 ◆

I FOUND RUSHTON sitting on a rock and staring out to sea.

"You haven't failed us," I said softly. "We haven't failed."

He was still for a moment. "Elspeth. I am glad you are well." His voice was dull, and he did not turn. I had never heard him sound so defeated.

"Listen to me—"

"I have called myself your leader," he said. "I thought to guide you all to battle, because I imagined your powers would fit you better for war, that all you needed was a leader to bind and direct you. But you are not meant for war. I failed you because I did not understand the truth of you."

"If there is any fault, it belongs equally to all of us," I protested.

He shook his head lethargically, but still he would not turn to face me.

"What will happen to you and the others when the Council sends its soldierguards to clear out Obernewtyn, Elspeth? Or when rebels like Malik come to wipe you from the earth? I wanted to protect you."

"Us," I said firmly, gently. "Us."

"I am not one of you," he said. "I have wanted to be

and I have dreamed of it . . . but I know now that it will never be."

"Of course you are one of us," I said sharply. "Besides, leadership has nothing to do with your being a Misfit. You began this. You freed us and gave us a place and time to grow."

"But I was wrong. . . ."

"So were we," I cried. "*I* was the one who wanted to show the rebels our power and our might. If anyone is a fool, it is me."

"You have the right to make such decisions," he said more strongly. "Whereas I . . . I cannot even access my Talents without help."

"You think there is something wrong with needing help?"

"It is a weakness."

"Now you sound like Malik," I said hotly. "And maybe that's the point. Maybe there is a little of Malik in all of us. In spite of what Bram said, I have the feeling we could be like him if we wanted to badly enough. A Malik, after all, would never need help. Our need for one another is what makes us better than him!"

Now he did turn around. "*You* can say that? You, who never needed anyone in your life?"

"No one could say it with greater truth," I said sadly.

"And what happens when you cannot *have* what you need?" he demanded angrily.

That was a question I could not yet begin to answer. I knew only that, though Rushton might not love me, there was far more at stake here than my feelings. "Look, I'm trying to tell you that what we learned in the Battlegames was important. We needed to know what we couldn't do so that we could begin to think of what we can do. Remember Maryon said this journey had something to do with finding the right road? Can't you see that we've done that?"

He shook his head. "Will that knowledge show you how to deal with the soldierguards?" Rushton asked, apathy returning to his tone.

I held on to my temper with difficulty. "It might. Misfits are hated and persecuted because people fear us. The Herder Faction and the Council enhance that fear, just as Angina enhances Miky's songs. Maybe the answer isn't to fight and force and make, but to show. To empathise. To let them understand us so that they will see there is nothing to fear from us. I think we should try to reshape ourselves and our purposes around empathy."

"You are not an empath," Rushton said.

"No, but I can try to understand and care for the unTalents. Any one of us can learn to do that."

Rushton made a choking sound and turned away again. "You do not understand. How could you?"

A spurt of anger made me reach out and pull him back to look at me. "What do you know of how I feel? Do you think I am a machine like the ones the Beforetimers made?"

"I do not know," Rushton said with a sudden fierce bitterness. "I know nothing, because you have never *let* me know. Because I am not like you."

I gaped at him, my anger slipping away. "Not like you? What are you talking about? I have just been telling you . . ."

"Then why?" he asked softly, a world of pain in his voice. "Why will you never let me come near? Why do you reject me with every look and word if not because . . . I cannot reach my Talent, because I am not . . ." His voice faded away.

Had I understood correctly? "But surely Freya . . . ," I said faintly.

He nodded. "She is an enhancer. She has tried to teach me to use my powers, and we have had some success." He paused. "Though I don't know how you could know of it—but it is too little when you are . . . what you are."

I gazed at him, incredulous, my mind rearranging itself like the colors of a kaleidoscope. He thought I did not love him because he could not use his Talent. He and Freya had been trying to reach his powers so that he would be worthy of me!

In that moment, I saw that if my quest to dismantle the weaponmachines and Obernewtyn's future were bound together, so were Obernewtyn and I bound up as one in Rushton's mind. In feeling he had failed one, he now felt he had failed the other.

But he had failed at neither. And I?

I understood that this was a moment that might never come again. I had learned the hardest way of all that beauty and happiness, like life, were ephemeral and could no more be saved up for later than a sunbeam could be hoarded. If I would have any life with Rushton, I must take it now, for now was all there ever was.

"What am I, Rushton?"

His eyes flared with a naked longing that seemed to suck the breath out of me.

He stood up suddenly, and I stepped back, almost frightened.

"You are everything," he said roughly, hopelessly. "Freya said to give you time, and I tried. But you have gone further and further from me. I have been a fool to imagine that you would ever care for me...." He shook his head, and the light faded from his eyes, leaving them dull and sad.

"You are a fool, all right," I said tartly, half laughing.

He frowned at me, and my smile faded at the hurt in his face.

"You are a fool for thinking you failed Obernewtyn. You will go on leading us as we strive to find some other way to make our place in the world."

He began to shake his head, but I reached out my hand and laid it against his cheek.

He stood very still, and I let my hand slide around until my fingers were against his lips.

"I love you, and I have done ever since I saw you at Obernewtyn carrying that silly pig," I said simply, looking steadfastly into his eyes. "I just had to grow up enough not to be frightened of what I felt."

Rushton's face did not change, and for a moment, doubt flickered in me. But then I banished it, for surely nothing required courage so much as love, and I was equal to it.

Swallowing the fears of a lifetime, I reached out my mind, passing the barriers Rushton could not broach, and opened myself to him.

Only then did he move, and faintly, so faintly I could barely catch it, I heard his whisper inside my mind. "Ravek, my Elspethlove."

✦ EPILOGUE ✦

MARUMAN GAVE ME a jaded look. "And what answer will that be?"

I leaned on the tower sill and looked out into the first flurry of wintertime snow, pulling my cloak about me.

"I don't know, Maruman. But we have begun to find it—Rushton and I, the guildmerge and beasts. And whatever it is, it will be the right answer, because it comes out of us and what we are."

"You will never make the funaga-li accept you," Maruman sent.

"Maybe that's the mistake we've made all along. Trying to make people accept us. I don't think *making* is going to be part of our answer."

I thought of Brydda. Just before we left Sador, he had come to the ship with Jakoby.

With them had been Miryum's Sadorian suitor leading little Faraf and the giant horse, Zidon, which Malik had ridden. He had gone to the Coercer guilden and held out the lead ropes to her. She had stared up at him suspiciously.

"They are a gift—" Jakoby began.

Miryum interrupted, stilted and awkward. "Well, that's all right, then. . . ." She took the ropes from the Sadorian's hand.

The man gave her a look of such burning intensity that her polite thanks faded. Then he turned and walked away. Miryum looked even more bewildered.

"They are his bondgift to you," Jakoby had told the astonished coercer then. "That you accepted them means you have accepted him as your ravek. When he is ready, he will come for you. That is the Sadorian way."

Miryum's mouth fell open.

Jakoby then turned to Rushton. "I ask a boon of you, Leader of the Misfits."

This was the last thing we had expected.

"Bram and I ask that one of your empaths remain in Sador as a guest of the Earthtemple. We would have speech with you, for there is much about your people that intrigues us. This guest would be greatly honored and shown things none has seen before who was not of our people."

She and Brydda had withdrawn a little at this so that we could discuss it amongst ourselves.

"I will stay," Dameon had said without preamble. "This must be my task, for there has been nothing else for me to do. This must be why I was sent here."

Miky and Angina had chorused horror, offering themselves in his place.

"You don't understand," he said. "I *want* to stay. I am not sacrificing myself. It is . . . a selfish desire. I can learn much of these people, and perhaps teach them something. They have such a strange mixture of barbaric instincts and true wisdom. There is much in them that calls to me. The very fact that they regard empathy so . . ."

Rushton reached out and gripped his shoulder. "Dameon, I . . . I know why you would remain here."

To my surprise, the empath had flushed. "Then you must let me stay."

There was a long moment, and I wondered at this strangeness between them. Rushton expelled a breath of air. "Very well. One season. When wintertime is over and the pass is thawed, we will come for you. The two horses will stay here as well, for, in any case, they would not like the sea journey."

I shivered. So already there was talk of returning. I seemed to see the ruined face of the overguardian of the Earthtemple, telling me that the Seeker would come to Sador in search of some fifth sign.

"You cannot stay alone," Rushton was saying to Dameon. "Someone must stay with you to be your eyes and guard you."

"I will stay," Fian offered eagerly. "I will protect Dameon with my life and soul. And I can research this region for Garth."

"I can protect him best," Hannay said, flexing his muscles.

There was some more talk and more offers to accompany the Empath guildmaster, but in the end, Dameon and Fian stayed because it was felt there would be no need for guards. The Sadorians had too much honor to let anyone harm a guest.

Saying goodbye to Dameon had been harder than I could have imagined. I would have opened my mind and heart to him, but he had set a wall between us. Perhaps so that he would not be hurt by our sorrow at this parting; perhaps because he still felt Matthew's loss.

"It will not be the same without you," I had whispered, holding him tightly.

"Ever was Obernewtyn empty when you were not there," he had said. "Yet I survived, and you will survive."

"Rushton needs you, especially now."

"He does not need me, especially now," the empath said. "He has what he has long desired."

I felt the blood surge in my face.

He smiled, his blind eyes turned to me. He reached up and touched my hair and face, running his fingers over me lightly. Seeing. I made myself smile so that he would think of me that way. His fingers had reached my lips and seemed to tremble before he took them away.

He had embraced a tearful Miky and a pale Angina then, reminding them that they would rule the Empath guild in his stead.

"Only until you come back," Miky choked.

Dameon kissed her cheek and then farewelled Freya, who had not known him long and yet wept, too.

"I am ready now," he said. Smiling farewell, Fian had offered his arm to the empath. As they departed, Rushton put his arm around my shoulders and held me tightly. "He will be well, Elspeth. He . . . he needs to do this. It is but a season."

Then Brydda had come to bid us farewell. "I wish things might have been different."

"Perhaps this is for the best." Rushton clasped the big rebel's wrist. "I thought an alliance was the answer, but we would want such different things after it was over, and we will always be Misfits to them. We must be what we are."

Rushton's eyes had shifted to me fleetingly, and this time I had not flinched from the desire in them. If there was a loss in loving, I was learning that there was a finding in it, too.

Brydda had looked from one of us to the other and then had leaned across to embrace me. "Goodbye, little sad eyes, though they are not so sad now."

"You will always have our friendship, Brydda. No matter what," I said.

He had crushed my hand then. "Friends. Always," he said gruffly. "No matter what."

And so we had gone our separate ways. He to his rebellion, and we, first by sea to Sutrium, only to find that Domick had not yet returned, and then home to Obernewtyn—where I belonged; where Dragon lay in her endless coma; where Matthew might one day return; my home, which I must someday leave forever to take up the dark burden of my destiny.

"What if the oldOne calls before this answer is found?" Maruman asked. "Will you obey? Will you walk the dark road?"

I shivered as the bitter wind changed direction slightly, pressing its icy fingers through the folds of my cloak. The snow was falling more heavily now, blurring the jagged darkness of the mountains, making them seem far away. "All roads are the one road. I gave my promise," I sent soberly. Then I smiled. "But there are five secrets to be uncovered, and I must one day return to Sador, and I must stand in battle with a gypsy whose life is bound to mine. These things will not happen in a moment, and so there is time in the midst of this for me to live.

"Atthis has not summoned me yet, and perhaps the call to walk the dark road will not come until I am old and gray. I have promised to go, but I have not sworn to live out my life in the dark shadow of that vow. I have learned that happiness is like the sun. It must be enjoyed when it comes and while it shines."

But Maruman was not listening. He was looking up, searching for the moon's cold face.

❖ ABOUT THE AUTHOR ❖

ISOBELLE CARMODY began the first of her highly acclaimed Obernewtyn Chronicles while still in high school. She continued writing while completing a Bachelor of Arts and a journalism cadetship. This series and her short stories have established her at the forefront of fantasy writing in Australia and abroad.

She is the award-winning author of several novels and many series for young readers, including The Legend of Little Fur, the Gateway Trilogy, and the Obernewtyn Chronicles.

She lives with her family, and they divide their time between homes in Australia and the Czech Republic.

Can Elspeth reconcile her feelings for Rushton with her quest as the Seeker?

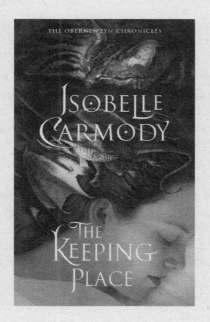

THE OBERNEWTYN CHRONICLES

ISOBELLE CARMODY

THE KEEPING PLACE

Read on for a sneak preview of Elspeth's journeys on the dreamtrails—available now!

SUDDENLY, A NIGHTMARISH beast appeared before me, massive and red, tearing through the shrubbery and screaming in fury. Its raking claws barely missed my face as it swooped past.

"Beware!" Maruman sent urgently. "It comes again. Wake!"

Instead I sank and found myself brushing against a memory of walking in the woods with Rushton. It was so pleasant that I allowed myself to be absorbed.

"I love you," he said, and kissed me long and softly on my lips. Then he drew back and looked at me so intently that I felt shy. "Are you sure you do not mind that I am unable to use my Talent?"

I took his face between my hands and kissed him. "I would not reshape you in another mold, else you would be another person."

His green eyes glinted. "I hope you will always feel that way."

There was a screaming cry, and the great taloned beast dropped suddenly from the clear sky and plunged toward us.

"Wake!" Maruman sent.

"Look out!" I screamed at Rushton. I threw myself

to the ground, but Rushton did not, and the thing lashed out at him before flying away.

I stared up in horror at his bloodied arm. Rushton swayed and fell to the ground. I had started toward him when Maruman leapt between us in his tyger form.

"Let me go to him!" I screamed.

"He is a dream, but the beast is not. Wake!"

The beast uttered its chilling cry, then plunged, claws outstretched.

Again I sank instinctively, only to find myself drifting in darkness. A roaring sound and unearthly singing told me I was deep enough inside my own mind to hear the mindstream and to feel its pull. I did not fear the beast would follow, for it could not do so without risking its own destruction.

Below, I could now see the mindstream's silvery flicker. A bubble detached itself from the roiling surface and floated toward me.

I had no hope of avoiding the memory it contained. I was in a strange, noisy machine speeding above the earth with a young girl, and beside her a man. They wore Beforetime garb. In front of them a third man peered intently out of the bubble that separated us from the air, touching this dial or that button. I guessed he was directing the machine's course. Outside, the sky was very blue and clear, and the sun shone down on a mountainous terrain.

"You can't afford to get mixed up with Tiban fanatics," the man said.

The girl responded hotly. "The Chinon Empire—"

". . . have closed themselves off and are no concern of ours. That is their choice."

"It wasn't the choice of Tiba to be swallowed up by

them. But you don't care about that. You're like everyone else who doesn't care what atrocities the Chinon Empire commits, as long as you don't have to witness them," the girl said with cold fury.

"I'm afraid I'm not a schoolgirl with the leisure to go on peace marches. I can't do anything about what happened hundreds of years ago in Chinon. I am simply doing what I can to stop the world from destroying itself."

"Helping to stabilize the balance of terror?" the girl muttered scathingly. "What sort of solution is that?"

The man's face developed a closed look. "The Guardian program will have access to all world information sources, and it will be able to evaluate danger swiftly and without bias. If it deems that one country has aggressed on another, it will activate the Balance of Terror unit, and BOT will retaliate, without any country having to make a decision."

"Eye for an eye? What if your precious Guardian makes a mistake?"

"It is far less likely to make a mistake than a human being."

"That's not an answer. And if the Uropan government is designing the program, it will think as a Uropan would, so it will still be biased."

"The program developers are of all nations, including Gadfia and Chinon, and we will evaluate and take into account cultural differences. In a sense, the Guardian program will be the very first world citizen. Not only that, it is capable of learning and, as time goes on, it will continue to grow and mature. It will be the most sophisticated program ever created, and it will be a buffer between humans and the BOT retaliation unit.

The World Council believes that Guardian and BOT will protect us from human greed and stupidity."

"Nothing can save us from that. . . ." There was a note of sorrow in the girl's voice.

"Cassy, is it so bad to spend the summer at the institute? The mountains in Old Scotia are very beautiful once you are accustomed to the bareness of them. We can spend time together hiking, and you can do some sketching. . . ."

"Sure thing," the girl broke in bitterly. "Only you'll be too busy directing your precious projects. Why can't I go to Mericanda with my friends?"

"Your mother does not want you there, and neither do I."

"The only thing you two manage to agree on is repressing me as much as possible."

"After the devastation of Raq and Turka, I don't think anyone could be blamed for worrying about the state of the world."

"It's all right for *you* to worry, but when *I* worry, I'm being childish."

The flying machine now hovered over a collection of flat, square buildings.

"This place is a prison," the girl said sullenly.

A sharp pain in my head made me cry out, and the dream faded as I rose quickly through the levels of my mind to consciousness.